INERTIA

COLORADO STORM HOCKEY SERIES

ELLIE MALOUFF

Printed in the United States of America

First Printing, 2020

ISBN-13: 978-1-949269-09-3 (eBook)

ISBN-13: 978-1-949269-10-9 (Print)

Persephone Publishing LLC

P.O. Box 270684

Louisville, CO 80027

For the boys who captured my heart in 17 Seconds.

1

Summer

THE BISCUIT IN THE BASKET DINER IS COMPLETELY PACKED, WITH a twenty minute wait. For a weekday, it's only ever this busy on the Fourth of July, since a lot of locals like to come in after the parade and get some of Momma's special red, white, and blue waffles. But it's not the Fourth of July. That was a week ago.

Even over the excited chatter of our customers, I can hear the distinct clatter of a coffee cup dropping and the gasps of a few patrons. I weave around the tables and dash behind the counter.

"I'm sorry, Summer," Mr. Wilkins says as coffee wells on the countertop, not yet spilling onto the floor. I pull a well-used rag out of my back pocket and start to soak it up.

"It's fine," I assure him, knowing that he's been having a hard time lately with his Parkinson's.

"And on Christopher's day, too."

"Don't you worry about it. Are you going to the event today?" I ask, knowing full well what his answer will be. It's everyone's answer.

"Wouldn't miss it," he replies and fiddles with his 36th Fighter Squadron cap. He was one of twenty-five African American Air Force pilots to fight in Korea. He wears his cap with pride everyday, as he should.

"Want a fresh breakfast?"

"No, dear," he says, looking down at his soggy eggs. He barely had a chance at it.

"Nonsense, it's on the house."

"Summer—"

"You said it yourself, it's Christopher's day." I scribble his order down and pop it into the ticket holder. From the kitchen, Momma grabs it and gives me a quick nod and a wink.

"When are you getting out of here?" she asks me through the window as she cracks eggs.

"Ten minutes. I've already got my equipment packed. Margie is here with her niece, and they've got a handle on it."

"Great," Momma replies and turns around to the stove.

"Give it a few minutes, Mr. Wilkins, she's working on it," I tell him and refill his coffee.

"Thanks, Summer Sweetheart."

"Anything for my favorite customer."

Over by the door, a pack of boys comes in and everyone in the diner looks at them with huge smiles on their faces. I think I'm even doing it. They don't have to wear their Fossebridge High School letter jackets to be recognized in our town. If hope was light, they would be blinded by it now, especially with how everyone is looking at them today.

It doesn't seem like all that long ago I was that age, but I guess it has been eight years since I graduated high school. We believed in our high school hockey team just as much back then. Every pep rally, every game, every high, and every low. Even when we had our most tragic loss, the town of Fossebridge, Minnesota was there. It's no wonder people took off work today to celebrate Christopher's big win.

My smartwatch starts to vibrate and I know it's time to go because I can't be late for this. Before I can make a step toward the door, there's a text from Tia. She's ordering me to get my butt to the airport. Her control issues really need to be checked at some point. I reply back with the eye roll emoji and go to get cleaned up. The last thing I should do is show up with frizzy hair and dried jam on my hands. I pull my hair down from the messy bun I've been sporting and run a small comb through it. Then I put on some of my favorite vanilla lotion, give my cheeks a quick pinch, and get on the road to the airport.

The drive takes a half hour and I pass the time listening to one of my favorite playlists. The one that's perfect for this time of year, when the fireflies illuminate the trees by the lake at night and the humidity just might kill you, but you still get cold in the mornings. Everyone here loves the winter, when the lake freezes over and you can drop a puck on the ice. Not me. Maybe it's being named after the season, but I love these long summer days.

It's hard to find a parking spot, but I make do. I pull out all my video equipment from the trunk of my beat-up hatchback and haul it over to the terminal. There's a hoard of fans and photographers camped around the baggage claim, so it's not exactly hard to find where I'm going. I locate my kind, and head straight for the men with the video cameras.

"Mind if I set up here?" I ask one of the guys wearing Sports World credentials.

"Not at all," he answers and winks at me. I flash him a polite smile, just grateful for the space.

Like a pro, I strap on my stabilization vest and attach my camera to the arm, all the while feeling my new buddy's eyes on me.

"Is that a DVX200?" he asks.

"Yep."

"Huh," he says loud enough for all the other guys to hear.

I don't stop the eye roll. He's not looking at my face, anyway. "Not what you were expecting?"

He gives me a funny look for calling him out. "Who you with?"

"*Fossebridge Weekly Telegram*," I answer and show him my press badge. It's the first time I've ever worn it. In fact, Tia and I made it just for today, because we certainly don't need them in Fossebridge, where everyone already knows each other.

"How does a small town paper afford a camera like that?"

"It's my own."

He chuckles under his breath, but I ignore it because the chatter dies down and people are starting to move around each other to look toward the door. My palms are slick, which is simply ridiculous. There's no reason at all to be nervous, but I am. I'm totally nervous.

I have a job to do, so I film the crowd that's come out and see quite a few people I know and a lot that I don't. Their excitement is palpable, and it's taking everything in me to not start bouncing up and down along with them. Some are holding signs and most are wearing shirts or jerseys with number 21 on their backs. I wonder if they know what I know. I wonder if they remember that it wasn't Christopher's number originally. I wonder if they know that 21 belonged to my cousin, Trey.

"He's coming out," some dude says to the crew beside me and they all lift up their cameras with little fanfare.

I turn my camera to the sliding glass door and hold my breath.

"Big Mac! Big Mac! Big Mac!" the crowd chants.

When the doors slide apart the crowd erupts in applause and hoots and hollers. I take two steps forward and zoom in on Fossebridge's favorite son, Christopher MacCormack. The first thing I notice is that he's beautifully clean-shaven, that nasty playoff beard gone until next April...if they make it to the play-offs again. He's also cut his dark hair high and tight, no flow at all, probably to the disappointment of many across Minnesota. It's nice to see. *Really, really nice.* I gulp and stay on track, starting to move to my left to get a shot of Christopher and the crowd in the same frame.

He's followed by a gaggle of men, one of which is his dad, Peter, and two that are pushing a big chrome case right behind him. His mom, Nancy, is waiting with the crowd, as well as his older brother Gabe with his wife and kids.

Christopher waves to the crowd and then shoves his hands into his shorts pockets. Yes, he wore shorts, a t-shirt, and flip-flops to this—his big day back home. So typical that it makes me want to laugh, but I don't want to ruin the video. On the plus side, the guy could use more sun since he's been stuck in arenas for the better part of eight months. His calves, while so well sculpted, could blind the crowd. Not that I can talk.

"Hey everybody," Christopher greets them. "Thanks for coming out."

Friends from home approach him and the handshakes start. There's a man, just shy of Christopher's six feet and a few inches, by his side providing protection, which is truly laughable considering that Christopher is one of the fiercest forwards in professional hockey.

I continue to move, circling around this moment, capturing the very spirit of the thing. I'm not interested in reporting news. I'm interested in making this feel like it did as it was happening. Forever.

"So, I don't think you're just here to see me," Christopher goes on. "I think you want to see what's in this trunk, yeah?"

Christopher's fans cheer in the affirmative.

He takes a few steps back and approaches the men at the chrome case. "Gentlemen, if you would."

They nod and one unlocks the case and unlatches the lid. Silver shines bright and my camera lens snaps right to it like it's magnetic. I'm immediately dazzled, as is the crowd. Christopher picks up the Cup and hoists it over his head. The crowd erupts, as if they were seeing the Colorado Storm's game winning goal in the seventh game of the finals all over again. Christopher lowers the Cup to his lips and kisses it like it's his—because it is for the day—and I capture it perfectly.

When he lifts it back up over his head to the sound of even more cheering, he turns to face me straight on and I zoom in, not daring to look away from my eyepiece. His lips turn up into a slight smile and I see everything in his hazel eyes. There's a sense of accomplishment, a big dose of pride, a little love, and sadness. This should be one of the happiest days of his life, but I know in my heart that it's not. It could never be more than bittersweet.

Then Christopher does something that I will have to edit out later. He looks directly into my camera and mouths the word, "Hi."

Christopher

There's nothing like being home, and being home today is extra special because I've brought the Cup. Winning the Cup was the culmination of all of the sacrifices and work and support and faith this town instilled in me. Nothing will quite feel like the moment when I hoisted it for the first time as captain, but bringing it home for Fossebridge, the town that made me who I am, is a close second.

My mom arranged for a convertible to drive us down Main Street on the way to the high school for my speech. The streets were lined with people to see me holding the Cup to my side like a girlfriend. She sure is sexy and all the things that most boys in this town dream about, but the Cup doesn't hold a candle to Summer Gunderson.

She's moving around the auditorium, graceful as a cat, with a camera strapped to her body. It's been a couple of years since I've seen her, but she's just as I remembered. She's still got the longest blonde hair in town, and dimples that cut so deep they slay me. Her green eyes are as mischievous as ever. I've always been convinced that she sees things most people don't notice and that's probably what makes her a great videographer.

She's filled out a little bit more and I like those curves. Too much. I can't take my eyes off her. Well, I guess it's good to know that some things never change.

There's a slap on my back, snapping me out of my Summer spell. "Ready, son?" my old high school teammate, Mateo, asks. He started coaching the hockey team after Coach Kiogima retired. I'm glad that both of them are here today.

I wipe my sweaty palms on my shorts, because this would be a terrible time to drop the Cup. "Ready as I'll ever be."

As captain of the Colorado Storm, I've grown accustomed to public speaking, but this is different. These people know me too well. They remember when I peed my pants on the field trip to town hall. They remember when I broke the window at the gas station with a wild slap shot when we'd already been told multiple times not to play in the parking lot. They remember when I got completely fucked up and passed out on Summer's lawn. They remember practically everything about me. I wonder if they remember Trey that well.

Coach Kiogima finishes up a rousing introduction that has the crowd on their feet and cheering. It reminds me of our old pep rallies, although those usually took place on the rink. Now *that* would have been fun. I'm already itching for the ice.

"So let's give a huge Fossebridge welcome to our own Christopher 'Big Mac' MacCormack," my old high school coach shouts into the mic.

The crowd does not disappoint him. I pick up the Cup, walk out on stage, and the volume goes up to game seven overtime levels. The rock song they used throughout the playoffs, blasts over the speakers. Honestly, I'll probably never get tired of hearing it.

After the first verse, I set the cup on the table and hug my old coach with a hearty slap on the back. He hands me the mic and leaves me alone to face my entire hometown and then some. My eyes dart around the auditorium and find Summer. She's off to one side, her face hidden by the camera. Without even knowing why, I'm stuck in place until she finally peeks up at me over the lens and releases me.

"Hello Fossebridge," I shout and they go wild. Sweat trickles down one side of my face and I wipe it away with my shirt. You'd think it wouldn't be embarrassing, considering how many intermission and post-game interviews I've given when I'm just drenched in it, but that's not the case today. It is terribly embarrassing, but no one seems to notice. They're all staring at me with complete adoration. Except for Summer. She's staring through the lens of her camera. Crap, I'm back on Summer again. I've got to get this moving along. I quickly recall the remarks I planned and start.

"Did you ever think that we'd get to have the Cup here in Fossebridge?"

There's a lot of shouts in the affirmative and others that are still in disbelief.

"Well, I always dreamed of this day, just like I'm sure you dream of this day too," I say and point to the boys' hockey team that's seated in the third row. "One day this can be you, and I'll come to your ceremony."

"Eagles! Eagles! Eagles!" the crowd starts to chant for them and I join in for a few rounds. When it dies down, I go on, "It was a tough season for the Storm. We lost Hux for eight weeks to that hamstring injury. Our coach, the great Bruce Bliss, had to take a leave of absence for his daughter. And those dreaded Growlers really had our number. But we were strong. We stuck together. We believed we could win and we wouldn't hear otherwise."

That gets a round of applause.

"Well, I'm sure you guys were watching."

"We sure were, Big Mac," Mr. Knudsen, the hardware store owner, shouts and makes the audience laugh. I laugh along with them.

"We are a hockey town, through and through. And even if I'm not playing in the great state of Minnesota, Fossebridge is always in my heart. I do it for this town," I say with spirit and they all cheer.

"I do it for Minnesota!"

More applause.

"I do it for you!"

Incredible sounds of joy fill up the space.

"I do it for Trey!"

And like that, I've dampened everything. The joy drains away, but I keep going, "This win—this was for Trey."

Summer looks up from her camera and stares at me, her mouth open, her eyes are large and bright.

The applause is different. Slower, quieter, but somehow more intense. Heads turn and look toward the back of the auditorium and that's when I see Trey's parents. I wasn't sure if they'd be here today. They aren't clapping. They're barely moving as all eyes are on them.

Shit.

I didn't want to make this even harder for them. I'm so

fucking dumb. I had some more material planned, but decide to move right on to the next part. "Who wants a photo with the Cup?"

And that gets everyone's attention real fast. Everyone, but Summer Gunderson. She's lowered her camera and is still looking over at her aunt and uncle.

Summer

It's been a really long day. After photos with Christopher and the Cup, there was a visit to the county hospital, a boat ride around the lake, a dinner with the Fossebridge Booster Club, and an ice cream sundae social on Main Street, where they closed down an entire two blocks.

I was officially off the clock about a half hour ago, when Christopher's scheduled events wrapped up. All day long, I'd been behind the camera, so I didn't get a chance to talk to him, but I caught him looking my way several times. When I was packing up, he was still surrounded by people. I caught his eye one last time and waved goodbye. He nodded at me in that classic way of his, ever so slightly with blinding eye contact.

Needing a slice of quiet, I drop off my gear at home and walk over to the cemetery.

Trey's grave sits beneath an old oak tree, and from a distance, I can see some fresh-cut flowers already there. No doubt my Aunt Leslie and Uncle Dave visited today. I haven't brought anything with me, but that's okay, Trey wouldn't mind.

The sun is setting as I take a seat off to the side and stare at his gravestone. The engraved dates still don't make sense to me. The years are too close together.

"Hey Trey," I whisper to my cousin and start talking to him in my mind, since I always feel a little foolish to talking out loud here.

You should see Christopher with the Cup. It's amazing. A dream come true. You would have loved it. I can totally picture you drinking beer out of the Cup out on the boat. Poor Christopher had to put up with all kinds of shenanigans like that. But he would have loved to watch you do it. I would have, too.

Tears well in my eyes, but I don't have time to wipe them away because there's a rustling sound behind me. I quickly turn to look over my shoulder, freaked out since I'm dumb enough to be alone in a cemetery at dusk.

It's Christopher and he's carrying the Cup. I get up on my feet and glance around, looking for the Cup handlers, for his parents, for all of his fans, but he's completely alone.

"Hey," I say and wipe at my eyes with my thumbs.

When Christopher sees this, he frowns at me, the creases around his mouth evening out. "Hey, I'm sorry to disturb you. I can come back."

"No, it's fine. What are you doing here? This wasn't on the schedule."

"I know. That was on purpose. I didn't tell anyone about it, except for my dad and the Cup handlers. I'm not surprised to see you, though. Come here a lot?"

"Not anymore. I used to a lot in college, whenever I was home on break."

He sets the Cup down beside the tree and stares at the gravestone, just like I had.

"I'll give you some time alone," I tell him and turn to go.

He grabs for my hand and turns me back around. "No, wait. Stay with me."

"Okay," I reply. My hand disappears within his grasp when he doesn't let go and when I feel how warm his skin is, I'm taken back to the last time we held hands. The memory stings. Especially here.

"I wish he could have seen it," Christopher whispers. "He loved hockey more than anybody."

"Yeah, he did," I answer, but I'm not so sure Trey loved it more than Christopher. Trey was so out there about everything, so bold, that it was easy to assume his surface feelings were how he really felt down deep. That wasn't always the case. As we found out, he sometimes did it for show.

"He would have been the first person in Fossebridge to drink beer out of it, you know," Christopher says and looks down at me. There's that small twinkle in his eye that I've missed.

"I was thinking the exact same thing," I say and smile up at him. "Congratulations, by the way. I haven't really been able to say that yet."

Half of his mouth lifts into a smile. "Yeah, you did. I got your email."

"You did? You read it?"

"Uh...yeah. You didn't get the one I wrote back?" he asks with a full-blown smile now. He lets go of my hand and crosses his arms like he's offended.

"You wrote back?"

"Yes," he replies like it's a no-brainer. "Did you think I wouldn't?"

I pull my phone from my pocket and open my personal

email. There are a ton of unread messages, going back weeks. "It's been a busy summer," I mumble as I scroll and scroll.

"Just search," he tells me.

"I know what I'm doing," I snap back playfully.

"I hate when people don't search."

"*I know what I'm doing,*" I repeat, emphasizing every word.

"Still stubborn, I see."

I quickly flip him the bird, which makes him burst out laughing, and keep on scrolling. Sure enough, in the mix of messages from the University of Minnesota Alumni Office and sale ads from my favorite camera equipment place is a reply from Christopher. I never expected him to write back. In fact, I kind of forgot that I wrote to him at all. There'd been a huge bash to watch game seven, just like there had been for game six...and game five, and all the playoff games before that. And well, I got a little drunk that night. Lord knows what I actually wrote to him. I'll deal with that later.

"Touché, Chris," I say and gaze up at him. He's gazing right back and I get lost there for a few seconds, looking in his eyes. The cemetery fades away, just as the sun did a few moments ago.

"We should get out of here," Christopher says.

"Did you drive?" I ask.

"Yeah, my old truck. Dad still has it. Need a ride?"

I wave him off. "Nah, it's only three blocks."

"Come on, it's dark," he pleads and he does have a point, although there's not much to worry about in Fossebridge.

"Sure there's enough room for me and this old piece of junk?" I tease.

He shakes his head in disgust. "The hockey gods are going to strike you down, you know that right?"

"Not after they see the most excellent feature I'm putting together about your day with the Cup," I reply with an edge of pride in my voice.

"Right, your brilliance and talent will win them over for sure," he says it without an ounce of sarcasm.

I squint at him. "I think you're being serious."

"You know I am. I've always been your biggest fan."

I slug him in the arm, because I don't know what on earth to do with that compliment. He laughs it off, but gets serious again when he picks up the Cup and turns toward Trey's grave. He holds the Cup there for a long quiet moment and I'm guessing, much like me, he's talking to Trey in his head.

We head toward the truck in silence. I open the passenger side door and Christopher slides the Cup to the center of the bench. I follow it in and let him shut my door. He jogs around to the driver's side and I smile at his hustle. He's ever the sportsman.

"Will you keep hold of it? On the way here, I strapped it with the seat belt."

"Dear lord," I blurt out and we both laugh. "Yes, I will hold onto the giant trophy in case we get in an accident on the three-block drive to my house."

"You're lucky it's just the two of us with the way you're talking about the Cup."

"You mean it can't hear me?" I ask and look around the behemoth to see Christopher's reaction. He's doing that half-grin thing again and I remember now how it's always been one of his most adorable features.

"You know how to humble a guy, you know that?"

"How so?"

"Well…Jesus. You're only riding with the most sought after trophy in professional sports, with the guy who scored the game-winning goal to get it, and you do not seem impressed."

"Of course I'm impressed, you weirdo. I think I'm nervous. This thing has a life of its own, right? Like, maybe I should introduce myself formally to it or something?"

"Hey, if it makes you feel better, Summer. He probably won't respond—he's a real dick like that."

"It's a little surreal though, right? It's like we're back in high school and you're driving me home from the Biscuit, except there's the object that has embodied all of your dreams wedged between us."

"There's always something," he mumbles and takes a left turn while I hold onto the Cup so it doesn't fall over on him. Christ, this is weird.

We get to my house much too fast. He pulls into the driveway and puts the truck into park.

"How long are you in town for?" I ask and lean forward to look over at him.

He leans forward, too, resting his head on his arms over the steering wheel. "Still trying to figure that out."

"Well, maybe I'll see you around."

Classic Christopher. He simply smiles at me and doesn't respond, so I have no idea if I'll see him or not. I hop out of the truck and we work together to move the Cup over to my seat and strap it in.

"Good night, you two. Be good. Don't do anything I wouldn't do."

"Wouldn't dream of it, Summer Gunderson."

Christopher waits until I've unlocked and opened the door to my house before he starts to pull away. I wave at him and he rolls down his window and waves back. It's a funny sight, to watch him drive away with the Cup.

"Hi, honey," Momma says from the family room. She's watching one of her favorite singing competition shows and looks absolutely beat. "How was Christopher?"

"Good. Did you get the see the Cup?"

"From a distance. Pretty cool," she says, but I know in reality that hockey has never really been her thing. She's a southerner in the great white north. "Your dad would have loved it."

"Yeah, he would have," I say somberly and look over at his portrait on the mantle. He died fighting in Iraq when I was ten years old. That's when we moved to Fossebridge, so we could be close to my grandparents and my dad's brother Dave and his family.

I plop down on the couch and pull out my phone. Time to face the music and see just how embarrassing that email is that I sent to Christopher.

Holy crap, you won! Like, you just won the Cup!!! Okay, excuse the exclamation points, I had one too many at the watch party on Main Street. Seeing you score that goal was one of the best things I've ever seen in my life. It was even better than when you won State. Everyone in Fossebridge is freaking out and we're all so proud of you. I practically lost my voice from cheering so loudly when you hit that slapshot. You have to bring the Cup home, right? That's what the champs always do. You're one of them now! They're going to engrave your flipping name on it. God, you looked so good skating around with the cup hoisted over your head like that. Hoist is a weird word. Now that it's over you can shave!! Bring back Clean Cut CHRIS. I can't wait to see you, it's been so long. I miss your face.

Dear Mother of Dragons, kill me with fire because that is the most ridiculous thing I have ever written to another human being. I roll over onto my side and groan into the back cushion of the couch.

"What's wrong?" Momma asks.

"Oh nothing," I reply. "I just can't ever face Christopher MacCormack again."

Momma laughs at me, not with me. "And why is that?"

I hold out my phone. She leans over and snatches it away eagerly. The next twenty seconds are silent and then there's a big burst of laughter coming from the woman who is supposed to love and nurture me.

"Momma!" I whine.

"Baby," she replies and tosses my phone back, knocking me in head. "Oops, sorry."

"Seriously?" I ask and turn over, so I can give her a crusty look. "Did you say 'oops sorry' when you dropped me on my head as a baby? 'Cause clearly there's something wrong with me. Why else would I send him such an embarrassing message?"

"Ah, it's fine. He probably didn't read it."

"Oh, he read it. He told me so."

"Oh." She pauses and stifles a laugh. "Did he write back?"

"So he says."

"Well?" she asks with saucers for eyes. Her impatience is always so obvious. "What did he say?"

"Haven't read it yet."

She's flabbergasted. "What? Why not?"

"Because, I'd rather have the couch swallow me whole."

"Do you want me to read it?" she asks with a little too much eagerness.

"Momma. Please be less desperate to be up in my business."

"Oh please, you want me to read it." And I know what's coming next, because she can't help herself. "You want me on that wall. You need me on that wall. You want answers?"

Of course, I play along. "I want the truth!"

"You can't handle the truth!" she shouts and smacks her hand down on the arm of her recliner.

"You know, there's a lot more to that scene and I'm pretty sure we're getting it out of order," I tell her.

She shrugs. "Who cares? We do the best parts."

I roll off the couch onto the floor and slowly get to my feet. My whole body hurts from the long day strapped in and filming. "I'm going to take a bath."

"You're gonna leave me hangin'?" she protests.

"You don't always get what you want," I answer.

"But you get what you need," she says, not able to help herself.

"Good night, Momma," I say and lean down to kiss her cheek.

"Good night, baby."

As the bath water runs, I take a deep breath and open Christopher's email back to me. It only has six words, but those six words pack a punch.

Thanks. I miss your face more.

2

Christopher

Spring, Junior Year

"Did you guys see that awesome Vartan save last night? I'm telling you, Chicago is going to win it all this year," Trey says to a locker room full of torn-up hockey players. We got thrashed at practice today.

"You and every other talking head is saying that," I tell him.

"But did you see that save? You can't get anything past the guy. And he's young. He's got so many years left in him."

"Bro, you have it bad for goalies," Mateo teases.

"I respect the job. You have to when you're a sharp shooter like me."

Everyone groans and throws things at him, including me. I get him good with the wad of athletic tape I've just pulled off my wrist. The conversation in the room breaks down, and Trey parks right next to me to finish getting out of his gear.

"Going to the Clearing tonight?" my best friend asks. The Clearing is exactly that, a clearing in the woods that's perfect for a bonfire and a keg of beer.

"Maybe. I've got a few things to do."

"What could you possibly have to do tonight?"

I don't answer that because I don't want to tell Trey where I'm headed. "We've got a big game tomorrow. You know how Coach doesn't like it when we party."

He's understandably skeptical, and I think he's starting to see through me. More often than not, I've been spending my free time at The Biscuit in the Basket when his cousin Summer Gunderson is working. The last thing I need is this overprotective caveman giving me shit about having a thing for her. "It's for the game. Not for any other reason?"

"I've also got a test to study for," I answer. It's not a lie.

"On a Friday night? God, you're so full of shit."

Trey's laughing at me, but it's easy to ignore in the locker room. Everyone is loud and obnoxious and a little bit their worst selves. I get blowing off steam, but we're at the most critical point in the season. I'd rather concentrate on that, instead of who is getting laid, parties, and beer.

"Sure you can't make it tonight?" Trey asks. "It'd be great for the boys if their captain showed up."

Trey always knows where to hit to make the most impact.

"I'll try to make it," I tell him.

"That's my boy," he says and punches me square in the arm. Fucker. "Oh hey, I've got something for you."

I roll my eyes. "Your dirty jock strap? I'm not falling for that again."

He chuckles at that and starts digging through all kinds of

crap in his locker. "Not this time. I've been meaning to give it to you." He pulls out a dinged-up puck with a piece of masking tape on it. He tosses it to me and I read the label. *GWG Juniors Championship.*

My eyes go wide. "Is it really?" I ask.

"Yep. My dad met up with our old coach last week, and he gave this to him to give to me. I guess he forgot that you scored the goal."

"But you set me up," I argue.

Never one to be humble, he says, "Like a fucking champion, yeah."

"So maybe you should keep it," I say and hold it out to him.

"Nah, hold onto it for us. I'll probably just lose it or something. Maybe I'll have my shit together better when we're college. Then you can give it back to me."

"Anything is possible," I joke and give him brief hug with a hard slap on the back. "Now, get in the shower, you smell like a fucking rhino."

"What does a rhino smell like?"

"I'm assuming it stinks, just like you."

Main Street usually empties out around this time of night, but there's a new feature at the movie theater and a retirement party at Ekeley's Bar, so I've got to make a couple of laps around the block to find a parking spot near The Biscuit in the Basket.

The little bell jingles and all eyes are on me when I enter. I used to blame the letter jacket, but they all know me without it, especially this time of year. One more win and we'll clinch top seed at state.

Margie, a waitress who's worked here for ages, is balancing a tray of dishes. "Take any of the open booths, Big Mac," she says.

I toss my letter jacket on the opposite bench and take a seat, my backpack between me and the wall.

"You want the usual?" Margie asks and winks at me. She knows the answer.

"Yes, please. With an extra pickle and a root beer with extra ice."

"As you wish, darlin'."

Mrs. Gunderson's southern slang must be rubbing off on her. Speaking of the Gundersons, the younger of the two steps out from the kitchen and wraps an apron around her waist.

"Sorry I'm late, Margie. You can head home now," Summer says.

"Shucks, just when Big Mac got here. He'll have the usual."

Summer glances over at me and I snap my head down to look at my hands.

"Got it," I hear her say. "Did he order a root beer?"

"You know it, and don't forget the extra ice and the extra pickle."

"Wouldn't dream of it," Summer says with a little laugh in her voice and the sound makes my chest feel tight.

I can feel her eyes on me from across the restaurant, but I don't look up. I won't. It's not that I'm shy around her...well maybe I am, more than I care to admit, but when we start talking to one another it's fantastic. Having her attention ranks up there with being on the ice with the puck on my stick. I just don't want to come across as a creepy stalker, sappy puppy dog, in-love teenager, because if I'm being completely honest, that's exactly what I am. Instead, I choose to play it cool by pulling out my binder and turning to some History notes.

She goes about bussing a table as I feign studying, but I barely see the words in front of me. My eyes betray me and snap up to watch her as she glides around the restaurant like she's on ice. I fixate on her silky hair that's swinging around in a ponytail. The plastic end of my ballpoint pen cracks between my teeth. *Shit. Not another one.* This bad habit of mine tends to happen whenever Summer Gunderson is around. It's a miracle I haven't bitten through one and tasted ink.

My notes go fuzzy in front of me as I sense her nearing my table.

"Hey Christopher. Here's your root beer," she says and sits down across from me. I'm very good with this. I like it when we connect on her terms.

"Thanks." I close my binder and put it away in my backpack.

"How was practice?"

"Good. Tough. Typical for this time of year."

"It's all anyone talks about, but you know me, I like getting the news firsthand," she says as she fiddles with the salt shaker.

"That's what makes you a good reporter."

She laughs at that and looks away. She's never been one to handle a compliment well, but it's something she should get used to, because Summer is brilliant. "Did I tell you? Mrs. Reed-Kiogima named me Editor-in-Chief for senior year."

"Get out, that's awesome."

ELLIE MALOUFF

"Yeah, I guess so."

Summer's mom whacks the bell at the window and my food is up.

"Be right back," she says and dashes off to get my cheeseburger with barbecue sauce, her hips swaying so sweetly as she goes. It's not unusual for me to get lost in her in a moment like this, but something else is tugging at me. Summer doesn't seem nearly as excited as she should be about getting named Editor-in-Chief.

Before I can dwell too much, she's back with my burger. Have I mentioned that Summer Gunderson feeding me is also a favorite pasttime of mine?

I'm grateful that it's slow and she can sit down with me again. She passes me the ketchup for my onion rings without me having to ask for it.

"Guess so?" I ask.

"Guess so about what?"

"About Editor-in-Chief. When I said it was awesome, you said 'yeah, I guess so.' Why aren't you dancing on the counter right now?" *Lord knows I would kill to see that.*

She sighs and shakes her head. "This is crazy, but I'm thinking about turning it down. The newspaper conflicts with the Video Arts class I desperately want to take. Plus, I think Tia would do a better job."

Summer not doing the newspaper? That's always been her goal, and I've done whatever I can do to support it—like hooking her up with interviews with the team or waiting around late after practice on nights when she's working late, so I could coincidentally bump into her and accompany her home.

This is bad. Really bad.

Summer is deviating from a plan I've had in place since freshman year. She's supposed to go to University of Minnesota to study journalism and I'll go there on a hockey scholarship. We'll start dating after a year or so, enough time to settle in, and by graduation we'll be engaged. Then I'll go off to the league and she'll become a fantastic sports reporter and follow the team on the road, so that we're never far apart.

Before I can totally meltdown, she looks up at me with such an excited smile that it freezes me in the moment. "I've been dabbling with this really amazing editing software, making videos about all kinds of things from some of my favorite shows, and I've got kind of a following on YouTube."

"You never told me about this." This hurts. Knowing Summer is something I pride myself on.

"I know," she says and flashes a shy smile. "It's just a little embarrassing."

"Why?"

"Because I'm making videos about different TV couples that I ship."

"Ship?"

"Like couples that I love...you know, I'm rooting for to have a happy ending."

"Weird."

She tightens up before my eyes. "See, this is why I didn't tell anyone. You think I'm weird."

"No," I reply and reach for her hand across the table. "That's not what I'm saying, it's just a weird word for it, *ship*."

"Oh," she says and laughs nervously. "I'm a shipper, I'm shipping fictional characters to be in a relation*ship*."

"Yeah, you can keep saying it, but I still don't get it. But you know I could never think you're weird."

"Whatever. I'm totally weird. I own it, Chris."

I love it when she calls me Chris. Absolutely love it. Like it practically brings me to my knees if I'm standing. So, if one of us at this table is weird, it's me.

"But it's the newspaper, Summer. It's been your thing for so long."

"But this is better. I've been saving up for this awesome camera, it does super high definition. I'm so excited to try editing something real. Like your games." Her eyes are the size of saucers, as if this particular idea has just dawned on her.

"Like sports videography?"

"Sure, why not? Anything, really. I just love the idea of being behind a camera, capturing my own footage to edit. Sound insane?"

As much as change pains me, I think that I can work with it. Maybe. I'll have to try my best to be supportive, but I've already been cooking up a plan to see if there's anything I can do on my end to get one of those classes moved so they don't conflict, because Summer should have it all if she wants it.

I pick up my pen. "What's your username?"

"There's not a chance in hell I'm going to show you my silly videos."

"Come on, Gunderson, let me see it."

"Nope. I'll show you a video once I've got something real put together."

Fat chance of that. I've already got an idea about her username, so I'll be looking that up later when I get home...after the party at the Clearing. *Goddamnit.* I really want to skip that and just stay here with her.

"Are you going to the Clearing tonight?" she asks, as if reading my mind.

"I guess so. Trey convinced me. He pulled the whole 'your team needs their captain' card on me again."

"My cousin isn't dumb."

"Bastard."

She throws her head back and laughs, and it is a thing of beauty. I'm definitely skipping the party now. There's no way I can walk away from my future wife.

Some new customers come through the door, and I kind of hate them for being hungry and having the common sense to eat at the best place in town.

"Well I'm going to the Clearing too, assuming we don't get a big rush after the movie lets out. I'll see you there," she says and scoots out of the booth to greet them.

Holy shit. Guess I'll be going to the Clearing after all.

Summer

Tiana Stanton lives, breathes, and sleeps the *Fossebridge Weekly Telegram*. She's also my best friend and we've done everything together since I moved to town in fifth grade, including going to college together, rooming together, and majoring in journalism together. So, when she tracked me down at the library two months before college graduation to tell me that her grandfather died unexpectedly, I wasn't surprised when she said that *we* inherited the *Telegram* from him. Legally it wasn't actually *we*, it was her, but she needed all the help she could get to keep it running. The only thing I had lined up was a peanuts-for-pay gig at a local magazine out of Duluth that I was not thrilled about in the least. It was a no-brainer. We moved back to Fossebridge and took on the *Telegram* together.

Some may say that print journalism is dead, but in a town like ours where the per capita subscription rate of the *Telegram* is ninety-nine percent, it's most definitely not. Even though the print model works, Tia and I have been working our hardest to take it into the 21st century. We launched the website six months into our tenure and that's been my baby since. Basically, I'm responsible for all things digital and that means video, my one true passion.

When I told Tia that I wanted to put together a video of Christopher's "day with the Cup," she was a little hesitant because she thought I would be more valuable to our traditional reporting strategy for our special Christopher issue. It was a hard sell, but I finally convinced her. I told her I'd use my own time, off the clock, to do the editing so I could help get the rest of the special issue put together.

So, it's been a lot of late nights for me at the *Telegram*, which is housed out of the same shopfront on Main Street as it was eighty years ago. What it didn't have eighty years ago was a video editing bay, my favorite closet-sized room in all of Fossebridge.

"I don't know how you stay cooped up in here all the time. I'd have a nervous breakdown after an hour," Tia says as she tries to maneuver her desk chair into the room.

"I think it's cozy," I tell her as I cue up my Christopher video.

She laughs and swings her hair over her shoulder. "I think you're deranged."

"Takes one to know one," I tease.

"All right, show me this thing."

Tia has seen my absolute worst work before, like when I went through my avant-garde phase and edited shots of a dead bird I found behind our dorm to the tune of Mongolian throat singing. She watched the entire video all the way through to the end with all the black lace overlays and blood-dripping font. Nothing can be worse than that, yet I'm still nervous to show her this. Maybe because I feel like so much is on the line with our coverage of Christopher's day. But most likely it's because, deep down, I think it's my best work ever.

She watches and I try to imagine it through her eyes and ears. Does she feel the emotion I'm trying to evoke with the music that overlays the clips of our town coming together to celebrate Christopher's victory? Is she captured by the editing that makes it impossible to turn away as I blend shots from his performance in the finals with shots I took myself from high school? Is she pulled along by the pride and joy that threads through the piece in every smile and every tear?

Or does she look at it as one more asset for the *Telegram*? One more tactic to drive traffic to the website that will appease our advertisers? Does she appreciate it with her heart or her head? I'm hoping both.

She doesn't say much after it ends, she just sits there with her chin resting against her fist. This is surprising, because she's usually ready to move on to her next task.

"So?" I ask.

She shakes her head and closes her eyes briefly before answering. "It works. It totally works."

"Why do you look so weird about it?"

She plasters on a smile and turns my way, but I know better. Her wheels are turning. "You're really talented, you know that?"

My nervous laugh is dulled by the soundproofing in the editing bay. "Thanks, I think."

"And that's so great. So great for the *Telegram*," she says dryly.

If I could somehow see what's going on inside her head, I'm sure I'd be treated to a conspiracy wall covered in printouts with red strings tying something beyond my grasp together. "What is going on in that head of yours?" I ask.

"I've got a great idea," she says and jumps out of her chair. She's trying to maneuver it out of the room as she goes on. "Let's do a premiere for the whole town, sponsored by the *Telegram* and our advertisers."

"A premiere?"

"Yes. At Webster Lake, in the park. Thursday night. With the inflatable movie screen they use for movie nights. Maybe we can get Christopher to come if he's still around."

"I don't know if he is," I tell her and that's the sad truth. I haven't seen or heard from him since that night he drove me home. Honestly, I've been too holed up in here to know where he's been.

"We'll track him down. I'll get in touch with his agent."

"His agent?" I say with a bad taste in my mouth. "This is Christopher we're talking about. The same guy who split his pants in Bio II, remember? I'm pretty sure we don't need to reach him through his agent. If anything, let's talk to his mom if we can't reach him."

She thinks on that for a moment. "He's always been fond of you, so it's your job to track him down."

Blood rushes to my cheeks. "Fond of me?" I ask, but it's not really a question. I'm repeating back her words because I'm shocked she said them. No one in town, besides Momma, ever talks about me and Christopher like that anymore.

"Don't play coy. Everyone remembers what happened in high school, especially me."

Whoa, she is going there.

"Yeah, but that was so long ago and we couldn't...act on it."

"Trey's been gone for a long time, too. Maybe it's time we all let go."

"Okay, this conversation has steered way off course," I tell her and turn back to my monitor. In rapid succession, I close down all the open screens. I don't like talking about what happened to Trey, and with Christopher home, it's really dragging all of that back to the surface. I move us back to the real topic. "Are you sure you want to do a premiere with everything going on?"

She places a hand on my shoulder. "I'm sure. We have to do this. It's time to show this town and the world beyond just how talented you are. Are you cool with that?"

For anyone who's experienced the nervous exhilaration of sharing your creation with an audience, you know it's one-part vomit-inducing and two-parts thrilling in the best of circumstances. Well, these circumstances are as good as butter on a hot roll. There's no way I can turn down the opportunity, even though I might have to hightail it to the port-a-potties when it's time to premiere my video.

The lunch rush chatter at the Biscuit is interrupted when the bell chimes at the door. I don't have to look to know why. Christopher does that to a room. He did that before he was even a pro. I twist around from the coffee maker to confirm it. Our eyes click right away and he smiles ever so slightly in that way of his. Patrons start talking again and quite a few to him, as he slowly makes his way around the tables to the counter. He takes a seat on the center stool and turns to shake hands with Mr. Wilkins. It's nice to see a smile on my favorite customer's face.

The coffee isn't going to finish making itself, so I complete my task as if the league MVP isn't sitting at my counter.

"Hey, can a guy get some service in here?" he says, his deep voice working a little bit of magic because it makes my chest tighten.

"Hold your horses, Big Mac," I say over my shoulder, knowing he hates when I call him that.

"Whatever happened to calling me Chris?"

"The *Chris* I know has patience."

"That's the Chris you *knew*. And it wasn't patience. It was shyness."

"The Chris I knew wasn't shy around me."

"Oh Summer, if you only knew," he says and pulls his lips into his mouth.

I blink a few times and store that info nugget away to process later. "So, do you want the usual?"

"You still remember?" he asks, as if I could ever forget.

"Of course. I'm an awesome waitress."

"Well, let's just see about that."

I love a good challenge, especially if there's a little flirting involved. I whip out my notepad like a gunslinger in a draw and scribble down his order, then pin it to the ticket holder and go over to the pop machine. *I've so got this.*

"One root beer. Extra ice," I say and place the glass in front of him. Then ridiculously slow—just because I'm having fun with him—pull out a straw from my apron and set it in front of him.

He snatches it up as he suppresses a smile. Christopher is a fierce competitor.

"Am I right so far?" I ask and stand up a little straighter with my hands clasped behind my back.

"Yes," he grumbles playfully.

Mr. Wilkins is enjoying the show and so are the Andersons sitting on the other side of him.

"But," he starts and points over to the cake plate of donuts beneath a glass lid. "I bet you one jelly donut that you forgot the key ingredient of my meal."

A sharp memory slices through the present and makes my heart squeeze. It was sophomore year, Father's Day, and I was sitting on the curb outside of the Biscuit missing my dad. I didn't want anyone to see me cry, but Christopher must have. He brought me a jelly donut, sat down beside me, and tried to cheer me up. I wonder if he remembers or if this is just a coincidence.

I pretend to ponder his bet by scratching my chin for a few seconds and stare off to the side. "I will take that bet, Big Mac."

Christopher's lips purse. They're just as full as I remember. *Kissable lips*, I once thought long ago. A little laugh slips out of me and I reel it back in. He winks at me and I roll my eyes before taking off to help some of my other customers.

Eventually, Momma taps the bell and Christopher's food is up. I spin on my heels, grab his plate, and place it in front of him. "One well-done *plain* cheeseburger, onion rings, and an extra pickle."

The smile on his smug mug is annoyingly adorable. "Oh Gunderson, you almost got it," he says and brings the burger to his mouth. "I can't wait to eat that jelly donut."

"Sad," I say and cross my arms over my chest.

He lifts an eyebrow and takes a big bite, never taking his eyes off mine. When the barbecue sauce bursts from the bottom of his burger and splashes onto his plate, he groans.

"Sad for you," I gloat. "Did you honestly think I wouldn't remember?"

He doesn't say a word but his eyes speak for him as they glisten. He's enjoying this very much.

Christopher was the definition of a regular. He'd be here in his letter jacket sitting in his usual booth, working on his homework, at least three times a week. Honestly, I never understood how he afforded it and why his parents weren't feeding him at home. "You ordered that burger every time you were in here and I personally served that to you like at least a hundred times."

The six-foot-two first-line center pops to his feet and slides down to the end of the counter. "I hope you like powdered sugar," he says and plucks the only jelly donut we have from the plate and puts it on a napkin.

"Powdered sugar is my favorite," I tell him and accept my winnings with a smile. I bite into my victory and let the powdered sugar fall as it might all over my v-neck t-shirt.

Christopher plops back down on his stool and removes the bun from his burger and scraps off the barbecue sauce with his knife.

My mouth, still sweet with raspberry jelly goodness, drops open. "What on earth are you doing?"

"Can I have a glass of water?" he replies.

Then it dawns on me. He's a world-class athlete. He has an Olympic bronze medal. This boy doesn't eat sugar. He can't eat "the usual" like he used to. He couldn't even eat that jelly donut if he had won it. After I get over my initial heartbreak, I'm delighted and flattered he played along.

In an effort not to embarrass him in front of the other sugar-consuming customers, I lean in close and whisper, "Can I get you a side salad or some steamed veggies?"

"Why are we whispering?" he whispers back.

"You know, health concerns," I say a little louder because he's made me feel silly. Mr. Wilkins lifts an eyebrow.

"Right." He nods quite seriously and I know he's toying with me, but I like it. "Well, I'd love whatever veggies you've got back there. Surprise me." He passes his onion rings—God, I don't think I could live without Momma's onion rings even if it meant winning the Cup—to the Andersons and they gladly take them.

Lunch carries on and I serve the customers I've been neglecting for my shenanigans with Christopher. None of them seem to mind—in fact, everyone is in a fantastic mood. I guess that's what Christopher does to a room. After he finishes his lunch, I clear his space and offer him a coffee.

"No thanks, I kicked caffeine a few years ago."

"My gosh, you're a machine."

That makes him laugh.

"So, Chris," I start up and lean onto the counter space in front of him.

He leans forward too so that our faces are only half a foot apart. "So, Summer," he responds quietly so that this conversation becomes just for us.

"What have you been up to the past few days?"

"Not much. I had some other regional speaking events to attend."

"You and I have very different definitions of *not much*."

His eyes never leaving mine, he asks, "What about you? Where you been?"

"Trapped inside the *Telegram*," I answer and find myself swallowing a little bit harder than usual. This closeness to him is making my body wonky.

"Speaking of that, my agent mentioned that Tia had been in touch. Apparently you're doing a premiere of the video you made about my day with the Cup."

Blood rushes to my cheeks and I stand back up. "All Tia, and I told her not to contact your agent," I say to diffuse my nerves. I've never been fond of being the center of attention and the premier is really starting to freak me out.

"It's tomorrow night, right?"

"Yeah, she's got it all set up. There's going to be a party and all that. You're not coming, are you?"

He hesitates and then shakes his head. "I have to get to Las Vegas for the league awards."

"Thank God," I tell him and place my hand over my chest. I finally feel like I can breathe again. The idea of Christopher watching the video was eating all my air.

"But I want to see it," he says and looks at me with those same brown eyes that haven't seemed to age in all the time I've known him.

Damn it.

"What time do you get off work?" he goes on.

"You know, it's really not necessary. I'll drop you the link when it's online." Fat chance of me doing that.

"Don't get shy on me now. You know I've always liked your work. I want to see it," he says.

In high school, when I started dabbling in video and recording their games for highlights on the morning announcements broadcast, he always made sure to compliment me. He had that way of making me feel like I was the one who had accomplished something when he—and Trey, for that matter—had played their hearts out and won the game.

"I get off at three," I finally answer.

"Great, I'll pick you up."

"Will the Cup be joining us again?"

"Nah, it's at some cabin in Colorado with Hux. I'm pretty sure its going to finally meet its end by the time he's done with it. He's a brute, on and off the ice."

I can totally picture it. The Storm's star defenseman Nikolas Huxley doesn't seem like he does delicate.

Christopher digs into his pocket to fish out some money and pushes a fifty across the counter.

I push it right back. "That's way too much."

"It's for me and my friends," he says and pats Mr. Wilkins and the Andersons on the back, and I let him have this one because I can't deny how happy he's just made them. He stands up to go and points at me. "Three o'clock."

"Three o'clock," I confirm and he lifts his chin in my direction.

He goes just the way he came, with all eyes on him, including my own.

Christopher

When I poke-checked the puck away from a Pittsburgh Growler's defenseman at the blue line and made my break-away in game seven overtime, I had two thoughts pop into my head. One—don't fuck this up. Two—she's probably watching. The *she* being Summer Gunderson. That second thought almost made me fuck it up, which was in direct conflict with the first thought. I pushed her out of my head and focused on Grinblat, Pittsburgh's goalie, while keeping an eye on the puck. Grinblat traveled dangerously far out of the paint in an attempt to cut off my angle. It was his weakness and I knew exactly how to exploit it. The fucker had a hero complex. Most goalies do. I pushed my puck to the tip of my stick, far out from me to tempt the most arrogant goalie in the league. Sure enough, Grinblat dove out to smack it away but I pulled back, just like Trey did to win our second state championship. I went to his left to backhand that baby right into the center of the net.

The fans went wild and so did we. I threw off my gloves

and tossed my stick aside. And while the noise was absolutely deafening and the moment was completely surreal, all I could think about was thought number two. She saw it. She was seeing me. And that's when I knew my body may be in the center of Denver's arena, but my heart was in Fossebridge, Minnesota.

Now that woman is sitting beside me in my old pickup truck as we drive to her house. Something feels so right about having her in the passenger seat. It always has. I try not to think about the night of the Winter Formal, but it happens regardless. It was the first time I held her hand. The last would be at Trey's funeral.

"I'm not going to lie. I'm super nervous to show you this video," she says, lightening my darkness.

"That's ridiculous. I'm the last person you should be nervous to show it to. You've had to look at my ugly mug for hours editing the thing. I should be apologizing."

"Yeah, you're so ugly, Chris. It really did take its toll." I don't even have to look over at her to know she's rolling her eyes.

"That's what I'm saying. You should look into worker's compensation," I tell her and can't hold back this stupid grin I've got going on.

We pull up outside her house and get out. My palms are sweaty as we walk up the driveway. In all the time I've known her, I've only been inside this house once, and only in the living room. I've never seen her bedroom, even though it was the setting for multiple fantasies of mine in high school.

A small black cat greets us in the foyer and swooshes around her legs smoother than most of my teammates on the ice. "This is Miss Mouse, my baby," she says and picks up the sleek beast with one hand and carries her along with us. "You're not allergic, are you?"

"Nope. Not at all."

"Oh yeah, you grew up with cats," she mumbles as we climb the stairs, I assume up to her room.

This is it, I tell my teenage self as we enter. The first thing I notice is the smell. It's just like her, only amplified. A more distinguished man would know the scent right down to the flower, but I'm a hockey player. All I know is that it smells like how I think women should smell and that's probably been her programming me for the past fifteen years.

Next, it's the bed. *Of course it is, you perve.* It's a full-sized bed and shoved into a corner, where the antique white rail headboard partially covers her window. The comforter is dark purple and her pillowcases are mismatched. There are a bunch of dirty clothes overflowing her hamper, which she's now picking up and stuffing back inside, and two water glasses on the nightstand. She was clearly not expecting company and knowing that honestly makes it easier to breathe. We've haven't really caught up with one another, so I'm unsure if she has a boyfriend. I'd hope that my parents would tell me if she did, but they're not always the most observant people. I'm pretty sure that there isn't a person with a Y chromosome in this whole town that deserves her, including me.

There's a small desk with shelves installed above it. She's got a hodgepodge of things, like an oversized round alarm clock, a wooden letter S, a few books on videography and some fiction. There's also some half-burned candles, two mismatched mugs with old teabags in them, a framed art print, and a green leafy plant that winds its way along some string lights. It's like Christmas in July because so many of my curiosities have been satisfied. My favorite thing is a needle-point that hangs just beside it that says *Fuck You Very Much* in a fancy font. I'm charmed by all of it.

I glance at the whiteboard calendar she's got bolted to the wall. There, in all caps and circled in green dry erase marker, it says *Christopher's Day*. It's the first time I've ever seen my name in her handwriting before and it does something to me. *Fuck, I'm so lame.* If my teammates could see me now, pining after a girl so bad that even her handwriting makes me hard. Ridiculous.

She grabs her laptop out of a backpack and plops down on the bed and then pats the empty space beside her.

Dream. Come. True. At least for the seventeen-year-old me.

I'm tempted to hop on with a running start, but I think I'd destroy the ancient bed frame in the process, so I gently crawl on and sit beside her, elbow-to-elbow. She crosses one leg over the other toward me and I wish she wasn't wearing jeans so we could get a little more skin-to-skin, but beggars can't be choosers in Summer Gunderson's bedroom.

Quicker than I can pass the puck to a winger, she opens her laptop and cues the video. "Here goes nothing." She places the computer on my lap and her hand gets dangerously close to the one place I'd love for her touch but would absolutely die of embarrassment if she did in this context.

She presses the space bar and the video begins. I'm four-teen years old and on the ice as number nineteen. The footage is old and choppy, just like my moves back then. I quickly lose sight of myself and focus on Trey. He was a natural since day

43

one. He's only in the shot for a few seconds before it's all on me again and I'm reminded what this is all about. The video morphs into current times and I'm transformed into the player I am today and then back again. The editing is beautiful and so is the music. It's a song I've never heard before but the lyrics fit perfectly.

I watch in awe as it shows my experience as a hockey player, from my heyday in high school with Trey to my time at college in Boston, my draft day, my brief stint in the minors, and then making it to the big leagues. My day with the Cup in Fossebridge is woven into an edit that makes me feels excitement and pride comparable to actually winning the Cup. It's fantastic.

Seeing myself through her *eyes* is unreal. I look good. Real good. It makes me wonder if Summer Gunderson sees me the same way that I see her—the very epitome of my heart's desire. After everything we've been through and *haven't* been through, it seems impossible, but I'm going to pretend like it's not.

Once it's over, I close the lid slowly and pass the laptop back to her. The only thing I hate about it is that she's not in it, not even for one second and for that it will be incomplete in my mind. But seriously, this video is better than most professional pieces I've seen or been a part of. The girl's got talent and I've always known it.

"Say something," she requests while she fidgets with the simple silver ring she's always worn on her right middle finger.

I sigh and try to think of someway to express how great it is. "What are you still doing here, Gunderson?"

"What do you mean?"

"I've seen my fair share of sports pieces over time and you've got a real eye for this."

"You only like it because you're the star."

"Me being the star is the thing I like least about it," I tell her. I know it's dramatic, but I want her to hear me. This isn't just about my role in it, it's what she's put together. It's fucking art.

"That's nonsense," she says and scoots off the bed, much to my disappointment. She puts the laptop away and starts pacing around. "Well, I think it's really gonna help out Tia and the *Telegram*. Our website traffic and social media is already sky high since you came back to town."

"Well this is definitely going viral," I tell her.

She points a finger at me. "Do not use the *V word* with me. Do not do it, Christopher!"

"Summer, I'm serious, you need to get out of Fossebridge. I'm sure Tia has told you the same."

"Tia would shit a brick if I left. So would Momma. That's not happening. Plus, where would I go?"

"Come to Colorado. Work for the team. We have a video production unit in our marketing department, and they'd love to have you."

"Right, I'm sure," she says, dismissing herself.

I'm going to make it my life's mission to boost her confidence.

I scoot to the edge of the bed and stop her in her tracks by gently taking hold of her hips. She freezes in place and I turn her toward me. She gazes down at me and bites her pale pink bottom lip. Her hair is a mess in its ponytail and her makeup is a little smeared. Her eyes are a bit on the frantic side of things, and yet she's still unbelievably gorgeous.

I didn't mean for this to turn into such an intimate encounter, but now that I have her like this in her bedroom, I can think of nothing else but pulling her legs around me and bringing her down onto the bed again. This time straddling my waist.

"Summer," I whisper up at her, the most beautiful name in the world. "Believe in yourself the way that I believe in you."

Her eyes flutter closed and her body sways ever so slightly, like she's lost her balance. I'd give anything to know what she's thinking. She was right about me. I am a patient man but only for her, so I wait for her to open her eyes again. When she does, they're wet. It dares to crumble my resolve. I want to scoop her up and hold her body to mine. I want to tell her that I love her and that I always have, but before I can do any of that her lips part and she asks, "Did you like the parts with Trey?"

Like getting a high stick to the chest, I lose my breath. I'm reminded again about why we were never able to act on this feeling between us. I'm reminded about how everything went wrong.

Summer

Summer before Senior Year

My stupid mouth. Worse yet, my stupid brain. This was all my idea in the first place, and now I'm scared to actually go through with it.

"Don't think, just do it," Trey barks at me as he wades around in Webster Lake.

"Yeah," I reply, but stay frozen in place with the rope in my hand.

"There's nothing to it," Christopher says and smooths back his wet black hair. "Just get a bit of a running start, jump, and let go."

"Yeah," I say again, because all the words they're saying make sense, they do, but I really don't want to do this. Too bad there's no way I'm going get out of it.

"Three, two, one!" Trey tries, God bless him, but I don't budge, not even a little bit.

Tia is at my side, rocking an aqua bikini that looks fabulous against her golden brown skin, while I'm totally drab and already sunburned in my modest navy blue bikini. "Should I go again?" she asks, and it's a swift kick to my ego. She had no problem at all taking the rope, swinging over the lake, and letting go. But that's Tia. Confidence is her strong suit.

I shake my head vigorously. "No, I've got this."

"Yeah, you do," Trey murmurs as he floats on his back. He's clearly lost interest.

I glance at Christopher and he's not smiling. Which isn't unusual for him, but this look is different. His jaw looks tight and his eyebrows are scrunching together. I think he's worried for me. "Summer—"

I cut him off. "I've got this."

"Only if you want it." There's a gentleness in his tone that is a little unexpected but I'm not surprised at his way with words. It's what makes him a natural captain.

"I do want it. I know I do." Tears are springing to my eyes and it's absolutely infuriating.

"Then you can do it. I believe in you," he yells over Trey, who's singing "Whole Lotta Love" off tempo and very off key.

Christopher's affirmation isn't superficial. I know, deep down, that those aren't just words he's saying. He's shown me time and again that he has faith in me in a lot of the things I do. I borrow against his belief to make this happen. A little prayer slips out as I grip the rope tighter and start running toward the shore. I take the leap and see Christopher's face for one split second as I swing out over the lake. He's smiling like a damn fool. Even Trey is watching now.

"Let go!" Christopher shouts.

So, I do. The fall is a little longer than I expected, but it gives me the most exhilarating rush. Too bad I can't control my arms or legs, because all that flailing around makes for a horrendous landing. Water splashes every which way when I go in butt first. *Youch, that stings.*

From beneath the surface, my friends' hooting and hollering is distorted but it still brings a smile to my face. When I break through the surface of the water, Christopher is there and he takes hold of my arm and pulls me toward shallower water. Even though we both know I'm an adequate swimmer, I go along with it anyway. Altogether too soon, my toes drag along the sandbar and we're standing together. It's time to let go now, but he doesn't. He stays close to me and rubs my arm ever so slightly. My breath catches and it has nothing to do with the jump. He doesn't congratulate me, nor does he take any credit for inspiring me. Instead, he gazes down at me and if his eyes could smile, they'd be beaming.

"Ready to go again?" he asks.

"Maybe in a little while," I answer, because I don't want to move an inch away from him.

"How's your butt?"

"Sore, but what else is new?" I don't even know what that means, but it makes him laugh, and me too. It doesn't go unnoticed when he places his free hand on my other arm. It's nearly an embrace now, but still so far from it. An urge to wrap my arms around him, and my legs too, roots down in my lower belly but I wouldn't dare make a first move like that, especially in front of my cousin.

I go into an unfamiliar zone where I'm hyperaware of sensations. Like the way his swimming trunks keep caressing my abdomen in rhythm with the water's current. Every time the fabric makes contact, my thighs press together beneath the surface. Or the way his thumbs are tracing the inside of my elbows, sending flutters through my chest right down to my toes that are pressing into the sand beneath my feet.

His eyes are darker now and he's squinting from the setting sun. His lips are parted and I notice mine are too. I've never kissed a boy before. I've never even understood how to get started, how to make a moment between two people tip over into a kiss. It's been nearly impossible for me to imagine how my first kiss with someone might play out, but now it's so clear. It's like this. It's like letting go of that rope and falling right into that moment. This is chemical. It's a physical pull that goes beyond logic and words and decisions. The decision is already made for me, no thinking or talking required.

His feet shuffle and align with mine. The fabric is there now, flush against my abdomen. He's holding me close and his eyes shut as our chests press against each other. Like magnets, our mouths are going to snap together and there's not a damn thing that will stop it.

But there is someone that will. My stupid cousin. Trey is suddenly invading our space, taking Christopher in a swift move and pressing his head under the water. As big as Trey is, he's no match for Christopher, who easily overpowers him and the two go to war. I make my way to the shore and get out of the water, happy for the space to process what just happened. I almost had my first kiss. With Christopher!

Tia is there, waiting for me, and the look on her face speaks volumes. I'm totally busted.

She pounces on me like a kitten on your toes under a blanket and I jump back. "Did you guys almost kiss?"

I laugh and then laugh some more, hoping that it seems dismissive, but I know it's not. Honestly, the laugh is making it even more obvious that she's spot on.

"You did!" My goodness, she's loud.

"Be quiet," I command, and pull her by the arm to a nearby tree.

"I knew it. He's always had a thing for you."

"Stop," I say, but in my heart I know she's right. I mean, he's got to be, right? He comes by the Biscuit all the time, he's always around to drive me home when I stay late to work on the paper, and all those times I've caught him looking my way at school... That all adds up, right? *Yes,* I tell myself.

Tia doesn't bother arguing, because she knows she's right, too. "Well, I think this year is going to be so awesome. You have Christopher and I..." She looks over her shoulder at the water and smiles.

"Trey?" I ask, a little shocked.

"Yes," she whispers.

"Why didn't you tell me?"

"You must be blind, because I've liked him for so long, dummy."

"I never knew," I tell her, and try to run through all the times I've seen them interact. Nothing obvious comes to mind. "Do you think he feels the same way?"

"Hard to say. He's so laissez faire about everything that I can't really tell."

"Laissez faire? I'm not sure you're using that right."

"You know what I mean," she says and swats my arm.

I take a moment to consider Trey's possible feelings for Tia. Honestly, he doesn't spend much time without Christopher, and he's always so focused on hockey. He's got goals and does not keep it a secret that his dream is to bring the Cup home to Fossebridge one day.

"Would you be pissed if we hooked up?" Tia asks.

"Why would I be pissed?" I reply, genuinely baffled by her question.

"Because he's your cousin," she says like it's a no-brainer.

"Oh jeez, I don't care about that. He can be with whoever he wants."

"But what if things went bad between us? I'd hate to make you choose. That's why I've been afraid to tell you. I didn't think you'd approve."

This girl. She's one of the most considerate people that I know. "Trust me, there's enough room in my life for both of you. I would never pick one over the other."

"Even if he broke my heart?"

"Tia, Jesus. Why are you thinking about how it ends before it even begins? Don't you believe in a happily ever after?"

"I'm too smart for that." She laughs like she's joking, but as her best friend, I know that she's not. She's pragmatic to a fault. "What about you...do you believe in a happily ever after?"

"You know I do," I tell her, because it's true. If there are no happy endings, then what's the whole point of this?

3

Summer

TIA DOESN'T DO ANYTHING SMALL. THIS "PREMIERE," AS SHE
calls it, proves that point eight times over. The giant screen is
inflated at one end of the park, and folks from all over the
town are camped out on blankets and sitting on folding chairs
on the lawn. Children are as hyper as all the mosquitos flying
around, and enjoying the party, too. Needless to say, the smell
of bug spray almost overwhelms the community grills that are
cooking up hot dogs and brats. There's a cookie table filled
with treats brought by the residents of Fossebridge, as well as
coolers filled with pop and beer. At least that's what I've heard.
I haven't had a free moment to visit it myself, not that I could
even begin to eat or drink anything. I'm so nervous.

Once the sun begins to make its descent, Tia finds me
within the crowd and pulls me out. "It's time. I'll speak first,
and then hand the mic over to you."

"Do I really have to?" I ask as I stumble over my own feet on our way to the screen.

Tia keeps going. "Yes, you have to. Come on, girl, don't chicken out now. And don't forget to mention it will be on the website tonight so they can share it with their friends and family and hopefully the whole damn world."

My stomach roils. "Just a heads up, I'm joining an ashram in India after this."

"Even ashrams have wifi these days. And there's no time to *Eat, Pray, Love* your way through the world. We've got shit to do," she says and keeps yanking me to the front.

Why did I let her talk me into this? If Christopher were here, he could redirect that figurative spotlight in the blink of an eye. It sure would be nice to breathe again. Breathing is my favorite. But he's not here, so I've got to suck it up. His words echo in my head. *Believe in yourself the way that I believe in you.*

I do believe in myself. I *know* the video is good. I'm just worried about it being overhyped. I mean, for Christ's sake, she put on a whole town event for it. Why, oh, why couldn't we just put it out into the universe and let people consume it on their own?

As if sensing these spiraling thoughts, Tia says, "Buckle up buttercup. You'll be fine." Then she turns on the mic and taps on it, making quite a disruptive sound. It definitely gets everyone's attention.

"Good evening, Fossebridge. Thanks so much for coming out to the world premiere of *Little Giant*, a video for the *Fossebridge Weekly Telegram*. Our very own Summer Gunderson put together this feature about Christopher 'Big Mac' MacCormack's visit to Fossebridge with the Cup. Before I hand it over to

Summer to introduce the video, I'd like to thank our many wonderful sponsors." Tia rattles them off and starts clapping awkwardly with the microphone in hand to get the crowd to clap along with her.

"Without further ado, Summer Gunderson," she says and hands me the mic.

It slips out of my sweaty palm and into the grass, making a godawful sound. I crouch down to grab it and realize that my sparkle-encrusted tank top reveals way too much cleavage for bending over like this in front of the whole town. So apparently they're getting *two* shows tonight. "Hi...sorry. Sorry," I say when I finally have control over the mic.

"So, um, this is a video I made about Christopher's day with the Cup. You'll see that it's not just about that day, but... well, you'll see," I peter out right away, not sure what else to say. Tia elbows me, and I turn to her. "What?" I say into the mic and she shakes her head sternly.

"The website," she mutters under her breath.

"Oh. Yeah," I say, once again into the microphone. "We'll be publishing the video on the *Fossebridge Weekly Telegram's* website tonight so you can watch it again."

Tia pulls the microphone her way. "So you can share it with your friends, far and wide."

"Or, you know, watch again, I guess," I say and decide to wrap up this humiliation. "Okay, here is *Little Giant*. I hope you enjoy it."

It takes a few seconds for the screen to warm up, which gives me the perfect opportunity to move away from the front of the crowd and watch from the edge of the gathering. When it finally begins, I'm just as dazzled with my work as if it's the first time I'm seeing it. I decide to turn away from the video itself and check out the audience just this one time and pray that they're enjoying it, but I don't get a chance. Instead, I'm startled half to death when someone steps up beside me and whispers, "See how much they love it?"

"Christopher," I say, too loudly for his liking. He puts a finger to my lips to shush me. "What are you doing here?" I whisper around his finger.

He pulls me back a few steps further so that we're now watching from the trees. "Did you honestly think I would miss this?" he asks quietly.

"You said you had to go to the awards."

"I changed my flight. I leave early tomorrow morning so I can make it on time."

"Are you insane?" I ask and grip onto his t-shirt.

"Shut up and watch," he says and turns my face back to the audience. "Look how much they love it. Just like I did. You're so incredibly talented, Summer."

My M.O. is to downplay, if not, outright refute compliments. But I stop myself, just this one time. It's not all together easy to read the faces of the crowd, but they seem enraptured. Even the little kids are sitting still as they watch their hockey god on screen.

As the video concludes, there's a quiet moment that seems to go on for an eternity. My pulse races as I wait for any sign of validation. Boy do I get it. They erupt in applause and ear-blistering whistles. My skin and bones vibrate from the pure joy I'm feeling. I glance up at Christopher and he's beaming at me. Pride radiates off of him.

"Get on out there," he urges me and sets me off with a push.

When I look back over my shoulder, he retreats into the trees. No one has seen him yet, as far as I can tell. He's giving me this moment to shine in front of our town. What. A. Guy.

"There you are," Tia says and scurries over to me. We practically jog back up to where the mic is. "Take a bow."

"I'm not taking a bow," I mutter.

She shakes her head, simply done with my silliness, and turns on the mic again. "Wasn't that fantastic?"

The crowd cheers even loud, hooting and hollering. Some start chanting my name and it actually takes off for a moment. How does Christopher handle this kind of thing?

Tia struggles to get the crowd's attention again, but is eventually able to say, "Remember, it will be on the *Fossebridge Weekly Telegram's* website tonight."

As the party breaks up, family after family makes their way over to me to congratulate me and give me their praise. It's all so sweet and I'm on top of the world. All the while, though, I'm keeping an eye out for Christopher but he doesn't show up. Maybe he already left, the weirdo. Maybe I hallucinated the whole thing. That would make more sense than him sticking around town for this.

Then it dawns on me. If I didn't hallucinate his appearance, he's probably over at the dock we used to hang out at. When I can finally get away, I grab two beers from the coolers and sneak away through the trees where I last saw him. It's a short walk through and when I emerge, I'm delighted to see that Christopher wasn't a figment of my overtired imagination.

He's there, in the flesh, sitting on the dock, leaning back and looking out at the water.

"Hey," I say and he glances over his shoulder, not startled in the slightest.

"Hey, Scorsese," he says and smiles.

"Please," I say and hand him the beers so I can sit down beside him. The water moves beneath us toward the shore.

"Believe me now?" he asks a little too smugly.

"I know it's good and I know I'm good at this. But yeah, tonight was nice."

He just smiles at me and opens his can.

"I don't know how you do it, though," I tell him.

"Do what?"

"Handle the pressure. They were chanting my name," I say with a laugh, because honestly, it's all absurd.

"Yeah, sorry, I started that chant. It felt good to be on the other end of that," he says with his classic laugh that starts deep in his chest.

"Jerkwad." I swat at him and then open my beer. I take a much needed drink and then lean back on my elbows to look up at the stars. They're more magnificent than I ever remember, sparkling and shimmering brighter, and I just know it's because Christopher is here. All the stars came out to see him.

He leans back on his elbows to do his own gazing, but he doesn't spend nearly as much time on the stars. His gaze turns to me and I feel him there, so unbelievably close but never close enough. He makes the whole left side of my body burn.

I turn away from the stars, who have nothing on him, and meet his twinkling eyes. We don't speak. There's no charade, no crafting our rapport. There's just this. The connection I've felt to him since I invaded his fifth grade class.

I was the girl with the hair that was so long it'd get tangled in my backpack. The girl with petal pink frames and thick lenses. The girl with the dead dad and a silly southern accent.

He was the boy that was too tall for our worktables and chairs. The boy that mercilessly chewed on pens. The boy who barely said more than *yes* or *no* or *sorry*.

The stars shine so bright for him...and why wouldn't they? He's a hockey god. He's a champion. But they don't know him. They don't know why he won't kiss me when our lips are mere inches apart, pulling closer and closer together the way the shore pulls in the water. The desire is there, boy is it ever there, and the tension that crackles between us is overflowing with untapped electricity. It wouldn't take much effort at all to cross that imaginary plane between us, to make this night be truly perfect.

But he clears his throat and sits up abruptly. Like I said, the stars don't know Christopher.

I sit up slowly and take another drink of my beer to shake off the need I feel for him and once again accept the complexities between us. I'm not only a master at video editing, as it turns out. I switch that gear right off and ready myself for more conversation.

"So..." he starts slowly. "What's next?"

"I'll put the video up on the website," I answer just as slowly.

"Not just tonight," he says. "I mean long term."

I let my legs dangle over the edge of the dock and if I'm not careful, I'll lose my sandals to the lake. Keeping my sandals dry is awfully important to focus on, at least that's what I tell myself. I'd rather not think about the long term, mostly because there's nothing to think about.

"You know my life," I answer simply and curl my toes. "The *Telegram*, the Biscuit, Fossebridge. I'll keep doing my thing."

"The *Telegram* is great, don't get me wrong," he starts and I can feel him boring holes into the side of my face. I can also feel that big "But" coming. "But you're so talented. You always have been."

Still focusing on my sandals, I reply, "And why doesn't the *Telegram* deserve someone so talented?"

"You can do more, Summer. You can go big. You can leave—"

"Stop, just stop, okay," I tell him and finally turn his way. "Don't do this."

"Do what?"

"Listen, I get it. You and I both know it better than anyone else, unlike anyone else. I know that being here is hard. The memories. The guilt. Everything."

His mouth drops open and I've stunned him momentarily speechless.

I go on. "You think you're saving me, but I'm trying to tell you, I'm okay with it. I'm okay thinking about Trey every day."

"Trust me, Summer. I think about him everyday too," he says with a rough edge to his tone. "It's impossible not to."

"So what is this about? Are you feeling guilty that you're the only one who left? Because you shouldn't feel guilty if you do. We're all fine. We don't mind living here."

"Not everything is about guilt. I know that's how it seems. I mean, it's the reason why we've never..."

"Never what, Chris?"

He hesitates, looks away, and shakes his head. Could he possibly be thinking what I'm thinking? How the night of Trey's death changed everything for everyone, but especially for us? How the possible became impossible?

"So if it's not the guilt, what is it?" I ask, much more gently this time.

Now he's the one who can't stop staring at his shoes. His jaw swishes side-to-side, just like he does on the ice.

My next question tumbles right out. "Why do you wish so much more for me?"

In the quietest voice, he finally speaks, "Isn't it obvious?"

I shake my head because I want to hear his actual answer.

He turns his head to look my way and our gazes lock again. The words that come next slip out of his mouth effortlessly. "Your dreams have always mattered to me. That's never changed. It will never change."

"Why?" I ask and unexpected tears well in the corners of my eyes.

His mouth opens, but no words come out. He either can't or won't answer that question. But I don't actually need the words. I'm pushing so hard for an answer that I've known for years. It was there that summer day at the lake in high school when he held me in the water. It was there the one and only time he held my face in his hands and kissed me after the Winter Formal. And it was there when he held my hand for the last time at Trey's funeral.

Christopher

The video went viral. Of course it did. Tia must be shitting herself with joy, while Summer is hiding under a rock somewhere. I can only imagine how much traffic the *Telegram's* website is getting.

Since Summer's name got out into the world, I've noticed a huge spike in subscribers on her personal YouTube channel. Yes, I check. I wasn't lying about wanting to see her succeed. It's always been a passion of mine. If only she knew the real reason why. If only she knew that sometimes I care more about her success than my own. That's a lie, I admit it...it's not just sometimes. It's all the time, especially these days. She thinks it's all wrapped up in guilt about Trey, but it's not. Before he died, I wanted the best for her. I always have.

Naturally I'm getting my fair share of sports media attention because of the video. That's a given. To make matters worse or perhaps better—I don't really know—I also won the league MVP trophy.

Yeah. That happened.

Vegas was a whirlwind of press and madness and temptation. Every step of the way there were women. Winning MVP multiplied that type of crazy. For once, I was relieved to have the team's personal security team with me. These weren't even puck bunnies. I've had a handle on that for years. These were determined she-beasts, trying to latch onto anyone with upward momentum, anyone with a fixed spotlight.

But now I'm back in Colorado. Beautiful, colorful Colorado. The place where I can breathe a little easier. The place where there's enough space for me. Playing for the

Storm is a fucking dream come true, but living in Colorado is an absolute blessing. Don't get me wrong, Minnesota will always be home, but there's a reason why midwesterners flock to Colorado, and it's not just for the legalized marijuana.

I've been away from my loft in LoDo too long. The exposed brick wall and brown leather couches are a sight for my sore eyes. My plants are thriving, the place is spotless, and my fridge is filled with fresh food and prepared meals. Thank God for the people that make my life work.

I don't stay long, though. The moment I set my bags down, I go to see my girl. She's next door and I've missed her so much.

I knock rapidly on the loft door next to mine and bounce on my toes while I wait.

The doors are too heavy to hear anything on the other side, so I'm not sure if I'm going to get to see her after all. I've almost given up when I hear the door unlatch. A smile spreads across my face. It's been too long and I can't wait to hold her in my arms.

Lily opens the door with a smile on her face that matches mine. She's changed her hair color from pale blue to a rainbow of colors. She's wild like that.

"Hey, you're back," she says.

"I'm back," I tell her and rub my hands together.

"Shall I call you Mister MVP, now?" she teases and wheels back to open the door wide for me.

"Bah, no," I say with a laugh and step across the threshold into Lily's place.

Two weeks shouldn't seem so long, but when I'm away from my girl it seems to last forever. Thank goodness Lily lives

ELLIE MALOUFF

next door. It's tremendously convenient and I need all the convenience I can get, even in the off-season.

"I've missed my girl," I tell Lily and weave my way around to her. She's staring at me with big dilated eyes and a look of an utter indifference. I'd move mountains to be with her and she lives to punish me like this.

I know it's only a matter of time before her icy stance melts, so I take hold of her in my arms and kiss her on the forehead. She uses all her strength to push away, but she's no match for me. "Don't make me hold you like a baby," I whisper and she tries to break free again.

"You were gone too long," Lily says.

"This happens if I'm gone for a fraction of that time," I say and try again to kiss her on the forehead. This time she puts up a very determined fight and presses her paw against my mouth. "Did you play with the red dot while I was gone?"

"The assigned training, yes, of course," Lily says with a laugh in her voice.

"Gotta keep up those puck-chasing skills."

"You do know that she's a cat, right?" Lily asks and stands by watching as I flip Joey over onto her back and stick my face in her furry belly. "You're so getting hissed at."

And Lily is right. Joey hisses at me hard and bats at my head, but I don't care. All that pain is worth it to enjoy her calico fur.

"Thanks for taking care of her," I tell Lily.

She smiles and twists some hair back off of her shoulder. As a work-from-home software developer, she and Luthor, her bulldog, are almost always around. "My pleasure. I'm sad to see her go," she says and gives Joey a little ear scratch.

"Just be careful, MVP. I think she's starting to get a crush on me."

"Thanks for the warning," I say with a laugh and take my sweet girl home. Once settled, I get a text from Robin in the front office. They want me to come in for an impromptu strategic meeting.

As captain and the face of the team, this isn't altogether unusual, but we just got off the fucking plane.

Christopher: *Gotta hit my work out first. Be there in two hours.*

Robin Farmer, Executive Director of Media Relations, greets me like we weren't just on a private jet together this morning. "Big Mac, thanks for coming in," he says and we fist bump.

"No problem, Rob. What's up?" I ask and plop down on one of his oversized office chairs. I glance across his desk to a credenza where he has lots of framed photos. Next to a photo of him and his husband is a picture of himself holding up the Cup. It's awesome to see that this was truly a team victory all the way around.

"It's about this viral video. We're seeing some fantastic traction on it, especially from a prime female demographic. As you know, you can't go wrong with that. Remember Luke Blotner riding naked on the Zamboni for the *Physique* issue? That did a lot for the Lynx."

"I do. I'm pretty sure I talked some massive shit to him about it in the division playoffs last year."

"We're always trying to diversify the team following and so

the higher ups have taken note. The video has a ton of heart and stokes emotions. You really made a dent."

"Summer Gunderson deserves all the credit."

"Yes, your old friend, right?"

"Right," I say and lean forward a little bit. Talking about Summer in this setting sets me on edge.

"Tell me, was this some fluke thing she made with some app, or is this the real deal?"

"Real deal, one hundred percent," I answer quickly. "Summer has been a talented videographer for years. She works for the *Fossebridge Weekly Telegram*, a small weekly paper."

He laughs at that, as if I just told him that she works for... well, a small weekly newspaper.

"But she has a degree from the University of Minnesota and has done a whole series of videos that are superb. She's been doing this since high school."

"I'll cut to the chase. We could use her lens, if you catch my drift, to pull in more female fans. Do you think she'd be interested in a job?"

"Yes," I tell him, even though not even two days ago she and I argued about this exact thing.

"And she'd be okay with relocating? And being on the road, following the team occasionally?"

"If the offer's right," I answer, knowing full well that they'd probably try to lowball her. I won't let that happen.

"She'd have a junior title and work under Welby."

"Welby?"

"Jim Welby, the head of digital media."

"Oh, that guy who made me skate around in the sumo wrestler getup for that goofy video right before the playoffs?"

Robin puts on a phony smile that dies at his eyes. "Yes, that's Welby."

The anger I felt that day comes right back. "I nearly broke my ankle doing that."

"We're well aware. Jim needs some help and we think… your friend…might breathe some new life into our media production unit."

"My friend's name is Summer Gunderson and you should let me talk to her before you make her an offer."

"Listen, I've got to ask, is there anything going on between the two of you that could cause some complications here? The last thing we need is a locker room divided if your friend gets involved with one of your teammates."

The idea of one of my teammates touching Summer in any way beyond a friendly, professional handshake makes my blood boil. Regardless, I'd never let my jealousies stand in her way of doing something big. It's my burden to deal with the disappointment that I can't be with her. I've been carrying that burden since the senior year of high school. It's why I've tried to move on countless times since then, but I've never gone further than a month in any relationship. It's hard to be with someone else, when the woman you've been in love with for years is back in Minnesota waiting for her life to really begin. Even if I can't be with her, at least I can help propel her career.

So I tell Robin the truth. "There's nothing going on between us now. Any chance to form a romantic relationship died and was buried long ago."

When I told Robin that I wanted to talk to Summer before he does, that was true. But before Summer, I have to talk this over with Tia. It's not that Tia is her keeper, I just know that getting Tia's support will definitely give me an advantage with Summer, and I'm all about using advantages. It's why I'm the lead points earner on the Storm.

Joey is still pissed at me and is hiding under the bed. So, I shake a can of kitty treats, knowing that it's the only way she'll come out to see me. The ploy works just as planned and we're well on our way to reconciliation. I hope the same can be said for me and Summer when I dangle this amazing opportunity out for her.

I wouldn't call our last conversation a fight. I've been in some drag-out nasty fights in my time. I would simply call it a friendly disagreement.

Christ, the last time we were together, I was seconds away from kissing her. I've spent countless nights thinking about kissing Summer one more time. One more shot at it. To feel her lips on mine again, to connect so passionately the world gets blocked out. I find myself slipping down into that fantasy once again, the one where it's just the two of us, alone, and free to be together without all the baggage. Without anything or anyone in our way. Where I slip off her shirt and bury my face—

Damn it, I'm doing it again.

Time to call Tia and get this show on the road. I've got plans tonight with Hux, and I'm going to be late if I don't make this happen. She answers on the fourth ring and it sounds like

I've caught her while manning the monitors at air traffic control.

"What do you want, MacCormack?" she asks. At least there's one person out there that doesn't kiss my ass.

"I'm calling about Summer."

"I've got about three minutes," she says and then shouts, not at me, "There are a thousand typos in this thing. Do better."

Damn, she's tough. I'm feeling pretty shitty about my chances, but go for it anyway, cutting right to the chase. "My team wants to hire her."

The chaos on the other line comes to a complete stop. I pull the phone away from my face and make sure that we're still connected. "Tia?"

"Hold on a second," she says. There's shuffling and movement and then silence. "Okay, I stepped out so we could talk."

"Did you hear what I said?"

"Yeah, I heard it," she says, her voice emotionless.

"And?"

"Well, I knew this day would come. I just didn't think it would happen so fast."

"You knew the Storm would hire her?"

"Not the Storm exactly, but I knew some great gig would come along. She's too talented to be sitting around Fossebridge."

"That's exactly my point, too."

"Did you set this up for her?" she asks, always the inquisitor.

"I didn't. I had a conversation with her at the premiere

about doing something beyond Fossebridge, but she didn't want to hear it."

"You were at the premiere?"

Busted. "Yeah, I was…sort of hanging in the shadows."

"Huh," is her only response. Tia takes a deep breath and sighs into the phone. "I'm guessing that you're calling for my blessing or something."

"I know your support means so much to her. She would never leave out of an obligation to you, you know that, right?"

"Oh, I know it. Summer is tremendously loyal. She lives to please her friends and family."

"But…?"

"Don't worry, MacCormack. I'm with you. It's time to push this little bird out of the nest."

"Do you think her mom will be okay with it?"

"Without a doubt. Peggy wants nothing more than for Summer to spread her wings. She's going to be especially excited that it will be with you and for the Storm. She's always liked you."

I sigh, relieved at that notion. "Well, then. Maybe this is going to work after all."

"What's the offer like?" Tia asks.

"I suspect it will be a good one, but I don't have all the details. I wanted to make sure that she would even be up for this. I didn't want her to be caught off guard."

"You're a good guy. Do right by her," Tia orders.

"That's always been my goal," I tell her, and feel the weight of our history bearing down on my chest. People often forget that Tia had a role to play in everything that went down back

then. If anything, she's the one who may have paid the ultimate price when Trey died.

"I know, Christopher," Tia says quietly. "I wouldn't trust
anyone else alive."

Summer

The Biscuit is once again swamped. It's been this way all
summer long. Something about Christopher's visit and my
subsequent video sparked a new sense of town pride. All the
residents are being super friendly with one another. They go
out more and they plan more community events. It's as if
they're trying to hold onto this magnificent summer as long as
they can. And there are actual tourists coming in to visit the
Biscuit. Usually we get a few, mostly family friends of the
people that live here, but it seems like people are going out of
their way to experience our little slice of Americana.

Mr. Wilkins gets in extra early these days to make sure he
gets his usual seat at the counter. He stays a little longer too,
entertaining me from time to time with really goofy jokes. The
kind that no one actually laughs at—the punny ones that I
find so delightfully funny, especially when he tells them. Or, if
I'm lucky, he'll tell me stories from his time in the Air Force.
Even though he served decades before my dad, it makes me
think of my dad fondly. The one thing he never talks about is
his wife, Louise. She died five years ago. And that's when he
started coming in. He doesn't drink as much coffee as he used
to—he says it upsets his condition—but he doesn't have to buy
a thing to get to sit at my favorite end of the counter.

Momma is a busy bee in the kitchen and Uncle Dave is

helping out. He's the spitting image of my father, which is weird when I see them together. I wonder if it's as weird for her.

Trey was also the spitting image of Uncle Dave with sandy blond hair, gray eyes, and a stout build, but I don't want to think on that for too long.

Momma's hired some new waitresses and has an ad out for another short order cook for the kitchen. It might just be seasonal, because who knows how business will shape up in the winter.

I've just served an order of her biscuits with gravy when my cell phone vibrates against my butt. I slip it out and see the name *Christopher* lighting up the display. It's so weird for him to call me, so I go ahead and step out into the alley out back to take it.

"Hey, Chris, what's up?"

"Hey. How are you?"

"Since the video went viral? Basically the same in real life," I answer.

That makes him laugh a little. "And not in real life?"

"The internet is a really weird place, that's all I'm going to say," I reply and shake my head. The outpouring of comments, likes, subscriptions, and such would make you think I was immensely popular. I tried to keep up with it at first, trying to respond to every comment. I've always tried to give back to my viewers as much as possible. I was thrilled that they took the time to watch, and for that I suppose I still am, but now it's impossible. It's just blown up and so have my other videos.

"Well, that's a relief, I'm sure, still having that bit of

anonymity. Sometimes, I'd love to put that all back into the can, if you know what I mean."

"Knowing you, it's probably more than sometimes, right?" I ask and kick some gravel.

"You know me better than anyone, so of course you're right."

It's a heavy thing to say, that's for sure. After I absorb his words, I wonder once again why he's calling me. He's not exactly the type of person who calls to check in or shoot the shit. At least, that's not how it's been up until this point. Maybe he's wrong. Maybe I don't know him nearly that well.

"Listen," he begins and I let out a big breath. There is a purpose. I do know him. "I'm just going to come right out and say it so we can start the negotiations."

"Negotiations?"

"The Storm want to hire you," he states plainly.

"The Storm...want to hire me? For what, exactly?"

"You know what, Summer. They loved the video. They love your work. They want you to join the media relations group and do videography for the team. Travel with us and produce videos on a regular basis."

My lungs expand as I process the words he's saying. It's like someone calls you out of the blue and says, "Oh hey, you know how you always dreamed of riding a magical rainbow unicorn through a chocolate forest? Well, you're in luck."

But of course, I can't immediately shriek *YES!!!* into the phone. Nothing is ever that simple. There are so many things tying me to Fossebridge. "That's an amazing offer, it really is, but—"

He cuts me right off. "Before you start up about the *Telegram*, you should know that I talked to Tia."

"You did *what*?"

"She's on board, one hundred percent. She's ready to let you go."

"Chris, I really wish you would have let me handle that."

"I wanted to make this as easy for you as possible."

"You know, sometimes you make me feel like I can conquer the world and other times you make me feel like an incapable child. Why are you so involved? Why haven't I heard from the team about this yet?"

"The last time we talked about this, you had a lot of reservations about leaving. I wanted to make it easier for you."

"Did you set this job up for me?" I have to know the answer to that. He's their star player and their captain. They've just won the Cup in large part due to him. He could ask for the moon right about now and they'd call NASA.

"Nope, this was all them," he says and I can tell he's being honest. It's not like Christopher to lie. "If you really want to know, they like your gaze—your lens, as it were."

"What does that mean?"

"Your ability to pull in the female fans."

"Oh," I say simply and think through what that means. The video I made wasn't gratuitous with the hot hockey player subject, but then again, Christopher kind of makes it that way, intentionally or not. "And I would just be making videos all the time?"

"Sounds like it to me, yes. They'll have all the details. Are you considering this, Summer?"

It's impossible not to consider it. I don't tell him that, because I have to think. "Let me talk it over with Momma."

I can hear him smiling from multiple states away. "You will love Colorado," he says. "There's so much to do in Denver. And you'll get to basically see all of North America. I'm not sure you've ever had a thing for travel, but it's as glorious as it is grueling."

"Don't get ahead of yourself," I say through a giddy laugh. "I need time. Is that okay?"

"Of course it is. Just get here before the summer ends, will ya?" he says and sounds happier than I've heard him in years.

I feel our conversation winding down but I'm not ready to let him go yet. "Chris?"

"Yeah?"

"Thanks, I think."

"You think?" he asks, amused. "For what?"

"For letting me hitch my wagon to yours."

"Don't say that. It's not about me. It's always been about you. Always," he says so earnestly that I might actually believe him.

As I'm closing up the diner with Momma, it all starts to break apart. Who will do this with her? Who will be the one to clean off the gum from underneath the tables? Who will refill the ketchups and sugar shakers? Obviously, you don't need particularly special skills to do these things, but it's our routine.

But it's not the sugar shakers that are making me lose my marbles. It's the undeniable fact that I've been all Momma has had since Daddy died. I can't bear the idea of her going to bed alone in our house. She did it while I was in college, but I came home often and there was a temporary feel to the whole thing. Working for the Storm feels tremendously different.

Tears are slipping down my cheeks as I mop the floor.

"Baby, what's wrong?" Momma asks from the kitchen window.

I shake my head and that just makes the teardrops fly off my face.

"Cheese 'n' rice, Summer," she says, and comes out from the back and puts her arms around me. She smells like french fries and maple syrup. "You should be so happy, with the video and all that."

"I am happy, Momma, but I'm also not happy."

"And why not?"

"Because I got offered a job."

Her eyes light up and she smiles. "Why the hell are you crying?"

"It's in Colorado, for Christopher's team."

"I don't see a tragedy here."

"You know why I'm cryin'," I say, my childhood southern accent making a guest appearance.

"Because of me?" she asks, rather flabbergasted.

"Yes, dummy," I tell her and laugh into another sob.

"Well, I'll always be your momma, no matter where you are. That will never change, so you should button this up right now."

"But I'm leaving you all alone," I tell her and break down again.

"Who's the dummy now?" she says and swats at my butt

with a dishtowel. "I'm not alone, not at all. I've got your aunt and uncle, and Tia, and Margie. Hell, I've got all of Fossebridge. I wouldn't be your momma if I wanted you to pass up such an amazing opportunity just to get you to stay with me. That's the exact opposite of what I'm going to do. I'm going to pack your boxes. I'm going to clean out your room and put in one of those elliptical machines."

The tears flow even harder, "No momma, don't clean out my room," I cry and squeeze her even tighter. It's amazing how quickly I can revert to six years old.

"I'm teasing, just teasing. Your room will always be your room, okay?"

"Promise?"

"With all my heart," she says, and uses her jam-stained apron to dry my face. "Is it okay if I keep Miss Mouse, though? Then I'll know for sure that you'll come back to visit."

I swat at her and laugh. "Of course, Momma. Fossebridge is her home."

4

Christopher

MOST OF MY TEAMMATES WILL TELL YOU THAT THEY ENJOY THE summertime.

They use their time off to travel across the world, which makes little sense to me, since I feel like I live my life on an airplane.

If they're not traveling, they hit the links, golfing and drinking their summer away. I've never understood the appeal. If I'm going to use a long object to hit a small object, I'd rather just have it be a stick and puck.

They go to parties and weddings and well, that's never really been my thing either. Basically they squeeze in the life they wish they lived year round, letting hockey slip away for a handful of weeks, pretending that it's not simply *everything*.

Not me. I miss the ice. I miss the routine. I miss the game.

It wasn't so hard to work out getting regular ice time at our training facility for the offseason. I can get pretty much whatever I want when it comes to an ice rink. What's harder is getting friends to join. So most of the time it's just me and my trainer, Pete, working on drills.

Today, I've been lucky to be joined by my boy Hux.

Nik Huxley is a Colorado man. He wasn't born or raised here, but came up as most hockey players do on the other side of our northern border. Honestly, you'd never know it. He's made this state his personal playground, usually spending his free time up in the mountains backpacking where civilization isn't, using a hammock for a bed and simple rations to keep him going. I wouldn't be surprised if the man hunts for his dinner every night.

He lives to be outside, opting to identify as a grizzly bear more than an elite defenseman, especially with that nasty playoff beard. Lord only knows when that matted mess will come off. Somehow, someway, the ladies actually love it. I guess lumbersexual isn't a passing fad.

Since Hux's hamstring injury that cost him two months of our season, he's been a little more keen on his craft. While he made it back in time for the playoffs, he didn't perform to his standards. Much like the rest of us, the dude has too much pride to sit back and live with it.

We just finished doing line sprints up and down the ice. He's fast, but I'm faster. At least I made sure that's the case. I think I might throw up. Fuck altitude and fuck Hux, since he's seemed to master it.

"It wasn't a race," he says, barely out of breath.

"It's always a race," I reply and reach for my water bottle.

"Hey, whatever happened with your friend getting the job?"

"It's all set," I say and rest against the boards. "She's moving to Denver this weekend."

"You helping out?"

"I'm meeting up with her after she gets settled in."

"So, do tell. You hit that?" he asks and wiggles his eyebrows.

I squirt more water into my mouth and turn away.

"So that's a yes," Hux says and starts fucking with the tape on his stick.

"That's a no, actually."

Hux stops what he's doing and looks over at me. "Is she—"

I don't even know what he's going to ask, but I feel the need to step in. "It's not whatever it is you're thinking. We were once really close to taking that step, but some shit went down and we've never crossed that line again."

Hux looks at me like he's never had a complication in his life, which I know for a fact isn't true. That being said, he pretty much gets and does whatever he wants. "She's gonna be traveling with the team?"

"Occasionally. Making videos."

"And you're not at all worried about the likes of Smitty and Hawk trying to get some of that?"

Philip Smith and Alexander Hawkins are two of the biggest cads on the team. Smitty is married, but has never once passed up an opportunity on the road. Total slime ball and not even that great as a fourth line forward. Hawk, our goalie, is just young and wild and happy to be here. He doesn't take his phenom status too seriously on the ice, but he sure uses it to his advantage with the ladies.

But am I worried about Summer?

"Of course I'm fucking worried," I confess.

"Set 'em straight. Tell them she's off limits."

"Already planning on it."

"They'll be sure to listen to their captain," Hux says and laughs a little.

"You don't think it will matter, do you?"

"Oh, Hawk will totally listen, but we both know Smitty is a piece of shit. Not that I ever plan on getting married again, but if I do, I'll never do the shit he does."

"Me either," I reply. Marriage is too sacred and should only be undertaken if you mean it, and with the right person. Since I'm clearly not relationship material, because I'll always be in love with Summer, I'm definitely not going to be getting married in this lifetime.

"Great," Hux says and wipes off his mask. "We can live together like the Golden Girls when we retire."

"Do you even own a TV?" I ask, shocked he'd make such a pop culture reference.

"Fuck no," he answers proudly.

I control my eye roll and then say out loud what I hope to be true. "Summer's too smart to fall for that asshole. Honestly, I shouldn't be worried at all."

"I'll keep an eye out for her," Hux says, always the defenseman.

"Thanks, man," I tell him and attempt to knock him against the boards. I barely move the beast.

"First one to the net buys smoothies," he says and takes off across the ice.

I never lose a race, especially when there's something on the line.

This can't be right. I'm standing outside of Summer's apartment door. It's covered in stickers and decals of all sorts of subjects, establishments, and brands. It's extremely unlike her. I fish out my phone from my pocket and check the address again. Yup. This is the place. Besides being totally out of character, this entire apartment complex leaves a lot to be desired. Saying it's run-down would be an understatement. It's not something a coat of paint could help, that's for sure. Not to mention that we're way on the outskirts of town. I figured Summer would opt for something downtown to be close to work.

Christopher: *Is this address right?*

She texts back right away.

Summer: *Yep. Why?*

I go ahead and knock, on guard for whoever might open the door, because it sure as shit ain't gonna be Summer. There's no way.

On the other side of the door, someone yelps and there's a lot of conversation. Maybe the TV? I was totally right. There's no way.

The door opens to let out a slip of light as well as a cloud of cigarette smoke. The chain is still latched, connecting the door to the frame. Before I can even gander a hello, a woman wearing at least three dozen curlers on her head pokes her face through the crack. "I guess you look like you might be him," she says. I don't think I've seen a hockey player with less teeth than her, and it's a really great look with that bright purple lipstick she has smudged all over her mouth.

What the effff?

Time to stop fucking around. "Is Summer Gunderson here?"

"Password?"

"What?"

"Do you have the password?"

"What? No. I'm looking for Summer Gunderson. I'm her friend, Chris. I must have the wrong place," I say and turn to go.

She plunges her arm through the opening and grabs onto my t-shirt. "No, she's here. I'm just protecting her. What's the password? If you say you are who you are, then you'll know the password."

"You've got to be kidding me," I mumble and pull my phone out of my pocket.

"No cheating!" the woman blasts.

I've had enough, so I take off, upset that it took me even that long. Summer's phone picks up after two rings.

"Hi, sorry," she starts. "I'm coming out."

"I think I went to the wrong place," I tell her and climb into my truck.

"No, you didn't. I heard you talking to my roommate. Be right down."

"You live with that woman?"

Summer snorts right before hanging up on me. Less than a minute later, she's sliding into the cab of my truck. She looks as lovely as ever. Her hair is pulled up into a messy bun and she's wearing light gray sweats that hug all my favorite parts of her.

"Moving day," she says and motions down to her at outfit.

"Summer, what the hell is going on? Who was that woman?"

She shakes her head as if I'm somehow wrong. "That's just Susan. She's fine."

"How the hell did you end up here?"

"I answered her ad. She's really quite nice," Summer says. "Although, she kind of stares at me a little too much. And she won't let me see inside her bedroom."

Never in a million years would I have said that Summer was naïve, but maybe I'm wrong. This is insane. I'm sure the poker face I've perfected in her presence has flat out failed. My teeth are gritted. My eyes are narrow.

"Summer." I don't know if I want to shake some sense into her or just drive her away from this place and buy her all new stuff.

"Chris, she's great. She made a peanut butter and mayo sandwich. I never would have made that for myself. Denver cuisine is quite different than I was expecting," she says and stifles a laugh.

"Summer," I growl.

"Oh, and she keeps the TV on all day at this really high volume. I asked her why and she said it's because she's worried about her privacy, whatever that means. I guess I'm in the big city now."

And then she can't hold it in anymore and falls apart in laughter. I have no idea what is going on.

"Tell me this is all one big joke," I urge her.

"It's not a joke. I actually live there," Summer somehow conveys through her hysterics.

"No, Summer. You can't stay there," I tell her—there's no laughter on my end.

"Oh, Chris, you're so cute," she says as she takes measured breaths to calm herself down. "You should have seen the look on your face."

"It's not funny," I tell her, still a little baffled about what she's doing.

"Do you honestly think I'd stay there? I didn't even unload my trailer."

"Oh, thank God," I mumble under my breath.

"I was just waiting for you to come over so you could see it before I left. It took you long enough," she says and playfully smacks my arm. "I learned my lesson, like everyone does. Don't trust the internet."

"That's the fucking truth. What was with all those stickers on her door?"

She shrugs. "Well, she doesn't have a car, so you know, no bumper."

"Wow. Okay. At least that one has some logic," I say, surprising myself. "So now what?"

She presses her palms together and looks at me, already pleading with those beautiful green eyes. "Well, I'm hoping I could crash at your place, at least for tonight."

"Of course," I tell her and finally feel like I can breathe again. Summer is in Colorado. Tonight, instead of sleeping by that eccentric woman, she'll be near me. Someone maybe even more crazy for taking in the woman I can't be with, but can't help but love.

Summer

Christopher's kitchen is seriously low on carbs. I've made myself some eggs and have gone in search of bread. There's not a piece in sight. Not a single refined sugar anywhere in this joint. I've checked all the cabinets, the fridge, the pantry, and even the breadbox that sits on the counter. There's nothing in there but the nastiest smelling vitamins I've ever come across.

In all my life, I've never had eggs without toast or a biscuit, but here we are, living the athlete life, apparently. Even his adorable kitty, Joey, seems to be eating healthy wet food that stinks to high heaven.

There's also no coffee, but I can't even speak about that. Life without coffee isn't life at all.

I set myself up at his breakfast bar with my sorry eggs and my very un-caffeinated glass of water, then pick up my phone, hoping that scrolling through the *Brunch Life* hashtag from the weekend can distract me from all this bland on my fork as I shovel it down.

It might also help distract me from the "spending the night at Christopher's place" freak out I've currently been experiencing since last night. I've barely been able" to process things like the fact that he lives in a super fancy downtown loft. Like, I always knew he made money playing hockey, but I didn't know he made this much money. From the billiard table to the massive entertainment area, it's dope. It's also been professionally decorated, so it's way classier than I'd ever give a boy from Fossebridge credit for.

Once I got settled in last night, with the majority of stuff still down in the small trailer hooked up to my car, I wandered around the place checking it all out. That's when I stumbled across Christopher in his bedroom, wearing only a pair of snug-fitting boxer briefs. He was faced away from me so I took every opportunity to check him out. From his sculpted back and shoulders that define him as an athlete, to his thick backside and mighty thighs that define him as a hockey player, it was *alllll* good. Like, really, quite something.

The sound of me panting must have alerted him to my presence. When he turned around to find me gawking at him, he quickly slipped on a t-shirt and sweat pants. Poor man. The whole rest of the night, he kept a safe distance from me and then went to bed at nine-thirty. I was exhausted anyway from the drive and my shenanigans with Susan, so I gave up on the day too. When I woke this morning he was gone. He left an actual handwritten note on the kitchen counter telling me that he would be out until seven, which meant he must have left really early for something that sportsy people do, like jog a 10k before the rest of us are out of our pajamas. Who knows?

When I can't stand the sight of another croissant or latte in #BrunchLife, I take my dirty dish to the sink. It's my first day of work and I don't want to be late. Better get that rideshare ordered now to play it safe, but before I can finish, the loft door opens and Christopher appears with a nasty green smoothie in one hand and a hot beverage in the other. Could it be? My one true love? Could it be coffee?

"Hey there," I say and he smiles at me in greeting. "Tell me that smoothie isn't for me."

"It's not for you."

"And in the other hand, we have...?"

"A coffee for you. I figured you'd be pissed when you realized I don't keep that kind of stuff around."

"Yeah, I wasn't going to say anything, but..." I joke and we laugh a bit. "Bless you St. Christopher."

Christopher's eyes sparkle at my silliness and there's that ever-present magnetism that I feel when he's in the same room. He throws off my gravity and I feel lighter than air.

He doesn't linger too long on my words and pulls out some creamers and sugars from his pocket for me. "I miss coffee, sometimes. But I've got my other love," he says and tips the straw to his green smoothie in my direction.

"I don't do kale, thank you very much," I tell him and go to work on crafting my coffee just the way I like it.

"It's not kale. It's kohlrabi," he says and takes a long drink.

"Kohl-what-now?"

"It's the new kale. Didn't you know?" he says and keeps drinking.

Cue my eye roll.

As I consume my beloved drink, I use my Sherlock sharp deductive reasoning skills to determine where he's been. He's wearing a new set of sweats from yesterday and has wet hair, seemingly from some post-workout shower. It looks really cute and reminds me of those days when I used to wait outside the high school locker room to interview the players after a game.

He always smelled so good after those showers. It was probably some form of industrial soap used in high school locker rooms, but it made my chest flutter every damn time. I take a step closer to him and take a whiff. As sad as I am that he doesn't smell like that industrial soap, there's something there, something familiar that takes me right back to those moments when he always stood closer to me than the other boys did. Those same chest flutters come right back like no time has passed at all between us. I want nothing more than to stay in this moment with him, but it's time to go.

"So, I'd love to stay and chat, but I need to order a ride and get over to the arena. I don't want to be late," I tell him for the sake of my career and my ability to stay on the right side of this line between us.

"I'll drive you. I'm going to go lift some weights and get a massage anyway."

"Didn't you already work out this morning?" I ask, a little bit annoyed for the rest of humankind.

"It's a process," he simply says, and grabs my backpack off the counter.

Once we're in his truck, he glances over at me and the corner of his mouth sneaks up.

"What?"

"You look so professional. I'm pretty sure the guy you're working for wears the same Dave Matthews Band t-shirt every day."

"Gross," I say, not able to help myself. "You know him?"

"Kind of. He makes us do the dumbest shit. Like last season, he made this stupid ass video of us competing against each other eating popsicles."

"Popsicles? Really?"

"Yeah, it fucking hurt like hell and I realized two things.

One, those things are filled with a boatload of sugar, and two, I had a cavity because one of my teeth stung like a little bitch from the cold." I start laughing but he shakes his head. "Sorry for the language. I've been back around the guys and my sense of decorum was left back in Fossebridge."

"No, don't do that. Don't be different around me because I'm a girl entering your space. I hate that. I always have."

"But you are a girl. Errrr...a woman," he says politely.

"Christ. It's going to be weird isn't it? Don't be weird, Chris, it's me," I say and hold onto the oh-shit bar as he takes a sudden left turn in front of some oncoming traffic.

"Yeah, well, we've all learned not to be cavemen in the workplace."

"That's a good thing. I'm just saying, I can handle some cuss words, got it?"

"Got it," he says and clears his throat.

"Something on your mind?"

"I want to warn you about a couple of the guys."

"On the team?"

"Yeah," he says and blows through a newly turned red light. I'm not sure I've seen him drive this poorly before. "Since you're going to be on the road with us, it might be for the best to avoid some of them. They're dogs."

"I know my way around guys like that," I tell him. "I can see them from a mile away. What about you?"

"What about me?"

"Do you change when you go on the road?" I ask, because I really want to know if I'm going to have to deal with a Christopher that likes to get his rocks off with random puck bunnies across the land. If that's the case, I'm going to have to learn to block out those encounters. Even though he's not mine, I don't think I can handle watching him with other girls. That's why I was glad when we went to different universities and took separate paths at the fork in our road. Hard to believe our roads have met up once again like this.

"I've always been focused on the game, you know that," he says and stares straightforward. He's so still I haven't seen him blink.

I'm not sure if I believe him. I mean, he's got to be getting it on somehow, someway. I just really don't want to see it, or know anything about it. Which reminds me...

"So, I'll spend some time looking for apartments on a break today. I should be out of your hair soon."

He noticeably grips tighter onto the steering wheel. "Are you going to get another roommate or live alone?"

"I think a roommate would be best. I'll be on the road so much, it breaks my brain to spend all that money on a place that sits empty so many days out of the year."

He pulls into the private lot at the arena and shuts off the truck. "Are you gonna vet them a little bit better this time?" he says with a laugh.

"Very funny. Yes, of course."

"Hey," he says and then snaps his fingers. "I might know the perfect place."

"Yeah?"

"Yeah. My next-door neighbor, Lily. Her old roommate moved out at the beginning of the summer. I think she's been too busy to find a new one. She's a developer for some fancy IT company. She's great."

"Oh, like right next door?"

"Yep, right next door. There's only three lofts on my floor. It's her and our neighbor, Alan, who is less than friendly. He's got a real stick up his ass. Anyway, she watches Joey when I'm out of town. She's fantastic." In my mind, I picture her as a hermit with a big overbite that never leaves her desk and only interacts with people online. At least that's what gets me through his nonstop praise and compliments about her. I've never heard him talk so highly about another woman before. It's weird and I'm on the verge of being jealous.

"Are you sure you want me living that close by?"

"Hey, we'll be on the road together, so what's the difference?" he says and shrugs his shoulders, but he won't meet my eyes.

"Well, I'd like to meet her," I reply, wondering if I'm making some sort of mistake here. It can't already be complicated between us, I've barely been here long enough to get over my initial altitude sickness. But it already sure seems that way. And why wouldn't it be? It is me and Christopher, after all.

As we walk into the arena together, he stays close beside me and presses his hand against the small of my back. I feel like he's ushering me into his world. I know without a doubt that he'll have my back throughout all of this. Hell, he even went to bat for me multiple times in the salary negotiations process until I told him to stop.

The only thing I really cared about was that I got my moving expenses paid, get to use the equipment I loved, and get to actually work the camera and not be trapped in an editing booth all day. That last point was a sticking point with my new boss, Jim. He believed I'd best be utilized cutting tape, but that's not my passion. As much as I love creating the final product, cinematography runs through my veins. I can't make art without the raw materials that I source myself.

Christopher leads me up to a reception desk at the front office and introduces me to an elderly woman named Betty that I learn has been with the team since they got their franchise in the nineties. We make polite chitchat and Christopher stays by my side. I'm mostly grateful, but a little worried, too. I don't want to be known only as Big Mac's friend. I'm hopefully here on my merit. "Don't you have some weights to lift?" I whisper to him.

He crosses his arms over his chest and leans back on his heels. "Like you said, I already worked out."

I give him this look that hopefully conveys my internal dialogue. *Don't fuck this up for me or for yourself.*

He gets the hint and flashes one of his most dazzling smiles at Betty before taking off, but not without looking back over his shoulder at me.

"That's quite a friend you have there," Betty says with a look in her eye. I've seen it before. It's the same look we got from folks throughout Fossebridge our senior year of high school.

Christopher

Fall, Senior Year

A lot of my teammates pick up other sports when hockey isn't in season. Some play football, a few even play golf. Not me. Hockey is everything. Hockey is life. The only other person that seems to feel the same way is Trey. That's probably why we became best friends.

It didn't start out that way, though.

In peewee, he was a little asshole to pretty much everyone, including me. *Especially me.* He was always so emotional about everything and hated when he didn't get attention. It made him fiercely competitive. Since I was the only kid to rival his talent, I had a big bullseye on my back. I didn't take his shit and we got into these knockdown, drag-out fights on and off the ice. The fights were fun. The competition was really fun, and our coach let it go on, knowing that one day he'd flip the script and we'd be incredible teammates. When that day came, he sat our stupid asses down and explained that we'd be unstoppable if we worked together. Of course, he was right.

Back then, we knew each other better than anyone else did and it's still the same way between us. It's helped us dominate on the ice. I know what he's thinking. I know which way he'll move. Which pass he'll make. Where he needs me to be at the exact moment I need to be there to tap the puck into the net. We've been playing on the same line ever since and it's why we've both been recruited to the same colleges. Recruiters aren't dumb. Pairings like this rarely come along.

Well, at least in terms of the hockey.

There's another pairing that I think would be great, but off the ice, and that's me and Summer.

It should be simple.

It should be easy.

But nothing is ever as easy as it should be.

Here's the thing. Whenever I get the chance to be near Summer, it's either when she's at work or with Trey and Tia around. If I could just get some alone time with her, things might be different. I refuse to believe that we're headed for the permanent friend zone, but if I'm not careful, any amount of denial about that will be futile.

That's why I've got a plan.

Homecoming.

It's simple.

It's easy.

Trey will take Tia and I will take Summer.

I mean it's pretty obvious that Tia has a thing for Trey anyway. She'd be sure to say yes.

Summer, on the other hand? Well, we did have that moment in the lake where I held her in my arms and we almost kissed. I've replayed it countless times since then. The way we connected. The look in her eyes that told me that she wanted to kiss me. I feel pretty certain that she'll say yes to Homecoming. And then, when I get her alone on the dance floor, maybe in a slow dance, I can hold her in my arms the way I yearn to do.

As I stand at my locker and organize my binders, I look over my shoulder at Summer. She's standing in front of her own open locker, eating one of those jelly donuts she loves so much and talking to Tia. There's some bright red jelly at the corner of lips and it just adds to Summer's adorable factor.

Yep, I'm going to pull this off.

Operation Homecoming.

All I've got to do is convince Trey, which shouldn't be a problem. He's usually game for a good time.

Simple.

Easy.

In fact, I'm tempted to just go for it. Summer looks over at me and smiles, then licks the jelly off of her lips and I die. She pulls me right in like a tractor beam and I find myself shutting my locker door and shuffling down the hall toward her.

Tia is going off about something, probably newspaper drama, but Summer is barely listening. She's got her eyes on me, just the way I like it.

God, I wish I could get her alone.

And just like that, my prayer is answered. Tia gives Summer a shoulder squeeze and takes off down the hall.

It's a sign.

I'm going to pull the trigger.

"Hey Big Mac," she says teasingly.

"Hey," I answer back and try to put all the right words together, but before I can Trey comes crashing in. Literally. He checks me into the lockers.

"Asshole," I say and shove him back.

Summer laughs as she always does at our antics.

Trey throws his arm around his cousin and shoves a piece of paper at my chest. "It's on, dude."

"What's on?" I ask and look at the paper.

It's a form for the hockey camp we've done every year we've been in high school. Only the best players from across the state get in. For us, it's a total given.

"I already filled mine out and sent it over while I was in second period," Trey says and takes the rest of Summer's donut, shoves it in his mouth, and keeps talking, spraying powdered sugar as he does. "It's the weekend of the twenty-third."

"Homecoming?" I ask as I glance around the hallway,

looking for one of those posters with glitter letters to confirm the date. *Fuck.*

Trey shrugs his shoulders and laughs. "Who cares? It's going to be epic. I've been waiting for this all year. We're seniors. We're gonna own that camp."

"Shit," I say under my breath and glance over at Summer. The smile that pulled me over to her locker has faded away. She looks as disappointed as I feel.

"What's your problem?" Trey asks and nudges her.

She struggles for words at first and doesn't meet my eyes before elbowing him in the ribs. "You ate my donut, jerk."

"Yikes. Somebody must be on the rag," he says and she swats at his arm. "Don't worry Sums, I'll get you a new one after school. I happen to have a super good hookup at The Biscuit."

The bell rings and students scatter to their classes. Operation Homecoming is a complete and utter failure. And as Trey starts to pull me down the hall toward our class, I'm left looking into Summer's eyes, silently promising her that there will be more opportunities, that timing will be on our side, I swear it. We just need momentum and once we get going, inertia will do the rest of the work.

"So, my mom told me that Boston called again last night. Have you heard from the recruiter again?" Trey asks.

"Yeah," I answer hesitantly.

"You're not still thinking of UMN are you? BU has the best program. Let's get the hell out of Minnesota."

Summer already got her acceptance letter from UMN. It was my original plan to attend there too. Honestly, I didn't think we were good enough for the likes of BU, but after we won state last year, they came calling for both Trey and I.

"I'm considering it," I tell him.

He stops in his tracks, his mouth ajar as he stares at me.

"What?" I ask him.

"We're a package deal—that's what the recruiter told me."

"They can't do that," I reply and roll my eyes.

"They can do whatever they want," he answers. "We can't pass up this opportunity, bro."

"Okay, just let me sort it out a little bit more."

"What on earth is there to even consider? Are you that much of a momma's boy? Or is it..." He lets that dangle there and I wonder if he sees right through me. If he knows that my heart wants to follow Summer wherever she goes. Trey's always been hotheaded and the last thing I'd want him to do is take any of his anger out on his cousin. And I certainly don't want him to tell Summer any of this. That would be so embarrassing. I wouldn't be able to face her again.

"It's nothing. I just want to be smart about it," I speak up. "Just give me a fucking minute, all right?"

"Just don't blow this for us, okay?" he says.

"I won't," I tell him and then take off toward our classroom.

5

Summer

CHRISTOPHER WAS RIGHT ABOUT MY NEW BOSS, JIM WELBY. NOT only is he wearing a Dave Matthews Band t-shirt, he mentions "DMB" repeatedly throughout the day, telling me stories about following them across the country and meeting members of the band numerous times. It's a lot to take in on day one, but I do my best to cut through all that and focus on the job itself. I meet a lot of different people, get a thorough tour, and get a badge. But the most rewarding part of my day is when I get access to the camera equipment. I have to endure some mansplaining about it all and how I have to take care of it—as if I wouldn't—but the thrill of it is too real for me to care. And when I get my very dope laptop, I'm basically on cloud nine. Tomorrow I'll get access to the video vault and photo database. This is really happening.

The day flies by and before I know it, my phone is vibrating in my pocket.

Christopher: *You ready to go home?*

Summer: *You're still here?*

Christopher: *I stuck around.*

It's just like high school when I was working on the newspaper and he *stuck around* to take me home. I can't help but smile that we're about to reenact that little bit of history.

Summer: *I think I'm ready.*

Christopher: *Meet you at the flagpole.*

That makes me giggle, but he doesn't say he's joking. Sure enough, when I exit the arena he's at one of the flagpoles with his gym bag, wet hair, and a friend that I recognize immediately. It's Nikolas Huxley, the Storm's unforgettable star defenseman.

Big Mac is big, but Hux is super sized. He looks much more cleaned up than when I saw him on TV at the celebration parade. He's trimmed his beard and his long thick mane of hair is pulled back into a bun. The two are laughing when I approach. Hux sees me first and his eyes light up.

"This must be her," Hux says.

Christopher glances over his shoulder and his laughter settles into a smile. "Yep."

"Hey," I say and extend my hand. "I'm Summer."

"Oh, I know," Hux answers and shakes my hand warmly. "Mac, won't shut his mouth about you."

Christopher shakes his head and blurts out "Asshole" at the exact same moment his teammate says, "I'm Hux."

"Oh, I know," I answer and wink at him.

"I loved your video. All I got out of my day with the Cup were some polaroids the guy down the road took."

"Really? Thank you, it's all Chris," I tell him and hope it's not too obvious how blood has rushed to my cheeks.

"*Chris*? Pretty sure I've never heard you called that before, Mac," Hux jokes.

Christopher shrugs.

"Hey, I knew this guy before he was Mac," I retort.

Christopher wraps an arm around my shoulders and pulls me to him. "Let's head home," he says.

Home. So weird, but I kind of like the notion, even if it's temporary.

Christopher lifts his chin in Hux's direction.

"Tomorrow?" Hux asks.

"Yeah," Christopher answers.

"What are you doing tomorrow," I ask as we walk out to his truck.

"Drills at our training facility," he says and pulls his keys from his pocket.

"How's he doing?" I really want to know, because Hux missed a lot of their last season with a hamstring injury.

"Really well. He's working so hard every day to get on the ice, dominate, and destroy," Christopher replies and opens the door for me. "I heard from Lily. She's excited to meet you tonight."

"Oh, cool. What's she like?" I ask and watch closely to see if he has a sparkle in his eye for her.

"She's smart, driven, and yet really chill. I think she'll make a great roommate for you." He pauses for a moment and looks over at me with a soft gaze that in my heart I know he saves for me. "I'd never steer you wrong," he says and I know he never ever would.

For a software developer, I was expecting Lily to be a little more frumpy and a lot less colorful. She's got piercings in her cheeks, unicorn rainbow hair, and tattoo sleeves of beautiful curvaceous naked women, peacocks, and flowers. She's like Starburst candy personified.

And she's got a bulldog that may just rival every grumpy old man I've ever met. God, I already love him.

"So," she says, "I think we'd make a good fit. Give me tonight to get the room ready and move in tomorrow night?"

I look over at Christopher, who's currently playing a little tug of war with Luthor. He looks up at me and shows his approval with me staying with him an extra night with a big silly smile.

"That would be so awesome. Thank you so much," I tell her and surprise her when I give her a hug. "You're so much better than Susan."

Lily laughs. "Who's Susan?"

Christopher joins us and shakes his head. "You don't even want to know."

"Hey, I counted seventeen jars of mayonnaise in her cupboard. That's a serious perk she didn't even put in her ad," I joke.

Both Lily and Christopher look like they're going to barf for a moment and it cracks me up.

"Come on weirdo, it's getting late and I'm starving," Christopher says and pulls me by the hand toward the door.

"See you tomorrow, Lily," I say as I follow him out. She laughs at us and shakes her head with a funny smile on her face.

Back in Christopher's place he goes right into the kitchen and pulls out some prepared meals from the fridge.

"Hope you like protein," he says.

"Man, I'm already missing Momma's onion rings," I reply and a pang of homesickness hits me right in the chest.

"Those are so good," he says with a smile. "I'm pretty sure I've had a thousand of those things in my life and I could easily eat a thousand more."

"But…" I reply and motion to some very bland looking chicken and veggie dish.

He shrugs and pops a container in the microwave.

"How can I help?" I ask.

"Get us set up in the family room with drinks and forks. No, let's do chopsticks. That will be fun. There's some in that drawer over there," he says and points across the kitchen.

"Oh lord, I've never used chopsticks in my life."

"Like I said, fun."

I playfully smirk at him and do what he says. Once dinner is properly nuked, he brings out two medium-sized bowls and takes a seat next to me on the couch.

"Are you going to teach me?" I ask him.

"Do you want to be taught?" he replies.

"Not really," I confess. "I'd rather wing it." And let me tell you how well that goes—I drop more food than I actually eat.

Christopher keeps laughing at me while he deftly feeds himself.

"Help," I whine.

"Happily," he says as he places his own chopsticks in my bowl and lifts a snap pea toward my mouth.

"You're not feeding me," I reply. "I'm not a baby."

"You've got to eat, right?"

He nudges at my closed lips and the frown I'm faking doesn't hold. I open up with a giggle and he smiles brightly before getting down to business. He focuses on my mouth with the same laser focus he puts on the puck. Man, he likes to score.

It goes on like this until my bowl is empty.

"Well, it tasted better than it looked," I admit. "But now I need ice cream."

"I'm sorry to say I polished off the cookie dough last night while you were sleeping," he jokes.

"Funny," I tell him. "But seriously. What does a girl have to do to get some ice cream? Or anything with sugar and fat?"

Christopher grabs our bowls and stands up. "You still like chocolate?"

"Of course," I answer with what I'm betting is a hopeful gleam in my eye.

"Get comfy and find something for us to watch. I'll be back," he says and heads for the door.

"You're a saint, Chris," I sing in his direction and hear him chuckle in that deep voice he's got just before the door closes.

I put on my pajamas, take out my contacts, and turn on a rerun of *The Office* on the TV. I cuddle up on the couch with Joey. Well, we're not exactly cuddling physically, per se, but we're sitting close enough together on the couch to do it if she'd let me. "One day, Joey, you and I are going to cuddle so hard."

And the idea kind of worms its way through my head, that this thing with Christopher isn't exactly fleeting. I've got a job with his team and I'm moving in right next door. It's so amazing to be back in his orbit.

Christopher returns with a small paper bag.

"My hero," I tell him as he winds his way around the kitchen to the family room. When he sees me, he stops in his tracks and his lips part.

"What?" I ask and look down at myself, afraid I missed a button on my pajama top.

"I just..." he says and shakes his head. "Your glasses."

"Oh yeah, still as pink as ever," I tell him and push the frames up on my nose.

"I haven't seen you in glasses in so long," he says, still standing several feet away.

"I can go put my contacts back in—"

"No!" he says and takes a step toward me, finally. "You look very cute."

"Cute?" I ask with a dopey smile.

He plops down next to me. "Yes, very cute in your glasses and your Garfield PJs."

"I've always loved Garfield," I mumble.

"Right, I remember you had a magnet of him in your locker."

"You remember that?" I ask.

He plays it off with a shrug and pulls out a pint of chocolate ice cream and two plastic spoons.

"I didn't know that Joey likes ice cream," I joke.

"She probably does, but she's not getting any," he says and leans over to pet her on the head.

"Oh, what now? You're having some of this?" I ask, shocked that Mister MVP would even dare.

He doesn't respond to that, but leans back next to me so that we're shoulder to shoulder on the couch. "I love *The Office*."

"Me too," I tell him and pull off the top to the ice cream.

We take turns with the ice cream, but sometimes we don't and spar with our spoons. It's fun to watch him really go after it—always the competitor. We polish the pint off quicker than I'd like to admit and laugh our way through the episode when Michael and Jan host a dinner party.

"I'm going to have Hunter's song stuck in my head for ages," I tell him. "I always do when I watch this episode."

"Oh, you mean from his album, *The Hunted*?" he asks.

I'm in awe. "Wow, you know your *Office* trivia."

He shrugs. "Being on the road so much, there's not that much to do."

"You don't go out when you travel?"

"Sometimes I do dinner with the guys, but hardly anything more. That's not my style," he says shyly as he fiddles with the remote.

And that settles a concern I didn't even know I was harboring. My Christopher would be the guy that watches *The Office* time and again. My Christopher wasn't really one for parties. I'm glad to know that this Christopher isn't all that different.

The next episode begins and a small shiver runs through me. Christopher notices and grabs the throw blanket that's hanging off the back of his couch. He pulls it over our laps and I nestle a little bit closer to him. High school me would be freaking out right now. Honestly, present-day me is kind of freaking out, too.

He doesn't seem all that fazed by it, so I try to play it cool and focus on the show. As I do, my eyelids get heavier and heavier. Before I know it, I'm drifting away to the sound of Jim and Pam being sweet to one another.

When I wake, I'm being lifted off the couch by Christopher. "You don't have to," I mumble.

"I've got you," he says and carries me across the loft to the guest room. He dips down to pull back the covers while still holding me and then lets me down gently onto the bed. I'm still so sleepy, but I don't want to let him go yet.

"Stay for a bit," I request.

His eyebrows furrow a little as he nods and takes a seat on the bed beside me. "You want me to tell you a bedtime story?" he jokes.

"Yes. What was it really like when you scored that goal?"

He knows exactly the goal I'm talking about. The game seven overtime goal that won the Storm the Cup.

He smiles ever so slightly as he thinks of it. "Surreal mostly. Confusing too."

"Confusing how?"

"It may seem like we know everything that's happening on the ice at every moment, but it's not like that at all. It's choppy and confusing, even though I'm the one that scored the goal. It all happened so fast, yet as I made my breakaway toward Grinblat, it seemed like the ice went on and on for miles. That puck at the end of my stick was like magic. It behaved just as I wanted. And then having my teammates around me and the sound of the crowd was so fucking overwhelming. For a few moments, my heart and my head were just overflowing with joy and excitement and a little bit of disbelief. It didn't hit me right away..." he says, trailing off and looking away.

"What didn't hit you?"

"The memory I carry with me every time I'm on the ice," he answers sadly.

"Trey?"

"Yeah. I was out of control with happiness and then I remembered. He was missing it. He didn't see it."

"Maybe he did see it, just not the way you think."

Christopher shakes his head and shrugs. "Sorry, I didn't mean to bring it all back to him. He's been on my mind a lot lately."

"Mine too, ever since you came back to Fossebridge."

"I guess that's our fate," he replies, and the corners of his lips sink lower. Disappointment unfurls inside me because I know he's right. Our fate has always been wrapped up with Trey's.

"But he's not the only person I thought of when we won," Christopher says, and his cheeks pink.

"He's not?"

"I was wondering if you were watching," he confesses.

Oh God. I turn my face over into my pillow and shake my head.

He turns me back over so he can see my face. "What?"

I groan. "You know I was. You got that ridiculously embarrassing email from me afterward."

He chuckles and says, "Don't be ashamed. I loved that email. It made my night."

"It made your night? You just won the Cup and my drunk email made your night?" I ask in disbelief.

"Hell yeah. When I was on that breakaway, I wondered if you were watching. Your email confirmed it," he says with a wicked smile.

"I want to die of embarrassment," I tell him.

"You're embarrassed? I just told you that I was thinking about you when I made the most significant play of my career. That's embarrassing." And now the pink in his cheeks has darkened to red.

"That's sweet," I tell him and reach for his shoulder. "Truly."

He shakes his head and laughs. "Oh, Summer Gunderson. It's not always sweet thoughts, but you've got to know that by now."

And there I go, right back over into my pillow because I can't show him how much I like what he's said or how I'm in the same boat.

Christopher once again turns me back over and I can only imagine how red my face is now. "Don't shy away from me," he pleads with a goofy smile on his face.

He cups my cheek with a warm hand and I gaze up at him, compelled to open my heart and answer honestly. "Yes, I know. I've always known. It's been the same way for me."

Maybe I've just told him everything he wants to hear or maybe what I've said is so totally obvious that's he like, *yeah duh.* But the way he pulls his lips into his mouth makes me wonder if he's trying to curb a smile, and the light in his eyes makes me wonder if he's harboring hope that there's a chance for us. I know that I'm hopeful, for the first time since that night back in high school. I just don't know how we can let go of what happened and find the courage to try again.

Christopher lets out a long sigh and I copy him. This suddenly feels very heavy. Too heavy to be lying down, so I sit up on the bed and crisscross my legs.

"I'm not sure what to say," he finally says and runs a hand through his hair.

"I know. It's kinda crazy that we're back in each other's lives like this."

"Totally," he says and just smiles at me like he actually can't believe we're in this situation.

Me either, bro.

"We're going to be working near one another and we'll be out on the road together," he says.

"True," I reply and nod.

"So maybe, we should just..."

That pause stops my heart. I have no idea what is dangling on the other end of it. No idea whatsoever.

"...we should just keep that in mind," he continues tentatively.

"Keep what in mind?" I ask, more confused than ever.

He clears his throat. "The way we feel about each other."

I give it a few seconds for his words to sink in but I'm still not sure what he's after.

"You look confused," he says.

"I am confused," I admit.

He does that little laugh he does when he's nervous, like before he gave his speech on Cup Day back at the high school auditorium. "Honestly, I don't even know what I mean. Just that, I want you to know that you're important to me and that my teammates—"

"Ohhhh," I cut him off as it dawns on me. We're back to this. He doesn't want me to hook up with one of his teammates. *Wow.* That is...annoying. And honestly, pretty crappy. Like, he won't be with me but he doesn't want me to be with anyone else. Not that I was planning on it, but he really has no right. I pull my knees up to my chest and shake my head. "Got it. Say no more."

I can't quite read the look he's giving me, but his mouth drops open for a few seconds before he buttons it back up again. "Okay," he says and stands up. "I should get to bed. Early day tomorrow."

"I'm sorry," I tell him.

"For what?" he asks from the doorway.

For everything. For nothing. For Trey. For all the complexity. "For the ice cream," I answer. "I hope it doesn't slow you down tomorrow."

"Nothing could slow me down," he says and then knocks on wood.

"Good night, Christopher."

"Good night, Summer," he says and turns off my bedroom light so that I'm left in the dark to mull over every bit of our time together since he came back to Fossebridge with the Cup. The only thing that's clear is that we're nowhere closer to putting our past behind us.

Christopher

I'm not sure how it happens, but every year I forget just how grueling training camp is. The blasted bike is what I hate the most. Thankfully, all of my conditioning this past summer has only improved my endurance, so when tested I'm able to give it all my all and easily meet the mark.

It's great to be back with the boys. Thankfully, most of last year's team is back and we didn't have to make too many trades to be under the cap. Although, we did lose two guys that just demanded outrageous bumps in their contract negotiations. I guess that's what happens when you win the Cup.

Much to my overall annoyance, Smitty is back even though he became a free agent last year. His antics bring the locker room down and as captain I'm always worried that he's going to cross the line with one of the guys' wives or girlfriends. Lord knows if ever lays a finger on Summer, I'll break him in two.

We've also got some fresh blood in the house to mix things up. Some of the vets get annoyed at the new guys, but not me. I'm all about potential and just because we were champions last season, doesn't mean we've got it made this year. If anything, there's a target on our backs and we're going to have to work twice as hard to prove ourselves.

We've been in the gym a lot, but today we're out on the ice. We start with the Storm's standard warm-up drills and then Coach Bliss and his assistants introduce a new drill we haven't done before.

As they're running through it, I spy Summer behind the boards with her camera chatting with Maddy, a young woman who works on the social media team.

Summer looks fucking gorgeous today. She's been wearing her hair in various kinds of braids throughout camp. Today, she looks like a Viking warrior—one of those shield-maidens —with a braid that pulls back most of her long golden hair. My guess is that she's doing it to keep it out of her face and out of the frame while she works, and that girl is always working, always in movement. Except right now because she's being friendly with Maddy, and I'm happy to see her make a friend.

Suddenly, the girls burst out laughing and I'd give up the C on my sweater to know what's so funny. Are they talking about me? One of the other guys on the team? I've heard rumors about Maddy hooking up with some of the guys, but I haven't given them much credence. I've never been one for locker room talk.

Honestly, I don't care what Maddy does. Summer, on the other hand...okay, obviously I do. Things are a little bit off with us, ever since we talked that night she stayed at my place. I'm not sure if we had a misunderstanding or what, but I thought we were making some progress. When she fell asleep against my shoulder that night and I carried her in my arms, nothing, absolutely nothing felt more natural than that. It's how I always dreamed it would be when I was back in high school, when I had all these ideas about how we'd end up together.

For the first time in years, I felt like we could make it work. That maybe our love could be stronger than the guilt we feel about Trey.

But it broke down somewhere along the way while we were talking and I can't quite figure out how.

I wanted her to know that she means the world to me, but so does this team, and that we have to be smart about not rushing into anything. That maybe just by starting with this idea in mind that we have a special bond, it could help us heal and get back on the right path. But she cut me off and while I wouldn't say she's been cold to me since, she's been a little bit distant.

Maybe she's not ready to let go of the past like I am.

"Where's your fucking head, Mac?" Coach Bliss yells at me from the blue line and when I look back, the rest of the guys are in some formation that I don't understand and they are all looking at me. *FUUUUCCCKKKK.*

Hux laughs first, the dick. Then the rest of the guys start chuckling. I glance back at Summer. Both she and Maddy are watching us. Maddy raises her phone and I roll my eyes. *Great.* I can't wait to be the butt of the joke on the Colorado Storm social media feeds today.

Coach skates over to where I am and gets up in my face. "Really? Really, Mac?"

"I'm sorry, Coach."

"Is this going to be a problem? I thought you had more focus than to look at pretty girls while we're on the ice. Be a fucking captain and the goddamn MVP and put your dick away," he orders.

"Yeah," I tell him and skate to the back of one of the lines. I still have no clue how the drill works, but I'm a fast learner and will pick it right up after I finish wiping the egg off my face.

Sure enough, I pick up what's going on and put all my concentration into it, showing Coach Bliss and the whole team that I don't actually fuck around out here. I had one momentary lapse in concentration at fucking training camp. Sue me.

As we keep going through it, I overhear some of the new guys making comments about Summer and before I can jab them with my stick and lay a shoulder into them, Hux does it for me.

"Shut your mouth, fuckers. She's off limits."

I'm relieved, because no one is going to stand up to Nik Huxley, especially some newbies.

For the rest of our time on the ice, I put Summer out of my head and focus on securing my job—not only as a first line forward for the Colorado Storm, but as the leader of this team.

It's not as easy as I make it look.

The locker room has got to be pushing ninety degrees on this hot August day. "What the fuck is the bullshit?" Smitty asks as he takes off his jock strap. This dude loves to get attention when he's naked. Like anyone actually wants to see his hairy balls.

"The air conditioner broke," I tell him. "They've told us this three times already. Aren't you listening?"

"Fuck you, Mac. I'm clearly listening better than you when it actually matters." It's a dig and I expect it after what happened with the drill. Especially from the likes of Smitty. "Tell me you've at least gotten your dick wet with that fine piece of ass."

"Shut your mouth," I tell him and Hux takes a step between us.

"Maybe she's seen what you're packing and would rather ride this stallion," he says and takes hold of his dick.

Half the room laughs, the other half knows better.

I try to take a step toward him, but Hux stops me. "You know he's not worth it," he says. "Not even a little bit."

"Psh, stallion my ass," Hawk teases him. "You wish you were working with what I've got. Ladies give me five star reviews after I'm done with them."

My eyes roll on instinct, but I'm happy to have the situation defused.

"I'm surprised both of your dicks haven't fallen off yet with all the puck bunnies you're hittin'," Wags, our star winger, says.

I shake my head and start blocking out the nonsense. Locker room talk has never been my thing, especially since Trey died. He lit up a locker room and made everyone laugh. My fondest memories with him weren't on the ice. They were off the ice, after practice or after a game. God, I miss that guy. I reach into my bag and find the puck he gave me all those years ago. Every time I touch it, I'm reminded that we never got to share it. That he never got a chance to keep it for himself. So I keep it with me. Every time I play, I've got it in my locker. It's my way of taking him along on the journey we were meant to go on together.

"Hey guys, listen up, I've got announcement," Hawk says. Our phenom goalie gets the attention of the room and even me. "My charity, Hawk's Kids, has gotten off the ground."

"Really? Hawk's Kids? Did your PR company come up with that? Or is this about all the illegitimate kids you got out there somewhere?" Wags continues to tease him.

"Shut up, fucker," Hawk says. "This actually really means something to me."

I can't count on one hand how many guys pipe up to make fun of him.

Hux does something he's known for. He puts two fingers in his mouth and whistles to shut everyone up. "May I remind you all, we're talking about a charity. What's your charity for, Hawk?"

"Pediatric cancer."

That brings everyone right down.

"See? Get your heads on straight," Hux says.

Seriously. The dude should be captain. Everyone quiets down for Hawk.

"So, as I was saying, to kick things off we're doing a really fun event. My people have reached out to your people about the details and the team's foundation is in the mix. So show up, a-holes."

"I'll be there," I tell him to lead by example because Hux is right. This is charity and Hawk is a good guy. But more than a good guy, he's an exceptional goalie and we're a team. We've got to be there for each other, no matter what.

Summer

Maddy waits patiently for me while I pack up all my gear to head out after practice. It's the night before our home opener, which is a huge deal because the Storm won the Cup. They're going to do a whole pregame show about it, including a video special I've been putting together about their championship season. It's pretty much wrapped up. I put in late night after late night to make it one of the best pieces I've ever done.

"You have too much stuff," Maddy observes. She's not wrong.

"It must be easy for you. All you need is a phone for social media," I tell her.

"It's not as easy as it looks and I have to use my laptop all the time. I feel like I spend my life making graphics. But yeah, for stories and stuff, I just whip out this bad boy," she says dangling her phone between her fingers.

"Did you post a story about Christopher whiffing the puck, falling on his ass, and then laughing so hard?"

"Sure did. It's gotten thousands of reactions. People can't believe Mister Tall, Dark, and Perfect could ever mess up. It's good for him. He needs to be a little humanized."

"Christopher needs to be humanized? He's about the most humanized guy I know. He has a pet cat that he adores. He loves watching *The Office*. He'll even splurge on chocolate ice cream occasionally," I tell her and smile at the memory of the night I stayed at his place. A blush spreads across my cheeks as I remember our confessions about how attracted we are to each other. But since then, things have been a little tense between us. If I understood him right, he won't be with me but he doesn't want me to be with any of his teammates either. Not that I would ever be interested in doing that. As long as I'm here, I'm working. I don't need to mix business and pleasure. Unless...

Maddy interrupts my train of thought. "They're right about you. You've got a knack for making him appeal to the ladies, because chocolate ice cream and loving his cat is some chick shit right there."

She's right and it makes me laugh. Yeah, those aren't his

most traditional masculine qualities, but it's some of the stuff I love about him.

Maddy goes on, "But you know all that because you've known him forever. The Big Mac we all see is serious and one hundred percent on his game at all times. Like I said, this was good for him and his fans loved it."

"It's still so crazy to me that he has fans outside of our hometown. But obviously it would be ridiculous if he didn't."

"Well it's been great for his endorsement deals."

"Endorsements?" I cock an eyebrow. "Like what?"

She puts a hand on her hip. "I thought you guys were friends."

"We were...we are...but we weren't in touch for a pretty long time and when we're together, we just don't talk about that kind of stuff. And lately we haven't had much time to talk at all."

"Well he doesn't seem like the type of guy that opens up easily in general. You probably know him better than anybody here."

If you had asked me an hour ago, I would have agreed but now I'm not so sure. Maybe I'm just projecting the Christopher I once knew onto the man I see before me today. I'm sure he's changed in ways I don't know, but I'm definitely up for finding out.

"Hey ladies," a voice booms from behind me. I glance over my shoulder and see Alexander Hawkins, the Storm's number one goalie.

"Hey Hawk," Maddy says with what can only be described as an "I know you biblically" smile.

"How are ya, babe?" he asks and throws an arm around her

shoulders for an informal side hug. He's an objectively good-looking guy. The type of guy that probably doesn't have to ask twice for a damn thing. Who's probably had everything come easily to him. Every. Thing. And it's not just his talent that propelled him, I'm guessing. It's the blond hair, blue eyes, and deep carved dimples on a sculpted body that should seriously be modeling. But like I said, he's objectively attractive and for me, I'm looking for someone with a little more depth. Someone with darker features, kinder eyes, and a sense of determination that goes beyond getting women into bed.

"You know me, always got my finger on everything," Maddy says.

"And what fingers they are." My God, the man can flirt. And then he turns those baby blues to me. "I don't think we've properly met," he says and extends his hand. "I'm Alex Hawkins and you're Summer...?"

"Gunderson," I fill in the blank.

"You do great work, Ms. Gunderson."

"Thank you," I say, admittedly flattered. Most of the compliments I get are from online strangers, not all-star goalies.

"Hey, are you coming to my charity event tonight?" he asks me.

"Charity event?"

"Didn't Mac invite you? I was sure he would have. Everyone's invited and I told the guys they could bring anyone they wanted."

"He must not have had the chance to tell me." I'm really hoping that's the case, and I'm trying my best not to be paranoid that he's possibly invited some else instead of me.

I don't know if Hawk can sense my confusion or concern that maybe Christopher has a date, but he takes an unnecessary step closer to me and lowers his voice. "Well you have to come. It's downtown at Flash Lanes."

"Isn't that a bowling alley?" Maddy asks.

"Sure is, baby," he says to her, but doesn't take his eyes off me. "It's going to be a great time. Do you bowl, Summer?" he asks and flashes his megawatt smile. The guy is a charmer, no doubt.

"I do," I answer.

He nudges me playfully. "Are you any good?"

"I'm not bad," I reply and give him a nudge back.

"Great, then we're on. I'll get us a lane and you wear something cute. Nothing cuter than a cute girl dressed all cute."

I roll my eyes and laugh it off. What a silly thing to say.

"We'll be there, Hawk," Maddy tells him and leads me away toward our cars. "Be careful with that one. I'm pretty sure his goal is to conquer the entire female portion of the population."

"Seems like maybe he's conquered you?" I throw out there.

"Oh sweetie," she says with a laugh. "I'm the one that does the conquering. And I conquered him hard in Vegas last season. He's an Adonis, but I don't got back for seconds unless I'm serious about a guy."

"And you're not so serious about him?"

"No way. He's such a player and not a serious person at all. He'll never settle down, mark my words."

"Do you think Christopher will be there tonight?" I ask her.

"You'd be the one to know. I'm surprised he didn't tell you about it."

"Me too. Well if he's there, he's there. I'm just looking forward to some bowling." It's not all together true, but it feels like the right thing to say to my colleague about my *friend*, Christopher.

When I get home, Lily is in the kitchen chopping up a mango, a feat that I don't think I'll ever be able to master. I tried it once at the Biscuit and nearly cut my fingers off.

"How ya doing, sunshine?" I ask her as I set down all my bags.

"When are you going to drop the nickname?" she asks and brushes a chunk of turquoise hair away from her eyes.

I snag a piece of mango off the cutting board. "What would you prefer I call you? Besides Lily of course."

"I'm partial to nightmare, T.B.H. I'd love to hear that. *How ya doing, nightmare?*"

"You're only a dream," I tell her and I'm not messing around. Lily is a great roommate. She just happens to be really cranky in the morning.

"Pshaw, whatever. So what's the on the sched tonight, honey cakes?" she asks.

I laugh. "Honey cakes, that's a good one. Well, my original plan was to set up shop in my room, order ramen noodles from that takeout place, and do some work."

"But now?"

"Now, I'm going to a charity bowling event apparently."

"Oh, is this a Christopher thing?"

"No, oddly enough. He didn't tell me about it at all. I was invited by his teammate Alex Hawkins."

She pauses and looks up at me. "The goalie?"

"Yes, the goalie."

"Like he personally invited you?" she asks with the knife jabbing in the air.

"I think he's inviting everybody."

"I've heard that guy gets around. God, I hate that I know that. I never even wanted to know anything about hockey, let alone the sex lives of their players."

"I don't remember the last time I wasn't caught up in hockey player drama. I guess it was before I moved to Minnesota. In the south, they just care about football and some basketball."

"In Boulder, we don't care at all. So is Christopher going?" she asks and goes back to her task.

"I don't know. He hasn't said a word about it to me. That's weird, right?"

"Well, he's not the most forthcoming person I know, but I thought you guys were close."

"We are. But then again, he's been known to not let me in on his schedule or where he'll be all the time. I think he's a little guarded like that. Or maybe he just doesn't want me around." It's a little *woe is me*, but that's how I'm feeling so that's what I'm saying.

Lily sets down the knife. "Can I be honest with you?"

"I would like you to be, yes."

"Christopher and I have been neighbors for a while, and in all the time I've known him, he's been steady and calm. Maybe even a little dull, if I'm being really honest. But white cis males have never really excited me. Then the night he brings you over here, there's something so different about him. It's like...okay forgive me for this ridiculous-ness...it's like his eyes were shining for the first time when all they've ever been are like, I don't know, like old pennies."

I laugh. "His eyes were shining for the first time?"

"Shut up. It's weird, I know. I think I've been watching too much anime or something. I mean, I don't usually get caught up in hetero romances but it seems pretty clear to me that you guys have something going on. So what say you, missy? Do you like the guy or what?"

Lily makes it sound so easy when it's anything but easy for us. "Chris and I have always been sweet on one another."

Lily grins like she might just make fun of me for the rest of her life.

I pull the cutting board of mango closer to me so I can keep snagging bites. "It's a phrase that Momma uses and it fits us. We finally took the leap our senior year, but there were all sorts of consequences I'd rather not get into right now if I want to go to this party without puffy eyes."

"Oh," Lily says sympathetically. "Was it a pregnancy?"

"No, no nothing like that. It's...my cousin died. He was our friend and his death kind of ruined things for us."

"Oh," Lily says again, probably more curious than ever about what really went down, but that's another story for another day.

"And so we went our separate ways. But that didn't stop us from liking one another. And since we've been back in each other's life, it's been so hard not to jump his bones every time I see him. 'Cause I'm pretty sure I'll never be attracted to anyone like I am to him."

Lily leans over the counter and rests on her elbows. "Well that's not a bad thing."

"Well, it's like some kind of bizarre sexual torture to watch him on the ice and that's all I've been doing day in and day out since I got this job. It's killing me. He's just...I don't know. He's sex on skates is what he is."

"Sex. On. Skates. Now that is a nickname," she says and then pops two bits of mango in her mouth.

I can't help but laugh and imagine a time when I might call him that instead of Big Mac, which I only do when I'm teasing him.

"So what are you going to do?" she asks.

"I don't know. But something's gonna give. Maybe he'll be there tonight and it could change everything. Then again, maybe it won't change a thing. We need some sort of catalyst to help us move along because we're stuck right where we've been for a long time."

"Hey, progress is progress. You'll find a way," she says as she grabs for Luthor's leash to take him out.

"Progress is progress," I repeat under my breath and head to my room to get cute, as requested. Like I was never not going to be cute anyway.

Christopher

"Who plans a charity bowling event the night before our home opener?" I complain to Hux as we approach the upscale disco bowling place in downtown Denver. "I'm fucking shredded from practice."

"I think you're just afraid you're going to throw gutter

balls," he replies and hooks his sunglasses onto his shirt. He has no idea how right he is. "Hawk is just excited to get something going with his new charity."

"I mean, he above all people, as our goalie, needs to stay healthy. He's probably going to throw his back out," I complain.

"You worry too much," Hux says. "And if anyone needs to stay healthy, it's me."

"Truth, brother," I tell him and pat him on the back.

"Is Summer going to be here tonight?" he asks.

"No. She's been up to her eyeballs in work, making the banner raising video, so I didn't even ask," I answer, but I wonder if that was a mistake. We've been orbiting around each other through training camp and the pre-season as I work my ass off and she learns the ropes of her new job. Bowling could have been such a good way to hang out together and cut loose a bit. Plus I think she'd look fucking adorable in bowling shoes.

The place is packed with people, which is great for Hawk's cause, childhood bone cancer—Osteosarcoma, to be specific. Apparently, it's a cause near and dear to his heart, but I have no idea why. I've never heard a story about it affecting him or his family personally.

Hux and I go through the motions to talk to some local press, take photos in front of the event backdrop that's covered in his charity's logo, and take three steps at a time between conversing with a teammate or someone new on our way to the bar. There are a handful of kids in attendance, some with prosthetic legs and others in wheelchairs using bowling assist ramps to play with some of my teammates. I could use one of those myself, since I've only bowled once in my life and ended up embarrassing myself because I was so bad at it.

"Can you believe this? The kid really pulled this together," Hux says in astonishment as he leans against the bar.

"Not at all," I reply.

The event is surprisingly slick and swanky for being in a bowling alley. Hawk clearly hired the best event planners in Denver to pull it off. From the drinks to the food, it's legit and well beyond my expectations.

One thing that's not surprising is the sheer amount of women. They easily, *easily* out-number the men and we're a male hockey team. He's always been good at drawing in the ladies and they are obviously willing to open their purse for his good cause.

I take a few drinks of my beer and look around. "Have you seen him?"

"He's probably already making his move on some girl."

I shake my head and laugh a little. "At a charity event for children?"

"Shit," Hux says from beside me and leans forward to look over at the bowling lanes.

"What?"

"Stay calm, Mac," he says and strategically moves himself between me and whatever it is he's seen.

"Hux," I command and look around him.

The first thing I notice is Summer's hair, braided back. The second thing I notice is Hawk giving her a double high five as she jumps up and down with glee.

The earth is unsteady beneath my feet and a vein in my neck starts to pulse.

Hux watches me closely. "I thought you said she wasn't going to be here."

"I said I didn't invite her." I am such a goddamn idiot. When will I ever learn with Summer?

"Well, looks like Hawk did," Hux says and continues to take up the space I need to get by.

I put a hand on his shoulder. "Move."

"Take it easy, they're just bowling," Hux says before stepping aside for me to pass by.

"She's just bowling. I highly doubt that's what Hawk is doing," I grumble and then slowly make my way down to the lanes.

I would be lying if I told you that I hadn't been in this position before. And while my instinct is to rush down there and put myself between Hawk and Summer, I know better. I only had to learn that lesson once. So, I hang back for a bit and drink my beer at one of the high tables and watch them bowl. She looks gorgeous, dressed in a floral sundress with a black leather jacket. I was totally right, the bowling shoes make her just that much more adorable to me.

"Big Mac?" a woman says as she approaches the table with her friend. I know their type. They aren't hockey fans or even puck bunnies—they're hunting for husbands, well to-do husbands. Both are dressed in cocktail dresses that should not be worn in a bowling alley, no matter how swanky.

"Hi," I respond simply and turn back to watch Summer. She's doing pretty well, considering Fossebridge doesn't have a bowling alley. I have no idea where she learned how to do it and I make a mental note to ask her.

"We were wondering if you'd be here," the other woman says.

"I always support my teammates," I tell them, even though I'm on the verge of knocking out the remaining real teeth in Hawk's skull because he's way too close to Summer now.

"That's so noble of you," she says, and takes a step closer to me as she puts her well-manicured hand on my forearm. I gently pull my arm out from under her palm, and take another drink while I watch Summer from afar.

Hawk has the nerve to take hold of her from behind and grab her hand. He's showing her how to release the ball. *That's enough.* I set my beer down on the table, ignore the women that are still trying to make small talk with me, and make my way toward Summer.

Hawk sees me first and wisely lets Summer go. "You made it," he says and extends his arms wide open for a hug. Summer watches me closely and I know that I've got to do the right thing here. I can't be the brute I want to be, the caveman that knocks him back on his ass for touching my girl.

She's not even *my girl.*

Not technically.

But Hux told the team that she's off limits and we try to respect that kind of thing around here.

The hug is brief and then I leave him behind to go to Summer.

"Hey," she says with a bright smile on her face.

"I didn't know you were going to be here." She gives me a funny look, probably because my tone is less than friendly.

"Alex invited me," she says, using Hawk's given name.

Of course he did. I pull my lips into my mouth and nod my head slowly.

"Yeah, I was surprised you didn't extend her an invite, man, since you guys are old high school friends and all that," Hawk says and sticks his hands in his back pockets. He makes our relationship sound so boring and non-important, when in my heart it couldn't be more important.

"I thought you were working," I explain to Summer.

"I'm pretty much done and then Alex told me all about his charity," she goes on and shrugs. "And how could I pass up bowling?"

"Well, you are great at it," Hawk chimes in.

Without taking my eyes off Summer, I ask, "If that's the case, why were you helping her?"

"Just giving her a few pointers to help her take her game up to the next level."

"Are you thinking about joining a bowling league?" I ask the two of them and I know it's not coming across as lightly as I'm aiming for.

They both laugh a little in unison and I hate it, and furthermore, I hate that she's slipping through my fingers right in front of me and I might have to endure Summer dating one of my teammates. There's only one way to handle this. "Mind if I join you?"

"We're in the middle of a game," Hawk says.

"You're only in the third frame," I argue back and go pick out the heaviest ball I can find. "Restart it."

"Don't you need shoes?" Summer points out.

"It's not a requirement," I mumble, having no idea if it is or not, but I'm not walking away now.

"Mac," Hawk protests, and I give him one of those looks that a captain gives the biggest punk on his team. One that says, *don't fucking test me.* Apparently that's what it takes. "What size do you wear? I'll grab you some."

"Eleven," I answer through gritted teeth and he takes off for the shoe rental.

Summer comes closer to me and just like always, I feel a charge beneath my skin when she's near. "What's up, Chris?" she asks with a sly smile.

I take a step closer to her and look her directly in the eyes. "Why didn't you tell me you were coming?"

She swallows hard, but her gaze doesn't waver. "I didn't know I had to run everything past you."

I circle my fingers around her wrists and erase some of the space between us. "So that's how it's going to be?" I ask quietly.

"That's my question too," she replies. "We're back to this? History repeats itself?"

My breathing is heavy but I don't answer her. I'm afraid of the words that will spill out of me if I do.

"I know what I'm doing," she says.

"Summer," I whisper to maintain some privacy.

"Christopher," she says and pulls her hands out of my grasp. "Be careful."

"Be careful?" I ask, absolutely incredulous.

"Don't let whatever is between us interfere with your team."

"That's exactly what I want to avoid and it'd be tremendously helpful if you didn't..."

"Didn't what, Chris?"

"Do this," I say and point back behind me toward wherever Hawk is.

"You insult me," she says and takes two steps back. "It's like you don't know me at all."

"We've been apart for a long time. I wouldn't dare to assume anything," I tell her and take a step in her direction.

"Assume what exactly?"

The distance between us closes again and I take hold of her shoulders. I angle my face down toward hers so that we're nose to nose. "That you're mine," I whisper as I gaze into her eyes.

"Is that what I am?" she asks, nearly breathless, her eyes blazing with questions and need.

Before I can answer, Hawk shoves a pair of shoes into my back. "Here you go, Mac. I got them to reset the game, too."

Any words I have for her fall away even though the inertia of the moment carries forward. She's still looking up at me with the same burning gaze.

"Thanks," I mutter and force myself to step away from her. As I sit down to put on the shoes, I come back around to reality. Telling Summer that I love her at a bowling alley isn't how I've spent years imagining it since the last time I told her. Plus, I've got a bigger problem I need to address. I've bowled all of one time in my entire life. I'm terrible at it and this is going to be ridiculously embarrassing.

"Ladies first," Hawk says and winks at Summer.

If I don't do it first, Hux will most definitely beat his ass for all of this.

Summer picks up her purple bowling ball and with beautiful form, bowls a perfect strike. To top it off, she twirls with her arms above her head exposing more of her thighs and it's one of the sexiest cellys I've ever seen.

Hawk rises up from his chair and puts out his hands for a double fist bump, which she excitedly performs.

"Fucker," I grumble under my breath, then suck it up the best I can and give Summer a little shoulder nudge. "Well done, Gunderson."

That earns me one of her beautiful smiles. "You're up, Alex," she says.

"We call him Hawk," I instruct her. There's no reason why she should call him anything different or personal.

"It's okay, you can call me Alex," Hawk says.

"Cool," I respond while everything in my body tenses. "Cool, cool, cool."

She takes a seat and I move quickly to sit beside her, as if it's somehow going to make a difference in the grand scheme of things.

Hawk knocks down six pins, and only one on his second try.

"I think you need to get some pointers from Summer," I joke.

"I'd be down for a private lesson," he says back and I want to punch myself in the nuts for setting him up.

Summer just laughs and thankfully doesn't agree to something so preposterous. I wrap my arm around her shoulders and smile down at her. She looks up at me with her darling green eyes and I notice she's done something a little bit different with her eye makeup, in that she's wearing some. With or without it, she's so damn pretty it makes my heart hurt.

But I'm clearly not the only one that feels that way. Hawk is standing right in front of us, not taking one of the other open seats. I'll be damned if I'm going to give this seat up to him.

Summer gently nudges me with her elbow.

"What?" I ask, as if I don't know.

"It's your turn," she says.

"Right. I'm just planning my strategy," I say and remain sitting.

"Strategy?" Hawk asks and rolls his eyes. "What kind of strategy could you possibly have? It's bowling, brother."

I point with two fingers to the seat across from us. "Why don't you have a seat over there and I'll tell you."

Hawk shakes his head and laughs before taking that seat. "Do tell."

"I'm going to knock all the pins down," I answer and stand up, assured that the fucker probably won't get up and move over to the seat beside Summer unless he has some sort of death wish.

But that's about the only thing I'm sure of, because like I said, bowling is not my forte. I whisper a little prayer to anyone deity listening for some kind of miracle. My prayer is not answered and if anything, I'm on the receiving end of some sort of cosmic bowling punishment. When I release the sixteen pounder, it flies too far through the air, hangs to the right, bounce-skips from the next lane into the lane over, and right into the gutter with a thud so loud it's enough to rattle my teeth.

I crouch down and cover my face in embarrassment, while earning not only the jeers of my direct bowling competition but from those bowling far and wide. It could not have gone worse.

Through all the shit-talking Hawk is spewing from behind me, I hear Summer's quiet and loving laugh. When I stand up and turn around, she's there and pulls me into a hug and I laugh into her hair, which smells so good to me I feel like I'm being rewarded. So many of my fears melt in that embrace. She's in no hurry to let go and neither am I. This is right. This is how it should be and it's undeniable that we belong together. I'm ready to let go of the past and be with her.

"Why wasn't I recording that?" Hawk muses.

"Hey, we didn't have a bowling alley in Fossebridge," Summer says, coming to my defense, but that just makes it more hilarious to him.

"You're lucky I didn't throw it at your head," I blast at him.

And then he comes over to where we are and slaps me on the back. "It's all good, bro. You can't be MVP at every fucking thing. Mad respect."

And isn't that the truth?

The tension between us fades away as we laugh together for quite awhile. Then we enjoy the rest of our game and I manage to score a whole fifty-three points. Summer wins with the highest score, just as it should be.

Summer

Winter, Senior Year

It's my first bonfire party in ages and I'm actually excited now that we're here. Tia had to beg me and Momma practically booted me out the house when she overheard her. It's not like I keep secrets from Momma anyway, but the fact that she's cool with her only child going out to a clearing in the woods for a kegger is a little bit of bad parenting, right?

"Who all's going to be here?" I ask Tia as she parks amongst a whole bunch of cars at the forest's edge.

"Well, pretty much the whole hockey team. They just finished their tryouts today, so they're in the mood to celebrate."

"I heard. It sounds like Christopher is captain again," I tell her.

"Yeah, sounds like it. Does Trey ever get jealous about that?" she asks.

"You'd know better than I would. I feel like you guys talk more than we do these days."

"He'd never admit it," Tia says.

"How's it going with you two?" I ask.

"Slow. I honestly thought he'd be more into it. He's got such a wild personality, you know? But at the end of the day, I think he's just so focused on hockey he doesn't really care about anything or anyone else."

"I'm sorry, sweets. Want me to hit him upside the head for you? I love doing that to him."

"Nah, we'll see what happens tonight. Maybe with tryouts being over, he'll open up to the idea. Maybe, just maybe, I'll ask him to the Winter Formal."

"Oh wow, that would be something. My cousin in a suit, dancing."

"You should ask Christopher. You know he'd say yes."

"Hmm…I'm not sure I have that much courage. Maybe if you ask Trey," I reply and laugh nervously at the idea. God, I hate Sadie Hawkins dances. I've never worked up the courage to ask anyone. Asking the captain of the hockey team? That's crazy. I'm sure half the female population at our high school has plans to ask him. "You know it's still a month away."

"Well, you know me. I like to plan ahead."

"That you do," I tell her. "Come on, let's go drink some weak keg beer and act like we're having a good time."

We link our arms at the elbows and walk down a snowy path to the Clearing, following the smell of the bonfire.

When we arrive, I'm amazed by the size of it. Fossebridge boys all grew up as boy scouts. They know how to rub two sticks together.

There's a great mix of people from our school standing in small groups talking to one another. Most are huddled around the keg that's been packed in a bunch of snow. No warm beer tonight. Naturally, that's where we find Trey and Christopher.

"Hey guys," Tia says and grabs two cups off the stack.

"Tiaaaaaa," Trey says and puts his arm around her.

It's immediately apparent that my cousin is already shit-faced. It's also not the first time. Everyone knows how much Trey loves to party.

"Nice," I tell him.

"Don't be such a prude, cuz," he says and drinks out of his cup, finishing it off. He turns back around for a refill.

I look over at Christopher, who has a rosy glow to his cheeks, but I think that's from the fire. He's as sober as ever. "You've got a handle on him, right?"

"As much as anyone can have a handle on him," he replies and steps a little closer to me. "Are you drinking tonight?"

"I don't know. Seeing Trey like this always makes me uncomfortable. Maybe I shouldn't."

"I'm the captain. I've got this, Summer, just have fun, and I'll make sure you're both okay," he says and motions to the keg. "Want a beer?"

"Okay," I tell him and he presses the tap as I hold my cup. I glance over my shoulder and Tia is holding onto Trey's arm. They're having a good laugh and seem to be enjoying themselves. This is fine. It's all good, I tell myself. "So, are you happy to be done with tryouts?"

"You know, I don't hate it like the others do. I like the challenge and the competition."

"I bet you thrive," I tell him.

He shrugs, never one to take a compliment. I know the feeling.

"I watched a program on the Hockey Network about training camp in the big leagues. That's a whole different casserole. This is nothing in comparison. All those camps that Trey and I go to, they've prepared us really well."

"You guys work so hard, I see it all the time. It's sure to pay off this season."

Christopher reaches over to a nearby tree and knocks on it.

"Still so superstitious," I joke.

"I'm a hockey player—it comes with the territory," he says to me.

While the fire is really something, a shiver goes through me. I don't think I'll ever adjust to a Minnesota winter. Christopher notices and steps a little closer to me, takes off his black scarf, and wraps it around me. "Let's get closer to the fire." A few people vacate a nearby log and we take a seat on it. I'm still shivering, so he puts his arm around me and scoots closer to me.

"Thanks, Chris. My southern blood just can't handle it," I tell him and we both laugh.

"It seems like my whole life revolves around snow and ice," he says while rubbing my arm up and down.

"Speaking of ice. Have you decided who you're gonna play for?" I ask him. "Isn't signing day approaching?"

"Yeah, it's in a month," he replies, but doesn't answer my original question.

"Trey is all about Boston. Aren't you?"

"UMN has been on my mind," he says and glances over at me.

The possibilities of us attending the same university make my head swim, or maybe that's just the beer. It's certainly helping me feel warmer, but that could be Christopher's body being close to mine. Like that day at the lake, when he touches me everything inside me warms up.

I want to ask him more about his college decision, but don't get the chance because Trey comes crashing into us, just like he's done a million times before and sticks his head between ours. "Aren't you guys looking cozy," he says. "You're not doing anything I wouldn't approve of with my cousin, are you, Mac?"

"Wouldn't dream of it," Christopher answers immediately and I'm struck with a bolt of disappointment.

"Good, because there's a code and that definitely goes against the code, bro," he somehow barks out coherently.

"You know, I can make my own decisions," I say and shove him off us.

Christopher looks pleasantly surprised at my reaction.

Trey starts to wander back over toward Tia, but not before pointing at Christopher and shouting, "I'm watching you, Mac."

"Ugh, what an asshole," I mumble. "I'm sorry about him."

"Don't apologize," he replies.

"He's just drunk, right?"

"Well, yes, most definitely. But there is a code. You know, not to cause any problems off the ice that could become a problem on the ice."

"Come on, be serious," I tell him. "How could us hanging out be a problem?"

Christopher clears his throat and takes time to form his response, but before he can, Mateo shouts over at Christopher. "Dude, the tap isn't working."

"Shit, let me go help him," Christopher says and goes over to the keg.

He hasn't been gone long before someone else joins me. I'm pleasantly surprised to see that it's Henry, a guy I know from video editing class. "Is this seat taken?" he asks.

I look over my shoulder at Christopher, who is hard at work with his teammates trying to figure out what's up with the keg. "Nope, not at all. It's cool to see you outside of class," I tell him.

"Yeah, same. Where's your camera?" he jokes.

"Poor lighting," I answer, and he laughs a little too much while I take a long drink of my beer.

He scoots a little closer to me and says, "Remind me on

Monday to show you this new feature in our editing software. I think it will be great for your hockey piece. It's a little bit like stop motion. Well, not really, but it's the only way I know how to describe it."

"Cool, yeah, I'm all about learning new stuff," I tell him and look back over my shoulder again. Christopher has stopped with the keg and is watching Henry and I closely, but keeping his distance. As much as I like Henry as a friend, I wish it was still Christopher sitting next to me.

"If that's the case, then there's so much I can teach you. I'm basically a pro," Henry boasts. "And it wouldn't be too much trouble for me. How about you come over this week after school and I can give you a one-on-one tutorial?"

I look back over my shoulder at Christopher and notice he's taken a few steps closer to us and is still watching.

Henry places two fingers on my jaw and turns my head back to face him. "What do you say?"

My gut reaction is to say no, but I don't want to be rude so I hem and haw about it as I formulate a response. "I've got a lot going on this week," I tell him.

"I'm sure you can find some time for me," Henry says and brushes a loose strand of hair back behind my ear.

Before I can speak or pull away or do anything, Henry is being lifted off the log. I blink rapidly as I try to understand what's happening and when I'm finally able to comprehend it, I'm shocked to see Christopher forehead to forehead with Henry, holding onto his shirt as he screams in his face, "What the fuck do you think you're doing?"

Everything from my legs to my voice to my brain is frozen in place as I watch the two scuffle.

"Let go of me," Henry barks and attempts to shove Christopher off of him but he barely budges.

"Do not touch her, you hear me?" Christopher tells him in the most menacing voice I've ever heard him use.

It's only then that I notice everyone has stopped what they're doing to watch the scene play out. This is bad. Very bad.

My senses finally come back to me and so does my voice. "Christopher," I shout and rise to my feet. "Christopher!"

He doesn't answer me nor does he let Henry go. He's going to get in trouble. He's going to risk everything he's been working for if this goes too far.

"Please stop, please," I beg as I grab onto his arm. His muscles are fully flexed, his jaw is tight, and his feet are grounded.

"Touch her again and I'll kill you," Christopher warns him.

Where is Trey? Where is Tia? Mateo rushes over and tries to pull Christopher off of him, but the guy won't give it up.

"Please, Christopher, stop," I plead with him as tears stream down my face.

Christopher finally sees me and blinks a few times as if coming out of some sort of nightmare. It's my crying he hates, I can see it in his face. A switch flips as if he's now able to process his actions. He lets go of Henry at last, which gives Henry the opportunity to shove at him harder than before. Christopher lets him and stumbles back a few steps.

"Forgive me," Christopher says to *me*, ignoring Henry altogether. "I didn't mean to..."

I'm horrified at his violent behavior and mortified that it happened because of me. "What got into you?" I ask him.

"Can we go somewhere to talk?" Christopher asks quietly.

I'm tempted to say no, not after all of that, but this is Christopher and first and foremost he's my friend. Something must be up with him and I'm going to make sure he's okay. "Sure."

He turns to Henry and reaches out his hand. "I'm sorry, bro."

Henry slaps his hand away and storms off. Honestly, I don't blame him at all for it.

I want this over with completely, so I take hold of Christopher's arm and pull him across the Clearing to the edge of the woods. It's so cold this far from the fire, but I do my best to deal with it. "What was that?" I ask him.

"I'm really sorry, Summer. I lost my mind," he attempts to explain while framing his face with his hands.

"Why?" I want to know.

He paces in front of me, his energy spiking again. "What was he talking to you about? Tell me."

"Don't change the subject. Tell me why you lost your mind."

He thinks on it for a moment too long and I'm sure the response I get won't be the whole truth. "Because you looked uncomfortable."

"That's what it was? You were defending me?" I ask.

"Yes. I was worried that he was upsetting you. That you didn't want him to touch you like that. You didn't, did you?"

"Well, no, but that was a severe reaction on your end."

"Like I said, I'm sorry," he says, but he doesn't seem nearly sorry enough.

Maybe it's the beer or the cold that's making me cut right to the chase, but I go right for it. "Were you jealous of him?"

He puts his hands on his waist and huffs out a laugh. "Jealous? Why should I be jealous of him?"

"Because he was hitting on me?"

"I knew it. I knew he was. What did he ask you? What did you say?"

"Nothing, Christopher. He offered to teach me some new stuff about editing after school at his house and I said no."

He takes two steps closer to me. "You said no?"

"Jesus, you can't be serious. I never took you for a caveman."

"Just answer the question."

"I already did. But you didn't answer me. Were you jealous?"

Without missing a beat he answers, "So what if I was? Would that be so crazy? Summer, I..." He closes the distance between us and brushes that same ornery wisp of hair back behind my ear before cupping my cheek and pressing his forehead to mine. "I think about you, about us...together. Do you ever think about me?"

I forget the cold, the forest, and my own name. The only thing I know is this sudden warmth in my chest, these butterflies in my belly, and Christopher's lips which are so close to mine.

"Do you?" he asks again and rubs his nose along mine.

"Yes, all the time," I confess.

I can't see it, but I can sense his smile. I know without looking that it's beautiful and wide. He wraps his other arm around my torso and pulls me flush against his body.

"Can I kiss you?" he whispers.

"Yes, all the time," I repeat.

He hums in a way I've never heard. It's primal and hungry and I'm desperate to connect with him for my first kiss.

"Summer!" Tia yells for me from the Clearing. "Help us, Christopher."

"What the...?" Christopher says, backing away from me and pulling me quickly by the hand back into the Clearing.

"It's Trey. He's too drunk," Tia says.

And just like that the rest of the night is derailed by Trey. Honestly, he's such a pain in the ass sometimes. He knows no limits. He takes everything way too far. So Christopher and I do our best to sober him up, and while we do our conversation at the forest's edge is never far from my mind. There's no doubt that if I gather up my courage and ask him to the Winter Formal, he'll say yes. But not tonight. Not when we have to take care of Trey.

6

Summer

THE VIDEO I'VE BEEN WORKING FOR TONIGHT'S BANNER RAISING ceremony is complete, but I just keep going through it, examining every frame and listening to every wave over and over and over again.

It's easy to make a video, pop it on a website, and walk away. But tonight's video showcasing the Storm's championship season is not only going to be played on the big screen in the arena but over national television as well.

I'm terrified.

I've worked with some great people within the marketing department and my boss, Mr. DMB himself, has been tremendously helpful. Although he did try to get us to license a Dave Matthews song for it. I had to bring in reinforcements to talk him out of it, including Maddy. She said something along the lines of, "Jim, it's not 1995 anymore."

As I go back through the piece one last time, I pause on one of Christopher's interviews and take a deep breath before pressing down on the space bar to play again.

"Winning the Cup was one of two dreams I had growing up and when the other dream didn't work out, I decided to dedicate my life, my drive, my everything to hockey."

Looking over my shoulder to make sure I'm truly by myself, I pause the video on him and study the face of the man I've known for so long. This isn't the first time I've done this while editing videos of him. I started doing it back in high school. I usually don't linger too long on his face because it's overwhelming to the senses, like staring into the sun. It's simply too much. But in this moment, I let it burn as I look at every line and curve and feature. He's handsome and always has been, but he's not without flaws. Like his slightly crooked front tooth or the way his nose curves a little to the left. He's got one dimple on his right cheek and while symmetry is considered beautiful, that single perfect dimple has ruined me time and again, especially since he's been back this summer.

But for all of this examination of his facial features, I find myself back on his eyes and wondering more than anything what his other dream—the one that didn't work out—was. I'd like to gut punch whoever was conducting this interview for not following up on that comment.

If I had to guess, I'd say it's about Trey. Maybe them playing together in college or the league one day. But then wouldn't that be wrapped up into his dream of winning the Cup? Still, while I may be off about the details, I have a feeling that what put an end to it was Trey's death.

I still feel responsible in so many ways for what happened

to Trey, but now I feel guilty for killing one of Christopher's dreams, too. Heartbreak is supposed to diminish over time, right? My heartbreak comes back around like I'm living on a circular track.

"Summer?" Jim says from the doorway.

"Yeah?" I answer and quickly press the space bar to start the video again.

"You're still working on that? We've got to get that over to the production crew and the network. We're three hours out from the doors opening. We need to test it."

"Shoot. Sorry Jim, I lost track of time."

"Did you make any big changes?"

"No, not at all. Just tightened a few things on transitions."

"Great. Export that baby and let the folks on that email chain know it's uploaded. Then let's get down to the rink. They're going to test the ice projection with the video."

"On it."

Thirty minutes later, I'm standing next to Maddy in the club level seats to watch as they run through a quick rehearsal of the banner raising and Cup presentation. Christopher is on the ice with the production crew along with the alternate captains. I don't think he sees me and that's fine. It's a big night for both of us and the last thing we need to do is sideline one another.

When their rehearsal is done and it's time to test the video and projections, everyone on the ice heads out, except for Christopher. He goes toward the tunnel but stops and looks up at the big screen as the video begins. Suddenly, all my fears of it being shown to a national audience and thousands of people in the arena vanish. The only opinion I care about is his. So,

ELLIE MALOUFF

instead of watching how the video plays out, I just watch him
from a distance. His arms are crossed over his chest as his
head is tilted back to watch it. He's got an excellent poker face,
so it's impossible to tell if he likes it.

"God, this is so good, Summer," Maddy says from beside
me. "People on social media are gonna eat it up."

"Thanks," I say, not looking away from Christopher.

The video is a summary of their championship season
with snippets of commentary from the star players and
management. It's not short, lasting five minutes, and for that
whole time he stays in place. I wish I was near him now. I wish
I could whisper in his ear that he inspires me.

When the video ends, I expect him to turn back toward the
tunnel and go, but instead he looks up directly to where I am
and smiles with so much heart, I can feel it from this distance.
It's silly that I thought he didn't see me before. Christopher
always sees me, better than anyone else.

Hours later, the actual banner raising ceremony goes off
without a hitch and the video premieres. My phone won't stop
buzzing in my pocket and I know it's all my friends and family
sending me messages about it. I love them all so dearly and I'm
truly so fortunate to have such a supportive community back
home. But my part is over now and it's Christopher's time to
shine. Opening night in the Denver arena is charged with so
much excited energy. The sold-out crowd is on their feet more
times than not as they take on Dallas, one of their rivals.

I've got my camera gear strapped on and I'm doing my best
to capture not only key parts of the banner raising and the
game itself, but all the footage that I use to tell the real story of
this night. The fans as they rise to their feet. The ice that

showers the bench when players come in hot. Dancing babies. Everything. It will make a nice piece for the Storm's YouTube channel about this night.

Christopher plays tough, maybe tougher than I've ever seen him play, like he has something to prove. Smitty gets two minutes for tripping and while they're shorthanded Christopher scores a goal on a breakaway. The crowd goes bananas and I capture his celebration as steady as I can, but even I'm shaking because it feels like fireworks just went off inside my chest. The pride I'm feeling is so heavy inside me, it's almost impossible to keep moving.

Hawk minds the net like the all star that he is, taking up all possible space with faster reflexes than I was ever able to appreciate when I was just watching him on TV last season. When one slips past him, he shakes it off with the help of his captain and I smile, knowing that the bowling alley square off didn't impact their on-ice relationship.

It's a tight game but it ends in Colorado's favor, and I make sure to capture every moment of the team raising their sticks in the air at center ice to thank the fans. The season is off to a great start, that's for sure.

As soon as the guys are off the ice, I head to my workspace and start working on my next video. I can do it from home, but I'm too excited to see what I captured. It's all as beautiful as I imagined and I get lost in my craft, weaving together a two-minute story about this night using the perfect song.

I'm so lost in it that I don't even notice a figure standing in the doorway. Truthfully, I smell him before I see him, the scent I've already come to learn is his as it is today—somehow the same as in high school, but evolved. A little more spice and unique to him.

"Hey," I say and take my eyes off the screens at last to look at him. His thick black hair is still a little wet and combed nicely. He's wearing his game day suit and looking like a million bucks.

"Hey yourself, Gunderson," he says, then slips his suit coat off and tosses it onto a nearby chair. His white dress shirt fits so well on his muscular body that I want to applaud whoever tailored it. I can see all the lines that make him one of the sexiest creatures I've ever laid my eyes on.

"You were awesome tonight," I tell him and spin around in my chair to face him. "Truly awesome."

He bends at the knees to crouch down in front of me. "*You* were awesome tonight," he repeats back to me and takes hold of my hands. "Truly awesome."

"Don't even," I reply and squeeze his hands.

"I didn't get a chance to talk to you after I saw your video. The team is so lucky to have you, Summer. You know that, right?"

"It was fine. It won't be remembered the way you will be. That's what really matters."

"It's not what I'll remember," he says while looking up into my eyes.

"You sure know how to flatter me," I tell him.

"It's not flattery. It's the truth," he says. "Did you get a lot of messages from back home?"

"As a matter of fact, I did."

"Of course you did. I got like two, one from my mom and one from my brother."

"That's because you're a star and no one thinks they can reach out to you."

He lets go of my hands and cups my cheek. "You reached out to me with that email."

My cheeks warm. "Don't remind me."

"Like I told you, it made my night," he says through his gorgeous smile.

"And like I said, you're just crazy."

"Crazy for you, Summer," he replies. "Always have been."

My heart beats in triple time as the room around us fades away. This isn't the hockey god that the world sees, this is Christopher. My Christopher.

In moments like this, it seems so simple. We should kiss now and never ever stop. It should be us together at the end of the story. It's only right. But our fairy tale hasn't worked out as it should. When he says to me that he's crazy for me and always has been, I know it's true, but it's that truth that wedged us apart. It was that craziness for each other that drove a person we loved to do something so unbelievably reckless. And it was that recklessness that doomed us all. That tainted Christopher's dream. That ended Trey's life. That turned my fairy tale into a nightmare.

My face must tell my story, because Christopher's smile falls. He clears his throat and stands up to grab his jacket. "Are you ready to go home?"

I nod and slowly collect my things, feeling downright sorry for myself. Christopher and I have been moving at this same pace for years, where the most I can ever hope for at the end of the night is a ride home. We're never going to get anywhere if there isn't a catalyst to overcome this inertia.

Christopher

Beads of sweat slide down my spine and my foot feels like a cinderblock weighing down the gas pedal. Summer sits beside me, staring out the window as the city lights of Denver pass us by. We haven't said a word to one another since we got in the truck. Normally this wouldn't bother me. She's the one person on this earth that I thought I could sit with in silence for hours and never once consider it awkward.

I was wrong. This is awkward.

Past be damned, I am going to kiss this woman because it's okay to be happy. We deserve more than this hell we've prescribed ourselves and our never-ending guilt loop. I'm ready to take that step...but she isn't. That was incredibly clear to me when her smile dissolved on the spot and the shadows in her eyes returned right before I was going to make my move.

Or maybe she just doesn't want me like that. It's a hell of a lot less painful than thinking about how we did Trey wrong, but when I think about it, I know that's bullshit. She admitted she was attracted to me when she stayed at my place. Her cheeks turned a lovely shade of pink and she turned into her pillow when I told her that I think not-so-sweet thoughts about her. She said she thinks of me that way too.

So are we destined to be a tragedy? The promise of young love never to be realized because the situation slipped out of our control? It's the way it went down with Romeo and Juliet. And the only point to debate is if Trey was the Mercutio or Tybalt of our story. I guess he was kind of both.

Well, fuck that shit. I'm not going to drink the poison. I'm not going to give in to the unhappy ending created by our own hands. We will overcome our fate.

And where do I get off knowing so much about Romeo and Juliet? When we read the play in Freshman Lit, I spent more time staring at the back of Summer's head than I did at the weathered paperback copy.

It doesn't matter. What matters is getting home, parking this truck, and making things right between us.

The garage seems darker than usual and the squeak of rubber tires on cement grates on me as we make our way to my reserved spot. When I shift the truck into park, Summer pops open her door and hops out. I grab our bags and we head for the elevator.

While we ride up, I try to think of a way to put us on the right track but nothing comes to me. We get all the way to her door and she pulls out her keys. I'm running out of time.

Come on, Mac. Do something.

"Hold up," I tell her and reach out for her arm.

She turns to look at me, puzzled as can be.

Christ. How do I start this? How do I ask her to forget the past and do this thing with me? Maybe that's the problem. Maybe it's all the words we've been trying to say.

I'm changing tactics.

I take hold of her hand and look into her eyes. She blinks a few times as she tries to understand what I'm doing, no doubt waiting for me to say something.

Not this time.

With her hand in my grasp, I lift it up to my lips and lay a long, lingering kiss on her knuckles. I never once take my eyes off hers. My lips on her skin is exactly where I've needed them to be for the past ten years.

She doesn't move and doesn't say anything. She simply breathes with me while her face softens into a small smile. Never, in all the years I've known her, have I kissed her hand, and that fact makes me smile. After a simple caress, I let go. She pulls her hand back slowly and traces over the spot where my lips touched her. I'm tempted to raise my fingers to my lips—if I'm being perfectly honest—but I want to play this cool, so I release the tension in my shoulders and tilt my head to the side. "I'll see you on the plane tomorrow," I tell her and take a step back toward my loft.

"Right. Chicago." Her voice is higher than usual.

"Good night, Summer."

"Good night, Christopher," she replies like she's on politeness autopilot. She's got that deer in headlights kind of look right now. It's as funny as it is adorable. Who knew such a little kiss could do that?

"Need some help unlocking the door?"

She blinks a few times and shakes her head. "No, no. I've got this," she says and fumbles with the keys again. I lean with my shoulder against the wall and watch. Finally, after a couple of tries, she gets the door unlocked and looks back at me with a grin that makes me downright smitten.

"Good night," she whispers to me.

"Good night," I whisper back.

She shuts the door slowly and I stay there for a few seconds more in case she opens it back up again. That went far better than expected and now that I'm brimming with confidence, I make a game plan for tomorrow.

Summer is sitting in the back of the plane with Maddy, and other team staff like our equipment managers. We've got a full crew and there's a current of excited energy flowing through the cabin. All twenty-one players are especially hyped and talkative, while the coaches sitting up front are busy conferring with each other on game plans for tomorrow. Summer has been working on her laptop with her headphones on since she took her seat. Every time I look back to check on her, she's staring at her screen. It's stupid, I know, but l I really want her to look up at me.

When will the fucking seatbelt sign turn off?

My plan is to go to her, so I can see her up close and touch her again. I really need to touch her again. Maybe we can sneak away into the galley or something when the flight attendants are busy.

But the goddamn seatbelt light won't turn off because of turbulence, so my hands and legs are restless.

"Dude, what is wrong with you? Do you need to take a shit or something?" Hux asks from beside me, not even looking up from an ancient book he's reading about mountaineering. It smells musty and outdoorsy, just like him.

I huff in response. "No."

"Oh, right. Summer's on the plane. I forgot," he says and tucks a leather bookmark between the pages before shutting it. He looks over his shoulder to the back of the plane. "She looks busy."

"I know," I reply and start biting on my thumbnail.

"What's the latest with her?" he asks and squeezes the book into the seat pocket in front of him.

"I'm making my move," I reveal.

Hux thinks on that for a minute. "Are you sure that's a good idea? It seems like really bad timing considering the season is two days old and she's working at a new job. I'm sure she feels like she has a lot to prove and sleeping with you would not do her any favors."

"Since when did you get so thoughtful? You're ruining your reputation," I reply, hating that he's chosen this moment and this topic to suddenly become insightful. Mostly I hate that he might be right.

He elbows my arm. Hard.

Never one to back down, I elbow him right back.

"So why now?" he asks again.

"It's been a long time, man. Like, a really long time that I've wanted her. And it was okay when we were states away and she wasn't in my space every day. I could get through it. I could be without her. But it's so hard now to just sit by and not do something about it. You know, I think our bedrooms share a wall since she lives next door now. I stare at the fucking wall all the time. I'm going crazy."

"I still don't understand what's stopped you from being together."

"Some shit went down in high school and there's a mountain of guilt between us. I'm ready to climb over it and move on, but I'm not sure she is."

"Are you talking about your old teammate? The one that died?"

I've never talked about Trey with Hux before, or with any

of my teammates. Not on the Storm or any team. But stories get out and Summer's video from my day with the cup brought Trey to the surface.

"Yeah. He was her cousin and my best friend."

"What happened to him?"

I look over my shoulder at Summer again. She finally looks up and catches me. I wink at her and her pretty pink lips lift up at the corners. She looks back down at her screen, but keeps the smile. I'm satisfied for the moment, at least enough to turn back around and relax into my seat.

"I fell in love with Summer and my priorities changed. He didn't handle it well and he died," I tell Hux, but won't say more. I can't get into the details, otherwise I might tumble back down to the bottom of this mountain of grief I keep imagining.

"Enough said, brother," Hux says, much to my relief.

"So what do I do?" I ask him, genuinely needing someone to help me navigate this tricky situation. Someone who won't let me fuck it up. And if that person has to be Hux, a guy who basically hates civilization, so be it.

Hux runs a palm over his thick dark beard as I wait patiently for his advice.

"Give up, Mac. You're doomed," he finally replies and fishes his book back out and opens it like he didn't just tell me, Big Mac, League MVP, and his captain to give up on something. Does he not know me at all?

"That's it? That's what you've got for me?"

Hux shrugs his shoulders and picks up where he left off in his book.

I grab it out of his hands and slam it closed.

"Hey, no need to take it out on that book. It's an antique."

"I'm about to shove it in the toilet."

"It's not the book's fault that any potential relationship with Summer is doomed."

Holding the book close to my chest, I tell him, "Fuck that. I refuse to believe anything like that. Have you not been listening? I've been in love with this woman for ten years, probably longer. I'm not going to give up. I'm going to fucking do something about it."

Hux makes a go for his book, but I just hold on tighter and tell him how I really feel in the quietest voice I can muster so that I don't completely embarrass myself. "She is the only girl I could ever want. She's brilliant and sweet and so fucking gorgeous that half the time I can't even look directly at her face. She's incredibly talented, and inspires me to be better at just about everything I do, including this sport we have in common. And she's adorably goofy, like she wears pink glasses just like she did in fifth grade and she sent me a drunk email after we won the Cup and she loves to make bets but only when she knows she's going to win. She's stubborn yet loyal, so much so that I trust her more than anybody else on this ridiculous planet. So no, I'm not going to give up, you dolt. Grow a fucking heart. I'm going to put it all out there once and for all."

Hux squints at me and then bites down on his bottom lip to stifle a laugh.

"What?" I ask, two seconds away from breaking his nose.

"You're welcome, brother," he says.

"*You're wel*...what? Why should I be thanking you?" I ask through gritted teeth.

"You knew the answer all along, which isn't that surprising, because you're one hundred percent obvious about it."

I wave the book in front of his face. "I'm going to ram this up your—"

"You can invite me to your wedding one day. I might even attend," he says and plucks the book from my hand, cracks it open, and continues reading.

"You're an asshole. You know that?"

Hux doesn't look up but smiles ever so slightly. "Just be smart about it. And *don't* let it fuck up our season. Got it?"

"Got it," I reply through a heavy sigh. Then I count to twenty before turning back around to check on Summer.

Summer

My phone must have disconnected because it is way too quiet on the other end. I pull it away from my ear to check, and I'm surprised to see that it hasn't.

"Tia?" I ask. "Can you hear me?"

"He did what?" she responds.

"He kissed my hand."

"Christopher MacCormack did that?"

"Yes," I reply and lie back on the bed that will be mine for the night in Chicago. Maddy took the one by the window, unpacked a few things, and headed out to meet a friend from college. Since I don't foresee a lot of alone time on this road trip, I jumped on the opportunity to call Tia and update her on everything. After calling my momma, of course.

"What is he, some regency gentleman or something?"

I sigh. "He's something, I'm not sure what."

"Start over. Tell me again how this went down."

So I do. I tell her all about our almost-kiss in my office, the way-too-quiet ride home, and then how out of nowhere he lifted my hand and kissed it.

"How did you not just shove him against the wall and kiss him back?" she asks. "Oh my God, you guys are the worst. I mean, this has gone on too long now. You're taking the whole slow burn thing too far."

"Slow burn, ha," I reply and shake my head. She wasn't kidding.

"The two of you have been doing this dance for ages. Remember what it finally took? You had to ask the boy to the Winter Formal."

And there it is. The exact night I don't want to remember. The exact night I'm trying to get over. We weren't the only ones that went through something that night. Tia was affected, too, yet she seems to have no qualms about mentioning it.

Tia must sense the way I've seized up, because she pushes through. "What I'm trying to say is that Christopher has always needed that extra nudge to open up. I think he puts you on such a high pedestal that he hesitates."

"Pshaw," I disagree. How could Mr. Hockey God himself put *me* on a pedestal? "Well, he didn't hesitate last night when he kissed my hand."

"Okay, as hot and steamy as that must have been for you, because the guy clearly melts your panties if he looks in your direction, we're talking about a kiss that perfect strangers have been known to do. Like in France or something."

She's got me laughing now.

"It's not like he put his tongue in your mouth."

"But God, I wish he would," I admit.

"Then you need to open things up on your end. He needs that nudge. Tell him you're ready. He'll do all the rest, I promise."

"I'm not sure if the timing is good, though. The season just started and I'm still learning the ropes. Plus, we're coworkers?" I state more as a question.

"Sure, but honestly, timing has been messing with you guys for way too long. Just get over yourselves already and bang. Sometimes sex is just sex. Okay? Maybe that's all you need to get over the past. And who knows? Maybe you'll stay together forever or maybe you'll get him out of your system and can finally move on."

That sounds good to me. Not necessarily getting him out of my system, but moving on from whatever this is that's been tugging at us for years. It's time to shit or get off the pot, as Momma likes to so eloquently say.

"How are things in Fossebridge? Tell me everything," I request.

"Well, I'm not sure if your mom told you, but Mr. Wilkins isn't doing so good. He was in the hospital for a bit, but is out now. He seems weaker."

"Is he still coming into the diner?"

"Everyday, like clockwork."

Relief floods through me and I let out a big breath. "Good. That's a good sign. I miss him and all of you, so much."

"We miss you too, but we're all rooting for you to be successful, just as much as we're rooting for Christopher."

"Don't be ridiculous," I tell her and roll over onto my tummy.

"Well, I am. I've always been in your corner," she says.

"And that's what makes you, you."

"Go do something. Be productive. I've got to get back to work."

"Yes, ma'am."

Maddy convinced me to go downstairs to the hotel lounge and get a drink.

At first I resisted, because drinking on a school night is never a good idea. Another reason to resist? Maddy suggested this adventure to the bar while wearing an off-the-shoulder hot pink dress while I had on black jeans, a black v-neck t-shirt, and the most boring black sneakers. You know the kind that waitresses and nurses wear? Yeah. Those. And since the contents of my suitcase wouldn't improve my situation much, save for the pair of black ballet flats I always pack just in case, I declined.

I should have known that excuse wouldn't fly. Maddy pulled another pink number out of her bag. "I always bring a backup," she said. "Come on, it's just a drink. Nothing crazy, since we're professional young women."

There were quite a few reasons to stay in, but there was one reason to go out that I couldn't quite shake. Christopher. After we landed in Chicago, he stuck with his team and we essentially parted ways. I couldn't get that anything-but-simple kiss out of my head, and my curiosity kept wondering what he'd do next if I bumped into him down in the bar. Especially if I was wearing the tiny piece of pink fabric that Maddy was waving in front of my face.

So here we are, riding down to the lobby, and I'm checking myself out in the elevator's mirror. *Professional* isn't the word that comes to mind. *Sultry. Sexy. Sinful.* Those adjectives are much more fitting. Speaking of fit, *snug* is another appropriate adjective. I'm not leaving much to the imagination.

The elevator dings when we reach the lobby and I contemplate going back upstairs to change into something more comfortable. Something more *me,* but Maddy grabs me by the hand. "Nuh-uh, I can tell what you're thinking. You're not chickening out now. You look fabulous and I need this. I spend all my time with a bunch of dudes," she says and drags me out of the elevator.

"One drink?" I ask.

"Just the one...that we'll buy," she replies and winks at me.

I stop in my tracks. "Maddy, you promised."

"When did I say the word promise?" she says with a laugh and pulls at me again.

She had me there. "Fine," I whine and give her my most exaggerated pout.

The lounge is nothing out of the ordinary with some basic black leather couches, armchairs, and a few tables. It's the exact kind of thing you'd expect in any decent hotel in Chicago. There's a graying bartender wearing a black vest that rarely gets dry-cleaned over a dull white dress shirt that could use some starch in the collar. A cocktail waitress that's spent a little too much time in a tanning bed is balancing a bunch of whiskey glasses. Business travelers in their grays and blues are holding a drink in one hand and a phone in the other. Some grandpa with puffy cheeks and glassy eyes is playing Gershwin on a baby grand piano in the corner.

And then there's us.

We glide into the place all blonde pink bubblegum, like an '80s music video that's about to get this party started. All I can hope is that no one approaches me with an indecent proposal, because if I'm being honest, we may just fit the part. My father would roll over in his grave if something like that happened. Momma, on the other hand, would find it hilarious. She'd never let me forget it.

"What are you drinking?" Maddy asks.

Since I'm clearly not playing the role of Summer Gunderson tonight, I ask myself, *what would a Maddy order?* "Rosé," I answer.

"Me too!" she says and we bounce our way over to the bar. The bartender lights up when he sees us, because we've clearly added some color to the place. I appreciate the generous pour he gives us because I need some liquid courage right about now. I'm not one that usually likes standing out and we are most definitely standing out.

I point at a nearby couch that's opened up. "Should we go sit down?"

"No way. We look a lot better standing here than we would sitting there."

"Are we trying to get attention?" I ask.

"Why wouldn't we want to get attention?"

"Ouf," I say under my breath and do my best to be a Maddy. The rosé is crisp and sweet, making it all the easier to drink quickly. Maddy is nursing hers while she tells me stories from last season. I expect to hear gossip about the players, but instead hear more about the actual games and the road to the championship from her perspective. Turns out, she's a huge hockey fan, and I'm annoyed at myself for being surprised about that.

"And then he got that breakaway in overtime, and I just knew that Big Mac was going to win it the second he got ahold of the puck," she says with a tear in her eye. "I could barely do my job, I was shaking with so much joy after he scored."

"I can't even imagine what it would have been like to be there in person," I tell her. "It was crazy enough watching it on TV."

"What was it like where you were?"

"You know the grand finale of a fireworks show?"

"Yeah?"

"Like that. Everyone exploded with joy at the same time."

"That's how it was in the arena. The noise was deafening. I swear the floors were shaking."

"Do you think they've got another shot at doing it again this year?"

"It's hard to repeat like that, especially after all the trades, but who knows? Nothing is impossible and last night they played strong."

"They sure did," I reply and finish off my drink.

"Speaking of..." she says and subtly lifts her chin in the direction of the hotel lobby.

Over my shoulder, I spy six or seven players walking through the hotel lobby. I don't bother to count, because I'm only focused on one. Christopher is still wearing the suit he traveled in, as are the rest of them, and he's looking mighty fine. There's just something about a guy in a suit that does things to me. And Christopher looks especially dashing. The one he wore to the Winter Formal wasn't as nice or expensive as the one he's wearing tonight, but I remember how the black jacket really made his blue eyes pop and the fabric felt so silky on my bare shoulders when he draped it over me on our way to the after party and then later…

I shake away the memory. I'm sick of being sidelined by it and after talking to Tia, I'm determined not to let it interfere anymore.

Christopher casually looks in my direction and then does a double take so exaggerated that it looks like it's out of a cartoon.

"Looks like we're about to have some company," Maddy says and finishes her drink.

Christopher slips off his jacket and strides over, leaving his teammates behind. I keep waiting for him to smile at me, but instead his eyebrows have dug in deeper than I've ever seen and his body is stiff like he's about to body check someone into the boards. I hope that someone isn't me.

"Hey, Chris," I say when he gets close enough.

He doesn't say hello. Without a word, he opens up his jacket and wraps it around my shoulders. This is not at all what I pictured happening when I took a chance and put on this dress. I figured that we might chat over a drink while he tried his hardest not to look at my boobs, because that's usually his M.O. Instead, he's putting the jacket around me like he's my big brother. I shrug right out of it and hand it back.

"What are you doing?" he whispers.

I match his arched eyebrow with my own. "Why did you do that?"

"Because you look…" he says in a low, growly voice and proceeds to scan over my body.

I don't keep my voice down like he does. "Amazing? Gorgeous? Breathtaking? Those are the only right answers."

"Yes, of course. You're all of those things," he says. He looks over his shoulder at the rest of his teammates, who are now taking a seat in the lounge and watching our little show.

"Then what's the problem? Am I embarrassing you?"

"No, it's just that…I…" he stammers.

"Use your words," I tell him and Maddy chuckles beside me.

"Can we talk?" he asks. "Privately?"

"Of course," I reply, because I've got a lot more I'd like to say to him about this.

Christopher takes hold of my hand and leads me past all his teammates, the business travelers, and hotel guests, right to the bank of elevators. We don't have to wait long before one opens. He pulls us inside, taps the number nineteen, and the close button a few times impatiently.

"So what do you want to say?" I start.

He turns to me as the doors close and folds his jacket over the handrail. I have no idea what to expect, but he doesn't keep me in suspense. Christopher takes hold of my hands, interweaves his fingers with mine, and raises our joined hands above my head as he backs us against the wall. He dips his head to my ear and runs his nose along my temple. He hums into my ear and the buzz travels throughout my body like a fat happy bumble bee.

"You're driving me crazy, Summer," he says.

"Crazy how?" I can't help but ask.

"Crazy, like I can't be rational about you. Never have been. Never will be," he answers. His warm breath on my neck makes my back arch on instinct.

"Then maybe you should forget about me once and for all." I lean my head to the side, exposing more of my neck to him.

He shakes his head like I should know better. "Impossible. Couldn't if I wanted to. Trust me, I've tried."

That's quite a revelation. Under normal circumstances that might be hurtful to hear, but after everything that happened with Trey, I completely understand. Hell, I did too, with every stupid boy I dated in college that couldn't come close to filling the Christopher-shaped hole in my life.

"I could make it easier for you. I could quit and go back home," I tell him, but I hate the idea so completely that I regret putting it into the universe at all.

He pulls back from my neck and meets my eyes. "Don't say that. Ever."

"Christopher—"

"I like when you call me Chris." He smiles so beautifully I lose track of what I was saying.

"I know," I whisper and smile back at him, suddenly feeling very shy.

He brings our hands down to each side of my head and touches his forehead to mine. "I want you so much, Summer. You've got to know it by now. Tell me you know."

"I know," I answer like a broken record.

"Then why do you do this? Why do you tempt me like this? You had to know that I'd lose my head when I saw you dressed like this. I can't resist you," he says and his nose grazes against mine. "You know that, right?"

Deep within my mind, in a well-hidden corner that I rarely reach, I do know that. And my denial about it could be mistaken for low self-confidence like I could never bring such a man to his knees. But that's not why I don't let myself accept it. It's because it's too much, too intense, and too magical. What if I mess it up? What if I ruin it all by taking it out of its box and exposing it to the elements? Well, he's cracked that box right open and I have no choice but to answer. "I know."

"Then why did you do it?" he asks, his lips coming temptingly close to mine.

I can't hold back the truth because it takes all my energy not to erase the space between us and press my lips to his. "Because you drive me just as crazy. Because I want you just as much. And maybe I'm ready."

"Ready? For what?

"To forget the past and make something happen."

He smiles like the devil himself, lets go of my hands, and cups my face. "You're ready? For something to happen?"

I nod, incapable of doing much else than breathe.

"Something like this to happen?" he asks and wedges a leg between mine. Dear God, it feels like heaven pressed against me, *there*.

"Yes." The word slips out with a moan.

"What about something like this?" he asks and runs his hand down the slope of my neck, over my nearly bare shoulder, my breast and belly, to take hold of my hip and squeeze. I gasp, unable to hide how much he's affecting me. He increases the pressure of his thigh between my legs just enough to make my head fall back against the elevator wall.

"Yes," I hiss. I want this and if my panties are any indication, I'm ready for it. But Christopher doesn't carry on. Instead, he gently lets me go, steps back, and grabs his jacket. Confusion doesn't even scratch the surface. It's not until the elevator dings and the doors open that I realize he stopped just before we reached the nineteenth floor.

I'm fully brought back to reality by Alex Hawkins waiting outside the elevator wearing sweats and a Storm cap. He freezes in place and his mouth forms a very dramatic O. I'm sure he's not actually surprised to see us together, but anyone that's known him for more than five minutes can tell that he lives for the drama. Thank goodness he didn't see his captain humping the videographer in the elevator. I'm not sure he'd be able to contain himself. I do, however, cross my arms, because the state of my nipples could easily become locker room gossip.

"And what are you two getting up to this evening?" the goalie asks.

Christopher shakes his head and steps out of the elevator. "Are you coming, Summer?"

I want to say yes. I want to tackle him in the hallway, yank up my dress, and mount him right there with Hawk as our witness, but I do have some shred of self-control left. I know it's not a good idea to get off this elevator with Christopher. I know the best thing for me to do is go back to my room and cool off a bit so that we do this right.

"Actually, I'm on twenty-one," I say. Now it's Christopher's turn to make a dramatic face.

"I better go with you, just to make sure you get there safely," Alex says and dares to take a step toward the elevator.

Christopher whips his arm out right across Alex's chest to hold him back. "Don't you dare."

Alex doesn't hold back his laughter and even I'm struggling not to crack.

"See you at morning skate," I say to them. "Good night."

Christopher doesn't say anything. He just watches as I disappear behind the elevator doors.

7

Christopher

WINTER, SENIOR YEAR

Coach Kiogima has been riding us extra hard this week. He heard about the party at the Clearing and all the trouble we stirred up, including my fight with Henry and Trey's trip to the emergency room for alcohol poisoning. Coach bitched us out more than my own parents did and I think I'll be sore for the rest of my life for all the extra sprints he's made us do up and down the ice each practice, with no end in sight.

We're goddamn lucky that this town loves us so much, because there was a moment there where I thought we'd get kicked off the team. And then goodbye future. There'd be no hockey scholarship if there was no hockey to be played. But at least one thing would be easier—I could stop debating between UMN with Summer and Boston with Trey. We could all just go to UMN and call it good. At least one of my dreams would come true.

But it wouldn't be good enough, would it? Dreams are pesky like that and that other dream I've been pursuing, the one where I bring the Cup back to Fossebridge someday, cannot be killed. So, I was pretty fucking worried about losing my spot on the team and pretty fucking relieved when I didn't. And after a lot of groveling and promise making, I got to keep the C on my sweater, too.

Both dreams are still within reach and I'm determined to make them come true, one way or another.

We go into our Saturday night game against our district rival more motivated than ever because we're counting our blessings to be there. Not to mention that all the aggression and frustration we've been brewing this last week finally gets to spill out. We're ready to prove that we're the best. Our players. Our coach. Our fans. And all that confidence gives us a serious edge. We beat them to smithereens.

After the game, the locker room is a much nicer place than it was on Monday and Tuesday and so on. We're all acting like we've just won State. Music is blasting and the guys are practically shouting as they recap what went down.

It's not until I'm in the shower that I realize that my head was so in the game, I didn't even notice if Summer was there recording the whole thing. I sure hope she was. After my shower, I get dressed as quickly as I can so I can be the first guy out there for an interview if she's waiting.

I don't keep her waiting long.

She perks up, lights up, and stands up when she sees me.

"That was amazing!" she says and dashes toward me to give me a hug.

The hug is long enough and thrilling enough for me to imagine what it could one day be like when she comes down onto the ice after I win the Cup. I'd kiss her so hard, even on national television. I wish I could kiss her now, but more of my teammates are starting to stream out and they're still riding that high from winning. Except for Trey. His smile fades when he sees Summer and I hugging, so I let go and take a step back.

"Can I interview you guys?" she asks the group of guys, excitedly.

"Of course," I answer and pull a few fellas over.

"I've got to get home. I'm still grounded," Trey tells her.

"No prob. Good job, buddy," she says and gives him a playful punch in the arm.

Trey gives her one right back before taking off, not looking back. *What's his problem?* He was totally living it up in the locker room. He couldn't be this upset over a simple hug. We've all been hugging each other for years.

Summer lifts up her camera and gets to work. I let the guys do most of the talking until she turns her lens on me. "Big Mac, you got three points tonight with a goal and two beautiful assists. What do you think led to such a dominating victory tonight?"

"Determination and gratitude," I answer.

"Gratitude?"

"This is the greatest sport on earth. I think we realized this week that we're just lucky for the chance to play it, especially for a school as great as Fossebridge High."

She smiles and lowers her camera. "That was great. You all played awesome. Thanks so much."

The rest of the guys get on their way while she starts packing her camera away.

"Want a ride home, or do you have any more interviews you want to do? Want to interview Coach?" I ask.

"Already got it," she says with a satisfied smile. "It's going to make a great piece. I was able to capture all the goals really well. I can't wait to start editing."

"Then let's head home," I suggest, even though she didn't really answer me about the ride.

"Cool. Thanks, Chris."

I blink a few times and absorb the sound of my name. I love that she calls me Big Mac on camera but Chris when it's just us. I love being special to her. And I especially love that I'm the one that gets to drive her home most nights.

We don't live far from school—honestly, not many people do in a town this size—so the trip is never quite long enough for me. I always linger at stop signs and have been known to make a wrong turn just to prolong it. If she sees through these antics, she certainly isn't letting on to it. I know it's silly, but I hope she appreciates the extra time, too.

I park outside her house and see that most of the lights are on and her mom is home. "It's a shame that the Biscuit is closed. I could really go for some onion rings tonight."

"Ohhh, that sounds so good," she replies and makes this hungry moan that makes me press down on the brake harder. I decide it's better just to put it in park. "Hey, Momma won't mind if we go down there and make some for ourselves. I think you've earned it with those three points you got tonight."

I smile. "Don't tease me, Gunderson. You can't dangle onion rings in front of me and take it back."

She laughs and says, "Wouldn't dream of it, Big Mac."

I love it when we play.

"For real?"

"Let me just go tell Momma and grab the keys."

"Hurry," I request, and she hops out of the car and hustles up to the house.

Her absence gives me time to come up with a million scenarios for why she might come back out here and tell me the plan is off. And about half a million scenarios where she doesn't come out at all and bails on me. But she does not disappoint. She hustles back to the car and slides in with a huge smile on her face. "Okay, we're on."

This time I don't linger at stop signs and I don't make any wrong turns.

We park in the alley behind the restaurant and go in the back door. She turns on the lights in the kitchen and some track lighting above the lunch counter. She grabs two aprons and tosses me one. "Since you've already showered tonight," she says, and I'm so worked up that even her saying the word shower is enough for me to bite on the inside of my cheek. This impromptu date is not the right time for an impromptu boner. *Or maybe it is*...and my mind gets carried away thinking about Summer Gunderson wearing only that apron and nothing else.

First, she turns on the fryer, since it will take time for it to heat up. Then she pulls a yellow onion out of a basket, washes, and dries it. With a chef's knife, she goes to work slicing it up into perfect rings. I stand by, ready to wipe away her tears in case the onion makes her cry. It doesn't faze her, but it sure gives me plenty of time to look at her beautiful green eyes while she works. She mixes up some batter like she's done it a hundred times before and then she dips the rings into it and drops them into the fryer, which makes one of the most satisfying sounds a hungry man can hear.

"When I was a kid, I never used to eat the onion," she says. "And my momma, she'd actually make them with extra-thick batter just for me."

"Your mother is one of the finest people in this town," I say.

Summer laughs. "I'll tell her you said that. She loves praise."

"What about you? Do you love praise?"

"I think you already know the answer to that is no, since you're the one who's usually praising me."

"You deserve all of it."

"I'm not sure that's totally true, but you make me believe that it is most of the time."

"And the rest of the time?"

"The rest of the time, I wonder how it is that Christopher MacCormack even knows I'm alive."

"Tsk. You can't be serious." If she only knew.

"Then tell me this, Chris. If I were to—hypothetically, of course—ask you to be my date to the Winter Formal, would you say yes?"

"Hypothetically?"

"Yes."

"Ah," I begin and start to scratch my head like I've really got to think about this in a hypothetical way. "I mean, hypothetically, would you be picking me up in a limo and taking me out to a five-course dinner?"

"Hypothetically, I'd probably ask you to drive and probably bring you here for onion rings and a burger."

"Okay, that changes things, because you know how much I hate limos and five-course dinners."

She laughs and wipes her hands on her apron.

"And hypothetically, would you be wearing a dress?"

"Well, I suppose, hypothetically, I would be. And you'd be wearing a suit."

"Would there be dancing in this scenario?"

"Unfortunately, yes," she says with a grimace.

"Slow dancing?"

She lifts an eyebrow and smiles. "I suppose there would be. Hypothetically speaking."

"Of course, of course...hypothetically. And in this slow dancing, is it something like this?" I ask, and reach one hand out and place it on her waist and take hold of her hand with the other, as if we were to waltz. She rests her other hand on my shoulder and I look down at the dimples that serve no other purpose than to rile me up.

"Hmm..." she hums, holding in a laugh. "I was thinking in this particular hypothetical, that it would be more like this." She lets go of my hand, takes a step closer to me so that we're apron-to-apron, and wraps her arms around the back of neck.

My free arms go around her waist and I pull her even closer to me. "Right, I've heard about this kind of slow dancing, in other hypothetical situations."

We slowly sway to the sound of the fryer settling down and

the fluorescent lights buzzing above. You could offer me an orchestra and I'd turn them away. It's perfect.

"So, what would your hypothetical answer be?" she asks.

I give it a few seconds as I watch her face. Her eyes crinkle and her easygoing smile sinks as I make her wait. This is more fun than I thought it would be. A smile slowly spreads across my face as I answer,"A resounding yes. Hypothetically, of course."

"Excellent," she whispers.

We continue to dance, if you can even call our embrace that, until the fryer gets louder and louder. She slips out of my arms and I miss her already. She checks the onion rings. "These are done. Let's eat."

She sets us up at the lunch counter, grabs us two root beers, and a side of barbecue sauce for me without even asking. I'm going to marry this woman.

We rehash the game again and eventually the topic turns to Trey. "He seemed a little cold tonight," she says. "I mean, I know my Uncle Dave. They're not that strict with him. This is like the first time he's ever been grounded, at least from what I can remember."

"Yeah, and he said it's only for this weekend."

"Did you get in trouble with your parents?"

"Not when I explained what happened. They were happy that I was a designated driver. Then my dad sat me down and talked to me about the fight." What I don't tell Summer is that my dad basically told me to cut the caveman bullshit because I'd never win her heart if I continued to act like such a brute. Considering how long he's been happily married to my mom, he's probably right.

"That's good," she says. "Do you think we need to be worried about Trey? Like, do you think he'll react poorly to us going to the dance together?" she asks.

"Wait, we're going to the dance together?" I joke. "I thought that was just a hypothetical question."

Summer turns beet red and nearly chokes. "Oh God," she spurts out between coughs. I pat her on the back a few times.

"Breathe," I tell her. "I was just joking."

She shakes her head and then punches me in the arm, not nearly as playfully as she did with Trey. "Dude!"

"I'm sorry. I'm truly sorry," I tell her and look at her with the most serious expression I can muster, which is hard because I've been smiling like a damn idiot since she unlocked to the door to the Biscuit. "We are most definitely going to the dance. I'm going to pick you up and we're going to eat here. You're going to wear a dress that will probably make me lose my mind and I'm going to wear a suit, and we will slow dance to all the slow songs if it's the last thing I do."

"Sounds like a plan to me," she says with a gorgeous smile, one that matches the happiness I see in her eyes. One that I could picture her having on all the important days of her life to come. Like when she walks down the aisle or when she holds her baby for the first time. It's an important one. One that she saves for moments when she's truly happy. Moments like this.

Summer

Peeling out of Maddy's pink dress is the second most physically satisfying experience of the evening. First place belongs to Christopher in that elevator. Actually, scratch that. That was nothing but very, very frustrating. Honestly, if something doesn't give soon, I'm going to lose my mind or hump a bell boy.

I take out my contacts and wipe all the makeup off I put on to complement Maddy's look. When I crawl into bed with my glasses and Garfield pajamas on, I finally feel like me again. My laptop completes the picture. I do what I do and check in on all my stuff, from view counts on my videos to my email and social media. The views on the video we aired last night about their championship season makes my jaw drop. It's surpassed the million-view mark in a little over twenty-four hours. The video I uploaded this morning of the banner raising ceremony and home opener win has already hit 200k.

Holy moly.

It takes a notification on my phone to make me look away.

Christopher: *Hey, are you still up?*

I'm not surprised he's texting me after what just went down. I'm also not surprised by the smile I'm sporting.

Summer: *Yes :)*

Christopher: *What are you doing?*

I could tell him the truth, but it's a little bit embarrassing to admit that I check the views on my videos. Plus, I'd rather have a little bit of fun with him, so I rewind time.

Summer: *Getting undressed.*

Christopher: *SUMMER GUNDERSON.*

That makes me laugh. I shut my laptop and toss it to the other side of the bed.

Summer: *What? It's not like I was going to sleep in that dress. It belongs to Maddy.*

Christopher: *Remind me to send her a thank you note.*
Summer: *You're funny.*
Christopher: *You're beautiful.*
Summer: *You're not too bad yourself, Big Mac.*
Christopher: **Chris**
Summer: *What are you doing?*
Christopher: *Talking to you.*
Summer: *We're not talking, we're texting.*

My phone starts to ring. Dear lord, he wants to video chat. *Shit.* I sit up in bed, pull my hair out of a ponytail, and shake it out. There's nothing else I can do to help this situation, except for ignoring him altogether, but I don't want to do that. I want to talk to him and I especially want to see him, so I stop wasting time and answer.

"Hi," I chirp and then thank the gods of technology for putting cameras in telephones because I get to see Christopher MacCormack shirtless and leaning against the headboard like a freakin' model.

He smiles like a goof and replies, "I'm glad to see the Garfield PJs again."

"Why do I think you're lying?" I tease.

"I mean, obviously I wouldn't mind seeing you in nothing at all, but I love you like that too. And you know I'm charmed by those glasses. I told you that back at the loft."

"I seriously don't understand you."

"I'm a simple man, Gunderson," he says and runs his fingers through his gorgeous black hair.

"Nothing about us is simple, Big Mac."

"What's a guy got to do to be called Chris again?"

"Hmm...now that I know how much you want to hear it, I

think I'll have to come up with something to make you earn it."

"You know I'm always up for a challenge. Your wish is my command."

"Are you solo, or do you have a roommate?" I ask, mostly to buy time so I can come up with something.

"I usually room with Hux, but tonight I'm solo."

"How's that?"

"Hux had some personal business to handle."

"Well, that's mysterious," I reply.

"It doesn't matter. What do I have to do for you to say my name?" His voice is deep and sexy and I flash back to him whispering in my ear when we were in the elevator. Warmth radiates down my chest and pools low in my belly.

"Since we're video chatting, we could play show and tell," I suggest.

He sits up straighter. "Show and tell? I like the sound of that."

"I thought you might."

"You know what's even better than show and tell on video chat?" he says.

"What's that, *Big Mac*?"

He pauses at my jab and holds back a smile that so obviously wants to spread across his face. "You could come to room 1908 and we could play show and tell in person."

"Now where's the fun in that?"

"Oh Summer, I assure you it would be very fun and interactive."

"Hey Big Mac, I make the rules."

"Okay, okay," he says and lets out a big breath. "What do you want to see? I'm ready."

"Easy, show me your toothbrush."

He scoffs. "My toothbrush?"

"Yeah, I'm in the market for a new one."

He sighs and shakes his head. "This isn't what I had in mind."

"Oh, I know."

He flips off the covers and gets up with an exaggerated groan. I get to go on a little journey where my view of his face is from a very silly low angle as he takes us into the bathroom. The light comes on and he flips the camera lens off of selfie mode to show me his toothbrush on the vanity. But I'm not checking out his top-of-the-line electric toothbrush. I'm scoping the mirror just behind it to get a good look at his abs and waist and belly button. Washboards are antiquated and six packs are cheap. His abs are like a flagstone path to an oasis that I'd like to visit someday. Someday very soon.

"So yeah, that's my toothbrush," he says. Has he been talking this whole time? I wasn't listening.

"Turn it on for me," I request so I can buy a little more time.

"O...kay," he says and does as I request.

Where was I? Right, he's got a smattering of dark hair that dips below the waistband of his boxer briefs and one of those belly buttons that's only barely an innie. I wipe my mouth, as a proactive measure in case there's any drool.

"There's a sensitive setting and a deep clean one too, which I like the most."

"Mmm-hmm," I say. "Show me."

"You want me to brush my teeth?"

After a moment's pause, I say, "Yes?" Really, I want to see his whole torso in the mirror. I continue with more conviction, "I want to compare techniques. Like, are you a righty or a lefty, do you move your mouth or your hand. Both? That would be wild."

He flips the camera back to selfie mode. "Summer, what are you doing?"

"Nothing," I say in such a high voice I'm sure it gives me away. "I'm genuinely curious."

"Are you...are you just trying to check me out in the mirror?"

I gasp. "Big Mac, how dare you!"

"Summer Gunderson, if you want to see any more of this, then you're just going to have to come down to room 1908 and I'll show you."

"Well, maybe I just will," I shout.

"Good," he says dramatically.

"Good," I say just as dramatically and am about to end the call when there's suddenly the distinct noise of a keycard at the door. Maddy's back.

"Hey. So you've got to tell me what happened with Mac!" she starts right away and then notices I'm on the phone. "Oh, is that him?" she asks in a whisper.

"No, it's my mom," I tell her and look at the phone.

Christopher's mouth drops open and he starts shaking his head.

"So anyway, Momma. I love you and wish you a very good night. Sweet dreams!"

He pleads with me by mouthing the words, "come down" again and again. I shrug and end the call before he can blow it.

"Was that really your mom?" Maddy asks as she takes off her earrings.

I pull up the covers over my chest and turn my phone face-down on the bed. "Of course. Why wouldn't it be?"

"Because it should be Christopher. What the hell happened with him?" She takes a seat on her bed and kicks off her pumps.

Everything that went down in the elevator flashes back and my cheeks are burning.

"Something did, didn't it?" she asks.

I'm not ready to go there with Maddy. My job with the team is too new, as are all these work relationships I'm build-ing, to go *there* about Christopher. So I rattle off a semi-true story to sate her curiosity.

"Christopher and I have a long history, and our friendship is a little bit complicated." Truth.

"I think he was just acting like a big brother, you know?" Lie.

"He apologized for overreacting." Truth.

"And he just wanted to see me back to the room, like a chaperone." Lie.

"Then I came in here and got on my pajamas." Truth.

"And video chatted with my momma." Lie.

Maddy's perfect posture loosens up and she leans back on the bed. "That is not the story that Hawk told us down in the lounge."

"You talked to Hawk?"

"Yeah, he said he saw you guys all flushed and awkward in

the elevator. He thought maybe something happened between you two. Bummer."

"Bummer?"

"Yeah, it's a bummer. We were all hoping you guys got busy."

"Who's we?"

"Me and some of the guys. Smitty, Foxy, and Wags mostly."

My phone vibrates not once, but several times beside me. I'd bet a dozen jelly donuts I know who it is. I let it go and keep focusing on Maddy.

"Aren't you going to look at that?" she asks with a laugh.

"Oh that?" I say and look down at my phone but don't dare to pick it up. "I'm sure it's just Momma, sending me goodnight kisses."

"Mmmhmm," Maddy replies and gets up. "I'm going to get ready for bed. Say hi to Big Mac for me."

My head falls back against the headboard. God, I must be so transparent. I pick up the phone and check out the onslaught of messages from Christopher.

Christopher: *Are you coming down?*

Christopher: *Summer?*

Christopher: *I can show you how I brush my teeth. I'll put on quite a show.*

Christopher: *Summmmmer?*

Christopher: *Just make up an excuse and get down here.*

He's such an adorable dork.

Summer: *Hi.*

Christopher: *There you are. What's the deal? You coming?*

Summer: *Nah, you need to rest and so do I.*

Christopher: *Pleaseeee*

Summer: *All those extra letters you keep throwing in doesn't change matters. You gotta get your head in the game, Big Mac. This isn't like a summer camp for teenagers. This is your job and mine too!*

Christopher: *<grumpy>*

Summer: *You're adorable. Have a little patience.*

Christopher: *Patience? You can't be serious. I've been wanting to play show and tell with you like this for years.*

Summer: *I think you'll somehow manage to wait just a little bit longer. Plus, I think Maddy is super onto us.*

Christopher: *Well, Hux just came back unexpectedly too, so I guess it wasn't meant to be.*

Summer: *Maybe not tonight, but certainly not forever.*

Christopher: *Mean that?*

Summer: *With all my heart.*

Christopher

She's ready. She actually said that she's ready to let go of the past.

I could barely sleep all night long as I thought about Summer.

Summer in that pink dress.

Summer in her glasses and PJs.

Summer's glossy pink lips that I'm betting taste like cotton candy.

Summer's laugh.

Summer's neck and her scent that makes my knees weak.

Summer telling me, "I'm ready to let go of the past and make something happen."

So yeah, I had a really shitty night of sleep because my head and my heart just wouldn't let me go. And then something crazy happened. I've never skipped a morning skate in my life, even though it's optional when we're on the road, but that streak ended this morning.

I vaguely remember Hux trying to wake me up. And I sort of recall turning off my emergency alarm that I habitually set but have never once used. When I finally came to and saw the time, I knew busting my butt to get there wouldn't be worth it. So, I flipped my pillow over and went back to sleep, all the while pressing my hard-on into the mattress. I'd been dealing with that guy since last night.

So yeah, my routine is totally off but whatever. Shit happens. I've got enough hockey experience to handle it.

I get in the shower, groggy and hungover. Not from booze, but something much like being love drunk. And instead of popping two aspirin, I opt for hair of the dog.

Summer's curves in that dress.

Summer in those adorable glasses.

Summer's pretty pink lips that are so plump I want to chew on them.

Summer's laugh.

Summer's creamy skin just below her ear.

Summer's soft body against mine. Her breast beneath my palm. Her hip in my grasp. The space between her legs where I fit so nice. Summer's warmth spreading across my thigh.

I'm lost in the moment and hockey is the furthest thing from my mind.

When I get out of the shower, there's a flurry of messages from practically everyone on our team that matters wondering if I'm okay but the only ones I open are from Summer.

Summer: *Hey, where are you? I thought I'd see you at morning skate.*

Summer: *I talked to Hux. He said you were still sleeping when he left. I hope everything is okay.* ♥

That silly little heart might just be the end of me. I stare at it until it looks like gibberish and then I text her back.

Christopher: *Good morning.* ♥

Summer: *Hey, are you okay?*

Christopher: *I didn't sleep well, so I decided to skip morning skate.*

Summer: *Yeah, but everyone was kind of freaking out. Apparently you never do that.*

Christopher: *There's a first time for everything, right?*

It takes her a while to text back and instead of using my time productively, I just stare at the screen, waiting for her to respond. It feels like ages until the three little dots appear.

Summer: *Why couldn't you sleep?*

Christopher: *Why do you think?*

As I wait for her reply, there's a knock on the door. I'm only wearing a towel around my waist, but I figure it's probably just one of my teammates checking on me. Of course, it's the one person I didn't expect.

"Summer?" I'm surprised.

"Whoa," she says and covers up her eyes. "I'll come back or just text you instead."

"Not a chance." I grab her hand away from her eyes and pull her into my room, letting the door shut behind her. She spins around in my arms and rests her hands on my bare shoulders. When I take hold of her hips, I'm reminded of the time we slow danced in the kitchen at the Biscuit. And just like then, I feel so much hope for us.

"What are you doing here?" I ask as my hands migrate and rest in the valley of her lower back. I could have written my college thesis about the geometry of this curve.

"I wanted to see you," she confesses as a blush spreads across her cheeks.

"Oh, is that so?" I ask and pull her closer to me so that my towel presses against her tummy.

"Chris..."

"There it is," I reply with a smile. "I was waiting all night to hear that."

She lifts an eyebrow. "Is that why you couldn't sleep?"

Here it is. An opportunity to tell her a truth so blunt it won't leave any doubt. As scary as it is, I want her to know my heart. "I couldn't stop thinking of you and I want you like crazy."

"Oh, is that so?" she asks, her dimples doing their damage.

"Do you hear an echo?" I joke. "Yes, it's so. How did you sleep?"

"Like a baby," she replies, but her mischievous eyes reveal the truth. She's just as wrecked as I am.

"What are we going to do about this, Gunderson?"

"I honestly don't know," she admits, then slips out of my arms and starts pacing around the room. "But today is not the day to figure that out."

My head falls back and I stare at the ceiling.

Five. Four. Three. Two. One.

I let out a big breath and remind myself that patience is a virtue.

"You've got a game to play today and I've got a job to do in an arena that I am not familiar with at all. Plus, it's CHI. CA. GO," she says, clapping between each syllable. "It's going to be super intense and loud, and every game in their house is like game seven."

I circle around her, the towel barely clinging onto me. "I'm a master at winning game sevens."

"I didn't say you couldn't win, but we've got to use a little common sense, Chris." Her body is tense and tight like the way I lace my skates.

I gently take a piece of her hair and run my fingers through it. Her shoulders relax as I do this, and when our eyes connect she lets out a big breath. I reach out for her again and hold onto her hips like before, never losing sight of her eyes. My voice is heavy when I tell her, "The most common sense thing in the world is for us to be together, and I think you know that."

Her eyelids flutter closed. "I do..." she begins and wraps her arms around my neck.

But since timing has always been our enemy, the door unlocks and Hux comes into the room. Summer quickly takes a step away from me so that there's a respectable distance between us.

Hux gets one look at us and freezes at the door. "Sorry," he says.

"It's okay," Summer replies for us and starts making her way to the door. "I was just leaving, anyway. I've got start

ELLIE MALOUFF

editing the footage I grabbed this morning. Talk later. Good luck tonight, guys."

And once again, she leaves me behind. If I had clothes on, I'd chase after her and finish the conversation, but obviously fate is going to make me work a little bit harder for it.

"Bravo," I tell Hux and start clapping.

Hux sets his bag down on the bed and puts his hands on his hips. "Sorry," he says again and laughs.

"Yeah, you sound really sorry, bro," I tell him and start getting dressed.

"We need to talk, so maybe I'm not that sorry."

"Talk about what?" I ask and yank a Storm t-shirt over my head.

"The fact that you missed morning skate."

I scoff. "Like you haven't."

"Actually, I haven't and neither have you. We talked about this yesterday on the plane."

"You think I'm losing my edge because of Summer. Gimme a break. I've been playing hockey with Summer hanging around long before I ever met you."

"Oh, in high school? Cool. Yeah, that's totally the same," he says sarcastically. I throw my towel at him and he bashes it away. "Don't fuck this up, Mac. You've got plenty of time to make something happen with this girl."

"I'm done talking about this," I tell him and charge into the bathroom. What Hux will never fully appreciate is how hard this has been for us and I'm not going to wait anymore. The last thing I'm going to do is let Summer Gunderson slip through my fingers. By day's end, I'm going to kiss her.

198

8

Summer

WINTER FORMAL, SENIOR YEAR

Christopher MacCormack is a surprisingly good dancer for a hockey player. When I pictured this moment, I figured he'd definitely do the white man's overbite, but the boy's got rhythm. As we dance to the second Britney Spears song of the night, I'm impressed, but I'm also ready to slow it down and move onto something where I get to cuddle up closer to him.

Tia bounces over to me and we bump booties. She's looking stunning in a royal blue strapless cocktail dress. When Trey and Christopher picked us up at my house, she wanted to make one of those staircase entrances so the guys could get the full effect.

In typical Tia style, she had me go first, probably to learn from my mistakes because the girl is smart like that. It took a lot of concentration to not stumble down the stairs in the scarlet red pumps that perfectly match my simple one-shoulder mid-length dress. As Christopher came into view, my breath went short. There he stood, all six-foot-something of him, wearing a midnight black suit that makes his blue eyes pop, a crisp white dress shirt, and scarlet red tie. I don't remember telling him the color of my dress, but I'm not surprised he somehow found out.

Upon seeing me, he swallowed hard and froze in place, never once taking his eyes off me as I descended the stairs. With each step closer that magnetic feeling I have to him intensified and I thanked my lucky stars that he said yes to being my date. I knew right then that I was the luckiest girl at Fossebridge High.

Without saying a word to me, he held out the plastic container containing a white rose corsage.

"It's beautiful, thank you," I said with a thread of nervous excitement woven through my voice.

We both took awkward turns trying to open it and get it around my wrist, all the while he just kept looking at me and ever so slightly shaking his head, as if he had to make sense of me. Maybe he didn't know that a girl who wears t-shirts and jeans most of the time could clean up so well. Well, the joke's on him then, because I cleaned up really well. Momma put about four thousand curlers in my hair and then pinned it into a half-up, half-down look she stole out of a People magazine that's been sitting around our house since the late '90s. I think it was based on something Alicia Silverstone did once upon a time. Momma stood off to the side with the other parents, snapping photos of her creation while rattling on and on about how cute we looked together. I gave her a look that said "shut it or I will end you" which of course only egged her on.

Trey was looking pretty good too, albeit not as dashing as Christopher nor as well put together. To say that he lacked enthusiasm for this dance was an understatement. Sure, he said yes when Tia asked him to be her date, but according to Tia, he hadn't really shown any initiative when it came to making plans. Since she likes being in the driver's seat anyway, she didn't mind taking it on herself. After all, this is a Sadie Hawkins dance.

Tia hoped that all would change when he saw her in that smashing dress and honestly, I hoped so too. I wanted to see his jaw drop. So, as she came down the stairs, I turned around to watch the two of them. Trey, who is always Mr. Wise Ass, could never live up to an expectation like that. There was no jaw dropping. There was no spark of excitement. There were only jokes. "You will never believe this, Tia. I almost wore the exact same thing," he said.

"Well we know who would have won *Who Wore It Better*, that's for sure," she replied and did a cute little shimmy that made everyone smile and laugh.

Trey handed her a corsage that looked pretty much identical to mine. She put it on with little fanfare and then pinned a white rose boutonniere to Trey's lapel. I didn't think to get Christopher one, but he didn't seem to mind.

At the request of our parents, we got together in different sets to pose for photos. When it was time for Christopher and I to pose together, a jolt of nerves shot through me. He wrapped his arm around my waist and held me close to him. Heat radiated off of his body and sunk into my skin, as if I were sunbathing at Webster Lake. As cameras flashed, I tried to hold onto the moment knowing that if I memorized it just as it was, I'd have something truly awesome to look back on high school about, but out of the corner of my eye I noticed Trey sitting on the stairs watching us with an expression on his face that rubbed me the wrong way. His eyes were dark, his brow low, and the thin crease at his mouth had me guessing if he was annoyed or impatient or jealous—of what, I couldn't quite put my finger on. Maybe he was pissed that Christopher and I were hitting it off so well and he didn't really have that kind of feeling about Tia. Or maybe he just hated this whole Winter Formal thing altogether and would rather be off doing pretty much anything else.

Trey was usually one to wear his heart on his sleeve, but he was uncharacteristically quiet. Why was he was retreating into the shadows when all around us was light?

Christopher took my hand into his and leaned down to whisper, "Shall we?" Getting to hold his hand was such a huge step, and throughout the night he found my hand whenever he could. I never want him to let it go.

After a special dinner Momma made the four of us at the Biscuit—that included a scrumptious chocolate pecan pie for dessert—we leisurely made our way over to the high school gym for the dance.

The place looks amazing. It's all decked out with colorful string lights and paper snowflakes hung up by ribbon ringlets. Tia is the chair of the dance committee and she made the place look incredible. Like a real winter wonderland.

Christopher didn't wait long to ask me to dance and we've been movin' and groovin' ever since. Tia, too, but not so much for Trey. I mean, I know the guy isn't into this kind of thing, but he can definitely get in touch with his silly side and how can anyone not be into a little bump and grind with a smoking hot chick wearing a killer dress?

"Where's Trey?" I ask Tia.

"The last time I saw him, he was talking to Mateo," she says and points over her shoulder.

"Looks like he still is," I reply and watch as the two stand off to the side of the gym, looking like they are up to no good whatsoever, whispering and looking around.

"Mateo's parents are out of town, so he's having an after party," she says with a smile. "Trey and I are definitely going."

No big surprise there. I'm also not surprised when Trey pulls out a flask from his jacket pocket and they both take a drink.

So it's going to be that kind of night.

The boy is going to get on my very last nerve.

I'm tempted to say something to Christopher, but I'm sick of Trey ruining any and all romance I get with the guy. So I block him out and focus on us. As the song fades out and a slow song finally begins, Tia gives us a wink and a smile and wanders over to a group of students that also work on the newspaper. I turn to Christopher. He's standing there with a goofy smile on his face.

"You ready for this, Big Mac?" I ask him.

"I've been waiting for this, Gunderson," he replies and pulls me to him with such exuberance, I can't help but laugh. That, and the nerves that have been hanging out with me all night. I fold my arms around his neck just like we did in the kitchen at the Biscuit, and his strong arms wrap around my torso like I belong to him. In so many ways I really feel like I do.

This is the guy that makes me feel completely adored and awesome and special. He's my biggest fan and at the end of the day, a person that I know has my back and I can rely on, even if things were to get bad. I can't see a way where we don't end up together, even if we went to different colleges.

When I rest my head over his heart, he tenses up and I chalk it up to his own set of nerves. It's really cute. After a few seconds though, he relaxes into it and I let out a long breath. Where our bodies meet is soft and warm and safe. Usually this is where I'd make some kind of joke, because that's something I really love to do with Christopher, but I don't want to change a thing about what we're doing.

We dance this way through the bridge of the song and as it goes on, I nuzzle a little bit closer until the only thing separating us is our formalwear.

The song winds down and I pray that the DJ isn't going to turn on a third Britney track. I want to keep this going. Fortunately, my wish is granted and a new song begins that's still on the slower side of things. I peek up at Christopher to make sure he's enjoying this as much as I am. His eyelids are heavy and his lips are slightly parted.

"What are you thinking?" I ask him.

He smiles ever so slightly and then bends his head to the side and looks away.

"Tell me," I poke.

"I'm going to UMN."

I blink a few times as I process what he's telling me. Could he possibly be doing that because of me? "What about Boston?" I ask.

"UMN has a fantastic program, too. I'd rather be here than there," he says.

"Have you told Trey?" I want to know because that could certainly explain his recent behavior.

"Not yet," he replies.

"Maybe he already knows," I answer and glance over at him. He's leaning against the wall with his arms crossed and watching us. Christopher doesn't seem to notice and I'm grateful.

"He knows that I haven't committed to BU. I'm just waiting to tell him."

"Isn't signing day Wednesday?"

Christopher sighs heavily. "Yeah, it is."

Anxiety bubbles around in my chest. This isn't going to go well, I just know it. Christopher picks up on it. "Hey, don't worry about your cousin. He'll understand, he's got to."

"Maybe UMN isn't worth it," I tell him, hoping he understands my real meaning. *Maybe I'm not worth it.* "You should do what's right for your future, Chris."

His hand slips into my hair and he turns my face up to look into his eyes. "This is right for my future, Summer."

At that moment, I know without a doubt he's choosing UMN to be with me, and suddenly I don't care what's right for him and his hockey career and I certainly don't care what Trey thinks. I want Christopher so much that I'm willing to be greedy.

The song shifts into an upbeat number and people all around us start bouncing up and down. Christopher seems oblivious to it all and we stay just as we are. "I hope you're right," I tell him.

"I know I am," he says and his confidence is alluring.

This is happening. It's really happening.

Mateo comes by and puts his arms around us. "You guys gotta come to my house for the afterparty. It's going to be epic," he says with a hefty amount of alcohol on his breath.

"Maybe," Christopher says to him and looks down at me. "What do you think?"

As much as I'd like to just spend time with Christopher alone, I don't feel right about bailing on Tia, especially leaving her with my jackass cousin.

"Sure," I tell them.

"Right on. See you guys there," he says and infiltrates a group of girls dancing together.

"Are you sure you want to do that?" Christopher asks.

I shrug. "Why not?"

"I personally don't think this is the best idea, after all the trouble we got in this season," he says and shakes his head.

"Yeah, no doubt. But I don't think we should leave Tia, do you?"

He glances over his shoulder and spots Trey and Tia dancing finally. Trey's sloppy and grabby, but Tia seems to be having a great time.

"They seem okay. I'd rather spend some time together that's quiet," he says.

I smile up at him. "That does sound nice, but why don't we go the party and find a quiet corner for just the two of us."

Christopher holds onto my hands and sways a little bit, not in rhythm with the song. "That sounds perfect."

Winter in Minnesota is not to be joked about. Frostbite is very
real. Hypothermia is very real. And the snow? Well, it's just
always there. Always. But somehow, on this night, all I need is
Christopher's jacket to keep me warm. And his hands. As he
drives us over to Mateo's house he takes hold of my hand in
his, interweaving our fingers and not letting go, even when he
has to shift.

For all the rides he's given me over the past two years,
this one is my favorite. Unfortunately, it doesn't last very
long.

"There's Tia's car," I point out as we approach Mateo's
house. He lives off the two-lane highway on the outskirts of
our town on a big piece of land where's there's at least plenty
of parking.

"Guess he invited a lot of people to the after party,"
Christopher says and shakes his head. "For the love of God, I
hope it doesn't get busted. I mean, the cops will see this,
right?"

"I think they're giving us a little grace tonight. Better here
than out in the woods freezing to death."

"No, thank you," he replies.

Christopher parks his truck next to Tia's car and we hold
hands all the way to Mateo's house. The place is bursting with
people. I can't believe anyone's parents would be dumb
enough to go away the same weekend as a high school dance.
That's just asking for it.

We make the rounds inside, never letting go of each other,
and while small talk has never really been Christopher's forte,

he seems especially impatient with it tonight even when we're talking to Tia.

"Where did Trey run off to?" I ask.

"He's around here somewhere, probably getting even more wasted," she says and shrugs it off, like it's not a big deal.

Christopher's forehead wrinkles. Without a word, he backs away to go check on Trey and I'm glad he does because it gives me a chance to talk to Tia alone.

"So how's it going? You guys were so cute on the dance floor," she starts.

"It's like a dream come true, Tia. He told me something that's so crazy, I can't believe it."

"What's that?"

"He's going to go to UMN instead of BU. We'll be at the same college!" I tell her and squeeze her arm.

Tia shakes her head as the news registers. "What about Trey? Do you think he'll go to UMN too?" There's a lot of excitement in her question.

"I hope so," I say, and we both squee a little and hug each other like we just won the lottery.

Christopher returns and still looks a little worried.

"Did you find Trey?" I ask.

He runs a hand through his hair. "Yeah, he's down in the basement, attempting to play beer pong."

"Oh!" Tia shouts. "I'm like a beer pong pro. I'll show him what I've got," Tia says and wiggles her eyebrows.

"Good luck," I say with a laugh as she takes off.

"Do you want something to drink?" I ask Christopher and motion over to the hodgepodge of liquor bottles on the kitchen counter. They clearly raided the liquor cabinet. Mateo is going to get in so much trouble.

"No, I'm good. I'm not drinking for the remainder of the season," Christopher answers. Honestly, I didn't know I could appreciate him more, but this boy always surprises me.

I lean into Christopher and smile. "I'm so happy you're my date."

"Oh yeah? I'd love for you to tell me more about that, maybe somewhere a little more quiet," he says, and leads us past all our classmates to an enclosed porch off the back of the house.

"No way, we'll freeze," I tell him.

"I would never let you freeze," he replies. "You've got to know that by now."

Of course I know it, but still.

"Plus, there's this," he says and turns on a space heater. "Mateo and I worked on a group project out here in December," he explains as he turns on a small lantern on one of the end tables.

There's a white wicker couch with a couple of blankets hanging off the arms, some lawn games in the corner, two snow shovels, and a big bag of salt. It's cozy and away from the party and I couldn't be happier.

He takes hold of my other hand and brings both up to his chest. "Earlier tonight, when I first saw you, I didn't really have the ability to tell you how beautiful you look," he says, his eyes sparkling.

I giggle at that. "The ability?"

"You ruined my ability to speak, Gunderson. Well done," he says and his cheeks flush pink.

"I figured you didn't even recognize me."

"Oh, I recognized you," he says and laughs. "I'm not sure what that actually means."

"I think I get it. You clean up pretty well too, Chris," I say and eye him up and down very dramatically.

"You're just so cute, you know that?"

"If you say so," I reply and shake my head.

"I do. Summer..." he starts, but trails off as he gazes down at my mouth.

I swallow hard and find myself looking at his lips. His very kissable lips.

"I've waited a long time to..." he says, trailing off again.

And I nod in agreement because it has been a long time. I think of how he's been a part of my life ever since that first scary day at my new school in my new town after Daddy died.

He sweeps a few strands of my hair behind my ear and tentatively drops his forehead to mine. Despite the space heater, our noses are cold as they bump against each other. He cups my cheeks so gently and with so much warmth as he tilts my face up to his.

"You're my everything," he whispers.

My eyes close and I feel the flutter of his eyelashes just beneath my brow as his lips tentatively graze mine and I'm ready to tip right over. He presses his lips to mine and I get the contact I've been craving as we finally take the plunge. It's just like letting go of the rope swing over Webster Lake. It's exhilarating and new and unforgettable. I don't know what I'm doing and I'm honestly not sure he has much more experience than me, but it feels like we're doing it right. This kiss is why people kiss. We pull back for a brief second and look into each other's eyes, and his are a mirror to all the need I'm feeling. We launch at each other again, this time with more pressure, and in mere seconds our lips are parting as we wrap our arms around each other and dive in, giving in to all that we want and all that is ours for the taking.

There's nothing else but him and us and the heat between us, letting me forget all about the Minnesota winter.

Christopher

There's fifty-five seconds left in the third period and we're tied with Chicago. They're fucking tenacious as ever, and through all of the thrashing something has dawned on me—we've clearly got a target on our back. Teams are going to try their hardest to knock us down a peg. Well, you know what I have to say to them? Bring. It. On.

I want to end this game with two points and leave Chicago with nothing, so fuck overtime.

Icing is called on Hux, so the clock stops and we meet in our defensive zone to face-off. I skate up to the spot, lower my stick and look Benda directly in the eye. His face-off percentage rivals mine, around 59%. Fortunately for me, he makes a movement with his stick and gets booted. Ozo replaces him and I smile. His face-off stats are dismal. I've totally got this. There's only five seconds between setup and puck drop, but somehow it only takes one for Summer to catch my eye as she films from between the benches. The ref drops the puck and I'm caught off guard. Ozo gets controls the puck and moves it over to Novak, their defenseman. He passes it across to Lison. And then the pieces fall into place and I'm just a witness to it. Ozo near the crease. Lison at the point. A shot aimed right toward Hawk that Ozo redirects to score a goal on a face-off that he won because I got distracted. The crowd erupts like they've just won the Cup and I bash my stick against the boards.

While they do their celly, Hux skates over and taps me with his stick. "Put it behind you, Mac. Look forward. We got time."

There's only thirty-six seconds left on the clock and Coach Bliss leaves our line on the ice, which says a lot. He knows we're fucking riled up now. This time Schneider meets me at center ice to face-off. "Ready to lose another one?" he taunts me in his German accent.

"Fuck off," I reply with my head down and my gaze on the spot.

This time I won't lose the puck, no matter what. Even if Summer takes off her top and starts bouncing up and down, I'm not looking up.

The ref drops the puck and I go after it like it's my job. I get it over to Wags, my right-hand man and Hawk flees the ice and Foxy jumps in to give us a man advantage. We take control and play the hockey we're good at with tape-to-tape passes and unrivaled skating. They pick Foxy's pocket though and get a chance to clear the puck. Some guys might think that's it, but not me. Not us. Hux chases it down, beating out Schneider before it crosses the blue line and passes it back to Foxy. Foxy makes a move, but drops the pass back for me to shoot. And then it's just years of ingrained hockey experience driving this. My stick is my bow and I hit the target perfectly.

My team jumps to their feet and taps their sticks on the

boards. I swing by for the celly and Summer is there filming the whole thing. I wink at her and then take a seat for a much-needed rest.

It's a tied game with twelve seconds on the clock. The second line takes care of it and we head to overtime for three-on-three hockey. I'm back on the ice and do my best to earn the Storm two points with two shots on goal, but they both hit the post. The extra time ends and we go to a shootout. As captain, I always go first. I circle around the puck at center ice and take a look at Danvers in net. I recall a shootout two years ago when I went five hole. Is his memory as good as mine? Let's just try it out and see. I take off with a skip and push the puck down the ice, right down the middle. As I get closer I tap side-to-side to add a little bit of mystery. Danvers shimmies unsure and I shoot. He's not fast enough to block it once he realizes I'm going right between his legs.

I swing back around toward the bench and try my best not go overboard with the celebration, because this thing isn't over and no one likes that guy. Chicago doesn't score when Hawk makes an unbelievable save that defies basic human anatomy. Unfortunately Wags gets blocked on the glove side, but we still have the advantage when Hawk once again makes a save that Maddy and the social media team are going to GIF the hell out of. Smitty comes to bat which makes me roll my eyes. I think Foxy would be a better choice, but I trust Coach Bliss. He's got to have his reasons. Smitty takes off but fizzles out and Danvers snatches the puck away easily. It all comes down to Ozo, who I'm sure is still riding high from his last goal. Ozo barrels down the ice, making lots of moves, but they don't call Hawk a phenom for nothing. He stretches out his left leg to make another incredible block. It's only the second game of the season, but we all raise our hands into the air and join Hawk on the ice for some earnest helmet butting.

As I make my way over to the bench to fist bump all the guys as they enter the tunnel, I let out a huge sigh of relief. My Summer slip-up almost cost us the game and my hope is that no one noticed—especially Summer—because if I was determined to score on the ice, you can't even imagine my determination to score off of it.

And so my pursuit begins.

Post-game interviews. Check.

Very required shower. Check.

Pack my bag and make sure I have Trey's puck. Check.

Sneak away from my teammates. Check.

Find Summer and pick up where we left off this morning in my hotel room. The goal.

I don't have to look too hard. Summer is waiting outside the locker room with all her equipment packed up. For all the times she's waited outside the locker room, this might be the most beautiful she's ever looked, with rosy cheeks and sparkling green eyes focused right on me. Her hair, which had been up in a ponytail during the game, is now free flowing.

"There you are," I say.

She perks up. "Were you looking for me?"

"Always," I reply and wrap my arms around her waist. Her mouth forms a cute O at the surprise. "So. Where were we?"

Before she can answer, I drop my forehead to hers. "Right here," I say, answering my own question.

She doesn't reply, but smiles and pulls me by my blazer closer to her. And that's all I need from her. I find her mouth with my own and close my eyes. Her lips are warm and soft like any woman, but she feels uniquely like the woman I kissed so many years ago on Mateo's enclosed back porch. She feels like perfection.

We don't wait to open to one another. She tastes sweet like a cherry snow cone, and I smile into the kiss picturing her enjoying one before the concession stands closed. Honestly, I savor her more for it. My hands glide up her back into her hair and our kissing escalates into something raw, hard, and severely overdue. Speaking of hard, I can't remember being this hard in ages.

I think of how many times I've wanted to do this. Every time she waited for me after a game. Every time she twirled around the Biscuit as my waitress. In Webster Lake, when I held her in my arms. At the dock, under the stars, after the premiere of her video. At her locker. At the airport when I brought the Cup to Minnesota. At my loft. In my truck. In the elevator last night. In my hotel room. Every fucking place and every fucking time that I've been with her since she's come back into my life.

Summer pulls me with her as she arches her back and I hook her leg around my hip.

I need her. Now.

Like right now.

But I know I can't.

We're seconds away from being caught and Hux's warning tugs at me. *Shit.* If anyone catches us like this, it could jeopardize her job. We've got to get home first and then the rest of the night is ours. It takes all of my willpower to pull away from her, but I somehow do it. Her eyes are still closed and her face is flushed. God, I love her.

She whines as she comes back up and straightens herself up.

"Anymore, and I wouldn't be able to actually stop. Let's catch our flight and get home," I tell her.

She nods, licks her lips, and doesn't take her eyes off mine. This is going to be the most brutal wait so far, but hopefully worth it, because I will have Summer Gunderson in my bed tonight.

Summer

Christopher is driving very fast. Like a teenager that's got to deliver a pizza in thirty minutes or less or the pizza is coming out of his paycheck fast. Thankfully it's nearly 2:00 a.m. and the roads are empty on the way from the airport to downtown Denver.

"What's the rush, Chris?" I joke, even though I know full well what he's got on his mind. Honestly, when we finally got to his truck after what seemed like the longest flight of my life, I figured we'd fool around a bit. Lord knows I want more of that kiss we shared in Chicago. But we did no such thing. Nope, he's a man on a mission to get us home, and I find it utterly sexy how determined he is.

He huffs. "Trying to get you alone."

"We are alone," I tease.

"You know what I mean," he growls, not even looking over at me.

"Hmmm...tell me more. What's going to happen when

we're *alone*?" I toss on some air quotes on that last word for full effect. He's just too much.

"You'll just have to wait and find out," he answers, and the corner of his mouth turns up.

I literally cannot wait any longer. This stupid truck of his has a serious design flaw. There's a huge console in between our seats. If we were in his old pickup with the bench seat, I'd be able to scoot right over and whisper in his ear just how impatient I am to find out what's in store for me. Then I'd place a hand on his thigh.

Screw it. I unbuckle my seatbelt and bend over the console to do exactly that. "I don't want to wait anymore," I whisper into his ear and run my hand over his belly instead of his thigh.

He stiffens and clears his throat. "Summer," he warns and slows down the truck. "Put your seatbelt back on."

I don't listen and start to kiss his ear as I let my hand drop down to his crotch. The fabric of his trousers doesn't hide his reaction to my touch.

"Seriously, Summer," he warns again and intensifies his focus on the road. "We could get hurt or hurt someone else."

His words spark a dark memory but I extinguish it just as quickly as it started. I'm letting go of the past and focusing on the future. And it's a beautiful vision, one where we're together and happy and he's wedged right between my legs. I kiss his cheek and settle back into my seat. The seatbelt clicks and he smiles. Then he takes hold of my hand and brings it to his mouth and lays a long lingering kiss on it.

Why does the stupid airport have to be so far from downtown?

Finally, we get to our place and he pulls into the garage

spot like he's driving a Smart Car and not a huge pickup truck. He turns off the ignition and we both sit quietly and very still.

I want to see if he goes first.

He does.

Not even a full second later, I release my seatbelt and we collide. Mouths, tongues, pulling, and pushing. He's got my hair in his hand. I've got hold of his lapel. And there's this ridiculous console between us. *Goddammit.*

"Upstairs," he says in between mauling me with his mouth.

"Upstairs," I agree.

We get out of the truck and leave absolutely everything behind. I don't even think he locks the truck. He takes my hand and leads me to the elevator and starts tapping the up button incessantly.

"Fuck this," he says and leads us to the stairwell. He takes them two at a time and I can't keep up. Not even close. When we get to the first landing, I tug at him and he spins around and kisses me.

"I can't wait," he says as he lifts my legs around his waist and presses my back against the wall. He's not straining one bit to keep me up like that. We kiss like we did in the truck. Desperate, hungry, and no longer beating around the bush. *Thank God.*

I forget where we are for a brief moment and then open my eyes to the harsh fluorescent lights of the stairwell. I pull away from his mouth, panting. "Upstairs," I request.

His eyes are wild and his lips are swollen. He nods and lets me down. "Upstairs."

We basically sprint the remaining four floors and my heart

pounds so hard in my chest I'm worried that I'll die before I finally get to be with Christopher.

Upstairs finally comes, and he opens his door as if it wasn't even locked. Everything is a blur. Christopher takes off his suit coat and his shirt quickly follows. I pull off my top and kick off my shoes. He pauses for a moment and just stares at me in my bra.

"Jesus," he blurts out, and I laugh.

He strides over to me and wraps one arm around my waist to pull me back up so that my legs go around his waist again. His other hand dives into my hair and he kisses me, slower and deeper this time, as he walks us toward his bedroom. I've never been with someone with so much prowess and I know it shouldn't matter, but dear lord, it makes me crazy for him.

I lose track of where we are until he stops kissing me and drops me onto his bed. "Ouf," I grunt as I sit up on my elbows and blow the hair away from my eyes so I can see him. He stands at the edge of his bed wearing only a pair of perfectly tailored trousers that showcase his mighty erection.

Holy fuck.

Christopher is a specimen that should be studied, sculpted, photographed, and documented.

He's gazing down at me as if he's thinking the same thing —but about me. Silly boy. Objectively, there's nothing truly extraordinary about my body. But he doesn't look at me like I'm ordinary. He looks at me like I'm the only woman he has ever seen. He makes me feel that way, too. Always has, if I'm being perfectly honest.

He goes for his belt and I'm brought back to the moment.

"Yes, take it all off," I command and then giggle at myself for being so demanding.

"I will if you will," he retorts with a smile as he kicks off his shoes and socks with much less eloquence than the belt came off. Our desperation is ramping up again. I start on my own pants, but before I can take them off on my own, he joins me on the bed, pulling them off me along with my socks, so that we're both now in our underwear.

I'd like to tell you that I had selected beautiful matching lingerie in case this moment happened, but when I packed for Chicago, I was in too much of a rush to think ahead like that. Instead, it's a basic white cotton bra and a pair of pink bikini briefs dotted with black hearts.

He runs his palm over my pelvis and drops his head to my chest. "Are you trying to murder me?"

"Murder wasn't what I had in mind," I reply. My cheeks are warm as I try to shimmy out from under him and cover up my very girlie panties.

He laughs into my belly and then sits up on his haunches and grabs my hands away. "Don't you dare. Fuck, Summer, you're the most beautiful woman I've ever met. How am I supposed to handle this?"

I sit up so that I'm mirroring him and point down. "Gimme a break, look at you! Don't you own a pair of tighty-whities or stupid boxer shorts with silly puns? Why does it always have to be these tight black boxer briefs that basically make me incapable of keeping my cool?"

He shakes his head and laughs. "Is this real?" he asks.

"I hope so," I tell him while I gather some courage. I reach behind my back and start to unhook my bra. His mouth noticeably parts and his hands ball into fists on his thighs as the bra slides slowly down my arms. I fling it across the room and let him take me in.

"This is real," he assures me, or maybe he says it to assure himself as he cups my breasts. "You have no idea how much I've daydreamed about these."

"Oh yeah?" My head falls to the side as my eyes flutter closed.

He squeezes and teases me, taking his time to get the full experience. "Countless times, but those daydreams don't compare to the real thing."

"I know what you mean," I reply quickly. Desperation doesn't even begin to describe my tone. His touch is making everything below my belly button heat up. But what I said is true. I know exactly what he means. We never got this far before. We never saw or touched each other like this. For the past several years, I've wondered what it would be like to kiss him again. I'd replay our first kiss, probably distorting it over the years. It was the best kiss of my life, and all the boys that I kissed after never compared to Christopher. Hell, I worried that Christopher wouldn't compare to the Christopher of my memory, but I was wrong. So very wrong.

"Fuck, you're sexy," he mutters and we're off to the races again. Our underwear comes off real fast as we tangle with one another on the bed. His hands, which are so large, seem to multiply and I lose track of them as his mouth makes its way down my neck to my chest.

He dips down and latches onto my left nipple, nibbles it and sucks, pulling it with his teeth and letting it snap back. It drives me absolutely crazy. Heat pools between my legs and I can't control myself. I slide myself up and down him, moaning every time the ridge on the underside of his tip rubs against the perfect spot. From the deep throaty sounds he's making, I suspect he likes it too.

The simple friction pushes me to the edge surprisingly fast, but if I think about it, I've been primed and ready to go for years. My legs are trembling and I'm gnawing on the inside of my cheek. I lost sight of him long ago to the orbs of light floating across my vision. All I am is sensation, my body no longer in my conscious control. There's only the feel of what he does to me, and there's no one I'd rather hand the keys over to than him.

My nipple stings as it makes contact with the open air. He drags his teeth down, down, down. His lips brush along his path, his tongue traces lines I didn't even know I had while everything between my thighs blossoms.

I reach for his hair, twisting and pulling as my back bends off the bed. He takes hold of my hands and places them on my breasts, prompting me to squeeze them as he pushes my knees farther apart with his elbows. Using both thumbs, he spreads me apart and licks with a broad stroke from the bottom. My gaze goes blurry and then he does it again.

"Does that feel good?" he asks and waits for my reply.

"Yes," I reply and lift toward his face, wanting more.

"You taste like...," he says but doesn't complete the sentence. Instead, he uses a precision I don't even have with his tongue—no less—while he carefully inserts one and then two fingers into me and goes right for the goal.

My orgasm comes quickly and dramatically. As strong as he is, he can't prevent me from closing my thighs around his head and riding it out. Then again, maybe he likes to see me like this, wild and thrashing. And he confirms it when he takes hold of my thighs and carries on, because his pursuit isn't even close to over.

"Still good?" he speaks into my flesh.

"Mmmhmm." It's all I can muster, but I pray it's clear enough so he doesn't stop. Of course he doesn't. The guy is relentless. My second orgasm follows but this time he holds my legs open with his forearms. He makes me absorb all the pleasure, which is something I've never ever done before. Usually I roll over to my side and curl into a doughy little ball. This feels unreal and I make that pretty well known with the way I'm quaking.

He goes back to it and I start blurting out all the grittiest cuss words that come to mind, because he's still not letting me come down yet. There's no ground in sight. And my brain finally boots up with only a rudimentary type of transitive property logic.

Christopher = athlete = endurance. If A=B and B=C, then A=C and he will never *ever* stop.

I can't go again. I need him inside me.

"Just fuck me already," I shout, which comes out just as crass as it sounds. Fuck flowery words. Fuck romance. I just want him. Now.

"Okay, Summer." His voice is tight and the veins in his neck and his hands and his forehead are all popping out.

He stops touching me for the first time since I took my bra off and retrieves a condom from his nightstand. His hands are trembling as he rips the foil and then rolls it on.

It dawns on me that this is actually the first time I'm seeing him. All of him. It's everything I pictured it to be.

Perfectly proportional.

Fierce.

Beautiful.

And that's when the romance comes crashing back. Stupid and perverted, I know, but when I see him like this it dawns on me that he's the only man I ever want to be with...for the rest of my life. And that knowledge does something crazy to my heart and my belly and my head.

But then he turns his eyes back on me again and my lovestruck moment washes away in a flood of lust. He looks hungry, like a vampire that needs to consume me to satisfy his singular appetite. Nothing else will do it. Not even hockey, I'm guessing.

And I want to be consumed by him. Completely.

I don't think there's anything that could tear him away. Not even our past. The only thing that could stop him is me, and that's the last thing I would ever do.

"You ready for this?" he asks as he pulls me by the calves over to the edge of the bed. His eyes are dark and his lips are parted.

"Yes, Chris," I reply and show him where I want him.

He stares down at me for a second or two. "Summer..." he hesitates, like he doesn't trust himself.

"Don't think, just do it," I beg and wrap my legs around his waist, locking my ankles against his rock-hard backside.

Christopher nods, roots his feet into the floor, and pushes himself into me. The pressure is intense, no doubt, but the pleasure follows quickly after that, thanks to how ready he's made me. My head flicks from side to side as I moan my approval.

His abs contract while beads of sweat roll down his torso into the dark patch of hair just above where we meet. He closes his eyes and let's out a strained breath through gritted teeth. "Summer," he says my name again, but this time like I've never heard it. It's raw and intense, and it could be mistaken as angry to someone who doesn't understand our situation. Who doesn't understand that *this* is years in the making. He draws back and fills me again with urgency.

My eyelashes involuntarily flutter and my toes actually curl. Dear sweet lord. A vigorous rhythm begins and he delivers on every expectation I've had for this moment.

I'm not sure how long we stay in that position because time is nebulous. So is reality and history and common sense. But after a while, he bends over and scoots me up further on the bed. Then he crawls on top of me, never once disconnecting from me, and the intimacy of this situation intensifies, which I honestly didn't think was possible. His mouth is on mine, then my jaw, my neck, my shoulder. Our nipples brush against each other and we're slick with sweat. His sheer amount of body strength is scary, but my heart knows better. I can give myself over to him freely because there's no one I trust more.

I pull at his hair and he drives into me harder and faster. He's trying to talk to me, but his words aren't making much sense. Something about how he never imagined it could be like this. Well, I'm right there with him because I think I'm on the verge of yet another orgasm. I try to hold him tighter to me as my fingers grasp for his flesh but there's mostly just muscle. I dig in with my fingernails and meet each of his thrusts. He looks down between our bodies at where we're joined and then back up to my face.

That's all it takes for me. I implode, tensing and tightening, and using all of my strength to hold his body to mine as I ride through it.

And that's all it takes for Christopher. He explodes, and the sound of utter satisfaction he makes is almost too much for me to handle. I wish I could record it. At the very least, I wish I could replay it just one more time.

He drops his forehead to mine as we attempt to recover. We breathe in sync and stay like that for quite a while and then he smiles at me. It's the kind of smile that dares to knock my heart right out of my chest. "I can't believe we just did that."

"I can." I thread my fingers into his hair. "It's been a long time coming."

"Fair point." He kisses me. It's a light graze of trembling lips at first, but he doesn't leave it at that. He kisses me again, slower and deeper, like he's savoring it. Like he won't be able to ever do this again.

He's wrong. So wrong.

Because I never want to stop kissing him, whether it's today, or tomorrow, or the day after that, or ever.

He gently breaks away from the kiss and gazes down at me. We look at one another for a long moment and that's when the reality really, really hits me.

I'm in love with him.

Christopher

Did that just happen? *Again?*

Summer collapses onto my chest as she lets out a huge breath. Her hair covers my face, the silky strands that are soft like her and smell like heaven. You couldn't pay me to brush it away. She's panting, just as much as I am, but I get the pleasure of feeling her warm breath against my neck. We're all loose limbs and expanding rib cages, beating hearts and emotions we don't speak out loud but somehow convey to one another.

This goes on for quite awhile until she lifts her head and looks down at me. "Hi."

I smile up at her. At Summer. My Summer. I'm still in disbelief that any of this happened. When you spend your entire adolescence and subsequent adulthood imagining what it would be like to simply touch her, it's a lot to fucking take in. I'm actually a little afraid that being intimate with her, twice no less, has broken my brain. I'm not sure I'll ever properly process it. But you know what? Processing is overrated. I already want to be inside her again. Actually I am still inside her. *Fuckkkk.* At this revelation, my mouth goes to hers like it has a mind of its own. We kiss and I push into her a little deeper. She moans against my lips.

"Hi," I finally reply.

She smiles into our kiss. "You're insatiable."

"For you." I nibble on her lips as I take hold of her ass and move inside her again.

She attempts to giggle, but I've just made her mouth drop open too. It's quite a sight. I think I could go for round three.

After all, my body has been waiting for her for years. It's ready for some serious ice time. No bench warming for me.

"I'm hungry," she murmurs against my cheek.

"Hungry?" I'm somewhat familiar with the concept.

"You know...for food," she clarifies.

Food is the furthest thing from my mind, but Summer's going to get what Summer wants. There's no way I would try to change her mind, even though I'd really like to.

I knead her butt and lay some kisses on her jaw. "Got it."

She must like what I'm doing because her eyes close. "Tell me you have more than just eggs and veggie bowls here."

"I've got protein shakes. Even chocolate-flavored ones," I say, hoping it sounds good to her. I definitely don't want to go out at this time of night.

She laughs, but I'm guessing it's at me. "Big Mac, your kitchen is the saddest place on earth."

"That's okay, because presently my bedroom is the happiest place on earth." It's a cheesy line, but I can't help myself.

A blush spreads across her cheeks and I want to kiss it, so I do. I can't believe I can. She maneuvers off of me and the happiest place on earth just got a little sadder. "Come on, let's go next door. I've got lots of snacks."

I glance over at the clock. "It's nearly three in the morning. I don't think we should wake Lily." The truth is, I don't want to leave this room, let alone my place. Reality lives outside these walls and I'm not ready to face it. Reality, like how I have practice at ten, how we need to go get our stuff out of the truck, how she could easily just stay at her place, or how we should probably have a conversation about what just happened. That last bit of reality really makes me want to stay in this bedroom and make love to her again because I'm afraid she'll reveal that she doesn't feel the same way I do. Man, that would suck because I'm full on, helmet-over-skates, in love with this girl and tonight means everything to me. What if it doesn't mean as much to her?

Damn. I should have stocked up on real-people food as soon as Summer moved to Denver.

"She won't mind. In fact, she probably won't even wake up. She knows I was coming in late. Come on," she says and swats my thigh as she gets out of bed.

"Cereal?" she asks me in a whisper, a rather loud whisper. "Or would you like one of my favorite late-night snacks?"

I pull at the hem of the t-shirt she's wearing, one of my old BU ones. It's got a hole in the armpit and the logo has faded over time, but she looks fucking amazing in it. "Do tell, Gunderson. What's one of your favorite late-night snacks?"

She pulls open the freezer drawer, bends over and grabs for something, all the while her beautiful ass wiggles in front of me. *Lord in heaven.* I want to caress it. Spank it. Bite it. Kiss it. I stick to a caress for now, which is a very good thing because just as I swipe my palms over her rear, a light switches on behind us. We freeze in place and look over.

Lily's there, with Luthor at her feet, staring at us with a slight smile on her face. "Well, it's about damn time," she says.

Summer stands back up with a box of frozen waffles in her hand and I finally...finally...remove my hands from Summer's ass. "Sorry, I did get home earlier, but I've just been hanging with Christopher at his place."

"That's not what I meant," she says and joins us in the kitchen. She goes right for the jar of dog treats on the counter and waits for Luthor to sit before she lets him pluck it from her hand.

"What do you mean?" Summer asks. Lily clearly put two and two together. I mean, she literally caught me red-handed.

"This," she says and nods between the two of us. "I was wondering when you two would finally hook up. It's been painfully obvious since you moved in."

Summer laughs nervously.

Lily turns to me. "Plus you should hear how much she talks—"

"Okay," Summer pipes up and grabs Lily by the shoulders. "That's enough from you, sunshine."

"Sunshine?" I ask and laugh a little, hoping if I lighten things up Lily will finish that sentence.

"It's her nickname for me, because of my very cheery mood in the mornings," Lily says and rolls her eyes. I've been around Lily in the morning, and she is anything but cheerful. "You should hear the nickname she has for you."

"All right, back to your bed," Summer says and actually slides Lily across the wood floor in her slippers.

Lily giggles as she lets herself be pushed back toward the bedrooms. "It's really something. Make her tell it to you."

"Oh I will. Good night, Lily."

"Good night," she sings.

Summer rushes back into the kitchen and sweeps her hair behind her ears. She can't look me in the eye and it's adorable.

"Okay, where were we?" She picks up the box of waffles. "Right, toasted waffles with peanut butter and jelly."

Ignoring that quite ridiculous late-night snack idea, I spin her around in my arms and lift her onto the kitchen island. She bites down on her lip to suppress a smile and still won't look at my face. "Come on, Gunderson. Out with it."

"Never," she replies, bashful as can be.

I point in the direction of my place. "I think after doing all that, there's nothing left to hide."

She flops her arms over my shoulders and lets her legs fall open. I take the opportunity to step right between them. "Honestly, Big Mac, don't you have enough nicknames? What's another one?"

I growl in response and she does what I expect her to. She throws her head back and laughs at me. This woman makes me frustrated and happy and smitten and love drunk. "What's it going to take, Gunderson?"

Summer thinks on it for a few seconds and looks around the kitchen. "Peanut butter and jelly waffles."

"That's it? I was hoping for something much more exciting."

"Like what?"

"Like," I say and lean in close to her ear, "using my tongue to make you come on this kitchen island."

A shiver runs through her and she nuzzles into my neck. "That does sound tempting." But before she can go with Option B, her tummy grumbles. Loudly.

"Wow," I say through a chuckle.

She tries to shy away, seemingly embarrassed, but I think it just makes her even more adorable.

"Option A it is," I tell her and kiss her on the forehead. "Stay put."

She does. "I'll coach you through it."

"Coach Gunderson? It has a nice ring to it," I tell her as I pop two waffles into the toaster.

"Whistle!" she whisper-shouts.

My hands fly up in the air. "What'd I do, Coach?"

"Those two waffles better be for me, otherwise we're going to need more."

"Got it." I spin around my heel and correct my mistake, adding two more waffles to the toaster.

"Whistle!"

"What now?"

"The toaster is set way too low. We want a good crunch. Set it to five."

My mouth drops open. "Five? They'll be pucks."

"Don't make me tell you twice. Otherwise you'll have to drop and give me twenty."

"Yes, ma'am." I'm not in the mood for push-ups, unless she's under me of course, so I set the toaster to five. "Where do you keep the peanut butter?"

"In the pantry," she answers and leans back on the heels of her hands. She's a damn pretty sight.

With a little smile on my face, I scour the pantry and find an organic almond butter and a standard peanut butter that moms across the midwest use. I grab the almond butter.

"Whistle!"

"Oh, come on!"

"MacCormack. You should know better. We don't use

almond butter for *peanut* butter and jelly waffles." She points to the floor, right beneath her. "Drop and give me twenty."

I roll my eyes.

"Make that thirty, MacCormack."

"Yes, ma'am."

If she wants to see me do push-ups, she's going to *see me* do push-ups. I reach behind my head, pull off my t-shirt, and toss it on the counter.

"Oh, I wish I would have thought of that," she says under her breath.

Down I go to the tile kitchen floor and then I begin to pump out perfect push-ups. She wants thirty? I could give her one hundred.

I glance up at her as I go, enjoying the sight of her leaning forward and watching me with pursed lips and big round eyes.

When I hit thirty, I spring to my feet and it coincides with the waffles popping out of the toaster. Couldn't time it any better if we tried.

"Aren't you even the slightest bit out of breath?" I detect more annoyance than awe in her question. I was really hoping for awe.

"Of course," I lie. It's going to take a lot more than that to wear me out.

My shirt stays on the counter as I smear the peanut butter over the crispy waffles. It melts a little bit like butter and I can't deny that it looks pretty fucking delicious as it does. The strawberry jelly is just the icing on top. I hand over her plate and she flips one waffle onto the other before taking a huge bite out of the sandwich she's made. The sound of pleasure coming out of her is an echo of earlier tonight. I might be a little bit jealous of this waffle. I think I have some competition.

Begrudgingly, I flip mine over and take a bite.

Damn it.

It's delicious. Before I know it, I'm halfway through it.

"How did you come up with peanut butter and jelly waffles?"

"I most certainly can't take credit for it. Have you honestly not heard of this before?"

"Nope," I answer and suddenly feel like the weird one.

"Tia and I ate these all the time in college," she tries to get out through a mouth full of peanut butter.

"Did you and Tia live together the whole time you were in college?" I ask.

"Pretty much, except when she went off to Semester at Sea."

"I know someone that did that, too. It always seemed cool, but I didn't have any room for it with hockey."

"Don't you ever get sick of it?"

"Sick of what?"

"Hockey. It's got to get old at some point, right?"

"Never," I tell her. "Every time I step onto the ice with my stick in hand and a goalie to stare down, a thrill rushes through me. I love the speed. The competition. The very game itself."

"Then you're really lucky," she says and takes another bite.

"Why's that?"

"Because you get to do what you absolutely love."

I nod and think about that. And then I think about her. If I could have hockey and be with Summer, my life would be unbelievably perfect. Would it be the same for her? "Aren't you doing something that you absolutely love?"

She smiles so brightly. "I am."

"Then we're both lucky."

"I guess we are."

"So, out with it Gunderson."

"Do I have to?" she whines.

"A deal is a deal."

"Fine. But don't let it go to your head."

"I'm the most humble guy I know."

She rolls her eyes playfully. "Sure thing, *Big Mac*."

"I'm guessing that's not what the nickname is. Come on, tell me."

"Fine," she says, playfully sullen.

I can't wait to hear it and if she's this reluctant, I think I'm really going to like it.

"Sex on Skates," she mumbles, not meeting my eyes.

I burst out laughing. It's a good one, from deep in my belly.

"Shhh, you're going to wake up Lily again."

"You called me that? To Lily?"

"Just one time, but lord knows she doesn't forget anything. I think she's a genius."

"*Sex on Skates?*"

"Yes, you dope. And so what if I did? I'm not ashamed."

"Nor should you be. How did it come up?"

She sets her plate on the counter and brushes her hands together. "Well, it was the night of Hawk's charity event. I was getting ready to go and I was telling her all about it. She asked if I was interested in Hawk and I told her I'm not. And then you came up."

I wait for her to go on, but she acts as if that's the end of the story. "Don't leave me hanging. What did you say about me?"

"I never knew you to be so self-interested."

"When it comes to you, Gunderson, I operate in the extremes."

"No kidding," she's says with a wry smile. "Well, she asked if I was into you and I may have gone on a little diatribe about how I am and I may have said something like, 'Christopher is like Sex on Skates.'"

"So you don't have a thing for Hawk?" I ask. I can't help it. She opened the record again and I just want her to put it down in permanent marker.

"Come on, Chris. All of this should have been completely obvious to you, but you still acted like a caveman at the bowling alley."

I shrug my shoulders. "Sorry. I mean, mostly sorry."

She laughs as her legs dangle off the counter. "That was the least genuine sorry ever. So, there. Are you happy now? I swear I'm going leave dirty dishes in the sink or something to get back at Lily for opening her mouth."

"I'm glad she did," I tell her and take a step closer. I spy a little bit of jelly on her bottom lip. It takes me back to all those times I was tortured watching her eat those powdered sugar jelly-filled donuts. Twenty-four hours ago, I would have stood back and done nothing but let my imagination run wild. But that was twenty-four hours ago. This is now. She thinks I'm *Sex on Skates*. I set my plate down next to hers and step even closer. She pauses and the heat of her dreamy green gaze melts me like creamy peanut butter on a hot waffle.

"You have a little..." I swipe my thumb across her bottom

lip and she opens her mouth, ever so inviting. She wraps her lips around my thumb and sucks on the tip. My vision goes blurry and blood pounds in my ears. She lets it go with a pop and it's like a starting pistol. My mouth goes to her mouth. Her legs lock around my waist. And I somehow have the ability to navigate us toward her bedroom and shut the door behind us.

As we both fall to her bed and our clothes come off again, I think to myself, we really are lucky because we can and will have it all.

9

Summer

It's too bright in my bedroom. Too bright for an early morning in October. Too bright for a workday. My instinct tells me that the world is out there passing us by. Christopher is dead asleep, snoring quietly. He's got an arm and leg draped over my body as he presses his face into my pillow. I nudge him carefully, because I have no idea if he startles easily in his sleep and I don't need a hockey player thrashing me.

"Chris," I whisper.

Nothing.

"Chris," I say a little bit louder.

The eye that's not pressed into my pillow opens and he looks at me for only a second before a big smile spreads across his scruffy face and he squeezes me.

Being close to him is everything I imagined it to be. It's a connection that's unparalleled to anything I've felt before. I don't want it to stop. I really don't. But I think it's time to face reality. "I think we overslept."

He lazily looks across my body to the clock on the night-stand. Whatever he sees makes him freeze in place, as if he's trying to hide from a freaking velociraptor. My heart starts thumping hard in my chest.

"Shit," he finally says and pops out of bed like it's a trampo-line. "It's ten."

"What?" I shout and get out of bed too, not nearly as athletically.

Even though he's naked as the day he was born, the boy darts out of my room and out of the loft. Lord help Lily if she saw it.

I desperately need a shower, but there's no time. I should have been to the office an hour ago. I'm pretty sure the same goes for Christopher. This isn't an optional morning skate on the road. This is full on practice. I think he could be fined by the team. As for me, I could get much worse. I do my very best to get dressed and cleaned up as quickly and with as much quality as possible.

A girl's best friend isn't diamonds. It's dry shampoo, wet wipes, and extra strength deodorant.

As I'm about to dart from the loft, I go to grab my equip-ment bags and remember where exactly they are.

"Oh no," I shout.

They're in Christopher's truck.

I fly down the stairs, hoping to catch him before he leaves, because if he's smart he wouldn't wait for me.

When I get to the garage, I breathe a sigh of relief that his truck is still there. And then I see him, standing there with the passenger door open.

"Chris!" I shout, but he doesn't turn around. He's got that same hiding-from-a-velociraptor stillness.

When I get to him, I'm out of breath. "You didn't have to wait for me."

He turns toward me. His forehead crinkles and his eyes darken. "I didn't."

Dread drops like a bag of pucks in my belly. "Why are you still here?"

"Because someone got into the truck and all our stuff is gone."

Nope. No. No way. I don't believe it. My head shakes and shakes and shakes some more. The only saving grace is that I sync all my footage and work to the cloud.

"For real, Summer," he says and runs his hands through his hair as he lets out a big breath.

"My stuff too? My camera and laptop?"

"Everything. It's all gone. It's all fucking gone," he says and slams the door shut.

"Oh my God." It's such a basic, silly thing to say in the moment, but that's all I've got. I should mention that I'll be fired for sure. I should ask him what he's lost. But I'm dumbfounded. I push him aside and open the door myself to look in the backseat of his cab. All that's left behind is an ice scraper. That's it. "Isn't there security or something?"

He blinks a few times and nods. "Yeah, there should be. We have to call them." He starts to pace around the garage, looking for a sign, and stops when he sees something. "Look, there are cameras."

For the first time since he told me our stuff was stolen, I don't feel like I want to crawl into a ball and disappear. There's hope—there's something. I nod, still not really able to articulate my thoughts and feelings.

"First, we need to call in. We need to tell them what happened and why we're not there," he says.

"No!" I shout and grab onto his shirt. "We can't tell them that I lost the equipment. I'll be fired for sure."

"No you won't. This is not your fault."

"Yes, it is all my fault. I'm supposed to take care of that equipment. It's part of my job."

"It's not like you threw it out the window or sold it on eBay. Someone stole it."

"But you didn't lock the doors!"

He pauses and then puts a hand on his hip. "What? Of course I did."

"No. I don't think you did. I think we were too distracted..."

He just stares at me. He's going to make me say it.

So I give it to him with as much flourish as it deserves. "...mauling one another."

"Mauling?" he says with a bit of a laugh.

"Now, is very much not the time, Christopher," I say sternly.

He shakes it off and says, "No fucking kidding."

"I mean, isn't it obvious? There's no sign of forced entry. We'll have to tell the authorities that we didn't lock the doors."

He steps closer to me and puts his hands on my shoulders. "Let's be very clear. I didn't lock the doors. This is not on you."

"But it's going to be. Why were you driving me home? Why did I leave my stuff in your truck?"

"Simple. We live in the same building and we were headed to the same place in the morning. We carpool. We're environmentally friendly."

My eyes plead with his. "And why were we so late?"

He thinks on that for a moment. There are clearly too many holes in this. "Because, I..."

"Because what?" I need to know. There has to be a solution. We've come this far.

"Because I love you, Summer. And I'm not afraid to tell them that. I'm not afraid for anyone to know."

Tears start streaming down my face. It's not the first time he's told me that, but this time it means even more. It's just too bad that we're in this situation right now, because this is not the most ideal way to hear those three little words. My heart squeezes with joy nonetheless.

He goes on. "I want you in my life. And I think we should tell them. What damage could be done?"

"My professional reputation could be ruined," I tell him, which is not the response I want to give him. I should be telling him that I love him too, because I do very much.

"Love can overcome this, I know it," he says.

I shake my head. "Love can overcomplicate things, I know that too." And there it is again. Our past can't quite shut up. I'm trying my level best to put what happened to Trey behind us, but the last time I heard him tell me that he loves me was when we were young and ignorant, and thoughtless about what that love could mean for someone else and how complicated it made *everything*.

His eyes are glassy and he swallows hard, because he remembers just as I do. "Okay, we're off track. We just need to focus on handling the things that need to be done. And I swear to God, if that dickweed boss of yours gives you shit about this, I'm going to rain down on him so hard. This was not your fault."

The lump in my throat burns. I can't reply. All I can do is nod my head.

He wraps his arms around me and I rest my head against his chest. Tears slide down my cheeks.

"It's okay, Summer. It's going to be fine. We're together. That's all that matters."

It would be easy to believe that he's right. That our love is all that matters, but that's easy for him to say. Colorado Storm management isn't going to kick him off the team. But I've finally landed my dream job and I'd hate to lose it now, so I don't respond. He smiles down at me, kisses me on the forehead, and pulls me into another hug.

"What did you lose?" I ask him, afraid to hear his answer.

"Only one thing that can't be replaced," he whispers.

I look up at him again and there's sadness in his eyes. "What's that?"

"It's just this thing. Sort of like a good luck charm that I carry in my bag."

"How long have you had it?"

"Since high school," he tells me and his eyes get watery.

Another wave of loss washes over me. "I'm sorry, Chris. I'm sitting here crying about the team's camera equipment and you actually lost something meaningful."

He sniffs and shakes his head. "It doesn't matter. I'll be okay."

I don't believe it for a second. I know how hockey players

can be. Superstitions are a very big deal. A terrible feeling settles in my gut, but I want to be strong for him. I want to be his solace, too. I take a deep breath and hold him this time. "All right then. Let's pull off this nasty bandage and get it over with. I'll call the police."

"Okay, I've gotta text Coach."

The walk into the office feels a little bit like walking into my own execution. I have no idea how Jim is actually going to react when I tell him I lost the camera and laptop and peripherals. Maybe he won't actually care, since it's team property and this is a professional hockey team that probably isn't struggling to get by. Or maybe he'll blow up and fire me on the spot for being so terribly irresponsible. It's what I think I deserve, but I've always been pretty good at self-punishment.

"Hey kid," Jim says. He looks away from his monitor to the clock on the wall. "Your first road trip must have been a doozy." If he's mad about me being late, it's not coming through in his voice.

"Yeah, it was definitely a late night," I reply and take a seat at my desk.

"I remember this one time coming home from Winnipeg when we all got hit with the Norovirus while we were on the plane. We didn't know it was coming for us until we were thirty thousand feet in the air, with only four bathrooms. That double dragon was vicious."

"Oh dear," I reply. "That's terrible."

"The smell. Jesus, the smell."

"Yeah, I can imagine."

He still hasn't really looked at me, but continues clicking his mouse and scrutinizing the monitor. I wish I could set up my laptop, but I obviously can't do that so I just sit there and continue to listen to his story. "I had to go to the hospital when we got back to the city, along with a few other guys. I've never been so grateful to have someone jam a needle into my arm so I could get fluids. Still puked probably four times while I was there.""God, that sucks so bad. I'm sorry, Jim."

"Yeah, it most definitely sucked. But that's not the craziest part of my story. Can you guess what happened next?" he asks and clicks a little harder on that mouse.

"What's that?" I ask timidly because I'm pretty sure I've just set myself up here.

"I still made it to work on time the next day," he answers and looks away from his monitor to shoot fireballs with his eyes at me.

Whoa.

If he's this pissed I'm late, I can only imagine how pissed he'll be when I tell him what actually happened.

"Jim, I'm so sorry," I start.

"This isn't the kind of job where you get to come and go to as you please. You know, if a player is late to practice or a meeting he gets fined. Unfortunately, I don't have those options. But I can document it and tell you that this is strike one."

Tears well in my eyes. I'll be fired for sure when I'm done telling him what happened. I know that now without a doubt.

His face softens a little when he sees a tear slip down my cheek. "What?" he asks.

"My equipment. It was in Christopher MacCormack's truck because he gave me a ride home since we live in the same building. I foolishly left it there overnight because we were both headed back here today."

"Okay..."

"And well, I'll just come out with it. Someone broke into his truck and stole it. It's all gone. The camera, the laptop, all the peripherals. Everything."

His mouth drops open. "Shit," he whispers.

"I'm so sorry. I am so stupid for not taking it upstairs with me. You can dock my paycheck until it's paid for."

He blinks a few times and turns back to his monitor and starts typing.

Of all his reactions, the silent treatment wasn't what I was expecting. Not even a little bit. He continues to type and click and I stay frozen in my seat as tears slip down my cheeks.

"Well, that didn't take long," he murmurs.

"What didn't?"

"The equipment is already at a pawnshop," he answers and points to his monitor.

I pop out of my chair and go to see what he's pointing at. "What? How do you know?"

Sure enough, there's a map with little blue dots radiating at what appears to be at a location downtown.

"This ain't no two-bit operation, Summer. We've got trackers on all our stuff," he says, like I should know better. I never knew about the trackers. It makes me wonder why he never told me, but I'm so happy to see the blue dots I really don't care.

"I wonder if Christopher's stuff is also there."

"They got his stuff, too?"

"Yeah, and he was really upset. The police didn't give us much hope, especially since the cameras in the garage have apparently been offline for two weeks."

"So this is what you were dealing with this morning?" he says a little softer.

"Yeah, it took forever." It's not altogether untrue, but I don't confess to oversleeping. "When the police realized that it was Christopher's stuff that was taken, they went all out trying to figure things out. They even dusted for prints, which I'm sure will be fruitless but it pleased Christopher and he ended making a nice video for the officer's daughter."

"Glad to know the DPD are fans," he says sarcastically.

"Yeah," I agree. "So anyway, I'm sorry. I should have called you right away, but I thought that I would tell you in person about the lost equipment."

"I get it," he concedes.

"Do you mind if I call Christopher and let him know."

"Good luck, he's probably being reamed out by Bliss for missing practice. Then again, maybe Mister League MVP gets a pass. The organization loves him."

"He's easy to love," I say stupidly and Jim raises one of his thick salt and pepper eyebrows in my direction.

"You know, this reminds me of this story I once heard about DMB. They were on the road in ninety-nine and Carter lost his favorite pair of drumsticks..." Jim goes on and on but I stop listening pretty quickly and take out my phone to text Christopher.

Summer: *Hey, I have news. We have trackers on the equipment and Jim located it at a pawnshop. Call me when you can.*

I bite on my thumbnail and watch my phone, hoping for a quick reply, but I don't get one. I hope that doesn't mean bad things for him.

Jim is still telling his story and I tune back in for a bit. "And so then Stefan was like, weren't you using them when we jammed with Trey Anastasio in Austin?"

"Oh, funny," I chime in and look back down at my phone. Still no response. I need to know he's okay. I need to know that what we did last night wasn't a mistake. That our leap into love didn't have irrevocable consequences like it did in high school. There's no way it could ever be that bad—after all, no one died here. Yet, it would be nice to have a little bit of peace. A little bit of assurance that Christopher and I can be together without our world falling apart.

Finally, my phone vibrates in my hand.

Christopher: *What?? But how? That's crazy. Busy now but I'll pick you up at the usual time and place.*

Summer: *Are you okay?*

Christopher: *How could I not be? :)*

For the first time in a while, I actually smile. A real, full-fledged smile.

Summer: *Good. That's all I really want.*

Christopher: *You are all I really want. I love you.*

I don't want to tell him that I love him for the first time in a text message, but I can't leave him hanging...so a little emoticon will have to do.

Summer: ♥

"And can you believe it? Carter's drumsticks were in Dave's dirty clothes bag the whole time. Just right there!" Jim laughs like it's the most incredible story he's heard all day and it makes me giggle. If I can somehow convey to Christopher that I love him as much as Jim Welby loves Dave Matthews Band, then he'll really know that my love is the real deal.

Christopher

"MacCormack, come on in," Coach Bliss calls from inside his office. Dennison, our assistant coach, is there beside him talking about some trouble we've had on defense. They don't button up about it on my account, which is fine. I know they trust me with that kind of talk.

I take a seat and cross a leg over my knee. Coach loves whiteboards and there's four in his office. They're scribbled with plays, various line combinations, stats, schedules, you name it. The room smells like sweat, dry erase markers, and stale coffee. He has a few family photos on his desk, including one of him with his daughter. She has purple hair and a nose ring and a smirk. When she got arrested last season, it sent Coach into a tizzy. He took some personal time off to deal with it, which must have meant it was serious.

"I'll talk to Hux," Dennison says.

And suddenly my interest is piqued. "Everything okay with Hux?"

"Nothing for you to worry about, Mac," Dennison says and pats me on the shoulder.

I'm not sure if I believe him. Hux has had a lot of injuries but has the fighting spirit of a tiger. He's invaluable to the team.

"Just a healthy scratch tomorrow against LA," Bliss adds

on, like that's not humiliating for a veteran player with an A on his sweater.

"Why's that?" I can't help but ask, really pushing my boundaries today.

"It's not for you to worry about," Dennison reiterates and leaves me alone with Coach Bliss, and I just know I'm moments away from getting my ass handed to me for missing practice. Good thing I've got a thick skin, and if there was ever a reason to miss practice it's being passed out in Summer's bed. I could do without the stolen stuff, though.

Coach Bliss has the best poker face in the business, so I'm not sure how to read him when he starts. "I heard about this morning. Tough break on that, kid."

"Thanks. The police are working hard on it, but they think it was probably just a transient trying to get by."

"Did they take anything of yours?" he asks as he shuffles some papers around.

I'm pretty sure he couldn't care less about Summer's stuff and most likely doesn't care about my stuff either, but I answer him nonetheless. "I did lose one thing but I'll get over it."

He pauses and looks up at me. "*Get over it*? What's that?"

"This special puck I've been carrying in my bag since high school."

"Aw, shit," he replies and leans back in his chair to stare at the ceiling.

"I'm not that superstitious, coach," I tell him, but honestly I've never been without it since Trey gave it to me. I've had so much success with it.

He blows out a big dramatic breath. "I hate this kind of shit. It's nearly impossible to coach around."

"Trust me, I'll be fine."

Coach sits up and looks at me. "You *will* be fine without the puck. No doubt about that. You hear me?"

"I hear you."

"But it's actually not the puck I'm worried about."

"What are you worried about?"

"Summer Gunderson."

I'm taken aback on the spot. I can't even believe he knows her name. This has probably been a discussion that I haven't been privy to with other coaching staff and team management. "What about her?"

"You fucked up the face-off last night."

"Yeah, I did, but it happens."

"I pay attention to the little things. That's what makes me a future Hall of Fame coach, Mac."

I know what's coming next, but I still go for ignorance as a strategy, "What do you mean?"

"She was nearby and she distracted you. Tell me I'm wrong."

I'm tempted to. I'm tempted to tell him to fuck off. And do it in a glorious fashion. But I'm not a complete idiot and I meant what I said this morning in the parking garage. I love her and I'm not afraid to tell people that. Then again, she didn't seem too keen on the idea for her own career and Hux's advice from the plane is still ringing around in my head. I may have all the perks and privileges around this place based on my status but she's new and this job means a lot to her. I don't want to mess that up. So, I'm going to confess my truth, not the one that belongs to us. "Yes, she distracted me for just a split second. I'm adjusting to having someone I know be close by while I'm playing. It's like when my parents come to watch me play. That's all. I'm working on it."

"She means a lot to you, doesn't she?"

I focus on my breathing, a technique I use in interviews. It's okay to take a breath before you answer, my agent coached me. That seems to work well when being grilled by your coach, too. It's my truth. I can say it. "Yes, she does. She always has."

"As a friend or something more?" he asks while he pops the cap to a red erase marker on and off.

My phone vibrates in my pocket, but I don't dare look at it now. "As something more," I admit.

He stands up and looks at the board with player stats on it. We've only played two regular season games and we've played well in both of those for the most part, yet I still feel like he's seeing something in the numbers that concerns him. Something I just don't see. And maybe that something is about me.

"Love and hockey isn't always a good mix," he starts and turns back toward me, placing his hands on top of all those papers he was shuffling earlier. "When you're on the ice, your love needs to be for the game. Your loyalty needs to be to your teammates."

I sit up straighter. "Yes, sir."

"When you let your dick pull you like a fucking magnet off the ice, you've stopped being Big Mac, you get that? You're just Christopher MacCormack. And let me tell you something, Christopher MacCormack doesn't belong out there. You can be him at home. Fuck, I don't care if Christopher MacCormack marries that girl. But he's not who I need. Not if we're going to contend for the Cup again. I need Big Mac. You got me?"

"Yes, sir."

"So be careful. Be thoughtful. Be the leader we all believe you are, otherwise I'll strip that C off your jersey and give it to the likes of Smitty."

Low. Fucking. Blow.

"Get fucking focused," he says and turns back toward one of his whiteboards.

"Will do," I reply and stand up. "Do you need anything else from me?"

"Go see Dennison. He'll recap today's meeting for you."

"Yes, sir," I say and back out of his office.

All things considered, it could have gone worse, but I do feel like my one true vulnerability has been exposed. This isn't high school. This isn't college. This is my career, and I have to do everything in my power to fulfill my promise and potential while still loving Summer Gunderson.

My phone vibrates again so I fish it out of my pocket.

Summer: *Hey, I have news. We have trackers on the equipment and Jim located it at a pawn shop. Call me when you can.*

That is great news. But since I have to go talk to Dennison, a phone call isn't possible.

Christopher: *What?? But how? That's crazy. Busy now but I'll pick you up at the usual time and place.*

Summer: *Are you okay?*

If I were completely honest, I'd tell her that I'm a little bit shaken by my chat with Coach, but I don't need to add any more stress onto her. Everything is going to be fine. Truly. Plus, I'm still riding high from last night. Every free moment I've had today, when I haven't had to deal with all this mess, has been reliving each and every moment with Summer from last night and this morning.

Christopher: *How could I not be? :)*

Summer: *Good. That's all I really want.*

Christopher: *You are all I really want. I love you.*

It's not lost on me that she didn't say it back this morning in the garage when I told her. Maybe I should have picked a more romantic time to confess how I feel, but maybe hearing it when you're in the thick of it is better. As much as I'd love to hear her say it too, I'm feeling confident enough in us to not need it...yet.

Summer: ♥

There's that little heart again. It makes my much more real heart squeeze inside my chest. I'm glad she didn't say it in text. I want to be able to see her when the time comes, to look into her eyes, to see just how she smiles, to take hold of her hand and press my lips against hers on the very last word.

Coach Dennison's office door is closed, but I can see through the window that Hux is standing on the opposite side of his desk getting the news about sitting out tomorrow's home game. It hasn't happened to me yet, but if I don't get my mind in the game, it just might.

Hux opens the door harder than he has to and storms past me.

"Hey, Hux, hold up," I say and chase after him.

"Don't say a word," he barks.

"What's their logic?" I ask, because I honestly don't get it.

"They're tinkering, plain and simple. What do they expect, a shut out every game? Anyway, he said it's not my performance. They just want to do a little experimenting."

"Don't worry, brother. They're not lying. You've been excellent since you've been back. The way you beat out Schneider last night, you saved us."

"It's fine. What happened to you this morning? I heard some wild story about raccoons ransacking your truck."

"Not quite raccoons, at least I don't think so," I say and ponder the possibility. They do have little hands that I guess could be used to open the door. It's as good an answer as anything at this point. "Someone stole all the stuff in my truck, including all of Summer's camera equipment and her laptop."

"Oh man, that sucks. Is she in trouble?"

"I don't think so. Turns out they have trackers on that stuff and they found it at a pawnshop. So as soon as I catch up with Dennison, I'm going to get back in touch with the police."

He squints. "Well, that's good news, I guess."

"Hope so."

He shrugs and smiles just the tiniest bit, which is saying something for his mood. "Why'd you guys leave your stuff in the truck?"

I cross my arms over my chest and shrug. I'm not going to kiss and tell.

Hux squints again and nods. "Don't say another word. Got it. Congratulations."

I nod in return and put a hand on his shoulder. "I hate playing hockey without you, brother. There's been too much of that in the past six months."

"Tell me about it." He takes a deep breath and lets out a long sigh. "I'm headed to my cabin to clear my head. I'll see you when I see you," he says and takes off without looking back.

"Officer Escobedo, it's Christopher MacCormack calling you back. Any news?"

"Yes, Mr. MacCormack, thanks for calling. We were able to recover the camera equipment and laptop from the pawnshop, but no such luck on any of the personal items you described."

"What about the hockey puck with the masking tape on it that says *GWG Juniors Championship* on it?"

"No, the pawnshop manager said nothing like that came in at all."

"Shit," I whisper under my breath. "Were you able to identify who brought it to the pawnshop?"

"We've got a name and description based on the manager's recollection. The security cameras could use some serious improvement. Bad angles, bad light. We ran the name and it's bogus, though."

My gaze goes up to the ceiling as I pace around the office hallways. "Awesome."

"Unfortunately, in a circumstances like this, it's likely they tossed the other bags when they realized there wasn't anything of high value in there."

"Have you searched the dumpsters around my building and the pawnshop?"

"We did have a junior officer take a look in a few key locations, but didn't find anything. The truth is, your stuff is probably gone for good and we don't have the manpower to—"

"Track down dirty clothes and athletic tape. I get it. I wouldn't expect you too," I grumble.

"If anything turns up, in particular that puck you described, we'll let you know."

"Thank you, officer," I tell him and make my way to meet Summer. I'm definitely disappointed about losing my lucky puck. A dark thought worms its way through my head that this is one more fuck you from Trey from beyond the grave, punishing me for being with his cousin. I don't actually believe in ghosts, but I do feel like I'm being punished for being reckless last night. When I'm with her, I get so overwhelmed that I don't always think straight. I'm totally consumed by her.

Summer is waiting for me by the truck as the sun starts its descent behind the Rocky Mountains. Her skin is bathed in rays of orange and pink light as she takes in the stunning sunset that isn't half as beautiful as her.

"Hey Gunderson," I call for her.

She looks over her shoulder at me, her eyes piercing me. "Hey Chris," she replies with a smile.

With a flick of my wrist, I toss my bag into the bed of my truck and slide my arms beneath hers to lift her up and spin her around. She giggles and squirms until I let her down.

"Enjoying the sunset?" I ask into her hair, which shines in the light.

"It's incredible. I've never seen one like that, with the mountains. The best I ever saw was over Webster Lake, but this is a close second."

"When was that? The one over Webster Lake?"

Her cheeks pink up, and I know there's something about the memory that has to do with me.

"Will you tell me?" I ask quietly as I step closer to her and rub a few strands of her hair between my fingers. "Please."

"It was the day at the lake, with the rope swing, when we almost kissed after I finally did it. At least, I think you wanted to kiss me."

"I did, very much," I say and lean down to whisper in her ear. "But that's not new. I wanted to kiss you every day back then, just like how I want to kiss you now."

"Well, I wanted you to kiss me so badly," she says and I lean back to look into her eyes. "I still remember how it felt to be in your arms. And the feel of your swimming trunks against my skin. I remember the look in your eyes, the wetness of your hair," she says and runs a few fingers through my hair as if we're right back there. "I remember how much I loved you then. It was overwhelming and heady, and too much for a seventeen-year-old."

"I loved you like that too," I tell her, because I want her to understand how not one-sided it was.

"But it was nothing," she starts again with some tears in her eyes. "It was nothing like how I feel for you now."

We stand with the weight of her words grounding us to this moment. The wait is longer than the actual seconds that pass between what she just said and what she's about to say.

"I'm in love with you, Chris. Fully. Deeply. Completely," she finally says.

Four months ago, I was knee-deep in the playoffs. Traveling. Playing. Leading. But I was empty. I was a machine. My passion was only for the game because I never, ever thought that I would get to love somebody the way I loved Summer in high school. There was no point. She wasn't in my life. She was tucked away in Fossebridge, and I figured she would never get over what happened with Trey. She was out of my reach, forever. That's what I thought. I didn't let myself think anything more.

But then I got her email on the night we won the Cup, and my hope for us was ignited again. It wasn't hard. I've been kindling for her since the day we met.

My fingertips graze the back of her arm until I cup her elbow while my other hand finds its way into her hair.

She smiles so sweetly and I'm truly done for. "My heart is yours."

I blink a few times as breath leaves my chest in one big rush. I kiss her because I absolutely must. It's slow and soft and full of all our promise and our potential. As we part, I touch my forehead to hers and close my eyes.

Summer Gunderson is mine.

Christopher

Winter Formal, Senior Year

Summer Gunderson is mine.

Our first kiss was so beyond what I ever imagined it would be and now we can't stop. I forget that we're on Mateo's back porch. I forget that we're at a party. I forget my own name. All I know is Summer. The sweetness of her lips. The smooth skin beneath her ear. The soft fabric of her dress on the small of her back. The apple smell of her hair. It's completely over-whelming to my senses.

This night could not get any better. But then...it does. She wraps her arms around my neck and I pull her body even closer to mine. Her fingers thread through my hair and she makes a really sweet sound against my lips. I back us up to the wicker couch and sit down. She follows and lifts up her dress enough to be able to straddle my lap.

Whoa.

It's like the beginning of every fantasy I've ever had about her.

Our kissing gets more frantic and I'd sacrifice everything, even hockey, to take this to the next level. My hands tremble as I dip beneath her dress and let my palms slide up her thighs. I'm touching her in places I've only dreamed of.

When I was learning how to skate, I was way faster than all the other kids on the ice. I would push myself to go, go, go. The only problem is that I didn't know how to stop. I couldn't even slow down. The only thing to stop me was the boards. I would crash into them time and again. Even though the impact was painful, I'd turn right around and do it again, probably faster.

There are no boards in sight right now.

I can do this. I can slow us down. Because we don't have to go that far tonight. We can go slow. We can take this one step at a time. We've got all the time in the world, especially since we're going to the same college.

"Summer," I whisper against her lips.

"Mmm?" she responds and leans back.

Even in the dim lamplight, her green eyes slay me. We've done this before, this thing where our eyes lock and we linger as if there's nothing more interesting in the entire world to look at. It's like that again, but this time it's heavier as our mouths stay parted and our breathing is short. Her hair, with all its ringlets, cascades around our faces. And as badly as I want to kiss her again, I could also stay like this all night.

She traces my jaw with a light touch. "What were you going to say?"

I can't remember. So I say the one thing that's been on the tip of my tongue this whole night. "You're beautiful."

Summer takes a deep breath and shakes her head a little bit before pressing her lips to mine and we get back to it, slowly this time with more intention in each and every kiss.

"You're beautiful too," she whispers.

My kiss goes deeper. My hands go further. My pants get tighter. We're sliding again with nothing to stop us.

My first thought still nags at me. This isn't the right time and it's most definitely not the right place, but I can't seem to slow down again. I want be free with her, with my body and my words. I want to tell her that I love her. But we finally hit the boards. A loud crash happens in the house that sounds like glass shattering. We stop kissing and sit up.

"What was that?" she asks.

"Party foul?" I guess. I'm already missing her mouth and have no willpower, so I pull her back to my face and kiss her again. She's more than happy to get back to it.

Suddenly there's shouting and it sounds like my teammates.

Shit.

"What's going on?" she asks and leans up to look through the window but shakes her head. "I can't tell."

"Goddamnit," I mumble. It's probably Trey causing trouble with Mateo. I should go to them. I should make sure everything is okay. I should. I should. I should. But I can't. Not right now. Not while I have the chance to be with Summer. I push the noise out of my head and press my lips to her neck, just beneath her ear. Her fragrance, the one I always know is her, fills my nostrils and I know I've made the right choice. She tilts her head to give me even better access and makes a sound I've never heard from her before. She likes it. A lot.

Yep, I definitely made the right choice.

I keep kissing and nuzzling her neck, her ear, her jaw and her hands keep moving over my shoulders, down my arms, and up into my hair.

Like I said. I just turned right around and skated even faster. And I would just stride and stride, harder and faster.

My instructor tried to teach me how to slow down, but I didn't really understand how to do it until I watched Trey shave and drag. It made sense to me the more and more I watched him do it. The last thing that Trey would ever be called is calm and controlled, but on the ice he's the one that's got far more control than I've ever had. On the outside, I may seem like the one that can keep his cool, that can be measured and reasonable and focused.

They're wrong.

He's the one that's mastered it. He's the one that has focus on the goal, the game plan, and the strategy, while I'm just out there flying down the ice with nothing but feeling and base instincts.

People always get us wrong.

And now, in this moment where the boards have once again disappeared, we're flying with no drag and I don't know what it will take to stop us.

Unfortunately in this world, it seems you can't go forever without meeting some kind of force, whether it's boards or best friends.

In this case, it's my best friend. He's standing in the doorway, staring down at us with bloodshot eyes and balled-up fists.

Summer hasn't noticed that I've stopped kissing her, nor has she noticed Trey yet. His silence is so loud, I don't know how she doesn't hear it.

I swallow hard and gently press Summer back. She blinks a few times and then follows my eyes to see who I'm staring at. It's her cousin and he is anything but happy to see us together like this.

10

Summer

"TELL ME A STORY," CHRISTOPHER SAYS AS HE STROKES MY HAIR while we watch *The Office* over at his place. "How was your day?"

"It was okay," I say with a sigh. "Jim has this whacky idea that I'm trying to talk him out of."

He clenches up. "Does it involve popsicles? Because if it does, I swear to God I'll have my agent try to break my contract with the Storm."

I shake my head and laugh. "No, no popsicles this time. Just Santa outfits, since the holidays will be here before you know it."

Christopher groans. "I do not want to dress up as Santa."

"I think he wants you to be an elf."

"Great, even better," he says and pulls me over to him so that my head leans against his chest. "Doesn't it bother you?"

"What?" I ask and look up at him.

"That you have this incredible talent to make"—he thinks on it for a second—"art, and this guy is your boss. It's so ridiculous."

"Nah, it doesn't bother me. I'm just happy to have this job," I tell him and pat his chest. He puts his hand over mine and squeezes. I lift up and look at him. "That being said, can you guys win a game sometime soon? Nobody wants to watch a video from a loss, even an overtime loss. They're just archiving all my footage."

He shifts in his seat. "You think I don't want to?"

Me and my dumb mouth.

"Sorry, I know you're trying," I say and rest my head on his chest again.

He holds me to him and releases his head back to the cushion. "We get so close, but we've just had bad luck. If we lose another game on a bad goal, I'm going to lose my mind."

"Yeah, it's just a bout of bad luck," I agree, even though I'm not really a believer in that kind of thing, but I know Christopher does, especially since he lost his lucky puck. I still don't know what makes it lucky to him or why it was so special. "Maybe you need to identify another good luck charm?"

It's a dumb idea, but I'm hopeful that if he can move on then maybe he'll gain his confidence back that they can win.

"Maybe I don't need a good luck charm," he says and threads his fingers through my hair. "Maybe I just need you."

"Mmm," I hum into his belly.

He rubs my shoulders and down my back until he gets to my ass and gives it a playful squeeze. As he does it, I feel him harden beneath me and that makes me want him so badly.

Even after a couple of months of being together, I still can't get enough of him. It was just this morning when I woke up in his bed and found him in his big walk-in shower. Needless to say, I joined him and we figured out the best position for that kind of play, with me bent over with my hands pressed against the tiles. He drove into me with one hand on my shoulder and the other between my legs. My legs trembled so hard after we came that I had to sit down. He joined me, even though he didn't need to, and we made out under the shower spray.

But here we were again, ready to go even after a long day where we didn't even get home until nearly midnight. It's late, and he's got an early start tomorrow.

"Chris, it's a little late. Maybe I should head back to my place and let you get some sleep."

He doesn't let up, kissing down my neck as he says, "I'll be fine. Don't worry about me."

"Are you sure?" I ask. "As much as I want to be with you, I could let you be and you can get a really good start tomorrow morning."

"Yes, I'm sure," he answers and pulls me further onto his body. "Being without you will make me restless. I need you."

I straddle his lap and let my hair down. He looks up at me with the same type of wonder he had when we were in this same position back in high school on Mateo's porch. Like he can't believe it. Honestly, neither can I. We move a little slowly this time, unlike this morning's shower frenzy. Without taking his eyes off mine, he lifts my top off of me and then reaches behind his back and pulls his own off. One of my favorite things is being skin-to-skin with him, and so I slip off my bra and toss it over near where Joey is taking a nap on the ottoman.

"God, I love your tits," he says all growly-man-like as he cups each one and squeezes my nipples between his thumb and his index finger. My hips instinctively move back and forth, which leads him to grunt a little. He starts sucking and licking and biting on me until my head lolls back and around. He takes control of it and brings my mouth to his. We kiss like it's the first time not the hundredth. It's intense, both physically and emotionally, at least for me. When we kiss, we're fighting against the fate we saddled ourselves with so long ago. We're choosing this.

What happens next is like a series of astronomical events. There's energy and pressure and a collision with explosions. When all is said and done, I'm lying on top of him, my back against his front, his mouth nibbling on my earlobe as his hands roam over my trembling body.

"Love you," he breathes into my ear.

"Love me enough to carry me to the bathroom?" I reply. "You've once again incapacitated me."

"You're blaming me?"

"I'm thanking you."

He smiles against my neck. "You're very welcome, then."

"Don't let it get to your head, Big Mac," I joke.

"Too late for that," he says and lifts me up in his arms and then over his shoulder.

I swat at his back. "This isn't what I had in mind."

Christopher laughs and swats me right back on my ass. "Would you rather walk?"

"No," I whine.

"Mmmhmm," he replies and carries me like this, so confidently and cocky, across his loft and into his master bathroom. He sets me down on the counter and warms up a washcloth so he can clean us both up while I sit there with a goofy grin on my face.

"Hey, did I tell you that Momma and Tia are coming to the game in Minnesota? I'm so excited to see them."

"You did tell me and I'm glad they'll be there. My parents are coming and I heard your aunt and uncle are coming too."

"Oh cool," I reply. "I didn't know that part."

It's good of my Uncle Dave and Aunt Leslie. I suspect that ever since Christopher came home with the Cup, they've healed a little bit more. Losing their only son was terribly hard for them. Beyond the obvious reasons—they had wrapped up so many hopes and dreams in his future as well. Uncle Dave had been so involved in Trey's hockey development and there's no doubt that Aunt Leslie put in countless hours taking care of everything else. They were a little team with a dream, and that dream died right along with their son.

"Yeah, quite a few folks are gonna be there," Christopher says, not dwelling too much on Trey's parents.

"Hey, I have an idea but I'm not sure if we can pull it off," I tell him. It's an idea that I've had ever since I started working for the team but one I haven't quite figured out how to pull off. I still don't know if we can make it work.

His eyes light up with excitement. "What?"

"I don't know. It's really hard, considering all sorts of factors."

"Come on, Gunderson. You've got to tell me now. I'm sure if we put our heads together we can figure it out," he says and walks off to the bedroom briefly and returns with two pairs of shorts and two t-shirts for us.

Even though I live right next door, he's always more than ready to loan me clothes so we don't have to leave. He's also bought me a toothbrush—a fancy one, like the one I had him show me on video chat in Chicago—and he's stocked his place with all sorts of delicious food, including frozen waffles and the not-so-good-for-you kind of peanut butter.

"Okay, so you know how they honor service members during the national anthem?"

As he puts on a basic white tee he says, "Yeah."

"Could we have them honor Mr. Wilkins?" This is my big idea.

Christopher's eyebrows shoot up. "That would be super cool."

I lift my arms up and he puts one of his Colorado Storm t-shirts on me, pulling my hair out and over my shoulder when it's on. "Yeah, did you know that he was one of twenty-five African American Air Force pilots to fight in Korea? He earned an Air Force Cross. And you know, he hasn't been feeling well lately, so I thought we could do something, before..."

"Yeah, I think we can try to make that work. Let me talk to our people and see what can be done. If we get the okay, we can see if he can it make there and come out on the ice."

"He would love that so much, Chris. He's so proud of you."

He nods quietly and closes his eyes briefly. "I'm not sure I've earned it lately."

The phone rings and rings and rings. I can just picture Momma hopping around the the Biscuit, multitasking like the queen she is while the phone on the wall rings. I've learned over the years to just be patient. She will answer it at some point. And sure enough, after about thirty rings, she picks up.

"Biscuit in the Basket," she chirps.

"Momma, it's me."

"Hey baby, what's new?"

"I've got some exciting news."

She squees into the phone.

"Momma? What are you doing? Why are you making that sound?"

"I'm happy. When your grown daughter tells you that, you can hope for a couple of things. I'm personally hoping for an engagement, but I'd be just fine with a grandchild. Tradition is silly."

"Calm down, Momma. It's neither of those things."

"Promotion, then?"

"Nope, not that either," I say and cringe a little bit. Work hasn't been going so great. The team keeps losing and dropping down the standings, and the worse they do, the less the marketing department needs my particular type of work.

"Well you're no fun," she says. "Just tell me your not-very-exciting news."

"Christopher and I were able to arrange for Mr. Wilkins to be honored at the Minnesota game."

"Really? That's great! He's here now, can I tell him?"

"Sure, Momma. Go ahead. The game is on the December 23rd. Will you help me get him there?"

"Oh Summer, of course. Ya'll have such kind hearts. He's

going to love seeing Christopher play. I am too."

"Don't lie, Momma. You couldn't care less about hockey."

"But I do care about Christopher, and I especially care about you. It will be so wonderful to watch you work. Jettin' all around the arena with your camera. I couldn't be more proud."

"Thanks, Momma."

"Oh, my french toast is burnin'. Gotta go!"

She just hangs up on me, which isn't as unusual as it should be, and I turn back to my monitor to edit some footage I took from last night's home game. We had some great plays that can go into the archive for the personal profiles on individual players. Sadly, none of those amazing plays are from Christopher. He had an off night and has had a rough month, not scoring any goals with only a few assists.

That is not the caliber of play that the world expects from him, and I know no one is more upset about that than Christopher himself.

What's worse is that he's been getting chippier on the ice too. He's drawing penalties like he's an enforcer and has really been pushing his luck. Ever since the break in, he hasn't been himself out there and I can't figure out why, beyond superstition.

I'm honestly worried about him.

But apparently I should also be worried about me, because Jim comes in and pulls up a chair beside my desk. "Hey, Summer, do you have a moment to talk?"

Jim has never, ever been this formal or respectful of my time. A bead of sweat drips off his thick sideburn.

"Yes," I say with a frog in my throat.

"Okay, great," he says and wipes his hands on his Carhartt

pants.

"What's up, Jim?" I ask, just wanting him to get to it.

"I just got done meeting with Robin Farmer."

"Am I fired?" I ask, just cutting right to the chase.

"No," he says, flabbergasted.

"Thank God," I say and breathe a sigh of relief.

"But..." He trails off and my heart rate spikes again.

"But what?"

"We don't need you to travel with the team anymore."

"Oh," I say and slump into my seat. "I guess I understand why."

"It's just not worth it right now." Then he looks over his shoulder to make sure no one is listening. "They're playing like shit. Especially your friend, I'm sorry to say."

"Yeah," I reply and will myself not to cry. It's not even a demotion. It makes total business sense. It's upsetting that their season is turning out to be so terrible. They should be riding high off the Cup win. They've got all the talent they need to be great and the coaching staff to get them there, but something is missing—a key element. They're not clicking and so the fans aren't, either. I'm also sad because that means I'll be home while Christopher is on the road. "Is it effective immediately?"

"Afraid so," he says. "We're also going to have you cut back on filming practices, pre-games and post-games, and use that time to assist Maddy. Social is so in the moment, win or lose."

"Social?" I ask, like I've never heard of it. Social is not what I do. Sure, the social team shares my work, but I don't know much about actual social media. It's never been my forte, even back in Fossebridge. That was primarily Tia's thing.

"It will be fun. You gals are friends right?"

"Yeah," I answer, still shaken from the news.

"It's just for practice, pre and post. No big."

"And if they win, shouldn't I gather some postgame footage?"

"Yeah, sure. I don't think anyone in management is really going to be paying attention," he says nonchalantly. He has no idea how much those words hurt. My stomach won't stop clenching.

He goes on. "Plus, I'll need your help with the Santa video."

Ugh. I guess he's going forward with that stupid idea after all.

"Okay, but I've made quite a few plans for the Minnesota game," I tell him and there's definitely a defensive edge to my voice. "My family and friends are coming to the game and we're honoring a vet from my hometown. Can I work that one?"

I can tell Jim hates it as much as I do as he shakes his head.

"Fine," I snipe. "Can I at least take some time off and fly myself out there? It's really important that I'm there."

"I'm sure we could make that work," he tells me and I breathe a small sign of relief. "Let's just hope they win tonight's game and the team gets back on track."

"From your mouth to the hockey gods' ears."

Christopher

Fuckin' fuck fucker. I stomp through the tunnel and into the locker room, punching the wall as I pass. Lenny, an equipment manager, and Falcon, one of our trainers, follow me. I toss my helmet at Lenny and he catches it. Falcon stands by to help me cool down, but I'm not in the mood to be smothered by either of them.

Boston's Danielssen had it coming, the fucker. He intentionally tripped Hux on his bad leg. It was a no-brainer. The gloves had to come off. And after going a few rounds and clearing our bench to join in, goalies included, I got sent out for a five-minute major with only four minutes left in the third period when we're down four to three.

"Thanks guys, but can I get some fucking room?"

"Sure thing, Big Mac," Lenny says and they both go back out to the rink.

First, I take off my jersey and throw it on the floor, then my undershirt.

"Chris?" Summer says from the door to the locker room. "Are you okay?"

"You can come in, I'm alone."

"Are you sure?"

"Yes," I call out as I unlace my breezers but leave them hanging off my hips.

This isn't her first time in the locker room. She's been in here filming our celebrations, us being interviewed by the press, us after a tough loss. Sometimes I think she's more like a documentarian than anything.

Unlike all those times, her camera is nowhere to be seen. And more than ever, I appreciate that she doesn't have her camera glued to her face. It's just her and the badge hanging from the lanyard around her neck.

"Hey, what happened out there?" she asks.

"You didn't see? He tripped Hux."

"No, I saw that. I mean, why did you nearly tear the guy's head off? Are you okay?" She's standing about three feet back, as if I'm a volatile volcano. I don't care for it.

"Yeah, of course I'm okay. He just had it coming," I snipe.

She crosses her arms over her chest. "I've watched a lot of your games over the years and I've never seen you so hotheaded."

"Then you haven't been paying attention." It's a low blow. I know it is, but I'm still pissed and the last thing I need is for my girlfriend to give me shit about it.

She holds her hands up. "Okay, whatever you say, Big Mac. Clearly there's nothing wrong whatsoever."

I hate when she calls me Big Mac. "Nothing more than hockey," I say and turn my back on her toward my stall.

"Hey," she shouts and grabs me by the arm in an attempt to twist me back around. Apparently she's not as afraid of the volcano as I thought.

I'm towering over her since I'm still wearing my skates. She looks up at me with fire in her eyes. "Don't push me away."

"I would never," I hiss and take hold of her shoulders to the muffled cheers of fans in our arena. We must have tied it up.

Her fingers dig into my sides where I'm slick with sweat as she doesn't take her eyes off my mine. "You did once."

Well, that's certainly up for interpretation. Perhaps her memory isn't as good as mine. "I would never," I repeat myself and blink away the sweat that's dripping off my hair.

Her lips are parted, as if she might just say something else ridiculous, but the words don't come. She reaches up and slides her hand to the back of my neck. As always, her touch destroys my senses.

Fuck, I want her. Right here. Right now.

My forehead lowers to hers and I take hold of her ass. I need her as close as possible.

"Chris," she warns, but I keep going. I lift her off the ground and she wraps her legs around me as our mouths connect. In my skates and pads, I make my way to the wall to get some support, so I can work through all these layers between us.

"We shouldn't," she says and shakes her head, but she doesn't stop pulling at me and kissing my neck.

"We shouldn't what?" I tease as I free my erection. She drops a hand and wraps it around me. "Summer..."

She continues to stroke me as best she can in this position, but it's not tenable, so I move us again, this time to the player's lounge and shut the door behind us. It's for players only but it's obviously not private. I don't really care. I set her down and then take a seat on the arm of the couch, so she has a better angle to keep stroking me. And she does it with perfection.

All my worries fall away.

I'm no longer thinking about Danielssen or Hux or my shitty stats or our standings in the central division. I no longer hear the sounds of the crowd. And I'm even able to forget about how terrible it is that I lost Trey's puck, which I still haven't told Summer about in more detail. None of that matters right now. There's only the pressure that's building within me as the most beautiful woman I've ever known does wonders on me.

Her green apple eyes look down at me and I'm lost, utterly

utterly lost. I'm very close to letting go and about to tell her so when there's a symphony of shouting and cheers in the room next door. The boys must have pulled it off and beat Boston. Before Summer and I can do a thing about the compromising position we're in, the door to the player's lounge bursts open. In order of worst to best person to be on the other side of the door, I would put Coach Bliss first. Thankfully it isn't him or any of the assistant coaches. But it is someone that's high on that list. Fucking Smitty. It might as well be all of the coaching staff and the media too.

I get to my feet in no time flat and attempt to make myself decent.

Smitty stands there with a shit-eating grin on his face and the door propped open. I don't make a sound, but wave him in so he'll close the fucking door.

"Looks like I missed the the party," he says and rubs a hand over his jock. "Are handjobs part of your new assignment, Summer?"

I'm not sure what he means about new assignment and I don't ask because I'm on the verge of flattening the asshole on the carpet. Summer knows better and grabs my arm right away, helping me regain my common sense. If I fight Smitty, I'll be suspended and then we'll have press problems, too.

FUCK.

"Shut your mouth," I tell him as quietly as I can muster. "Summer and I are together. She's my girlfriend. We got carried away. Doesn't that ever happen to you and *your wife*?"

"Christopher," Summer whispers and I know the tone. She wants me to cool it.

Smitty's the least faithful person I've ever come across, so it's a dig. I gotta get them in wherever I can since I can't pulverize the bastard.

"Aww, how sweet for you two," he says sarcastically. "I'm sure Coach would love to share his sentiments as well. I'll go get him." He turns toward the door and just as he opens it, someone is pushing it from the other side.

It's Hawk. Fucking great. At least my dick isn't in Summer's hand.

All his pads are off and his skates. He quickly assesses the situation and closes the door and stands back against it so no one else can come in. "Hey guys," he says with a little laugh in his voice. "What's up?"

I huff. He knows damn well.

"Big Mac finally got his first handjob," Smitty says and starts to clap.

Hawk ignores him and looks over at Summer. "We've got to get you out of here."

"You think?" she barks. "Any ideas?"

"Yup. Smitty, block this door," he says.

"And why the hell should I?" he asks.

He grabs Smitty by the jersey he's still wearing and swings him around to the door. "Because he's your teammate and your captain, and Summer is a good person."

Smitty doesn't reply to that, but stands against the door with a shitty frown nonetheless.

"Mac, help me with the fridge," Hawk says as he stands in front of an alcove with a drink fridge in it that has lots of bottled water and sports drinks. "There's a door behind it, remember?"

That's right. They closed it off when they remodeled these

spaces last year. "Good thinking." The two of us easily move the fridge and sure enough, there's a door that's locked from the inside of the lounge. *Thank fuck.*

"Where does it lead?" Summer asks.

"Just to the hall behind the locker room that has the trainer's rooms and offices. Take it out to the concourse."

"Okay," she says.

I squeeze her hand and say, "Head home. I'll come over."

"Okay," she says again and her cheeks aren't quite as rosy pink from embarrassment.

As we close up the door and put the fridge back in place, Smitty opens the lounge door and leaves, not waiting a second longer than he has to.

"Do you think he'll tell Coach?" I ask Hawk.

"Not if he has any shred of team camaraderie," he answers and takes a seat on one of the couches.

"That doesn't give me a lot of hope," I tell him.

"I'll make sure he doesn't do anything stupid," he replies, and I know then that Hawk should be wearing an A on his sweater. "Maybe we should talk for a few minutes."

"Why?" I ask, even though I know exactly why. I just wouldn't have pictured this from him. It's totally a Hux move.

"Because I think you're blowing it hard, no pun intended," he says, and laughs full on from deep in his belly.

"It was just a handjob," I correct him.

"Sure it was. Come on, Mac. Sit down for a second before this room gets swarmed."

I take a seat and wait for him to say whatever it is he wants to say. What he says next, though, is not what I would expect. "I admire you."

"What?"

"You're this one-woman guy that's just been so singularly focused on Summer. She's great, I get it."

A little flare of jealousy spikes in me, but I shake it off.

"I've never felt that way about anybody. Never really wanted to."

I tug at my messed-up hair and look over at him pointedly. "What's your point, bro?"

"What I already said. You're blowing it. Ever since Summer came, you haven't been on your game. And I mean, even when you're not on your game you're still one of the best that's out there. But you're making mistakes and poor choices, like this little escapade at the exact wrong place at the exact wrong time. That's a *me* move. All this time, I've been looking up to you and you're blowing it."

"Stop saying blowing it," I growl. "It was just a handjob."

He puts his hands up jokingly, "Okay, okay. But you know what I mean. Be that guy that I think you are and find a little balance."

"You sound like Hux."

"That's a compliment, man. But seriously, can you imagine how destroyed you'd be if they found Summer in here and you got benched? Or worse, that she got fired? Use some common sense, man. We need you. We need our captain."

I shake my head as I drop my face into my hands. He's right. Of course he is. Especially about Summer getting fired. How selfish and greedy I was. One day, I've got a figure out a way to be with Summer and not let the world around me burn.

Christopher

Winter Formal, Senior Year

"What the hell, Trey?" Summer shouts and climbs off my lap.

Trey doesn't flinch nor does he respond to her. He doesn't even glance in her direction. His eyes are on me and I feel oddly vulnerable sitting on the couch. I'm clearly about to be confronted, so I'd better stand up in case he wants to throw down.

"Hey man," I say as I stand up. "You okay? I heard shouting and glass breaking."

He still doesn't say anything, but his face gets even redder.

Is this about kissing his cousin? I will not apologize for that. Ever.

Summer takes hold of my arm. "Trey, seriously, why do you insist on ruining everything? What Christopher and I do is none of your business."

"Come on, man, you have to know that I've liked Summer for a long time. I know it's weird because she's your cousin, but this isn't just a hookup. We care about each other."

"That's obvious," he says. It's not that his eyes are just glassy from the booze, there's actual tears there. Why on earth would he cry about this?

Unless...

Did he somehow find out about about my college decision? The only person I've told is Summer. Did she tell...Tia?

Fuck.

"Hey man," I say again. "We should talk."

"You think?" he asks and takes a step closer to me.

"Talk about what?" Summer asks, clearly pissed off. "Shouldn't you be spending time with Tia? Where is she? Why do you keep ditching her?"

"She's downstairs," he answers. "And she told me everything."

"Everything?" Summer asks and then whispers, "Oh."

"UMN, is it?" Trey asks, his voice going up.

"Yeah, I've been meaning to talk to you about it. It's been a really hard to decision for me to make and I just think that going to UMN would—"

"Oh, you don't have to tell me. It's fucking clear what you intend to *do* at UMN."

"Gross," Summer whispers and shakes her head.

"Oh, I'm sorry. Did I offend you, cuz?" he asks and gets right up in her face. "I don't know how you could be so offended when you're practically humping him out here. Does your mom know what a slut you are?"

Summer slaps him straight across the face and he stumbles back against the wall.

"Dude, that's uncalled for. Your issue is with me, not with her."

"Oh, it's with her."

"You're so ridiculous, Trey. It doesn't have to be like this at all," she argues.

"You won, Summer. Congratulations," he says and claps. "What did it take? Finally agree to fuck him if he goes to UMN?"

She shakes her head. "I didn't ask him to go to UMN. I played no part in it."

"Of course you did, honey."

He turns back to me. "She teases you all the time, flirting and playing hard to get. Making you think with your dick instead of your head. You're a fucking idiot, you know that? We had a plan. What kind of friend are you? What kind of team-mate are you? And you, Summer. What kind of cousin are you? When you moved here, who looked out for you? Who was there for you? And this is how you repay me? By ruining the only thing we've been working toward."

"Stop it," I shout. "For the last time, it's not her fault."

"No? Because I can't believe you'd betray me like this."

"It's not a betrayal! You can sign with UMN. We can still go on to play. We can still do great things. They have a great program."

"And what? Be stuck in Minnesota for four more years? Be stuck watching you pine for Summer?" he says as if he's disgusted. He grabs me by the shoulders and I try to take a step back because he reeks of whiskey, but he follows. "College was supposed to be our time, Mac. Just us," he pleads with me.

"Dude..." I say, unsure how to respond to that. I had no idea he felt so strongly about me and hated my feelings for Summer, but maybe it's been right there the whole time. Every time he stepped between us, interrupted us, and pulled me away. I always thought it was because he was thoughtless, or because he was trying to protect Summer. But it was never that. It was about me.

"How could you do this to me?" he screams as tears stream down his face. "You've ruined everything!"

I get choked up. "It doesn't have to be like that. It can still be us as teammates. We can go to UMN together," I try to explain, but it's useless.

He shakes his head and shoves me. "Change your fucking mind, man. Change it now"

I look over at Summer and I know. I just know that if I have to choose, I will choose to follow her instead of Trey. "Go to Boston, man. You'll play great there. You've always been better than me. You don't need me."

Trey cries harder and kicks the space heater across the room. "How could you? She's not worth it. She's just some fucking worthless girl. What we have is more important."

"No," I shout back. "I love her, man. I love her."

Summer's mouth drops open at my confession. It's probably the worst possible time to tell her, but I don't care. "I love you, Summer."

She starts to respond, but Trey shoves me hard enough to knock me back onto my ass.

"Trey, stop!" Summer shouts and comes to my side as I start to get up. "Just stop it!"

People are crowded around the doorway, watching us. Including Tia, who looks visibly upset as if she's already had her own fight with him.

"There you have it," Trey says to the crowd. "Your captain. He's a liar and a fool."

"Come on, man," Mateo says. "You need to chill."

"Fuck you, Mateo," he says. "I'm so done with this town. So done with this shit. And so done with you," he spits in our direction and takes off. The crowd parts to let him go and no one tries to stop him.

No one stops him as he stumbles through the living room.

No one stops him as he crashes through the kitchen.

No one stops him from going out the front door.

And no one stops him as he gets out on the road to walk home.

Summer

Folding my laundry is the only way I can keep calm. There's just something therapeutic about it to me. Something to do. Something to focus on. Making order out of chaos. It works for me.

Unfortunately, the clean clothes basket run out, so I turn my attention to my dresser drawers and pull out all my clothes so I can refold them. As I fold some pajama bottoms in thirds, I glance down at my watch. It's late. Christopher should be home from the arena by now.

He said he would come over.

My mind runs through a thousand scenarios of what happened after I left. Most involve Smitty shooting his mouth off. Christ, I hope I don't get fired. Or worse, I hope Christopher doesn't get punished for any of this. The last thing I ever want to do is interfere with him achieving his hockey goals and dreams. That's been my stance for a long time.

Seems like I just can't help myself.

Stupid.

Reckless.

Thoughtless.

Name a negative adjective and I'll pin it to my sweater.

As I start on my sock drawer, there's finally a loud knock on the door. I cringe because as much as I want to learn what happened, I most definitely don't. Lily answers the door as I wander out of my bedroom.

Christopher stands in the doorway. Instead of his suit, he's wearing a pair of sweats and a sweatshirt. He must have gone home to change before coming over. I figured he'd have a little more urgency to catch up with me or at least text me to let me know, since that's usually his style, but not tonight. Can't say I blame him, I guess.

"Hey," Christopher says to both of us and puts his hands into the front pouch of his hoodie.

"Come in," Lily tells him but he hesitates a little. She looks back at me standing near my bedroom holding a goofy pair of socks and wisely grabs for Luthor's leash. "Perfect timing— this guy needs a walk. Come on, Luthor."

Christopher steps aside for them as they pass and I'm a little surprised he doesn't bend down to give Luthor a pet like he usually does. He's clearly not in a good space and my stomach jumps into my throat.

"Hi," I squeak as he closes the loft door.

"Hi," he greets me again but doesn't move toward me.

"Are we just going to keep saying hello?" I ask.

"I'm sorry," he replies and runs his hand through his hair. "It's been a rough night."

I nod and shift my gaze away from him. "Right. What happened after I left?"

Christopher takes a seat on the couch and presses his palms together between his knees. "I talked to Hawk for a bit."

"Is that all? Did Smitty talk to anyone?"

"No, I don't think so."

I breathe a sigh of relief for his sake and mine.

"Turns out that Smitty is more of a team player than I am," Christopher says as he stares at the coffee table in front of him.

I make my way over to the opposite couch and take a seat across from him. "Don't say that. You're the best team player out there."

He shakes his head and pulls his lips into his mouth. "Not lately, not since..." he trails off.

"Since when?"

He doesn't answer but he doesn't have to. I know the answer. "Since I came back into your life?"

"It's not you, Summer."

"Oh, wow. I never would have taken you for that guy."

"It is me, though," he says and places a hand over his heart. "I just have a hard time finding balance. I want to have it all, I do, but I can't figure out how to make that work."

"Are you breaking up with me?" I ask point blank, because I do not want to drag this out. I want to hear him say the words and then leave so I can crumble into a thousand pieces.

"No, never. Never," he says firmly.

"Then what is this?" I really need to know because everything is just....off.

"This is us just talking. That's all this is," he replies.

"About what exactly?"

"Consequences."

"Consequences?" I ask. It's not a word I take lightly.

"Yes."

"Well, I've spent the better part of my adulthood considering the consequences of my actions and trying to live with them. I've seen therapists. I've talked to a psychic. I've done my best to process consequences."

"I'm not talking about Trey," he says. "I'm talking about me and you and what happens when we get carried away. When I get carried away."

"People die, right?"

Through gritted teeth he says, "I don't want to talk about Trey. I want to talk about what's happening right now."

"Okay, let's talk."

"Fine. Smitty said something strange tonight. He said you had a new assignment. What's going on with work, Summer?"

Fucking Smitty.

"Jim told me that they're not going to have me travel with the team until performance improves and there are actual videos to make again. They also assigned me to assist Maddy with some local social media stuff."

Christopher takes a measured breath. "Were you going to tell me? How did he know, but not me?"

"I was planning on telling you tonight and I don't know how he found out. Maybe Maddy heard the news and told him. I have no idea."

"What about Minnesota? Surely they've got to send you for that trip," he asks, quite frankly flabbergasted.

"Nope. But I'm going to take a few days off work and pay my own way because I wouldn't miss it for the world."

"And they did this because of performance, huh?" Christopher asks and moves to his feet and into the kitchen to get a glass of water. I let him do it. He drinks the entire glass down before speaking again. "Because of me?"

"No, it's the team. It wasn't like an intentional thing about our relationship. They don't even know, as far as I can tell."

"Coach Bliss knows."

"How? When?"

"I was getting lectured awhile ago and he asked point blank. I don't lie to my coach."

I rise to my feet and stand across the kitchen island from him. "That's just great. Did you tell him about the handjob, too?"

"He didn't ask, so no."

"Oh, well thank goodness he didn't ask," I say sarcastically. And drop my head into my hands and mumble, "God, I do the dumbest stuff."

He shakes his head. "Do not blame yourself for that, Summer. I made that happen tonight."

There's more anger in my voice than I intend when I bark, "It takes two to tango, don't forget it."

He cocks an eyebrow and shakes his head again. It's almost infuriating so I change lanes. "So what? Do you think he told management and they've essentially sidelined me?"

"Either way, it's my fault, Summer. That's what I've been trying to say. The team has been terrible because I haven't been doing my part. Because the team is terrible, they don't need your videos anymore. Get it? It's my problem. Believe me when I tell you that I'm not trying to blame you for this. I'm telling you that I need to learn some fucking restraint. That's all."

"Restraint?"

"Yes. For example, if I'd had any form of restraint, I would have had the sense to lock my truck and I wouldn't have lost my puck and maybe all of this would have been better."

"Superstitions are just—"

"Stop!" he says and holds his hand up. "You don't know the whole story."

I stand there for a few seconds and wait to see if he's actually going to tell me *the whole story*.

"That puck, it's not just lucky. It meant something to me."

"Why?" I ask, almost afraid to hear his answer because I somehow already know. Maybe not in specific terms, but I know. He said tonight's conversation wasn't about Trey, but it always comes back to him, doesn't it?

"Trey gave it to me. It was ours together and we agreed to share it, to take turns, and I promised that one day when we got to college, I'd give it back to him."

I wrap my arms around my torso, trying everything to soothe myself from the pain that begins to ripple through me.

He goes on but his voice is trembling. "That day never came, did it? So I held onto it and treasured it. It was like having him with me."

"Christopher." Tears well in my eyes. I never knew, and I thought by this point I knew all there was to know about our tragic tale.

"Now, because of *us*," he says, "I've hurt him again."

A tear slips down my cheek and wipe it away with frustration. "Why didn't you tell me the puck was so special after you lost it? I just thought it was a stupid puck that you were convinced helped you win."

"It wasn't a stupid puck. Not at all. And I didn't tell you because we'd finally been able to overcome our past. I didn't want you to slide back down into it. I was finally able to have you and I didn't want to stop, no matter the consequences."

Consequences. We've come back around to that, haven't we?

"So now what?" I ask, totally unsure of where we actually stand.

"I need to do something I should have done years ago. The team has a mental health therapist on hand. Alex Hawkins recommended him, and I think I'm going to talk to him."

"I think talking to someone is a good idea," I tell him because it's the right thing to say, even though it makes me worry for the most selfish of reasons. If the therapist helps Christopher change himself—most likely for the better—will Christopher still feel the same way about me? God, I hope so.

He circles around the kitchen island and takes hold of my hands. "I might need a little space to work all this out."

"Space?" I ask and my breath goes short.

"I know what you're thinking. It's not like that," he assures me. "I just need to focus on hockey a bit and sort my shit out. But you have to know, Summer, that I never want to leave you. Come what may...this is it for me."

"This is it for me too," I reply and pray that just like Coach Bliss, Christopher would never tell me a lie.

Summer

Winter Formal, Senior Year

"Shit," Tia says to me as we continue to let the dust settle. "My keys are in Trey's pocket and I left my purse in the car."

"It's okay. I'm sure Christopher doesn't mind giving you a ride home."

"That's good, because I had a couple of beers while playing beer pong anyway."

I nod and then shake my head as tears well in my eyes again. "I can't believe that just happened with Trey."

"I know," she says and hugs me. "I'm so sorry. I didn't know it was a secret. I regret telling him so much."

"He was going to find out sooner than later. Who knows if his sober reaction would be any better? I feel like he hates me, Tia."

"He's your cousin. He'll come back around, Summer. And trust me, you did nothing wrong at all."

"He definitely does not feel that way."

"Well, I know it's not the same thing at all, but I don't think it's going to work out with me and Trey. When I told him about Christopher's choice and asked if he would be attending UMN, he made it abundantly clear that he would not. He almost seemed disgusted by the notion. He's just not that into me, obviously."

"I'm afraid you're right," I tell her, and now it's my turn to hug her. "It seems like he's only got hockey on the brain. You know how these boys can be." I don't mention the depths of Trey's confrontation nor his feelings about Christopher.

"Not your boy," she says and smiles. "You've got a good one."

"I don't know," I reply. "I mean, yeah on the surface of things—yes. But maybe Trey is right. Maybe Christopher isn't thinking with his head. Maybe BU would be better for his career. If we wanted to stay together, we could make it work long distance. I just hate that we did this to Trey. I honestly had no idea that we were hurting him so badly."

"How could you know? All you were doing was falling for Christopher. You had no idea anything of this could happen."

I glance over at Christopher, who's helping Mateo clean up the house. "Yeah, I guess you're right. I just hope our thoughtless actions don't cause too much damage to their friendship. They've been friends since they were little kids. They can get over it, right?"

Tia is just about to respond when we hear sirens wailing down the highway, with red and blue lights flooding the front living room.

"Shit," Mateo shouts. "Someone called the cops on us."

Christopher, Mateo, and a few of their other teammates go to work putting away all the alcohol as quickly as they can, but there's also a keg and empty plastic cups just about everywhere. Tia and I start dashing around the room to pick them up.

"We're so busted," Mateo goes on.

Christopher looks scared shitless, and it doesn't take a dummy to figure out why. His season could be over if we get caught with all this, which is really unfair because he didn't even want to be here. He only did it because I asked him to.

Ugh.

Everything is my fault. Absolutely everything.

It takes longer than it should for us to realize that the sirens have passed us and there's no more light. They didn't stop. Mateo opens the door and looks out to see if we're that lucky.

"They passed by us," he says.

Christopher visibly relaxes and shakes his head. And that's when I know that we should go. We shouldn't stick around here just in case they come back. This was Mateo's idea. Mateo's party. Mateo's choices. Mateo can clean it up.

"Chris, take us home, will ya?" I ask and he nods, as if we're on the same wavelength.

The three of us get into the truck and it take a few minutes for the car to warm up and for Christopher to chip off the ice on the windshield. Sometimes I hate this place too, and my sadness for Trey rears its ugly head again. Even though he said some truly hateful things to me tonight, it still makes me feel terrible that I slapped him. I hate it. I wish I could take it back. I wish I had noticed how he felt about me and Christopher. I'll have to bring him jelly donuts tomorrow. He'll be so hung over, he'll probably kick them across the room, but I don't care. That's even if he opens the door to talk to me.

Christopher gets back into the truck and we're all nicely packed into the front of cab. He squeezes my knee before he puts the car into gear and slowly pulls onto the highway. I'm so rattled from the confrontation with Trey to even enjoy what Christopher has done.

"I'll take Tia home first," he says, and I'm relieved. I think Christopher and I should talk about everything.

"Thanks, Big Mac," she says and presses her side against mine for more warmth. "I'm really sorry, by the way. I didn't know it was a secret, but that doesn't change it. I should have thought more about him and you, and everything besides just thinking about what it could mean to me."

"It's not your fault," Christopher says. "It's mine. I should have told him a while ago. I was just afraid."

Afraid. It's an admission I wasn't expecting. Clearly he's been really struggling with all of this. And that makes me feel even worse. If his decision to go to UMN is about me, then Trey is probably right. What have I done to Christopher to cause him to change his plans so drastically?

This really is all my fault. I just hope Trey forgives me for it one day. And Christopher too, when he comes to his senses.

On the highway back toward town, we're stunned silent by all the flashing lights and cars and people.

"Oh no," Tia says plainly. "I wonder what happened?"

"Looks like an accident," Christopher says as he inches us closer.

It's hard to see anything in the confusion, but deep down in my gut I already know and I already want to scream and cry. But first there are the motions, the things we must see to believe it.

The first hint is single black dress shoe abandoned off the side of the road.

And then the stranger's car spun around in the wrong direction.

The broken headlights flickering in no discernible pattern.

The shattered glass that's reflecting it all.

The white rose boutonnière lying in the snow that's been stained red.

I've seen enough to put the pieces together. I've seen enough to last me a lifetime of sorrow and regret.

I don't remember what happens next. I just find myself outside of the truck, standing in the snow, staring at the scene before me, and all alone.

Later, I'm lying with my head on Momma's lap and she strokes my hair slowly in a rhythm that I can tolerate, only just barely. Occasionally, I feel the small splash of a tear falling off her face onto mine. I don't do anything to wipe the wetness away. We stay like this in silence for so long, I don't know if it's still the same night or not.

All I know is that Trey is gone and it's all my fault.

11

Christopher

Dr. Lawrence's office is in a swanky shared workspace in Cherry Creek. I'm a little nervous about sitting the waiting room, afraid that I'll be recognized and someone will put two and two together. I'm not ashamed of seeing a therapist, but it's no one's business beyond my coach, my teammates, and Summer.

More than anything, I'm doing this for her...maybe more than for myself. But I think that may be why I'm here, right?

A man walks down the hall out into the waiting area. He's a big guy, like he could have played professional basketball. I have no idea it's Dr. Lawrence until he looks in my direction and asks, "Christopher?"

"Hi, yes. Dr. Lawrence?" I get to my feet and reach out my hand to shake his.

"Call me James."

He has a corner office that's more cluttered than I'd expect, but seems comfortable. There are armchairs and a couch to choose from. For the sake of breaking stereotypes I avoid the couch.

"Is this your first time talking to a therapist?" he begins.

My face warms from embarrassment. It's been a long time since I was new at anything. "Afraid so, and you'll wonder how I avoided it for so long after you hear my story."

"No judgement at all. There are so many reasons why that could be the case, the least of which is that you're a professional athlete who's been focused on seeing physical therapists and not ones for your mental health. I'm just trying to get a sense of your experience level so I can ease you into it."

"Yeah, that's pretty much it," I tell him.

"So let me tell you how this is going to work. These are your sessions. So I'm here just to listen, talk you through it, and offer some strategies."

"Right, okay."

"How about I give you a little background on me, so you don't feel like you're talking to a perfect stranger."

"That would be nice."

"I've got my degrees on the wall, those probably aren't what you're interested in. You want to know if I can relate? Well, no situation is the same, but I did play basketball in college and was in the NBA for two seasons before I blew out my knee and couldn't come back from it. Thankfully I had that degree to fall back on and I went back to school to pursue this, because at one point I needed someone like me to help me through some tough times."

"Who'd you play for?"

"Boston," he answers.

I smile. I remember him from my time in college. "Get out! The Leap?"

"That's me."

"I went to a couple of your games when I was at BU. You were awesome."

"Most of the time, yes. Not all of the time and that's okay."

"I'm sorry about your injury. That must have sucked."

"It did at the time. I thought the world had ended, but it obviously didn't. Now I get to work with athletes and push them toward their own form of excellence, and that is incredibly rewarding."

"I can imagine. That's one of the things I like about being a captain. I love lifting up those around me. I know it's not the same thing."

"It's something that defines you and that's what we're here to uncover and explore. So tell me, Christopher, why are you here today?"

I tug at the hair on the back of my head as I think of how to distill down what's been going on. "Well, I'm not sure if you did any homework on me, but last year I was league MVP and I helped the Storm win the Cup."

"Congratulations."

"Thanks. Well, if you take a look at my stats this season, you'll understand why I'm here. I haven't been playing my best."

"Okay, and what do you think therapy can do to improve your stats?"

"I know it's a long shot, but maybe you could flip some switch in my head to make me better?"

"Wouldn't that be nice? Unfortunately, it doesn't quite work that way."

I laugh a little. "I was afraid of that."

"What's different between this season and last season?"

I might as well just come right out with it. "Her name is Summer and I love her."

"You met someone new?"

"No. I've known her since we were ten years old, when she moved to my hometown in Minnesota."

"And how long have you loved her?"

"Since I was ten years old."

He chuckles. "So...how is it different?"

"We parted ways our senior year, each going to different colleges. We basically fell away from one another. Then this summer I went back home with the Cup and we reconnected. Long story short, I convinced her to move out to Denver and take a job with the Storm. She did. We became neighbors and she quickly became my everything."

He scribbles on a notepad I didn't even notice he was holding.

"Your everything?"

"Yes," I reply. "Which I think if we look back over time is kind of par for the course when it comes to her."

"Let's look back over time, then."

I swallow hard. Knowing that we're entering Trey territory so fast concerns me. I'd rather stay in the present because the present is the problem. "Okay, what do you want to know?"

"Tell me about her. How did she become your everything?"

"Well, when she moved to Fossebridge it was just after her dad died serving in Iraq. She was shy and a little bit scared to be in a new place, and I had this feeling I can't describe. I just wanted to make her happy right away. Her cousin, Trey, was my best friend, so I got to know her through him."

"You're not friends with Trey anymore?"

"He died. A while ago."

"Oh, I'm sorry to hear that. Is that why you and Summer lost touch? You didn't have that connection anymore?"

"Not exactly," I tell him and rub a hand down the stubble on my face.

He scribbles a few more notes.

"Anyway, Summer is like the quintessential girl next door. I fell hard for her in high school."

"That's not really getting to the heart of the matter. You said that she's your everything. What does that mean to you?"

"It means that she's my morning, noon, and night. It means that I want to be near her all the time. And it means that I can't focus on much else."

"Including hockey?"

"Hockey's different. Or at least it used to be. When I was in high school, I was able to perform on the ice because I knew she was watching and I wanted to impress her."

"If she works for the team, isn't she watching now?"

"Yes."

"So not to sound like a broken record, but what's different?"

"I guess not much is different," I answer and scratch my head a little bit. "I think I'm making selfish choices because of how I feel about her. Choices that could have bad consequences, just like when..."

Dr. Lawrence presses his pen against his chin and remains quiet.

"Trey died." My throat is thick like there's cardboard lodged in it. I expect Dr. Lawrence to ask follow-up questions and jot down more notes. He does neither. He just continues to listen.

"If I hadn't decided to follow Summer to UMN, then Trey wouldn't have gotten so mad and he wouldn't have left the party to walk home and get hit by that car. Not only did I lose my best friend, but I also lost Summer then too, because I wasn't making the right choices. And now…" My head falls to my shoulder while I grip my hands tightly. "And now…" I try again but I can't make myself say the words.

He picks it up for me. "You're worried you'll lose her again, and maybe hockey this time too?"

"Yes," I confess. "They're my two loves."

Summer is twirling around her bedroom just like she used to do when she was waitressing at the Biscuit. This time, instead of slinging burgers and onion rings, she's packing for the Minnesota trip. From my vantage point on the bed, it looks like she's an over-packer. She's using one of her bigger suitcases and tossing things into it like she's fleeing the country after committing a crime.

"Do you really need to take that?" I ask, pointing to the swimsuit in her hand.

"Just in case," she says and picks up some flip flops off the floor.

"You're going to Fossebridge. In December. I'm pretty sure that Webster Lake is frozen over by this point."

She giggles. "I was thinking more about the hotel we're all staying at in Minneapolis. They've got a pretty cool-looking indoor pool."

"Ah, that makes more sense," I say and lean back against her headboard.

She flicks some hair out of her eyes and slowly spins around the room looking for anything else she might be forgetting. Rays of Colorado winter sunshine beam in through the windows to spotlight her. I soak in this moment, taking advantage of her focus, so I can admire her beauty and appreciate that I get to be in this room with her.

God, I'm going to miss her while we're apart. The next time I see her will be at the Minnesota game.

But even I can admit that having this space between us could be helpful for me. I've been working on some new strategies that Dr. Lawrence recommended. Instead of pining for Summer on the last road trip, I focused on my routine. I was the first player at every optional skate and the last to leave, giving words of encouragement to each guy as they stepped off the ice. I also gave myself a purpose—to do whatever I could do to win the game. For her. For my team. For the fans. But mostly for me, because when I give it my everything, I can be okay with the outcome.

That's not the only thing we've been working on. We've touched on Trey a couple of times. I told him the story of what went down from my perspective, about losing the puck and how that's spiked my guilt reflexes again, and that's when he suggested that Summer come in so we can talk through it together.

"Where's his office?" she asks as she zips up her suitcase. I'm going to take her to the airport right after we meet with him.

"Cherry Creek."

"Great, so not that far."

"Nope."

"Shall we?" she asks and places her hands on her hips as she takes one last look around her room.

"Let's do it," I reply and grab the handle of her suitcase. "Are you nervous?"

"I'd be lying if I said no. I'm not new to therapy, so it's not that exactly," she says as if she's trying to figure out what's making her nervous about it.

I take a guess. "It's that we're doing it together?"

She smiles and leans into me. "I think that may be it."

"You don't have to do this," I tell her and drop my forehead to hers.

She smiles up at me. "True, we could just run away together instead. Go to Fiji, never come back. How does that sound?"

It sure as hell sounds tempting to me.

She shakes her head. "But no, this will be good for us."

"Probably right."

"Are you sure you don't want to come to Fossebridge for Christmas?" she asks me again about my decision to return to Denver between the Minnesota game on the 23rd and our home game on the 27th against Dallas. I traditionally have spent Christmas focused on hockey. I don't think this year should be different.

"I think that with everything going on, it's for the best if I use that time to work with my trainers and get my head back in the game. I'm sorry," I tell her because I genuinely am sorry that we won't be together for the holiday.

"Don't be sorry. Of course it's okay. I know how much you're trying right now. I totally understand."

I pull her into a hug and squeeze her tightly. "We'll have next Christmas, I promise."

"I'll hold you to that, Big Mac."

Summer

Christopher's hand is planted firmly on my thigh as we sit side-by-side on Dr. Lawrence's couch. I'm not sure he's aware of how much pressure he's using, but I don't mind. In fact, I'd prefer he didn't let me go, especially now while I'm in the middle of recalling what happened with Trey from my perspective. I'm glad he's next to me, holding on, like an anchor that I need in a turbulent sea of emotions.

"Trey was an emotional guy. I sat by for his wild antics and overblown frustrations. But I also got to ride along for fun adventures and fits of laughter. I reaped the rewards from going along with the silly ideas he had. That's why when I look back on what happened, I get so upset. The problem was right in front of me. He was quiet, which wasn't normal at all. It annoyed me more than concerned me, especially the night of the Winter Formal. Before he put all that alcohol into himself, he was eerily quiet. It should have concerned me, but instead it just annoyed me. I thought it was taking away from my time with Christopher. Maybe if I had been concerned instead of being so selfish, I could have prevented all this."

"Is that what you really think?" Christopher asks me.

I quickly reply, "Yes, that's what I really think."

Christopher shakes his head and looks down at his feet.

Dr. Lawrence sits totally still, as if he's observing wildlife from afar, afraid that the slightest movement might scare us away from this discussion.

"Do you think you could have prevented it?" I ask Christopher.

"Absolutely. I could have prevented it easily," he replies.

A chill runs down my spine. "How's that?"

With complete confidence, he says, "All I had to do was be honest with him about my feelings for you, especially when I made my decision to go to UMN."

"Huh," I murmur, honestly surprised by his answer, because I was expecting him to say that he would have done so many more things than just be honest with him.

"What?"

"Nothing, I just expected you to say something else."

He squints his eyes. "What did you think I was going to say?"

"Honestly?"

"That's all I ever want," he answers.

"I thought you would say you could have prevented it by not choosing UMN, or not going to the dance with me, or even not liking me," I tell him, unable to meet his eyes.

"You think those are things I could have *easily* done? Not like you? Not be with you? Are you kidding me, Summer?"

"I don't know, yeah. Maybe I'm not..." I hesitate to complete my thought out loud. We've dug to the roots of *me*, where all the insecurities and doubts are snarled and difficult to excavate.

"It's okay, Summer. You can say whatever is on your mind," Dr. Lawrence chimes in.

My bottom lip trembles as I start again. "Maybe I'm not worth it."

Christopher shakes his head and simply says, "No. No." He lifts my hand to his lips and kisses it with urgency. "You're worth everything to me."

"But I ruin things for you."

"Never, Summer. Never."

"What about hockey? What about peanut butter and jelly waffles, and chocolate ice cream, and oversleeping, and quickies in the locker room? What about all the ways I've distracted you? What about your puck? All of that is on me," I argue with a hand placed over my heart.

"Stop, that's not your fault. Not even a little bit. That's why I'm here, to work all that out. It's on me."

"Well, I certainly ruined things for Trey, didn't I? He couldn't be more clear about that."

He opens his mouth to argue, but nothing comes out.

I swallow hard and wipe away a few more tears. "See?"

Christopher's eyes are wet too, and I hate that we've come here and surfaced this tragedy once again. Two steps forward. One step back.

Dr. Lawrence clears his throat and starts fussing with a desk drawer. "I want to ask you guys a question and instead of answering it out loud, I want you to write it down on this piece of paper," he says and hands us each a sheet and a pen. "Don't read each other's answers."

We both nod and get ready.

"For this question, imagine that Trey had never disapproved and is still with us."

The idea seems impossible. My life has been divided in two parts. The time before Trey died and the time after. I've been in the second part for so long, it's hard to revert to a time when my relationship with Christopher was...pure.

"What happens the day after the dance? Describe it for me."

Christopher doesn't think on it long before he starts scribbling. It's not nearly that easy for me. Try as I might, I can't imagine it because I can't escape what actually happened. As horrific and tragic as Trey's death was, the next day was even worse for me. And that thought makes me feel even more guilty, for I was so scared that the boy I loved was going to be taken from me, too. And it was on that day that I ultimately pushed Christopher to Boston for so many reasons—one of which was because I didn't want to do anything else to hurt him.

So no, I can't imagine it and the page stays blank.

Doctor Lawrence is watching me but doesn't seem to be upset that I'm not doing his exercise.

"One more question for good measure. Would you two still be together today?"

That one I can answer. That one I know. Somehow I've always known, despite everything.

In big block letters, I write the word YES and look up at Dr. Lawrence. He gives me a slight smile and flicks his gaze over to

Christopher, so I do too. I see on his page that he's written the word "yes" as well, just below a big paragraph, which must be his answer from the first question. I can't help but smile as my heart pitter-patters at the sight of those three little letters.

Dr. Lawrence raises his hands in the air and says, "And that's all that matters. You choose to be together. You always have, and while I'm not an expert at couples counseling, I've got a pretty good feeling that you always will."

Christopher nods and takes hold of my hand.

"Now, like I told you, my specialty isn't exactly this type of therapy, but hopefully we've made a little bit of progress today. Summer, if I may, I can refer you to a great therapist that can help you address some of these issues you surfaced today. You both experienced a trauma and I think some progress could be made to desensitize the memories and let go of the guilt you both are carrying."

"I would like that, thank you," I reply and mean it. I'm so ready to move on from that fateful night.

"Back to what I do specialize in—one of the most effective ways to achieve your goals is to have your life in balance. Christopher, you've said that Summer is your everything and you've said that hockey is your everything."

Christopher shrugs. "Yeah, I'm not sure how that works."

"I'm glad you said it and I didn't have to. So that's your homework, young man. I want you to think about how you can have both and be happy to the fullest of your potential, but understanding that 'everything' is an impossible feat."

Christopher's lips form a thin straight line as he runs his hands through his hair. For the first time since he's been back in my life, he doesn't look like he has all the answers. All I can hope is that he figures it out soon, for the sake of his team and for the sake of my heart.

The drive to the airport is a little more quiet than usual. Christopher seems lost in thought, which I suppose makes sense after Dr. Lawrence's assignment. Regardless, it makes me a little nervous that maybe he won't be able to solve it. Maybe the only way for him to be successful at hockey is to give up on us.

Impossible.

At least that's what I tell myself.

As I stare at the desolate plains out east of Denver, I think back to Dr. Lawrence's question about the day after the Winter Formal. Christopher wrote so much on his page. It's like he always had a plan about how that day was supposed to go, almost like he had it memorized. It clearly wasn't the first time he had thought about it. I'd love to know what he wrote down, even if it brings up the very worst memories I have about what really happened that day.

I turn my gaze back over to him. He's got his left leg bent at the knee, propped up against the door and he rests his elbow on it as he drives with just his right hand. It's easy to get distracted by how handsome he looks in these little moments, when he doesn't even know I'm watching. He's still so lost in thought and a part of me doesn't want to interrupt, but this is the last time I'm going to see him before we meet up again in Minnesota, so I go for it. "Hey," I start.

He startles the tiniest bit and looks over at me briefly

before turning his eyes back to the road. "Hey, sorry. Did I miss something?"

"No," I reply and smile at how cute he is. "I was just wondering something."

"What's that, Gunderson?" he says so sweetly.

"You don't have to tell me if you don't want to, but I'm wondering what you wrote on that piece of paper back in Dr. Lawrence's office."

"Oh, um..." he stammers.

"Like I said, you don't have to tell me if you don't want to."

He shifts positions and takes hold of my hand. "No, I do want to. It just might seem silly now."

"I love silly," I tell him.

"Well then you might love this," he replies with that Christopher grin I adore so much. "We'd stay up all night talking and then when Schoop's Bakery opened, we'd get some of your favorite jelly donuts and watch the sunrise from my truck."

"Oh my God, I would love one of those right now."

"Gunderson, I'm guessing you want one of those pretty much all the time."

"No lie there."

He laughs a little and goes on. "After that, I'd take you home and we'd get a little rest, and then I'd pick you up that afternoon and we'd go skating on Webster Lake. I'd hold your hand the whole time and catch you if you fall."

"Hey, I'm an excellent skater," I argue as I try to pull my hand out of his grasp out in mock disgust.

He doesn't let go. "I know you are, Gunderson. We'd just be each other's safety nets. That's what I meant."

"Then what?" I ask.

"We'd go to the Biscuit and work on our homework together while sitting in my favorite booth, and I'd reach across the table and take your hand in mine and ask you to be my girlfriend." He swallows hard and the mood shifts unexpectedly to somber. "And you'd say yes...at least that was always my hope. Then, on Monday morning, I'd pick you up for school and we'd walk in together and let the whole world know that we belonged to one another. That was always my plan."

So, I was right. He had thought about it, even before the incident with Trey happened. My God, how different that day turned out to be. It was nothing like that and my heart aches for what we lost. Not only Trey, but the missed opportunity at the kind of happiness Christopher dreamed up for us.

"It sounds like a perfect day," I say sadly.

Christopher nods solemnly as he veers right at the fork to go to the East Terminal where my airline is. Our time is running out and I dread leaving him so much. I'll see him for the Minnesota game, but after that he'll come back here for Christmas. I understand his reasoning because he's at a critical turning point. The team has been on the upswing and I don't want to interfere with that. I just wish it wasn't an either-or situation.

He pulls over in front of the sliding glass doors of the terminal, puts the truck into park, and hops out. It's a chilly day in Denver, but the sun shines so brightly that it's still hard to see even with sunglasses on. Our breath billows in the cold air and I zip up my coat a little bit more while he pulls my bags out of the cab of the truck and puts them on the curb for me.

"Okay, so I'll see you at the game," I tell him.

"Yep."

"But I know how those games are for you, so if I don't get to talk to you before or after, I totally get it. I just want to tell you good luck and I hope you can figure all this out. Just know that I'm here for you, whatever the answer might be. Merry Christmas, Christopher." The lump in my throat is overwhelming as I try not to cry.

I half expect him to say, "nah we'll talk and spend time together, don't worry." But he doesn't. He pulls me into a hug and replies, "Merry Christmas, Summer."

We kiss once and he lets me go. I grab for my bags and head into the terminal, looking back over my shoulder. He hasn't moved from where I left him. He just watches with an unreadable expression on his face. A sinking feeling weighs down my belly. It's one I've had before, long ago, when I knew we were at the precipice of a change. Once again, a catalyst has pushed us out of our current state. But this time, I'm not sure if we're moving forward together or apart.

Christopher

The Day after the Winter Formal, Senior Year

Whiskey. It's what Trey liked to drink. I don't understand why, but that's what he liked so that's what I'm drinking now too. He liked me too for some reason and I certainly don't understand why. All I did was fail him. I failed my best friend.

The whiskey burns a lot. It hurts. But it doesn't burn enough. It doesn't come close to hurting me as much as I deserve.

I drink and drink, which defeats the purpose. The more I drink, the less it burns. The more I drink, the less it hurts.

But it does nothing for making me miss Summer less. I haven't talked to her and I haven't seen her since last night. Everything at the crash site was chaotic and horrific and I lost her. When I looked around for her, she was gone, almost as if she had never been there in the first place. As if she was maybe just a figment of my imagination all these years.

I need to see her. I need to hold her and tell her that none of this is her fault. It was all mine. All of it.

The walk to her house is long and cold, and it gives me way too much time to think. But my thoughts are circular and fuzzy, and all I keep going through over and over again is how badly I messed up and how much I want to see her again, which makes me think about how badly I messed up.

I have no idea what time it is, but it must be getting close to dawn because the sun is beginning to rise. Dawn on a new day that I don't want to face.

When I get to her house, I stand in front of it and stare. I've been here so many times to drop her off, but I've never been inside. I've never quite crossed the threshold. Somehow, Summer just always seems beyond my reach—especially now. Her yard might as well be a moat between me and her front door.

I thought I had it all figured out. I thought I could have it all, but he's gone now. He's gone. And I worry that she's gone, too.

All my plans are unraveling.

I fall to my knees on the edge of her snow-covered lawn

and drop my face into my hands. I've lost the two people I love most in this world.

I have no idea how long I stay like that, sobbing into my hands, or how it comes to be that someone is there and holding me. It takes me a while to realize that the touch is familiar and that the lines of her body are ones that I know better than anybody's. Am I hallucinating? Did Summer hear me? Did she come to me?

When I open my eyes and look around, there's no one there.

It wasn't real.

My head feels fuzzy and I'm tired, so tired.

I lie down on her lawn because I just can't keep going.

It's all over.

A monitor is beeping and there's a lot of light.

I'm cold to the core but I'm being weighed down by something warm. My arm hurts, like it's being pricked.

I try to move but my limbs are weak. Voices and voices and voices are all around me but they could be speaking Turkish for all I know. It's confusing and I want to go back to sleep, so I do.

"Christopher?"

Someone is calling for me but their voice is muffled. Maybe I'm under water? Maybe I'm in Webster Lake?

"Chris," the person tries again and it comes in clearer this time.

My eyelids are as heavy as sandbags. They're nearly impossible to open, but I try anyway.

A different voice says, "He's stirring. I'll call his mom."

"Mom?" I say in my fog. A bright light shines above me and I still can't see the faces of those that are with me.

"It's okay, honey. I'm calling your parents. They just had to run home for a bit." She's got a southern accent and my brain puts two and two together. It's Summer's mom.

Summer.

Memories of last night come in sharp slices. The dance. The party. The kiss. The fight. The accident.

Trey.

Pain ripples through my body, but it's not the physical pain I'm used to when I get knocked down. I clench and try to fight it off, but it's stronger than I am. In the battle between mind over matter, I don't know which side I'm on. I rub my eyes to clear away the clouds and lift my head. Summer's mom is stepping out of the room and I'm alone...or so I thought, when suddenly someone is touching my arm.

I expect a nurse. I expect a doctor or a friend or a coach. I don't know why I didn't expect it to be Summer, since her mom is here. In my heart it feels like I lost her too.

"Hey." She clears her throat and sits down in a chair next to my hospital bed.

"What happened? Why am I here?" I ask.

She sighs and shakes her head. "Do you remember the accident?" Her voice is so quiet I can barely hear her.

"Yeah," I groan.

"After we saw what happened to Trey, you came over to my house."

Another sharp slice of memory and I remember.

"I was tired," I tell her.

"We found you on the snow. We don't know how long you were there..." Her voice trails off and the wet in her eyes mirrors mine. "You nearly died from hypothermia."

"I'm sorry." I don't know how two tiny words could possibly cover my litany of sins, but it's a start.

"Don't apologize," she says and shakes her head while clearly holding back some emotions.

"I'm so sorry," I try again and hold out my arms for her. She hesitates for a few seconds and then leans over into them.

She weeps against my shoulder while I press my face against her neck.

"We killed him. If we hadn't made him so upset, he wouldn't have stormed off and been hit by that car," she says. "We killed him."

"No, no. You didn't. You didn't do anything, Summer. This is all my fault. I just...I was just greedy. I wanted to be with you."

"I wanted to be with you too, but we didn't think of anyone else."

"It was me. I did it," I tell her in as tough a voice as I can muster.

Her breathing shallows and I squeeze her tighter so she remembers that I'm here.

"Christopher." It sounds like a request, like she's begging me for something. "We have to make this right."

"How, Summer? How can we fix this when we can't bring him back?"

"You have to play for him now that he can't play for himself. You have to go to Boston. It's the only way to make this right. Get back on the course you were supposed to be on together."

"No, Summer," I cry. The idea of being apart from her now too is unbearable. If I got to Boston, all of this—all of this—would be for nothing. "I can't. I can't do it."

Her eyes are wild and her heart beats rapidly against my chest. "Yes, Chris, you can. You've got to do what's right. And if you don't do it for Trey, do it for yourself. Make your dreams come true for the both of you."

I shake my head and she just nods and then I see it there, in her eyes and I feel it from her heart. Everything is different now. Our road forks here. I bite down on my lip as tears stream down the sides of my face. I will give her whatever she wants and this is what she wants. "Okay, Summer."

She nods and starts to cry again. It's a sob this time and the same for me. We hold each other as long as we can, because we both know that this is the last time.

12

Summer

TIA AND I ARE LUMPED TOGETHER ON THE COUCH UNDER A
fleece blanket, watching the latest craze in celebrity talent
shows and trying our best to guess who's wearing a red and
green sparkly penguin costume. He's singing a Christmas
classic and we're singing along, very poorly, between spouting
off our theories on who it might be.

She blurts out, "Oh, I think it's Tom Cruise."

"That person is easily six feet tall. Not a chance. And what
on earth would he being doing on this crummy show?"

"I don't know, he's a competitive type of guy. Maybe he'd
give it a go."

"You're hilarious," I tell her and take a drink of the spiked
eggnog she brought over for our sleepover. It's the first time
we've been able to properly hang out since I got to Fossebridge
two days ago.

"Speaking of the competitive type, how's Christopher?" she asks and swirls around the eggnog in her glass.

"Oh, you know. As Christopher as ever."

"Mmhmm. Oh, Benicio Del Toro!" she exclaims.

"Tia, this show isn't getting that kind of talent."

"Well, he's making commercials these days, so who knows?"

My phone buzzes beneath my butt and I hope it's a text from Christopher before I remember that he's playing right now. That being said, I'm surprised to see it's Maddy.

Maddy: *Are you watching tonight's game?*

Summer: *No, I'm busy with a friend. What's up?*

Maddy: *Christopher is on fire tonight. He's got two goals and I bet you before the night is over, he'll have a hat trick.*

I could never be upset at Christopher's success, but my heart cracks at the edges. It really does seem like I have a bad effect on him. Now that I'm away, he's able to do what he does best and win hockey games.

Summer: *No way, that's awesome!*

Maddy: *Wish you were in Pittsburgh with us.*

Summer: *I wish I was too, but I'll see you tomorrow in Minneapolis.*

"Something wrong?" Tia asks me.

I dodge that question, not wanting to reveal what a shitty girlfriend I am. "Mind if we turn on the Storm game?"

"Of course not," Tia says. "I didn't know they were playing tonight. Why are we watching this instead?"

Fiddling with the remotes gives me the perfect excuse not to may eye contact with her when I say, "I don't know...it's just all a little painful right now."

"Summer, what's going on?" Tia asks and grabs the remote out of my hand. "I've always been able to tell when you're feeling stressed or worried. Did something bad happen with Christopher?"

"Just turn on the game and I'll tell you."

Tia grumbles something under her breath and she flips the channel over.

There's two minutes left in the third and the game is tied 3-3. It's the Storm's first time facing Pittsburgh since winning game seven in the final. Seeing Grinblat in the net gives me goosebumps as I remember Christopher's game-winning goal against him. It was a thing of beauty. "Two of those goals are Christopher's," I tell her with pride, as if they were my own accomplishment.

"Oh man, I'm sad we missed it."

"Me too," I reply as I watch the two teams go back and forth across the ice. It's up and down hockey right now as each team tries it's hardest to put some plays together and get the two points before the clock runs out. Christopher comes onto the ice after a change and quickly steals the puck from a Pittsburgh forward. He starts on a breakaway down the ice. It's just like game seven! This time though, that same Pittsburgh player chases him down and dives out to try to steal back the puck, but ends up tripping Christopher, ruining his chances. The ref's whistle blows and he raises his crossed arms above his head and then points to center ice.

"Oh wow," I blurt out.

"What does that mean?" Tia asks.

"Christopher gets to take a penalty shot."

"Nice," Tia says and we both lean forward in our seats as

Christopher starts circling center ice, waiting for the ref's whistle.

The TV announcers do their bit. "If MacCormack scores, this will be his third goal of the night but only his seventh goal of the season. The league MVP has been going through quite a slump lately, but as he said in his pregame interview, he's been turning that around lately with some new focus strategies."

"What do you think that means, partner?" the play-by-play announcer asks.

"Well, I do know it can be quite a head game after winning the Cup and being league MVP to live up to your own personal standards."

The whistle blows and the play-by-play guy goes on. "Mac-Cormack will pick it up at center ice, coming in slow on Lucas Grinblat. He's going wide and he scores!"

Both Tia and I throw our arms into the air and shout, "Yes!"

"It's a hat trick for the captain, who is definitely back on his game tonight."

A few more hats than I would expect fly from the stands onto the ice while Christopher fist bumps his way down the Colorado Storm bench.

"Damn, a hat trick. Way to go, Mac," Tia says and does a little dance.

"Yeah!" I exclaim, but as the clock ticks down and the final buzzer sounds, my emotions are bubbling over. I'm simultaneously happy and heartbroken. Tears fill my eyes as the team crowds around Christopher to celebrate his outstanding play.

"Why are you crying? They won," Tia points out.

"Because he played so well and it was wonderful. But it was

also without me. His slump they were talking about...that was all my fault, and I'm afraid he's going to leave me behind as he probably should."

"Summer," Tia says and puts an arm around me. "That's total nonsense."

"No, it's not. He can't manage both. There's no way he can have a relationship with me and be a Hall of Fame hockey player."

"The Christopher I know would never give you up, you understand that, right?"

"He did once before. After Trey died, he left for Boston and never came back for me."

"Did you expect him to, when you're the person who told him to go?"

"Yes...no. I don't know."

"Well he did come back, Summer. And I have a feeling that he won't be letting go this time."

"Everything is so mixed up right now. All the Trey stuff has resurfaced again and I just wonder when we'll be able to really let it go. How did you let it go? You moved on years ago."

"It wasn't easy at first. I used to obsess over every little detail and blamed myself for his death. I'm the one that told him about Christopher's decision to go to UMN. Amongst many other things that happened before that. Do you remember that day back in college when I got in the fender bender?"

"Yeah."

"Well, you probably don't remember it in as much detail, but everything was going wrong for me before it happened and my reaction was to lash out at people. I was also drinking to try to and ease all my stress and not keeping up on my classwork. I was even skipping class. And then one afternoon, I got a test grade back that was woeful. I was so pissed that I decided I was going to head back to Fossebridge for the weekend, so I grabbed a bag and got in the car and took off like a hotheaded lunatic. Sure enough, I rear-ended someone almost immediately. And while I was dealing with the officer at the scene, all I could do was think about how all of this happened *to me*. But then the cop said something that broke it down for me. He said something like, 'Since this was your fault, I have to write you a ticket.'

"My first reaction was to be super pissed. How could this be my fault? But then when he handed it over. I realized that, yeah, it totally was my doing. No one made me get behind the wheel of the car. No one told me to drive when I wasn't in the right headspace for it. No one. It was my choice to take off. And you know what? Same goes for Trey. We didn't kick him out of the house. We didn't tell him to walk home on that highway. We didn't send him to his death."

"We didn't stop him, either," I argue.

"We're not some omniscient higher being that could have known what was going to happen to him. We should cut ourselves some slack. We were just children back then."

"Sometimes I wonder if we still are," I reply and shake my head.

She laughs a little. "It does feel that way, sometimes. Then I get my credit card bill."

"Ain't that the truth."

"Speaking of adult stuff...how's work going? I noticed you

haven't been posting that many videos lately. I saw the Santa one. Tell me that wasn't your creation."

"Ha, no. That was my boss's brilliant idea. But it actually turned out pretty well."

"I will say that seeing old Big Mac in an elf costume made my year," she says and reaches out for her cup. We cheer to that and finish off our cups of eggnog. "So, what gives?"

"Pretty simple, really. If the team isn't winning games, it seems a little ridiculous to upload a video about the game. So I've been helping out the team in other ways. I won't lie, it sucks. I want to get back to what I'm passionate about. Naturally, Christopher blamed himself for it."

"Well, I might give him that one if he's been stinking it up."

"And now we've come full circle," I reply and groan dramatically.

"I say this with total love, Summer. You guys need to get over your shit once and for all."

"Well said, my friend," I reply and get up to go a refill.

Momma is packing up the car like she's driving across the country, not the two hours to Minneapolis. This is clearly where I get my overpacking tendencies.

"Do we really need to bring a cooler with drinks in it? Like, a water bottle would suffice," I bitch at her.

"Hey, I'm not the one that packed a swimsuit. When do you think you're going to go for a dip, baby? We've got no time."

"We're late. We need to get over to Mr. Wilkins's house."

"Okay, okay, stop your whining."

Mr. Wilkins is sitting on his porch when we pull up.

"Christ, Momma. The poor man is probably freezing because you had to pack the kitchen sink."

"You are a true delight today, my Summer child," she says sarcastically and puts the car into park with about as much force as she uses to open a jar of pickles. "Come on, let's go help him."

Can't say she's wrong. Maybe it's my eggnog hangover —*barf*—but I woke up on the wrong side of the bed. Nerves about this trip are wrecking me. Not only about getting to the arena successfully and making sure Mr. Wilkins is okay, but obviously seeing Christopher. I don't know what to expect and it's making me crazy. Unfortunately, I missed his text last night because my phone died without me knowing it. All his text said was: *Boarding our flight for Minneapolis. Thinking about you, Gunderson.*

I replied this morning. *All good things, I hope. Congratulations on your hat trick, Big Mac.*

I haven't heard from him yet, but I'm sure he's at morning skate or in meetings.

"Our beautiful Summer has returned from the Rocky Mountains," Mr. Wilkins says and starts to stand up with the use of his cane. It shakes pretty badly as he does. His condition is definitely worse and my throat tightens up.

"It's good to see you," I tell him and pick up his faded navy blue duffle bag. It has an old Air Force patch on it and I wouldn't be surprised if it's the same one he used when he served.

"Where's Judy?" Momma asks about Mr. Wilkins's home health care provider.

"I sent her along because we're hitting the road. She said she's gonna watch it on the TV."

"I'm sure all of Fossebridge will be watching it right along with her," I tell him.

"This sure is special," he says with tears in his eyes as we help him down the steps. My own eyes tear up.

"So the plan is, we'll drive down to Minneapolis and get checked into our rooms. Then the team is going to come pick us up at 4 p.m."

"Will we get to watch the game?" he asks as we get him seated in the front passenger seat.

"Yep, from right behind the Storm's bench," I reply and pass his seatbelt over to Momma.

"Hot dog, it's gonna be a real great game. Did you see Big Mac's hat trick?"

"I sure did," I say and Momma shakes her head no.

"One of Fossebridge's own. He's got about as much talent as you do, Summer."

"Oh, Mr. Wilkins, I didn't know you were so funny," I say and put his cane in the back seat.

"You know I'm not joking, Summer. The two of you sure are something."

Christopher

My pregame routine goes like this. I get to the rink about two and half hours early. I change into shorts and a t-shirt, and then tape my sticks while listening to my my pregame playlist. It's the same songs I've been listening to since I played in college. When the Eminem song comes on—like I said, college

—it's time to hit the bike. As much as I hate the fucking thing, I give it a solid ten minutes and then get a massage. After that, I get in the cold tub. Then it's out to play a little soccer with a handful of my teammates to cut loose. Back in the locker room, I get dressed and after I lace my skates, that's when I would dig into my bag and touch Trey's puck before heading out on the ice for warm ups.

My routine is about to change tonight. I put a call in to Dave Gunderson and told him about the puck. He remembered it well and choked up a bit when I told him how I'd been honoring Trey by having it with me all these years. He offered to bring me something else I can carry with me—Trey's laces.

And now I'm holding them in my hand.

"Thanks so much for this," I tell Dave and Leslie outside the locker room. "I promise, I'll never lose them. I'll keep them close."

"We're so proud of you, Christopher. Thank you for all you do to remember Trey," Leslie says.

I can't even respond. I just shake my head and look away.

Dave puts a hand on my shoulder. "We only wish one thing for you, son. Be at peace. And play your heart out every time, just like Trey."

A sense of relief I wasn't expecting floods through me and I let out a big breath. Leslie wipes away a few tears and I squeeze her shoulder. For the first time in a long time, I feel like peace is possible.

"If only I was half as good as he was," I quip.

They smile at that and we exchange hugs.

"Have you seen Summer yet?" I ask. It's been three days

since I've seen her and I'm missing the sight of her beautiful face. Who am I kidding? I'm missing everything about her.

"Not yet. I think they're with Mr. Wilkins getting ready, but we'll be sitting together behind your bench," Dave says. "Good luck tonight."

"Thanks," I tell them and head into the locker room to carry out the rest of my new pregame routine, Trey's laces and all.

The arena lights dim and the carpet is rolled out. I take my position as captain on the ice with the rest of the first line, and glance back at Hawk in the net. Most games, I block out the pageantry of the singing of the national anthem, but not tonight. Not only will they honor dear Mr. Wilkins, but I also arranged for one more person to be honored, too.

In the darkness, I can make out the shape of Summer as she assists Mr. Wilkins onto the carpet that covers the ice. My heart starts pumping faster knowing that she's near. She gets him to his position on the carpet and then backs away, so he can stand on his own next to an active servicewoman from the Army. A young man, who clearly got tonight's anthem gig, stands on the other side of her with a microphone.

The public address announcer comes to life. "Ladies and gentlemen, please rise and kindly remove all hats to honor Army National Guard Sergeant Candace Kline and United States Air Corp Veteran Leroy Wilkins." Mr. Wilkins raises his free hand into the air and waves.

The crowd applauds and I tap my stick on the ice for him.

There's a lump in my throat the size of a puck. I tune in on Summer again, who stands at the edge of the spotlight, because this next part is for her.

"Tonight we also honor Army Sergeant Daniel Gunderson and all the fallen who have given their lives in service of our country."

Summer's hands fly up to her face to cover her mouth. I can't quite make out much else about her reaction, but my heart squeezes so tight for her and for Dave, Leslie, and of course Peggy, too.

"Please join tonight's guest performer, Kendall Bloom, in the singing of our national anthem."

The anthem begins and my personal time is over. It's back to business as I return to my routine and focus on the game in front of me.

The game begins the way it always begins, with me at center ice, facing off against my opponent. Tonight, I win the puck and we're underway. The Minnesota guys are being extra chippy with me, probably because of last night's hat trick. It only motivates me more. Is it weird playing against the team I grew up cheering for? Hell yes, but my goal doesn't waiver. I want to kick their asses all the way to Duluth.

We play a strong shift and then we head to the bench. I see the row of my people and my girl. They're all cheering for me. My eyes connect with Summer's and she mouths the word, "Hi." I place my hand over my heart and smile at her. Then I turn my back and take a seat. It's the last time I look in their direction for the rest of the game.

The game is a slaughter by the second period and they bench their star goalie. It doesn't help matters for them because the Colorado Storm is back and we're stronger than ever.

After the game, I rush to get ready so I can meet up with the Fossebridge crew. I'd be lying if I said it wasn't to be extra close to Summer. I need to touch her, to hold her, to kiss her. I've missed the smell of her hair, the giggle in her voice, the way she stares me down and lights me up and makes me feel so mortal.

I make my way over to the meet and greet room where they're all there with their passes dangling from around their necks. When they see me, they start to clap.

"Stop, stop," I tell them and give my mom a hug and then my dad, and then pretty much everyone else. Summer is last and I do more than the polite hug. I wrap my arms around her and bury my face in her hair. She feels like home to me. When I pull back, there are some tears in her eyes that she quickly wipes away.

"Big Mac," Mr. Wilkins says from the seat he's in. "You played like a champ. Making Fossebridge so proud."

"Thank you, sir," I tell him. "It's such an honor to have you here."

He smiles ever so slightly. "Thank you for setting this up. It sure was special."

"Don't thank me, it was all Summer's idea," I explain and take hold of her hand. Both of our moms have the same goofy looks on their faces as they did the night of the Winter Formal when they took about a million photos of us together.

"Will you get to stay here for Christmas?" Leslie asks.

"Sadly, no. I fly back to Denver tonight with the team. They give us a couple of days off, but it's best that I stay in my routine." I glance down at Summer, who is looking anywhere but at me for that answer. There's tension radiating off her and I wish I had more time to talk to her about it. I wish we had some privacy for the time that we do have.

My mom links her arm through mine. "We usually video call on Christmas as we open all our presents. We'll definitely do it again, this year."

"Maybe we could video call too," I say to Summer and wink at her, remembering our time in Chicago when we did that.

She smiles in response but it doesn't reach her eyes. "Hey, I just wanted to say thank you for what you did for my dad. That was really wonderful, Chris."

"You don't have to thank me for that, Summer. I'm glad we could honor him too."

"Hey, Mac," Hux says from the doorway. "We're loading up."

"Okay, I'll be right there," I tell him and turn back to my Fossebridge family. "Thanks so much to all of you for coming down here."

"We love you, son," my dad says to me and we start the goodbyes.

Once again, Summer is last and I pull her aside, hoping the family will give us a little space. I wrap my arms around her waist and look down into her eyes. "Hey, Gunderson."

"Hey, Chris." Her eyes are sadder than I ever want them to be.

A part of me chalks it up to the Christmas thing. Unfortunately, that's life with a hockey player. If we're going to be together, it's going to be tough like this sometimes.

What am I saying?

If?

If is a terrible word. I want words like *now* and *forever.*

She rests her hands on my shoulders as she says, "You played great again."

"Thank you. It seems like my strategies are working."

She nods slowly, but remains silent.

I rest my forehead against hers. She closes her eyes. "It's good to see you, Summer."

"I'm happy we had this time together," she says, and I can tell she's holding back some tears.

"Me too," I whisper. "It's not long enough, but it is what it is."

She releases me and steps out of my arms. "I'll see you when I get back to Denver."

"Okay," I tell her, disappointed that she's not exactly into my video call idea. "Merry Christmas."

"Merry Christmas, Christopher." She steps away from me and I feel like my heart goes with her. She goes to Mr. Wilkins to help him stand up and doesn't look back my way.

It's not exactly what I had in mind for a goodbye for us but I don't want to keep the team waiting anymore, so I wave goodbye to my family and head out the door. It's not until I'm on the plane back to Denver that I realize I didn't even get to kiss her.

Summer

Senior Year

I don't own anything black. Not even a t-shirt. It's just never been a color I gravitated toward. Now I do. It's a simple black dress hanging off a hook on the back of my bedroom door. For my hair, I decide on a simple French braid with a yellow ribbon tied around the tail.

The day of Trey's funeral is surprisingly sunny, but still Minnesota cold. Outside the church, everyone's breath billows. There's got to be a few hundred people here and I wonder how we'll all fit inside.

Uncle Dave and Aunt Leslie are the only people I haven't seen yet. They must be inside already. My heart breaks for them. Trey was their only child, just like me. They don't seem to be angry at me and Christopher. There's just no room yet for those kind of emotions. I get it. When my dad died, I was only ten, but I remember feeling so overwhelmed by my feelings that there wasn't much room for anything else. This one is more complex for me. My feelings go beyond grief. There's so much guilt that often my grief takes a back seat to it.

I haven't talked to Christopher since the hospital. I heard he checked out the day after he woke up. He's standing with his family. I don't think he's seen me yet and that's okay. Now is not the time to be seen. I know there are rumors out there about what happened, and I can't blame people for trying to look for a reason to explain such a tragedy. Because it doesn't make sense.

Sometimes, I think I should be mad at Trey for being so reckless, but what I may regret most is being so angry with him before the accident. I can't take any of those terrible things that happened. I also regret not seeing the signs that he didn't like Christopher and I being together. Maybe we could have talked it out.

I hate that Trey thought I betrayed him.

I hate that he died alone.

I hate that I put my feelings for Christopher above everything and everyone else.

I hate that I pushed Christopher to Boston.

I hate that it was the right decision.

The service is so hard. Hard to listen to. Hard to focus on. I'm trapped in my own emotions about it. Momma sits next to me and holds me to her, but it doesn't comfort me as much as it should.

It seems like ages before we get to the cemetery. The plot sits next to an old oak tree and I memorize the location so I can come back to visit on my own. So I can come apologize.

As we stand around his casket and the minister does his business, I feel a brush against my shoulder. I look up to see it's Christopher. He doesn't look down at my face, he just stares straightforward. A selfish part of me feels rejected and I hate myself even more for it. I already miss his attention. I miss the way I could always count on him. I miss the feel of his gaze on my face. The smile that he saved just for me. It's gone, and I have to learn to live with that.

There's a loud clicking sound and his casket starts lowering into the ground. I close my eyes, refusing to watch because I don't want to remember this part. My body is hollow and my skin is ice cold. I feel a little dead myself. I hope Christopher doesn't feel as bad as I do. As if reading my thoughts and feeling my pain, he takes my hand into his. He's warm and vibrant and alive. And almost as if his touch is magic, I can feel his love starting at my fingertips and traveling up my arm to my chest and my lungs. I breathe in deeply and I've come back to life. The pain is still there, and I have no doubt it will always be, but I hope so much that it will fade with time and maybe, someday, I'll find a love like this again.

13

Christopher

"How on earth did you get them to open the practice facility on Christmas Eve?" Hux asks as we lace up our skates.

"Psh, it was easy. A few more guys are coming down too. So is Dennison."

"Basically you put together an optional practice on Christmas Eve. Seems a bit extreme, Mac."

"You're here, aren't ya?"

"Yeah, but I don't have anywhere else to go."

"Not spending Christmas with Debbie?" I ask timidly. Hux doesn't reveal much about his personal life, but what I do know is that it's complicated.

He tugs at his laces really hard and starts tying them up like he's battening down the hatches in a storm. "No. Debbie is firmly my *ex*-wife this year. She's been seeing this guy for a bit. I think they're getting serious."

Oh, damn. Could Hux be jealous? "Are you okay with that?"

He looks at me and growls, "Do I have a choice?"

"I guess not," I reply. We don't talk for a few minutes as we finish getting ready and waddle out to the ice. When we start skating around, feeling that cool breeze on our faces, I feel he's calmed down enough to ask him, "Are you cool being on your own tomorrow? You could come over."

"You know I'll be fine. I'm going up to my cabin.The better question is what the hell are you doing here, Mac? Why didn't you stay up in Minnesota for Christmas?"

"I'm back on track. I don't want this momentum to slip away. So I figured it'd be best to just stick to my routine as much as possible before our next game."

"What about Summer? Are you guys okay?"

"I'd like to think so, but I don't know."

Hux comes to a sudden stop.

I circle around him. "What?"

"You're fucking it up," he says and shakes his head.

"I'm not fucking it up," I reply, but deep down I'm worried that I am. I've only heard once from her since I last saw her. A text telling me goodnight, but I didn't get it because I was on the plane. "I'm just trying to make this all work."

"Middle ground isn't your forte, eh?"

"What do you mean?"

"You're either all in on hockey or all in on Summer."

"Yeah, pretty much."

"Well, I think you've been doing the right things about sticking to your routine and conditioning plan. That's good for the hockey. I've got a theory about the relationship, though. Do you want to hear it?"

"Coming from you, old wise one, sure."

"I'm thirty-three, not eighty-three."

"Out with it, old man."

"Marry the girl."

"That's your theory?"

"That's my advice. My theory goes like this. You dove in head first with her. I don't know all the details of course, you locked-up bastard—"

"That's rich coming from you."

"—but I suspect you did it because you were afraid she was going to slip through your fingers again."

"Fair."

"Maybe you need to get married."

"I thought you were against marriage."

"For myself, because look what I've been through with Debbie. But I think you and Summer are the real deal. Do you want to marry her?"

Marrying Summer was always the plan, from an early age, but for the past several years I thought that plan died just like all the other dreams I'd had. When Summer came back into my life, the impossible became possible once again and all the plans that couldn't be fulfilled before once again had a chance. "Yes," I answer. "I've wanted to marry her since high school."

He dramatically lifts his arms up. "Then what the fuck are you waiting for and what the fuck are you doing here?"

"We've got time," I argue.

"It's never enough. Love like yours only comes once in a

lifetime. Trust me, I know," Hux says and takes off down the ice.

Maybe he's right. Maybe the answer to all of this is to go for my dreams and believe I can have it all. Maybe if Summer and I get married, I wouldn't feel like I'm stealing every second I get with her because it could all fall apart at any moment. Maybe, just maybe, I don't have to pine for Summer anymore. Maybe it's time to go the distance and make the grandest gesture. Maybe it's time to make Summer mine, forever.

Summer

'Twas the morning of Christmas, when all through the house, not a creature was stirring, not even Miss Mouse. My stocking was hung by the chimney with care, in hopes that Momma slipped some hoop earrings in there. I was totally nestled all snug in my bed, while visions of hockey players danced in my head. When out on the lawn there arose such a clatter, I sprang from the bed to see what was the matter. Away to the window I flew like a flash, tore open the shutters and tied closed my robe's sash. When, what to my wondering eyes should appear, but Christopher MacCormack—exactly why is not clear.

"Chris?" I ask. "What are you doing here?"

He smiles up at me while stuffing his hands in his pockets. "I came to wish you a Merry Christmas, Gunderson."

I'm still completely shocked. He's here, standing on my lawn in the dark. "You came home for Christmas?"

"You're here, so I'm here," he says sincerely. "You're my home, Summer."

My heart squeezes so tight. "Really? You mean that?"

"If you don't think that, then you haven't been paying attention this year. Or pretty much ever. Now, can you let me in before I get hypothermia out here...again?" he says while bouncing up and down to stay warm.

I shake my head in mock disgust. "Wow, that joke is so not funny."

"I'm not even joking."

I smile one last time before closing up the window and dashing down the stairs. The clock strikes seven and the coffee pot clicks on. I flick the lock on the door and open it wide. Christopher is on the other side of the door waiting with his arms crossed over his chest, shivering. I wrap him up in my arms and he melts into my embrace. "Some hockey player you are," I tease him.

Apparently he's so cold, he doesn't have a witty comeback for me. He just moves us into the house and closes the door with his heel. I press my warm palms on his cheeks and rub my thumbs up and down his ice-cold nose. "Oh, God, that feels better than anything."

I lift an eyebrow and just have to ask, "Better than *anything?*"

It takes him a second to understand my meaning and then he pulls me by the hips against him and clarifies, "Christ, never. Never better than that." Without any pause, he dips his head down to mine and kisses me quick. That quick kiss becomes a second, and then a third, and a fourth one that goes on quite a while. It hasn't been that long in the grand scheme of things, but it feels like the first rays of warm sunshine after a big snowstorm.

"Go get dressed," he murmurs against my mouth.

"Why?"

"Come on," he says. "I've got a few things I want to do with you."

"Oh really? Like this?" I ask and run my hands over his ass.

"Well yes, but more. So much more. Come on," he says and turns me around and swats me on the behind like I'm one of his teammates.

"Okay, okay, I'll go."

"Get a move on, Gunderson. Time is critical. And dress warm, for God's sake."

I giggle as I take the steps two at a time. When I turn the corner, I poke my head into Momma's room. She's sprawled across the bed snoring away. "Hey," I whisper at her real loud. "Hey!"

She starts to stir.

"Did you know Christopher was coming over?"

Momma cracks one eye open and moans, "What?"

"Christopher. Is. Here."

Momma sits fully up and shouts, "What? He's here?"

"Shhhh," I implore her.

Christopher yells up, "Merry Christmas, Mrs. Gunderson."

I cover my face with my hands. "Momma."

Momma shouts back, "Merry Christmas, Christopher."

Christopher replies, "Thank you. Time is of the essence, Summer!"

"Be down in a second!" I beeline straight to my suitcase for the warmest clothes I've got and throw them on without much thought, then hightail it to the bathroom to brush my teeth and comb my hair. I rush down the stairs to find him sitting in the living room, holding Miss Mouse.

"You really are the ultimate cat guy."

"I could easily make an inappropriate joke at that, but it's Christmas, so I'll behave." I swat his chest and he snatches my hand. He pulls it to his mouth and gives it a little nibble. "Ready?

"Where are we going?" I ask.

"Oh, Gunderson. You'll have to wait and see," he says and leads me out the door to his old truck. He's obviously been to his parents' house first.

"Just tell me now," I plead.

"I bet you used to peek at your presents," he teases and opens the passenger side door.

I hop in, just like old times and just like this summer. "Used to? I still do."

There's a rectangular-wrapped Christmas present sitting on the bench beside me. The tag says, "To my Summer. From your Christopher." I give it a quick little shake before he gets in but have not one idea about what it can be. All I know is it's a little bit heavy.

There's also a dinged-up plaid thermos that I remember from years ago. Like elementary school. How on earth do I remember that?

It takes a few tries to start up the truck, but it roars to life and we get going. The sun awakens ever so slowly as we pull up to a look out, near Webster Lake. He keeps the truck going, but puts it into park.

"What are we doing?" I ask.

"We are going to watch the sunrise, Summer."

And then I remember what he told me on the way to the airport. He had wanted to watch the sunrise with me while eating powdered sugar jelly donuts the day after the Winter Formal dance.

"Is this...?" I ask and point to the wrapped present.

"Open it and see."

I unwrap the present, probably too aggressively, but I'm just too excited. Sure enough, the Schoop Bakery logo across the box gives it away. "How did you...? It's Christmas."

"I called Mr. Schoop and asked if he could make a batch for us. He dropped what he was doing and made us half a dozen. My mom picked it up last night."

"He did that for you? Well, duh, of course he did," I comment, knowing that Christopher's got star power in this town.

"Honestly, Summer. I think he did it for you."

"Can I?" I ask, with my finger ready to pull off the piece of scotch tape holding the box together.

"Do it," he tells me with a big old grin on his face.

He props his arm on the seat rest behind my shoulders as I pull a donut out of the box. My sneaky shake made quite the powdered sugar mess, but I don't care. They're absolutely beautiful. I don't hold back at all, taking a huge bite out of one. Powdered sugar explodes in a cloud of dust and the raspberry jelly covers my lips.

Christopher scoots closer to me. "And this is what I've been waiting for." And just like the night he made me peanut butter and jelly waffles, he leans in and kisses me so sweetly. Raspberry, sugar, and Christopher. The best.

The sun rises in an orange blossom across a low cloud

deck. It's stunning, but not as stunning as Christopher sitting beside me. He's actually here but he hasn't really told me what changed his mind about staying in Denver for Christmas. "So tell me, Chris. Why are you here?"

"I told you. I want to be where you are, Summer. Especially on days like today." He takes hold of my hand and says, "I hope you feel the same way."

"Of course, I do. I'm so happy that you came. Did you get a late flight or was this always your plan?"

"Plan?" He laughs. "Yeah, I guess you can say, I've had this plan for quite a while."

I have no idea what that means exactly. Did he already have his flight booked to come back here or is he talking about donuts at sunrise at Webster Lake? Regardless, I'm just happy he's here. I want to know if he's figured out how to balance it all, but I also just want to be in the moment with him on Christmas morning. We cuddle up together and watch as the sun rises and rises, until it settles behind the clouds and Webster Lake is spread out before us, an expanse of glistening ice.

"Ready to go?" he asks.

"Not really, it's so pretty," I reply.

"No, I mean out on the ice."

"What? Really?"

"Would I mess with you on Christmas?"

"Maybe I'm still dreaming."

"As much as this whole year has seemed like a dream to me, Summer, I promise it's real." From under the seat, he pulls out my figure skates.

"How on earth?"

He shrugs as he pulls out his own hockey skates. "I got a little help."

"Oh, man. Momma is gonna get it."

He smiles at that as he starts taking off his sneakers. It's been years since I've worn my skates, but they fit like a glove. "Need some help lacing them up?" he asks.

No, I don't, but why on earth would I pass up on that? I twist my body so that I'm leaning back against the door and I can put my feet in his lap. He goes to work with expert ease. "You like 'em tight, like me?"

I smile. "That's right, Big Mac."

His head shakes as he giggles a little at the nickname. It always gets him good. When he finishes, he moves my right leg to the floor and bends forward so that he's cradled right between my thighs. I pull him to me by the back of his neck and kiss him silly. And then we do something we've never done before. We fog up the windows of his truck just like silly high school teenagers.

Much too quickly, in my opinion, he pulls away. "Okay, let's get on the ice."

"Is it safe?"

"Yep, I had my dad make sure."

"Your dad was in on this too? Who *didn't* get in on this?"

He tosses his head side-to-side. "I'd rather not say at this point. You trust me, right?"

"Completely."

"Good, let's do this. Stay there—I'll come around."

I pull my snowflake knit hat down over my ears and put on my mittens.

He opens the truck door and I swing around. He puts his

hands under my arms and lifts me down to the ground. "Here, take my arm," he says and I hold onto him as we walk across the snow to the lake's edge. He steps onto the ice first and turns around so he's facing me and takes both of my hands.

"Promise me you won't let me fall."

"I will never, ever let you fall."

"I'm a great skater," I tell him, so that my pride doesn't get too bruised.

"I know, but I won't let you fall. You don't let me fall either, okay?" He pulls me gently onto the ice and starts skating like he's got eyes in the back of his head, never letting me go.

"You're hilarious, Chris."

"Hey, I've been known to have some epic wipeouts."

"Yeah, while going like twenty miles per hour in a professional hockey game."

"That just makes it hurt all the more."

My balance starts to improve and he lets go of one of my hands and turns to skate beside me. We skate in a big circle around the outer edge of the lake. Everything is beautiful— the snow, the quiet morning, and the man beside me.

"Trey and I used to sneak onto this ice," he tells me.

A sudden sadness sinks in. "Oh yeah?"

"Yeah, we probably shouldn't have, because we didn't know for sure it would hold us. But that was Trey, willing to do whatever it takes."

"He was so bold," I add.

"Yeah, he was."

Christopher turns back around so that he's skating backward and can look into my eyes. "I want you to know something."

"Okay," I say, unsure of what's to come next.

"Trey's death doesn't define me." A lump in my throat forms that I wasn't expecting to have today. I listen as he continues, "My love for you is what defines me."

I squeeze his hands tightly and he slows down so that I gently collide with him. He kisses me, tenderly, sweetly, while looping his arms around my waist.

"He'll always be a part of our lives, but it's our love that will live on forever," he says.

"Yes, it will."

Christopher keeps us moving along the ice as he says, "We could always focus on how he's gone, but I don't think that's good for us. I think, instead, we should celebrate his life. Like right now, skating on this lake."

"I think that's a good idea. I'm sick of being sad all the time about it."

"Especially when we have so much to be happy for."

"And are you happy, Chris? Do you think you can manage this all?"

"I suspect by the time this day is over, I'll be able to manage it just fine."

"Aren't you mysterious," I say.

"Gunderson, I've worn my heart on my sleeve this whole time. You just haven't been paying attention."

After one more loop around the lake, he says it's time to go. I'm not sure what schedule he's on, but my thighs are burning and I'm ready to warm up in the truck. Again, the truck takes a few tries to start up. "I feel like this guy might be on his last leg," I say.

"Never."

"Why'd your parents keep this truck all these years?"

"I asked them to."

"I didn't know you were that nostalgic."

"When it comes to you, I always will be."

"What do you mean?"

"Summer, when we parted, I didn't have much to hold onto that would remind me of you. The truck was one connection to you that I couldn't part with. All those times I got to drive you home from school, those memories were all I could hold onto for so long. But maybe now, I'd be okay with passing it down to some high school student."

"Don't you dare!" I exclaim.

"Oh Gunderson, seems like I'm not the only one that's nostalgic."

"You are not," I confess. "Okay, where to next?"

"You'll see and probably won't be that surprised."

Sure enough, when we pull up to the Biscuit, I'm not surprised. If we're playing out the day that Christopher had hoped we'd had the day after the Winter Formal, then this would be next on the list. Only trouble is, we don't have any homework to do, so I've got no idea what he's got in mind.

"And how are we going to get in?"

He reaches into his pocket and pulls out Momma's set of keys and jingles them.

"Like I said, she's got it coming."

"It's not just her. I got a little help from another friend."

We enter through the front door into a winter wonderland of colorful string lights and paper snowflakes dangling from pretty ribbons across the ceiling. It reminds me of how it was decorated for the Winter Formal dance.

"Who did this?" I ask, having a pretty good idea already.

"Tia and the rest of the *Telegram* staff."

"Get out! I'm shocked she found the time."

"Tia would stop the presses only for you."

Tears spring to my eyes. She is incredible. And so is Christopher. When I look back over at him, I notice he brought in that plaid thermos that was in the truck. "What's that for?"

He bites down on his lip and sits down in his favorite booth from high school. I take the seat across from him and he places the thermos in between us. "This one might be a bit of a stretch. Do you remember this?"

"Sort of. Didn't you use this in elementary school?"

"You do have a good memory."

He twists off the lid and pours some hot cocoa into the mug top. "Hopefully it didn't get too cold."

Based off the steam that's rising from the thermos and mug top, I'd say it's fine. "I can get us some cups," I tell him, so we don't have to share.

"I'm fine sharing," he says, as nonchalant as ever.

"Okay," I giggle.

"Ladies first," he says and pushes it across to me.

I laugh nervously. "You're not poisoning me, are you?"

He chuckles in response. "Yep, that was the plan all along. I flew up here at midnight last night, took you to see the sunrise, took you skating, and brought you here just to poison you."

"Mmmhmm," I say with a smile and take a sip. It's an interesting flavor, one that I've had once before. Hot Chocolate with pepper in it. A fuzzy memory comes into focus, and I remember being in fifth grade and having this once before.

Christopher shared his hot cocoa with me and it had pepper in it. It was my first day of school and I sat huddled in my big puffy coat during recess after lunch. I was cold and hating my new town where I didn't have any friends except for my cousin, Trey. And then Christopher was suddenly there, a tall boy who seemed shy. He sat down beside me and opened his thermos and offered me some. I didn't know if it was a trick or something, but for some reason I just trusted him right away. I'd never tasted hot chocolate like it before. "The pepper makes it warmer. That's what you told me."

"So, you do remember!" he says with a smile. "I didn't think you would. I just wanted you to know that I've loved you since day one, Summer. Since the very beginning."

I bury my head into my hands because I'm overwhelmed with so many emotions and so much love, just so, so much. I can't stop the tears that dissolve into my sweater as I press my face against my arms. When I come back up, I get the sight of a lifetime. Christopher is sitting across from me with a ring box on the table between us.

"What?" I ask.

"Summer," he starts. "All those times I'd sit in this booth, pretending to do homework just so I could be close to you. It seems like everything I did back then and everything I do these days is just to be close to you. You're always so close, but yet I've always felt like I could never quite make you mine. Now, here we are at the prime of our lives, finally over the past that kept us apart for so long. And yet, I still get nervous that you'll slip through my fingers. It makes me crazy. It makes me distracted, because all I've ever wanted is for us to belong to one another, forever. I've wanted to marry you since I was sixteen years old. Hell, probably longer. You and me together, that's all I need in my life, and I hope you feel the same way. Gunderson, please tell me that you'll marry me."

"Are you sure?" I can't help but ask. "I don't want to cause problems for your career."

"Don't you see, Summer? Maybe all we ever needed was to be together. Maybe making a commitment to this love can make us strong in everything else we do." He opens the black velvet box and it's a beautiful diamond mounted on a delicate gold ring with clusters of diamonds circling around it. "Marry me, please. Be my wife."

I take hold of his hands and bring them to my lips to kiss them. "Yes," I whisper into his skin. "Yes."

His eyes are glistening as he smiles and pulls the ring out of the box. He scoots out of the booth and gets down on one knee to slip it onto my finger. It fits perfectly. I'm not surprised.

He slides in beside me and kisses me and holds me and I just want to stay like this forever with Christopher—the captain of my heart.

"Can we come in yet?" Momma yells from the kitchen.

"Yeah, you can. She said yes," Christopher yells back.

I swat at him, "What did you do?"

Momma, Tia, Uncle Dave, Aunt Leslie, his parents Peter and Nancy, along with Mr. Wilkins, come in from the back and shout, "Congratulations!"

Tears, just so many tears, stream down my face and quite a few do too for Momma. Tia is all up on me, checking out ring and giving Christopher her approval. She's already starting on the wedding plans she tells me. "I can't believe you all knew," I say.

"We love you both so much," Tia says and hugs us both.

"Come on, Mrs. MacCormack, we've got family to serve," Momma says and I assume she's talking to Nancy, Christopher's mom, but then I realize she's talking to me and I practically lose it all over again.

Less than an hour later, we're sitting down to a delicious brunch with all the fixin's, from champagne mimosas to my momma's homemade biscuits. Christopher sits beside me, with his arm across the back of my chair. Everyone is as happy as can be, but no one is happier than me. I tap my knife against my champagne flute. It takes a few seconds to get everyone's attention, but when I do, I say, "I'd like to say a few words."

Christopher squeezes my thigh and looks over at me with so much love. "Thank you, everyone, for all you've done to make today one of the absolute best days of my life. I know that Christopher needed you all to pull this off, and I couldn't be more honored or feel more loved. I love you all so much."

My family around me *awwws* and says sweet sentiments back.

"And to my husband-to-be," I start and look over at Christopher. "They say love like this happens only once in a lifetime. I believe it. There was a time when I pushed you away. And in all those days between then and now, I was waiting. I didn't even know it, but I was waiting for you to come home to me. I just didn't know it would take you having to win the Cup to actually do it."

Everyone laughs and Christopher shakes his head with a smile.

"But I'm so glad you did and that we found each other

again. You are the best person I know, Christopher MacCormack. And you bring out the very best in me. You inspire me and you amaze me. I can't wait to be your wife."

Now it's Christopher's turn to cry a little. He holds my face in his hands and presses his forehead to mine. "I love you so much, Gunderson."

"I love you too, Chris."

EPILOGUE

Christopher

FIFTH GRADE

Mrs. Knudsen stands up and turns toward the flag that hangs in our classroom. "Please stand, class, for the Pledge of Allegiance." I do my bit, reciting the pledge even though I don't know what a lot of the words mean. All I can think about is going to the rink after school today. We get to play against another team and I'm super excited about it. Especially if Gunderson and I get to try out the new play we've been practicing. I'll be sure to score and there's nothing I love more than scoring goals.

We take a seat and I pull out a piece of paper and pencil to draw the play with x's and o's.

The door to the room opens and Principal Keck stands there with the new girl Gunderson told me about. She's his cousin and her dad just died in a war. He didn't tell me that she has long blonde hair and pink glasses. She's holding her lunch box with both hands and her purple backpack looks too big for her body. It's kinda funny. She's biting down on her lip as she looks directly at the only empty desk in the classroom. It's right beside mine.

"Class, I'd like you to meet our new student, Summer Gunderson. Summer just moved to Minnesota. Let's give her a warm welcome."

We all clap for her as she looks at my best friend, her cousin.

"Hi Summer!" Gunderson says and waves with his arms in the air.

Mrs. Knudsen laughs at him. "If the name sounds familiar, it's because she is Trey's cousin. So now we have two sets of cousins in the class," Mrs. Knudsen says pointing to Neil and Jacob Werkowski. Gunderson and I call them the Jerkowskis instead.

"I'll put your backpack in your cubby in the back. Go ahead and take a seat, Summer, at the desk by Christopher," she says, pointing in my direction.

A funny feeling happens in my tummy as she approaches. She's got pretty green eyes behind her glasses and the longest hair I've seen on a girl my age. She reminds me of a little bird for some reason. She's breathing in short little spurts and blinking a whole lot. I hope she's okay. I guess I'd be nervous if it was my first day in a new school.

As we go through math and then reading, I keep checking on her to make sure she's okay. And then, for social studies, Mrs. Knudsen gives us an assignment to work with our desk group with some butcher paper. We've been learning about land forms and we've been assigned the Rocky Mountains. We get out our colored pencils and and start to take turns drawing. "Do you want a turn?" I ask Summer.

"I don't know know what the Rocky Mountains are."

"Oh, we've looked at pictures. They're really pretty," I tell her. "They go through this part of America," I tell her and show her on the map hanging behind us.

"Cool," she says. "I'll watch you draw."

"Go ahead, you can't get it wrong. Just draw some triangles like this."

She messes with her hair, putting it behind her ears, and pushes up her glasses. Then takes the purple colored pencil and adds some triangles to our picture of mountains. When she finishes, she smiles and I don't know why, but I like that a whole lot. And I want to make her smile some more, but it's time for lunch.

I always sit with Gunderson and a few other boys from our class that we play hockey with. Summer is sitting by herself with her lunch pail and I feel kind of sorry for her. "Hey, Gunderson, should we invite your cousin over?"

"Gross, no. I like her and everything, but we can't have a girl sit at our table."

"Okay," I say and feel dumb for even asking.

After lunch, we go out for recess and I take my thermos with me. My mom always packs me hot chocolate with a little bit of pepper in it on cold days. Gunderson's all about kicking the soccer ball around. He says it will help us with hockey like the pros do before games. We play awhile, but I notice that Summer is sitting on the bench, huddled in a huge puffy coat. Looks like she might need my hot chocolate more than I do. I take a break from the game, grab my thermos, and go take a seat on the bench beside her.

That odd feeling in my tummy comes back, but I just ignore it. "Are you cold?" I ask her.

"Yes, I've never ever been cold like this," she says, and I notice she's got a funny accent. She must be from somewhere warm. I think her teeth are chattering.

"Want some hot chocolate to warm up?" I ask her and show her my thermos.

"Really? I love hot chocolate."

"My mom made it," I tell her and unscrew the lid and pour some into the cup for her.

"Thanks," she says, taking it from me and taking a sip. "It's good, but it tastes different."

"It's got a little bit of pepper in it. It makes it warmer."

She drinks some more and then wipes her mouth on one of her mittens. "I've never had pepper in my hot chocolate before."

"Want some more?" I ask.

"Sure," she says. She's got some chocolate on her lip as she smiles at me and that funny feeling in my tummy gets even stronger. For some reason, making her smile makes me smile.

"Your cousin, Trey, is my best friend," I tell her.

"Oh, do you play hockey too?"

"All the time. It's my life. I usually call Trey by his last name, Gunderson, but now you're here so I guess that could get confusing."

"You would call me Gunderson too?"

"Well, I guess I could. I could always give Trey a different nickname, like a good hockey one like Treysie or somethin'."

"That's funny. No one has ever called me Gunderson before."

"Well, now I will. Welcome to Fossebridge, Gunderson."

"Thanks..." she says but must not remember my name.

"My name is Christopher, but you can call me Chris."

The End.

THANK YOU FOR READING!

I hope you enjoyed Inertia! If you liked this, you'll love the next two books in the series. Yep, that's right, Hawk and Hux get their own love stories! Visit www.elliemalouff.com/books to learn more.

For book goodies, and giveaways, I invite you to subscribe to my newsletter at www.elliemalouff.com/newsletter.

If you want to discuss the novel or hang out with me and some really incredible readers, join our Facebook group at www.facebook.com/groups/ellies.ensemble.

Thank You For Reading!

Into bookstagramming? Show me your photos of Inertia! I'm on Instagram @EllieMalouff

---

Finally, if you like supporting indie authors and want to support my work, I'd appreciate a book review!

THE COLORADO STORM HOCKEY SERIES CONTINUES

Velocity

Things move pretty fast for phenom goalie **Alex Hawkins** when he meets artist Alexandria in a crazy Colorado snowstorm.

Push

Storm defender and mountain man **Nikolas Huxley** never planned on getting married again. But all that changes when he meets bookstore owner Avaline.

Learn more at www.elliemalouff.com/books.

ALSO BY ELLIE MALOUFF

The Love Overseas Series

Between The Waves

Life for former pro-surfer Jake Garrant moves pretty slow in the small town of Manalua, Hawaii until one day a mysterious black haired beauty in a Cubs cap asks for surfing lessons. He commits to six lessons and does his best to keep it professional, but he can't help falling for a woman named Audrey Logan. As each lesson goes by, the heat between them grows and they give into their desires, until one day they're forced to face the ultimate riptide.

Be What Love Is

Cara and Reid's worlds collide when they inherit an English estate. She's pure California with a flare for Mexican food and books. He's a sexy Brit that's as posh as the day is long. Their story may be paved with gold, but their romance is a rocky ride.

Pull At My Heart

Moving to Ireland has been my dream come true. I've managed a killer job, new friends, and a flat above the hottest pub in Cork. The ruggedly handsome roommate wasn't part of my plan. Every time he takes me out on his motorcycle so I can photograph Ireland, he grows increasingly irresistible.

ACKNOWLEDGMENTS

First and foremost, I have to thank my husband, Mike. He was the person who inadvertently turned me onto hockey. I didn't know that we'd be watching every Blackhawks hockey game when he moved in with me in 2009. Before I knew it, I was hooked.

I'd also like to thank my editor, Elizabeth Shay VanZwoll. She does incredible work and made this book better. Ivonne DeLuca, you are my romance guide. Thank you for pushing me and giving it to me straight. You made this book better.

Thanks to my author and book pals on Instagram. In particular, those BABs.

Thanks to Pat and Eddie.

I have to thank my daughters. Erica, for being my biggest fan. She demanded pages and pushed me to keep writing because she wanted to know what happened next. Every author should be as lucky as me to have someone that pushes and encourages them to draft the stories they have in their head. And I have to thank Isabelle for keeping me grounded and not letting all of Erica's praise go to my head. You both keep me balanced and make me feel loved. Thank you.

Grief is a tricky experience. In the middle of drafting this novel, I lost my three beloved cats to Feline Leukemia within six months. I couldn't have pressed forward without the help of my therapist. Without her help, I'm not sure I could have completed a story about overcoming tragedy and handling feelings of grief and guilt. Thanks, Jen.

ABOUT THE AUTHOR

Ellie Malouff has been dreaming up stories for as long as she can remember. She loves immersing herself in romantic stories in every format, especially Turkish dizis. One day she decided to give back to the romance genre with her own contribution. When she's not writing, you can find her parked on the couch in Colorado with her husband, kids, and cats. She loves traveling to Ireland whenever she gets the chance.

Visit Ellie online at www.elliemalouff.com.

Made in the USA
Columbia, SC
24 September 2020

21362656R00204